*W*e have to retreat," Giovanni said. "Get back to the wasteland *now,* Eliana. Trust me on this one!"

And I would have, but that was when the fires came down.

I grabbed for my whistle, blew *retreat, retreat, retreat.* The first wave had not hit the area nearest me, but I could see flames rising farther in the woods. White sparks streamed toward the sky like fleeing stars, and I heard screams of agony. "Oh, my God," I said. "Lucia. *Lucia.*"

Giovanni took off at a run; I didn't see to where. I turned, and in the twilight I could see a handful of figures on the hill behind us, clasping hands, silhouetted against the darkening sky and the bright burning forest.

I counted. Five mages—that was all it took. Five of them.

As I watched, they turned toward us, scanning the field we'd camped in. Over my head I saw the fire spring into life like a billowing gold cloud. The color darkened to red, and the cloud slowly unrolled. As the edge of the cloud touched the tops of the trees, they burst into bright white flames.

The cloud of fire paused for a moment, and I could almost feel the mages taking a collective deep breath. Then the flames flashed down toward me and I closed my eyes tightly, knowing that in an instant I would feel my flesh burning around me.

And there was nothing I could do about it....

Also by Naomi Kritzer

Fires of the Faithful

Turning the Storm

Naomi Kritzer

BANTAM BOOKS

TURNING THE STORM
A Bantam Book/January 2003

Published by
Bantam Dell
A Division of Random House, Inc.
New York, New York

ISBN 0-553-58550-9

Manufactured in the United States of America
Published simultaneously in Canada

OPM 10 9 8 7 6 5 4 3 2 1

To Ed Burke,
with love and gratitude
for all your support

Acknowledgments

First I'd like to thank my superb editor, Anne Groell, for helping me make this the best book it could be. I'd also like to thank my agent, James Frenkel, and his assistant, Tracy Berg, for their support and enthusiasm.

I'd like to thank the members of the Wyrdsmiths, past and present, for critique, encouragement, and friendship: Bill Henry, Doug Hulick, Ralph A. N. Krantz, Harry LeBlanc, Kate Leith, Kelly McCullough, Lyda Morehouse, and Rosalind Nelson.

Quite a few people answered questions, helped me with research, and let me borrow ideas. Thanks to all of them, but special thanks to Michelle Herder for historical information; Jennifer Horn for dance steps; Geriann Brower for Italian language consultation; and Sharon Albert and Louis Newman for Aramaic language consultation. Any mistakes, of course, are because I failed to take the advice of my consultants.

Thank you to all of my beta readers, who read and commented on earlier versions of this book: Ed Burke, Jason Goodman, Rick Gore, Michelle Herder, Jennifer Horn, Curtis Mitchell, Rudy Moore, Rebecca Murray, and John Savage.

My most heartfelt thanks go to my family: Bert, Amy, Abi, and Nate Kritzer, and Ed and Molly Burke. Molly is eighteen months old as of this writing, and helped mostly by napping at appropriate times. Ed, on the other hand—well, when people ask me about writing with a toddler in the house, I have to say that step one is to have a supportive spouse or partner. More than just being a wonderful partner and fellow parent, though, Ed has always taken my writing seriously—well before I ever sold a word of it. It is a great gift to have someone close to you who believes in your dreams, and I am grateful for it.

PART ONE

The Life of the Land

CHAPTER ONE

The doom of the leader is to lead.
—The Journey of Gèsu, chapter 4, verse 10.

Eliana? Eliana!" Giovanni stared down at me, flushed in the late summer heat. I squinted up at him and he sat back, looking relieved. "That was one hell of a fall."

I groaned and lay still for a moment. Two months of leading an army—two more successful battles, even—and I still couldn't stay on my horse and reload a crossbow at the same time. I pushed myself up with my elbows. "Nothing hurts," I said. That was blatantly false, but nothing *especially* hurt. "I must have just had the wind knocked out of me." I turned to glare at Forza, my horse. She had skidded to a stop shortly after throwing me, and was staring at me with wary sheepishness from farther down the hill.

"It's getting late, anyway," he said. "Let's just make a quick circuit around the hill and head in."

"Where'd the bow land?"

"Got it," Giovanni said. I stood up and Giovanni handed it back to me. "Let's go." He whistled for Stivali, the horse he'd claimed from the Ravenessi stables, and we remounted, turning to head back to the army encampment.

"Hold on," I said, reining in Forza. "Who the hell is that?"

Giovanni turned to look north and squinted at the figure walking toward us. "I don't know." He unslung his own crossbow and cocked it. "But whoever it is, he's alone."

The man headed straight toward us. He seemed to be carrying weapons, but they weren't drawn. I loaded my crossbow—easy enough now that Forza was standing still—and checked behind us, in case the man was supposed to be a distraction. I saw nobody, but stayed on my guard. We had an outer ring of sentries, but this man, at least, had gotten past them unchallenged.

"Hello there!" the man said, saluting us as he approached. "I come in peace, to meet with your leaders. I assume you are soldiers of the Lupi?"

Giovanni's eyes narrowed and he squinted down the sights of his crossbow. "Maybe."

I decided to let Giovanni go ahead and intimidate the stranger. He wouldn't fire without cause, and I found the stranger's breezy manner irritating. "What do you want with the Lupi?" I demanded.

The stranger bowed low, showing off a freshly sunburned neck. "My name is Felice. I have come from Cuore as the delegate of the reformers."

Giovanni lowered his crossbow just a hair. "Fire falls from the sky," he said challengingly.

"And the land weeps," Felice said.

Giovanni lowered his bow completely. "I guess you are who you say you are. We're—"

"—pleased to make your acquaintance," I said, cut-

ting Giovanni off. "We'll take you back to the camp."
I swung down from my horse and confiscated Felice's
visible weapons—a decorative sword and an ornately
carved crossbow. I was not so impressed by a two-year-
old password that I was going to tell this man that he'd
just met both generali of the Lupi army, alone. For all
we knew, he was a spy on a suicide mission to kill us
both. "You can ride double with me."

Felice mounted Forza effortlessly and I climbed up
awkwardly behind him. I regretted not making him
ride with Giovanni, but said nothing, not wanting to
look foolish. We rode back toward camp.

Felice even smelled like an aristocrat: clean, despite
his long walk, with a very faint whiff of perfume. His
tunic was made out of a delicate fabric that caught the
light oddly, covered with a well-tooled padded leather
vest. His hands carried the light calluses of a gentleman-
fencer, like Giovanni—except Giovanni did some real
work these days.

Back in camp, I dismounted and passed the horses
off to Vitale, the youngest of the Lupi. He'd joined us
when we'd liberated that first slave camp after Ravenna.
I'd tried to send him off to Doratura or one of the
other resettled towns, but he'd stubbornly followed us
across the wasteland until I shrugged and said that
anyone so determined was clearly old enough to make
himself useful. "Take Forza and Stivali," I said to Vitale.
"And tell Michel we need him right away."

Vitale vanished into the camp, and Giovanni and I
stood awkwardly, facing Felice. I wanted a private moment with Giovanni, to ask him the significance of the
password and how secret it really was, but I needed
Michel to take custody of Felice first. Fortunately, Michel

arrived almost immediately, still tying his sash. He was rumpled, and I suspected he'd been napping. "Michel," I said. "This is Felice, allegedly one of the reformers from Cuore. Take him to the generale's tent; they'll be with him shortly."

Michel picked up his cue, and saluted without addressing either of us as "Generale." "Please follow me," he said, and led Felice off toward my tent.

I turned to Giovanni. "What was it he said to you?"

"It's a password—"

"I guessed that. How secure is it? Couldn't he have found it out some other way?"

"We can trust him," Giovanni said confidently. "He's been sent by Beneto's commanders. I'm just surprised it took them this long. We ought to have a contact with the main Reform organization."

"Really." I stared off past Giovanni's shoulder. An argument was brewing between two of my men over whose turn it was to dig latrine trenches. "Hey!" I shouted, and they both jumped to give me a guilty stare. "It's both your turns. Fight over it and you'll be filling them in, too." I turned back to Giovanni. "Well, let's go see what he wants, then." I caught Vitale as he passed by. "Send Lucia to my tent when you get a chance. I don't want Isabella, not yet. Try to get Lucia alone."

Giovanni beamed as we entered the tent. My tent was larger than Rafi's tent in Ravenna had been, but not a whole lot higher; we didn't have much in the way of real tent poles. Felice sat cross-legged on a cushion, looking around dubiously at the rough accommodations.

"Welcome to the Lupi encampment," Giovanni said. "I am Generale Giovanni, and this is Generale Eliana."

I nodded to Felice, returning his aghast look with a predatory smile. "Charmed," I said.

Felice closed his mouth with a snap, but his eyes were still wide. "Really? I'd pictured you—" he studied me, his lips parted—"differently."

"Were you expecting me to be taller?" I asked. I glanced toward the tent flap, wondering how long it would take Lucia to arrive. "Male?"

"No, no, no. Of course we knew your, ah, basic description. Older, I'd say. I guess I'd assumed you'd be older."

"Hmm." I decided to let him stop flailing. "I suppose you're expecting us to bring you up to date."

"That would be helpful, yes."

Lucia came in and sat next to me. "This is Felice," I said. "He claims to be a reformer from Cuore."

"Do you know him, Giovanni?" Lucia asked.

"No," Giovanni said.

"I joined the Cause after you departed for Ravenna," Felice said. "I am originally from Parma."

Lucia gave Felice a long, careful stare. I looked at her; she shrugged.

"Well," I said. "You probably know that we led the uprising at Ravenna." Felice nodded. "That was about a month and a half ago. We've liberated three more slave labor camps since our escape, adding former slaves to our army when possible." Our army had doubled in size from the original group, but then the other camps had been smaller than Ravenna.

"At the last camp, reinforcements had been sent down," Giovanni said. "Fortunately, they had not been well integrated. The new troops and the old did not trust each other, and fought together poorly. Still, we can't count on that being true everywhere."

"What sorts of training have you done with your men?" Felice asked.

"Tactics," I said. "Some sword training, and bow."

"Three victories," Felice said. "That's quite something."

"Minimal losses," I said. "That's something we hope to keep up."

"Any problems?" Felice asked.

"Well, you know, we're fighting a war," I said. "People get injured sometimes, or die. *That's* a problem."

"But other than that?" Felice asked.

There were the constant petty squabbles, the rivalries between the original Lupi and the mutineer soldiers from Ravenna, the constant shortage of supplies, and the fact that half of the people I'd impulsively made leaders couldn't lead their way out of a stable if you drew them a map, but I wasn't about to share those problems with Felice. "That's pretty much it."

"Well," Felice said, his face lighting up. "Sounds like you're in good shape, then." I nodded. "So anyway, I'm here to take over."

I froze, not entirely sure I'd heard quite right. Lucia's jaw dropped, then she closed her mouth and sat back quietly, her eyes flickering from me to Giovanni and back. The slight quirk of her lips made it clear she was waiting for the show.

"You're here to *what*?" Giovanni demanded, just barely restraining himself from attacking Felice. "I am doing *just* fine myself, thank you *very* much."

"Oh, er, yes, of course," Felice said, glancing from Giovanni's face to mine. "Of course you're doing fine. We really appreciate what an excellent job you've done since Beneto's execution. The reformer leaders in Cuore have voted to give both of you a commendation, in fact.

But you have to understand, a position like this requires someone with experience—"

I cut him off with a raised hand. "So how many armies have *you* led into battle?"

"Oh, I'm very good at strategy," Felice said confidently. "I won nineteen out of twenty-five mock battles with my tutor—"

I laughed. "You're not taking my army away from me."

"Excuse me?"

"You heard me. Signore Felice, you can *try* to command here if you enjoy being laughed at, but this is *my* army. If you think we're putting our men into your manicured hands, think again. You don't command here—I do."

Felice was putting on a patient expression, and that did it. "Michel!" I said.

Michel was waiting outside the tent and poked his head in. "Yes, Generale?"

"Take this man to the stockade and place him under guard. He is not to be left alone at any time."

Michel took Felice's arm. "If you'll come with me, signore," he said.

"But—but—wait—" Felice said as Michel started to haul him off.

"Oh, one more thing, Michel," I said. "He's a guest. Treat him with courtesy."

"He won't have anything to complain about, Generale."

The tent was quiet for a moment after Felice was gone.

"I don't know if that was quite appropriate—" Giovanni started.

"If he's going to stay here," I said, "I want him to be

absolutely clear on who's in charge. Besides," and I relaxed slightly, "what an ass."

Lucia laughed. "I agree. Let him cool his heels in the stockade, for an hour or two at least..."

Giovanni was opening his mouth to say something else when Isabella came in to the tent. At least Michel was gone by the time she arrived. "Who's the fop?" she demanded.

"An old friend of Giovanni's," Lucia said. "The reformers sent him to take over."

Isabella looked at me with a single raised eyebrow.

"I declined his generous offer," I said.

"Just what is it you hope to accomplish by locking him up?" Giovanni demanded. "Fine, you get to gloat, but is there really any point to this, or is it just to humiliate him?"

I leaned forward. "I've seen no reason that I should trust him. There's nowhere else in this encampment designed to keep people under guard. So until I'm convinced that he's not a threat, he stays in the stockade."

Giovanni snorted. "A threat? That pretty boy probably had a servant to reload his crossbow, back in Cuore. You're actually afraid of him?"

"I've got enough things to worry about without Felice," I said. "I promise, I'll have Michel let him out soon. Do you want to go see about the scout reports?"

Giovanni left, still grumbling, leaving Lucia and Isabella in the tent with me. Unfortunately, Isabella showed no inclination to leave. She pulled up a cushion to sit on and poured herself a cup of tea. "Generale," she said. "I wonder if I could have a word with you."

I suppressed a groan; when Isabella called me generale, it usually meant that she wanted something. She was going to have her word with me sooner or later, so I poured my own cup of tea and sat back to listen, gesturing for her to go ahead.

"Yesterday you ordered one of my people to scrub pots for insubordination."

"Which?" I asked, trying to remember who'd gotten in trouble recently.

"Gemino."

"Ah, right." Gemino was a short, stocky boy who'd come with us from Ravenna. Isabella led a unit within my army, but it was made up mostly of "her people," the old-time malcontents who'd followed her in Ravenna. "Isabella, you aren't going to have me reduce his punishment, are you? It's not like scrubbing pots is that dreadful a task, and someone has to—"

"It's not this instance so much as it is a general pattern. The problem was not Gemino, it was Michel. You should *realize* that by now."

"I thought I told Gemino he didn't have to take weaponry lessons from Michel anymore."

"You did. This wasn't a weaponry lesson. Michel was trying to give my people orders, and Gemino refused—"

Now I remembered. "Isabella, Michel was trying to tell Gemino he needed to move the horses. It was a perfectly reasonable request—"

"—and coming from anyone else, it might have sounded reasonable. Michel can make the most reasonable request sound like an insult."

"So what do you want me to do?"

"Michel needs to be taken down a peg." Isabella's large eyes glared at me from behind a stray lock of gray hair. "He's unsuited to a position of authority."

This was true. Michel *was* unsuited to a position of authority. But so was Isabella, and most of my unit commanders. "I need him where he is," I said.

"But Gemino—"

"I'll tell Michel again to stay away from your soldiers." We'd be fine if I could find enough other things for Michel to do. Or if I could somehow keep him and Isabella permanently separated. The trouble was, I really did need him where he was. I needed his loyalty, his skills as a bodyguard, and his ability to get things done for me. He wasn't a bad soldier, but the power had gone to his head. I just wished I knew what to do about it. Isabella's suggestion had merit, except that if I hurt his pride, I might lose his loyalty—or he might simply leave. And I needed him too badly. Besides, if I disciplined Michel, I'd have to do something about all the lousy unit commanders, including Isabella. I *had* removed the really atrocious ones—the lecher, and the coward, and the one who turned out to be dumb as a donkey—but if I set about trying to ensure that only the best were in positions of authority, we'd be left with me, the woman who led the scouts, and Giovanni on his good days.

"Well, thank you, Generale," Isabella said stiffly, and took her leave.

Alone with Lucia, I sighed. "Are you sure you don't want to command a unit, Lucia?"

"And have Isabella on *my* back, as well as yours and Michel's?" Lucia raised an eyebrow. "Positive."

"So." I wiped out my teacup and put it away. "What's on my list?"

Lucia considered for a moment. "The scouts are due back this evening, but probably won't get in until late tonight. If they're not back by morning, we'll have to assume that they were captured. That's the most significant news."

I nodded.

"Other than that ... We're in pretty good shape for grain, but we're low on horse feed. If we absolutely have to, we can feed some of our wheat to the horses, but for obvious reasons that's not the best option. In any case, it's critical that we capture food at the next camp. And if they have horses, we should send them north with the refugees, rather than keeping them ourselves. Cavalry is nice, but we just don't have the food stocks."

I nodded; she was right, although this would only increase resentment among the people who didn't have horses but thought they should. Never mind that most of these people could barely ride, let alone fight from horseback; a horse was a symbol of status, so everyone wanted one.

"Other than that—Nerio and Viola split and have made quite a fuss about it."

"Move them into separate units. I don't care if they reconcile and miss each other; we're keeping them separate from now on. This is, what, the fourth time?"

"Fifth. Let's see. Ulpio and Bruttio were fighting."

"Latrine duty."

"Paulo and Severo are rumored to be spoiling for a fight."

"Paulo and Severo?" They were two more of the men I'd put in charge of units ... and now regretted putting in charge. "What's their problem?"

"Paulo's convinced you're favoring Severo's men. He wants a horse, and he thinks you're sending his men to dig latrines and scrub pots a bit too often. He blames Severo for turning you against him."

I sighed. "Remind me to ease up on Paulo's men. He's wrong, but it's not worth losing his loyalty over. Maybe I *should* give him a horse." I looked up; Lucia gazed at me levelly, a glint of humor in her eyes. I sighed again. "Once we're out of the wasteland, the horses can graze ..."

"According to Giovanni's calculations, that won't be until the end of the summer."

I shook my head. "No horse for Paulo, then. Maybe I'll arrange to outfit all his men with swords and crossbows."

"Think you can get Giovanni to train them?" Lucia asked. "If you give them the swords without training they'll only trip over them in battle."

"I could try making Felice do it," I said.

"Think he'll be any better than Michel? Or Giovanni?"

"Could he be any worse?" I said. "Don't answer that. I suppose I should go spring him from the stockade. What else do I still need to take care of?"

Lucia considered. "Five more people who want you to mediate disputes."

"Oh, for— Can't you do it?"

She shook her head. "They specifically requested you. Look, at least they aren't fighting."

"Right, I know. Fine. Later, before the scouts get back. Was that it?"

"That's all," Lucia said.

"In that case ..." I stretched. "I'm going to visit Felice."

The stockade was really just a fenced area with two guards standing over it. The fence was a flimsy, makeshift affair; any determined prisoner could escape by uprooting a fence stake and running. Most of the time, when I tossed someone in the stockade it was more for the symbolic humiliation than actual confinement.

I expected Felice to greet me with a glare, but he merely looked sad and hurt. "I had no idea you'd take it like this," he said when I arrived.

"Then you were poorly briefed."

"Is this really necessary?" He gestured at the fence and the guards. "I promise not to try to take away your army."

"I don't think you'd be able to," I said. "I had you locked up because you're a stranger and you might be here to cause trouble. Why should I trust you? I was never one of the official reformers of Cuore; I don't know the passwords and countersigns that so thoroughly impressed Giovanni." I stepped close to the fence, noticing that Felice was sweating. "Why should I trust you?"

Felice placed his hands flat against the fence posts. "Signora Generale," he said. "I may be soft and I may be weak compared to you and your men. The orders I was sent with may betray a terrible arrogance on the part of my leaders. But the fire that burns in my heart springs from the same flame as the fire in yours. My brothers were among those murdered by the Circle to keep secret the devastation caused by magefire. And I will do whatever it takes to bring them down." He met my eyes with urgent sincerity. "Let me fight with you, Generale. You won't regret it."

"Well," I said. I uprooted a fence post and gestured that he could step out of the prison. "Welcome to my army." I fitted the post back into the ground and started to walk away.

"Wait," Felice said. I turned back. "What do I do now?"

"That's for you to figure out, isn't it?" His look was

so pitiful I relented. "Fine. Report to—oh, you can be in Paulo's unit." I flagged down Vitale. "Escort Felice here to Paulo. Do you know how to use a sword for anything other than jewelry, Felice?"

"Of course," he said.

"Tell Paulo that Felice will be helping him with arms training." With any luck, Felice would be better at it than Michel. Vitale saluted and marched Felice off.

*   *   *

"Martido won't return my bracelet."

I stared at Fiora, baffled. "Why does he have it?"

"I gave it to him when we were—you know. And now we're not. But he won't give it back to me."

I glanced at Lucia, who sat beside me. She gave me her faintest wicked grin, and my spirits lifted slightly. I didn't understand why *I* was the one who had to mediate these stupid arguments. Lucia would have been better at it.

"Where did you get the bracelet?"

"From Teleso's keep." Fiora glared at me stubbornly now. "It's mine. I want it back."

"You only had it because I said you could have it, you stupid cow," Martido said, speaking up for the first time since they'd come in. He sat as far away from Fiora as he could and still be in the tent. "I saw it first."

"Why do you want it?"

They answered in unison: "Because it's mine."

How did I get involved in this sort of thing? And this was only the first dispute of the five Lucia had mentioned. "Give it here," I said to Martido, and he reluctantly handed it over. I studied the bracelet. Teleso must have kept it to adorn his mistresses, or else it had belonged to his sister. It was a woman's jeweled bracelet, ornate and fairly delicate. It would look silly on Martido's wrist.

"Generale!" The voice came from outside the tent, and then Vitale poked his head in through the door. "Generale, the scouts have returned."

I slipped the bracelet onto my own wrist. "We'll finish this later," I said to Martido and Fiora. "I'll hold the bracelet for now." Martido started to protest, then thought the better of it and followed Fiora out of the tent.

Vitale held the tent flap open for the scouts as they came in—six haggard and exhausted men and women. "Vitale," I said. "Get Giovanni, then fetch food and wine for the scouts. Then tell all unit commanders I want them here in an hour." He saluted and slipped back out. "Report, Camilla," I said to the scout leader.

Camilla was a farm girl who had entertained herself as a child by testing how close she could get to wild birds before they saw her and flew away. Now she used her noiseless step and her ability to disappear into the dusty ground of the wasteland to scout out the slave camps before we attacked. She was slightly built, with tiny hands and feet and a dark cap of short-cropped hair.

She pulled up a cushion and sat down, tucking her feet neatly under her. "Chira is about the same size as Ravenna," she said, "but more heavily guarded. They've received reinforcements, and Demetrio—their commander—has taken the trouble to train them." She sketched the camp's layout in the dust. "Like the other camps, Chira is set into a valley. They've done a better job with the perimeter, though; they built the camp up against a section of the wall they're building, and used that for some of the defenses."

"The wall could work to our advantage," I said. "If we could get some of our people on to it, to fire down—the valley location makes it easier to keep your prisoners contained, but it's hard to defend."

Camilla looked up. "In addition to the keep, they have five other buildings, also solidly built. And they must know that we start with a cavalry charge, but they haven't set up lances to impale the horses; I think they want to draw us in, then use those subsidiary watchtowers to shoot us down."

"Sounds plausible," Lucia said as Giovanni joined us. I briefly repeated what Camilla had told me, then gestured for Camilla to continue.

"The thing that worries me the most," Camilla said, "is that Demetrio runs drills. I saw them practicing, and it looked like they were rehearsing exactly what to do if there was an uprising, or if we attacked."

"You saw the drill?" Then we knew his strategy. One of them, at least.

"Yes." Camilla described the procedures the soldiers ran through. "He even had a soldier whose job was to go torch the grain. They're onto us."

"That's what they think, anyway," I said. "Which building holds the grain?" Camilla pointed to one of the scuffs she'd drawn in the dust. "Then we know what to protect. What are the people like?"

"Scared. Beaten down. Demetrio keeps a tight grip; we saw two executions during the time we were watching. Both were escape attempts who got caught."

"The soldiers?"

"Brutal. And loyal to Demetrio."

Vitale arrived then with food and wine for the scouts, and they paused to have something to eat and drink. We finished the briefing before the rest of the commanders arrived, but I already had a pretty good idea of what I was going to do. Camilla seeing those drills had been a stroke of luck.

It was very late when we finished; I sent the scouts off to sleep and slipped out of my tent. Michel trailed me as I headed past the edge of the camp and into the wasteland, keeping a respectful distance.

The hills of the wasteland were silvery in the moonlight. Even on the darkest nights, you could tell that the land here was dead. I sat down at the crest of one hill and opened my violin case. Learning to fight with a sword had callused my right hand, despite the gloves I always wore. It felt a little strange now to take my bow in hand and tuck my violin under my chin, but I could still make my violin sing. I tuned up and played for an hour, just for myself. I played the songs I'd learned with Mira, and the violin part of some of the ensemble pieces from the conservatory. Finally I played the Mass. I glanced at Michel, standing watch a short distance away. I always wondered if he wanted to dance when I played the Mass, but tonight he probably just wished I'd stop playing and go to bed so that he could get some sleep as well. I had to admit that I was tired. I put my violin away and headed back for the camp. As I reached my tent, I turned to Michel. He was still trailing me sleepily.

"Martido and Fiora," I said. "Whose unit are they in, anyway?"

"Severo's," he said.

I nodded. "Good." I took the bracelet off my wrist

and handed it to Michel. "Take this to Severo and tell him that *he* can deal with it. I have an army to lead." Michel blinked at me, puzzled, as I went inside to bed.

*   *   *

We attacked Chira at dawn a few days later, sweeping down from the black hills like the monstrous Heralds of the Lady's Vengeance that Her book promised on the last days. (Lucia insisted that Gaius had lifted this image directly from something in the stories of Gèsu, but she wasn't sure quite what.) We had split off the cavalry from the infantry as we traveled, and the cavalry circled around to strike from the far side of Chira. When we were in position, I blew three piercing blasts on the whistle I carried into battle, and we urged our horses to a full gallop as we fell upon the camp.

Sentries from the fence shouted an alarm, but we broke through and rode them down. From the corner of my eye, I could see Severo leading a squadron of Lupi archers along the top of the wall. One of the Chirani soldiers had been on guard; Severo took him out with a blow of his staff. I found myself smiling. My commanders had their problems, but they knew how to fight.

Giovanni had been training me to fight from horseback with a sword, but my enthusiastic swings were as likely to pull me off the horse as to do any damage, so today I settled for my crossbow and the whistle. Chirani prisoners scattered in every direction as we rode in, adding to the general confusion. A few had the presence of mind to escape the enclosure, but most just panicked. Demetrio's troops tried to regroup, retreating to their fortresses to fire on us from relative safety. This was where Camilla's skill would pay off, assum-

ing that she and the other members of her team had
been successful in their mission.

A few of the soldiers had reached their forts now—
but they were making their first mistake. The first soldiers to make it in panicked, slamming the door behind
them and trapping their fellow soldiers outside. Our
cavalry closed in for the kill; a few of us fell to arrows
fired from the towers, but only a few. Holding back a
bit, I whispered my secret selfish prayer: *don't let anyone I know get hurt.* These days, I knew everyone in
my army, but when I whispered that prayer, I meant
Lucia, Michel, and Giovanni. I felt ashamed to make
such a selfish request of God, so I said this prayer to
the Lord; the Lady's consort was known for taking
care of the little things.

Each of the extra guard towers Demetrio had built
had been equipped with a large stash of extra crossbow bolts, enough to take out most of the Lupi if need
be. As the soldiers' quivers ran low, they looked to
those stocks—and the rain of crossbow bolts slowed
abruptly. Camilla and her scouts had removed them in
the night. The soldiers would have to make every shot
count now; we could all move in. I blew a long blast on
my whistle, then a short blast, then a long blast. Of
course, Camilla couldn't remove all the arrows from
the main keep. But just before dawn she'd slipped inside it and hidden; when we reached the back door, she
would open it. As the Lupi infantry charged, some of
the Chirani prisoners came out of hiding, cheering for
us or even picking up tools from their work on the wall
and joining the charge.

Paulo and his unit had been assigned to secure the
granary; since I saw no smoke or flame, they'd probably succeeded. I led the way to the door of the keep,

and we burst in, flooding through the hallways, killing the soldiers who didn't surrender.

Chira was ours by the time the sun had risen over the hills.

The Lupi had the routine down by now. Secure the grain, horses, weapons, and papers. Capture the keep commander if possible, and his lieutenants, and place them under guard. Tell the prisoners that they were free to go or to join our army, and let them loot the rest of the keep to their heart's content—although the Lupi generally joined in that part of the fun as well.

We found Demetrio in his study, dead by his own hand. I was secretly relieved; I didn't like executing people and I liked extracting information from them even less. Giovanni and I covered the body and Giovanni started on the desk. "How are Lucia and Michel?" I asked.

"Fine," Giovanni said, pulling out the first desk drawer. "Lucia is off ministering to the injured."

"Where's Felice?"

Giovanni snorted. "He fell behind last night. I wasn't optimistic about his usefulness in a battle, so I told him to follow our track and get here when he got here. He pouted at me."

"Figures." I poked at the papers on the desk, then decided to let Giovanni handle the job. "I'll be back in a few hours."

"Have fun." Giovanni didn't look up from the desk.

I went out for what Giovanni called my personal victory parade, visiting each unit and congratulating everyone who'd fought with us, including the Chirani who'd picked up tools as improvised weapons. The Chirani were a grim lot, even more haggard and desperate than most of the prisoners we'd freed. I was passing the granary when I heard a hesitant voice say, "Eliana?"

The voice was familiar, and I turned. My mouth dropped open. Of all the people to find here—"*Lia.*"

Lia had been my roommate at the conservatory before Mira. She'd left the conservatory a year ago, when her family announced plans to move north. Her high cheekbones were prominent to the point of being ghoulish-looking, and her green eyes were sunken, but even starving she was beautiful in her own strange way. Lia had always been an odd one at the conservatory—she played lute, and had stubbornly refused to take up an ensemble instrument, saying that she wanted to be a minstrel when she finished her education. "Lia," I said again. "What are you doing here?"

Lia gave me a ghostlike smile. "I could ask the same of you. I think it's pretty obvious what I'm doing here—building a bloody wall. But the Eliana I heard about was *you*? I can't believe it."

I glanced around. I'd finished my parade, and my time was my own—as much as it ever was these days. "Come on, I'll get you something to eat. Do you have family here?" Lia shook her head. "Let's go talk for a while."

I led the way down into the larder. "All these keeps are laid out the same," I said. "This set of stairs *always* leads to the larder, and there's a hidden cabinet of food that the first looters to come through *always* miss." I pulled out the loaves of bread and bricks of cheese. "Don't eat too much, too fast," I warned her. "Especially not the cheese." There was a flask of wine in the cabinet as well, and I poured us each a glass.

"So tell me," Lia said. "What have you been up to?"

"You first," I said.

"My story's not that unusual. We tried to go north; they stopped us. We tried again; they stopped us. We tried again; they sent us here. My parents died here, as did the sister and brother who came with us. I do have another brother and sister, with families, but who knows what's happened to them." She pushed a lock of dark hair behind her ear and took a sip of wine.

"Your lute?"

"Stolen." She said it quickly, but I saw a look of pain cross her face, almost worse than when she said her parents had died. "I still have my voice, at least." She looked up. "Your turn."

"I don't really know where to start," I said.

"That doesn't sound like the Eliana I used to go to for all the best gossip," Lia said. "You could start by telling me about everyone else at the conservatory, if you're really stuck. How is Bella?"

"She's dead," I said.

"Dead!" Lia set her wine down, her face white but resigned. "Bella? How?"

"It was the Fedeli ..." I put down my bread and cheese, and picked up my own wine. "I suppose the story really starts with Mira. After you left the conservatory, I had the room to myself for a couple of months—and then a new student arrived, a girl our age, Mira. She said she'd come from a seminary in Cuore, but I realized almost right away that she was lying." I felt my cheeks flush and my hands warm, just a little, at the thought of Mira. "You remember how people would play Redentori songs, Old Way songs, back at the conservatory? Secretly?"

Lia nodded. "Of course. You seemed to be very good at picking them up; I eavesdropped on you to learn the ones I know."

"Mira got a group together to play the songs—me, Bella, Giula, Flavia, and Celia."

Lia's face brightened. "I wish I'd been there for that! But—*Giula?* What was she thinking?"

"It was Celia who nearly got us into trouble. A few weeks after Viaggio, Bella got a letter saying that one of her sisters had died. We met to play the funeral song, but Celia walked out right afterward, saying that we had crossed the line into worship of false gods. And then Giorgi, the cook's assistant, came in and told us all we were playing with fire. That kind of shut down our secret ensemble." I sighed and swirled my wine in my glass. "Bella wasn't ready to give up on the Old Way, though; she went to Giorgi and said she wanted him to teach her more about it. I overheard them talking." Lia shot me a look and I suppressed a smile. "I guess I was eavesdropping."

"That's the Eliana I remember," Lia said.

"Then the Fedeli came." I poured myself more wine; my hand trembled slightly. "Just before Mascherata. Celia tried to convince us all to turn ourselves in. But Mira would have had to flee, and Bella was ready to die for her newfound faith rather than forswear it. So we decided to brazen it out, though Celia nearly turned us all in anyway."

"But she didn't."

"No. On the night of Mascherata, they sent us all to dance in the courtyard—girls and boys together. Bella was playing. Very late that night, one of the Fedeli suddenly tore Bella's trumpet out of her hands and told her to swear loyalty to the Lady. When she said she was a Redentore, they cut her throat." I knew that Lia would look horrified, that however many awful things she'd seen here at Chira, the murder of her old friend would be no less dreadful. So I didn't look up. I fished Bella's cross out from under my shirt and held it out. "This was Bella's. I found it in the courtyard the next day and pocketed it."

"Bella was wearing a cross while the Fedeli were at the conservatory?" Lia raised her wine cup in salute. "That's our Bella."

"In the spring, I came back to our room one day, and there were a half dozen men lying in wait for Mira. They made me wait with them. One of them was a mage." The wine tasted like ashes; I forced myself to take another sip. "It turned out that Mira was a mage, too, from the Circle. She'd run away and hidden at the Verdiano Rural Conservatory because she'd found out that it was the Circle's magic—" I set down my wine very carefully. "It was the Circle's magic that drained the Verdiani lands, that created the wasteland."

Lia had not known this. She went white, and then carefully raised one eyebrow. "I should have guessed. We can't use witchlight here."

"Nor anywhere else in the wasteland." I sighed. "Liemo—that was the mage who'd come for her—tried to persuade Mira to go back to Cuore with him. She refused. So he had his guardsmen take me hostage. They were going to shoot me in the hand." My hand curled tightly now around the wine cup. "Mira used her magic to destroy the bolt before it hit me. And then she just crumbled. She started to weep, and she followed him like a tethered animal. He'd brought an extra horse for her, and she rode away with him."

The room was quiet. We could hear noise from beyond the building walls, but it seemed a long way away.

"Did Mira say anything? Did you say anything to her?"

"I begged her not to go," I said. "I followed her to the courtyard and shouted for her not to listen to him. And when I knew she was leaving, no matter what I said, I sang to her—we all did. Giula, Flavia, Celia, and I. We sang her one of the Redentori songs she'd taught us. But she just rode away."

Lia had eaten the last of the food from the cupboard. I got up, stretched my arms. "Did you want more cheese?"

"I wouldn't refuse it."

I poked my head out the door and spotted Michel. "Go find me some cheese, would you?" I said. "I'm with an old friend."

Back downstairs, Lia said, "There must be more to your story. Were you expelled from the conservatory for singing to Mira?"

"Oh, goodness," I said. "No. But I didn't want to stay any longer. The Circle sponsored me, and I didn't want to take anything from them. And I wanted to tell my parents what had caused the famine. So I left, and so did Giula. We walked together as far as Pluma, and then went our separate ways. My home village, Doratura, was just a few days from Pluma."

"Was?"

"When I got there, it had been destroyed. There were refugees that had come up from the wasteland, and soldiers that came down from Cuore to push them back. Doratura was caught between them. My whole family was dead."

"I'm so sorry," Lia whispered.

"I didn't know that for certain, though, when I first reached my village; there had been a few survivors, and I was told they'd all been taken to a place called Ravenna, in the wasteland. So I went to Ravenna. That was a place like Chira—refugees held prisoner, building the wall. Starving." Lia nodded. "Within a day or two I fell in with this group that was supposed to be planning a breakout. The person who approached me was Lucia. Her cousin Giovanni was there as well—though he was rude, petulant, and useless. Then there was a man named Beneto and a woman named Jesca. Giovanni, Beneto, and Jesca were all from the university in Cuore, and were officers in the Reform movement. They kind of adopted me—well, except for Giovanni, who'd hated me on sight. It turned out that Giovanni was supposed to be doing arms training for young men in Ravenna, secretly, so he was trying to make them all learn how to fight with swords. Gentlemen's weapons." I shook my head. "I'd barely met Beneto and Jesca before Teleso, the military commander, had them both hanged for causing trouble. This was a catastrophe, because the next person in line to command was Giovanni. And then Teleso had me brought into the keep."

"Why?"

"He said he wanted to hear me play." My ears and cheeks started to burn. "He acted like he wanted something else, though."

"I think I can guess," Lia said.

"Well, he didn't want it enough to force the point. He said he wasn't interested in unwilling women—though I think he was ready to stretch the definition of *willing*. Anyway. He also wanted me to play for the funeral of Beneto and Jesca. Both Teleso and the Ravenna reformers wanted the same thing—a riot. The reformers who were left thought that they could use the riot to break out. Teleso thought he could use the riot to kill a whole lot of Ravenessi and ease pressure on the food supplies.

And he had soldiers assigned to shoot people he particularly didn't like, such as Lucia."

"He needed a riot for that? Why?"

"*That* is an interesting story in itself. There was a soldier named Mario who had a strong influence over the other soldiers. Mario was a good man, and he thought it was wrong to shoot without provocation. So if Teleso wanted the soldiers to shoot down a prisoner, he needed to make sure that the prisoner provoked them."

Lia looked down at the table, a bit ruefully. "There wasn't anyone like that here."

"We were lucky."

"Was Mario Redentore?"

"No, definitely not," I said. "He believed devoutly in the Lady. His faith inspired him—a lot." Michel arrived with a basket of cheese, bread, and wine. I poured more wine for both of us and carved off a wedge of cheese. "Where was I?"

"I think you were telling me how you became the Head Troublemaker in Ravenna," Lia said.

"That's right. The funeral. Teleso had me play the Redentore funeral music, so that people could dance. Well, I knew the riot was coming, and when I saw the soldiers surrounding the dancers, I was able to defuse things so there wasn't a riot. Teleso was furious. He had me thrown into the dungeon, and the next morning, he had me dragged outside again. I defied him publicly, and he had me flogged. It sounds strange, but *that* gave me what I needed to take over as 'generale' of the Ravenessi army. Because I'd defied him, and because I didn't cry under the lash."

"What did Giovanni think of that?"

"He was furious. But he got used to the idea eventually. To train people to get ready for the breakout, we used a game, Shepherd-and-Wolves, so that they learned to fight together. And then the morning after Dono alla Magia, I led the uprising."

"And you won—that's pretty obvious."

"We did, though a lot of people died, including Mario. Teleso caught me alone, and nearly killed me. I beat him thanks to Giovanni's weaponry lessons." I gave Lia a rueful grin. "We've learned to get along. Officially we're both generali of the Lupi."

"And unofficially?"

"We're both addressed as 'Generale,' and people do what I tell them to do." Mostly. "After the breakout, we sent the children and the people who didn't want to fight up to Doratura, my old village. It's not in the wasteland, and it could be rebuilt. That's where Giula went; she ended up in Ravenna for a bit, too." I left out the part about Giula becoming Teleso's mistress. Lia's opinion of Giula was low enough already. "The rest of us freed two more of the slave labor camps, and now Chira. And that's it. That's my story."

Lia raised her wine cup to salute me.

"You looked surprised when I said that the famine was caused by magery," I said. "You didn't know that?"

"No," Lia said. "I did know it couldn't be just salt; that couldn't do this, no matter what the Circle said. But magery ..." She considered. "It makes sense." She poured herself more wine. "So do I get sent off to Doratura? Or can I stay with you and be a soldier?"

"You can do whatever you want. It's only the children we send away. Would you want to join the army?"

"I don't know," she said. "I'll have to think about it."

"You'll have until tomorrow morning. That's when we'll be moving on." Something occurred to me. "What exactly had you heard about us? The Lupi, I mean?"

"They started bringing in more soldiers about a month ago—just a few at first, but more and more lately. Of course, we all wondered why. We'd never caused any trouble. But rumors came with the soldiers." Lia stretched, gathering her thoughts. "First we heard there'd been a breakout at another camp, and they were here to make sure nothing like that happened in Chira. Of course, that gave people ideas; if someone else could manage it, maybe we could, too. There was talk for a while, but then Demetrio hanged all the talkers he could find, and then some." She shook her head, rubbing the back of her neck with her hand. "The next set of soldiers brought word of a rebel army. They called you the *Cani*, dogs, but we could tell they were afraid. You'd had some success; that was all we heard.

"The last group of soldiers knew some names. Eliana, Giovanni, Lucia. We whispered your names back and forth as we worked on the wall. The initial story was that you were in charge, and Giovanni your lover."

I choked on my wine. "Giovanni is *not* my lover."

"Well, it made a good story." Lia half grinned at my expression. "Lucia was said to be Giovanni's sister—"

"Cousin."

Lia raised an eyebrow from behind her wine cup. "And the story said you were all apostates—Redentori."

"Some of us are, but not all. Mario would be here now if he hadn't died freeing Ravenna—and he was *not* Redentore."

"Somehow they missed the violinist part, though, or I'd have wondered if it was you. I'd assumed it was someone older ... Anyway. About five days ago, Callista thought she saw someone watching us from the crest of one of the hills nearby. There was a great deal of whispering about that, but it was kept very quiet. If it *was* the first advance of the Cani—the Lupi—as we hoped, the last thing we wanted to do was tip off any of the guards."

We had been fortunate. "I'm glad you kept your mouths shut."

"So am I." Lia smiled. "Most of the victims of Demetrio's purges were men, so there are more women here. I think women are better at keeping secrets."

That reminded me of Giovanni. "I should go back up to Demetrio's study and see how Giovanni's work is going." I finished the last of my wine. "Want to come?"

Lia shrugged. "I certainly don't have anything else to do with myself."

We went up the short stair from the kitchen to the main floor, and down the hall to the study. Lupi saluted as I passed; Chirani refugees stared after me, wide-eyed. Some of them also saluted; a few of them knelt to brush the fabric of my trousers as I passed, as if I were a high-ranking priestess. The Lupi guarding the study stood aside to let us in.

Giovanni sat at the desk, papers piled around him. "Found anything?" I asked.

Giovanni looked up and glared at me bitterly. "I think Demetrio burned most of the important papers before he killed himself. But it's difficult to tell, as he kept the rest in some sort of code. Either that or his handwriting was really atrocious."

Lia slid unobtrusively into one of the chairs near the fireplace to watch us. "Let me see," I said, and picked up one of the papers. "How are you sorting, if you don't know what anything says?"

"Based on where I found it. Those were in the second drawer."

The paper was covered in scrawled symbols. "Do

you think there's a symbol that goes with each letter?"
I asked.

"How would I know?" Giovanni said.

"You went to the university, didn't you?"

"Give it a rest, Eliana," he said. "No, we didn't
cover secret codes at the university. If you don't have
any ideas, put it back where you found it; I want to
keep stuff in some sort of order."

"May I see?" Lia asked.

Giovanni looked up. "Sorry," I said to Lia. "I should
have introduced you. Lia, this is Generale Giovanni.
Giovanni, this is Lia, my roommate from the conservatory."

His eyes flew wide. "The mage?"

"No, don't be ridiculous. Lia was my roommate *before* Mira."

"Oh," he said, losing interest. I handed Lia one of
the papers. She pursed her lips as she studied it. "Do
you think you can figure it out?" Giovanni asked her.

"Maybe," she said with a shrug. "Can I look at the
other papers?"

"Help yourself," Giovanni said. Lia started sorting
through the piles, pulling out a clean sheet of paper to
take notes.

There wasn't really room for me at the desk, so I
went to poke through the cabinets. I found an almost-
empty bottle of potent wine and a bundle of letters tied
with a ribbon. The letters weren't in code. The handwriting was feminine, and after a few moments of
reading I concluded they were from Demetrio's sweetheart.

I nearly tossed them aside; I didn't like thinking of
my enemies as the sorts of people who had sweet-
hearts. Besides, the family letters we'd found at other

camps had been uniformly useless. But there was so little here that we were even able to read, I sat down with them anyway, just for a moment.

Demetrio's lover was named Clara, and she was a lover but not a wife, because the Lady had failed to bless their assignations with a child. It was not a common situation, but it did happen; Clara had come under quite a bit of pressure from her mother and the local priestess to end things with Demetrio and seek a husband that the Lady might show more approval of. It wasn't until the third letter that I realized the priestess she referred to so casually was one of the most high ranking in Cuore—a name even I was familiar with, though admittedly I'd heard it from Lucia. Clara was a lady of quite a significant rank, who lived within the enclave of the Circle and the Emperor, and her letters detailed extensive gossip regarding court politics.

"Giovanni," I said, hesitantly, "do you know of a lady named Clara, a noblewoman at the Imperial Court?"

Giovanni looked up. "Maybe."

"She was Demetrio's lover."

"You're joking," he said, and jumped up, scattering papers everywhere. "Well, *that* explains why she refuses all the men her mother tries to set her up with." He grabbed the bundle of letters from me. "Incredible."

Lia looked up. "I think I've figured out the code," she said.

After all that, the papers Demetrio had encoded really were largely worthless. Either he was an exceptionally suspicious man, or he took malicious delight in the image of his enemies frantically trying to decode grain allocations, duty rosters, and other fascinatingly useless information.

There were a few items of note. All the intelligence he'd received on the rebel army was tucked away at the bottom of one of the drawers. It was not in code, since he hadn't written it; I was relieved to discover how little they knew about our tactics. They knew my name and a bit of my background; a disgusted footnote added that my family was dead, and thus couldn't be used against me. They knew that we primarily relied on crossbows, firing down from the hill, rather than using swords or lances, and that few of us were mounted. They knew that we were inexplicably winning, again and again and again (this was hinted at, but never stated directly), but not why; they didn't know about the scouting party that infiltrated the camps and threw the doors wide open. Or at least, they didn't know yet. Unfortunately, the information revealed little about how they planned to deal with us other than reinforcing the remaining camps (that was obvious), and trying to keep us bottled up in the wasteland.

"Hey," Giovanni said. "Look at this." He pushed one of Clara's letters across the desk.

> You must believe me, my darling, I am doing the best I can. The Fedeli have come to agree with me that it is vitally necessary to reinforce the troops in the wasteland now. However, the Circle has opposed me at every turn.
>
> Because magic can't be used in the wasteland, the Circle can't fight there; I can't overstate how frightening this is to them. In addition, my sources tell me that the Circle has begun to fear

*the army: the army is loyal first to the Emperor,
and because of the wasteland, the army is no
longer as dependent on the Circle as they were in
the past. I believe that the Circle wishes to see
the army fail without magical support, and
obviously, magical support can't be provided
until the Cani leave the wasteland.*

*The sacrifice of the keep commanders seems
an appalling betrayal to me. I am doing my best
to convince the Emperor to send additional
troops, even if it means raising an entirely new
army. Wish me luck, darling. I pray to the Lady
for your safety . . .*

I looked up. "It's fascinating information," I admitted. "And certainly explains a lot. But I'm not sure how we can use it."

Giovanni's eyes glinted. "There's got to be a way." He checked the date on the letter. "This is months old. If only we had more recent information. For all we know, Clara convinced the Emperor and fresh troops are on their way. I'll keep the letters. I almost feel sorry for the lady."

Lia had been wandering the study and looked up suddenly. "You said that Demetrio killed himself?"

"Yes," Giovanni said.

"Where is the body?"

"Right there." I pointed to the corner, and suddenly felt apologetic. We'd gotten awfully cavalier about bodies lately.

Lia carefully lifted the corner of the blanket and stared down at the face impassively, then covered it again, standing back up. "I hate to tell you this," she said, "but that's not him."

"*What?*" Giovanni dropped everything he was holding. "Are you sure?"

"Positive. This is his second. But I wonder if the second took his commander's place willingly, or if Demetrio killed him and put the knife in his hand?"

"Lady's tits," Giovanni said, "I don't believe it. I can't *believe* I was taken in by such a stupid trick. Michel!" He stomped out the door.

Lia still stood by the body, her green eyes wide and very slightly amused. "I should've known Demetrio wouldn't just give up like that. It's not his style."

Giovanni was back within minutes. "One horse is gone," he said.

"From the stables?"

"No," Giovanni said. "We secured those, remember? The bastard stole *my* horse." I tried—and failed—to cover my laughter with my sleeve. "I'm glad you find this *amusing,* Eliana. Doesn't it worry you that he might, just possibly, have realized that we had a scout slip into his keep to open the door?"

"I don't find it amusing," I said. Well, I did, but only because it was Giovanni's horse. "Figures he took the best horse he could find, doesn't it? You can take his horse from the stables; that seems only fair. You've sent Michel after him, of course?"

"Of course."

"But Stivali was the fastest horse, wasn't he? That's why you wanted him." Giovanni's vicious glare was confirmation of this. We weren't going to catch Demetrio; he had too much of a head start. Giovanni went back to sorting through the desk, still disgusted with himself and our army; I started on the cabinets along the wall. "Hey," I said. "Lia!" She looked up. "Demetrio was a man of many talents."

There was a lute in the cabinet; I pulled it out to examine it. Demetrio's lute was more decorative than Lia's had been; it was adorned with carved designs of birds and flowers. I doubted that the carvings would improve the sound, but after the months without her lute, I think Lia would have snatched at the chance to play gut strung over a large mixing bowl. The sheet music stored behind it only added to her delight. "It's yours," I said, and she tucked the music under her arm and took her leave to go play.

*   *   *

Lia came briefly to see me the following morning, to say good-bye. "I won't be coming with you," she said, "but I'll be serving your army. You'll see."

"Are you going to Doratura?" I asked.

"Maybe," she said. "For a while."

Lia had no sash to go with her ragged dress, but she had found a red hat somewhere in the keep; it was a bit large for her, and she pushed it back to keep it from slipping into her eyes. "Take care of yourself," I said.

"You too," she said, and gave me a tight hug.

A few minutes later it was time to go rally the troops. The Chirani gathered by the keep to stare at me from hollow faces with eyes that scorched mine with hope and anger. There were many more women than men in Chira, and there were almost no children.

"We came here to free you," I said. "And we have. Your lives are your own; you serve the Circle's cruelty no longer." At the very back of the crowd I saw Lia, watching my speech with a tiny smile. "You have a choice. We've freed many other camps now, and the prisoners have resettled abandoned villages that are not in the wasteland. They are rebuilding; it will mean work, but not at the threat of the lash or the noose. That's one option. Or you can go wherever you want; return home, head north, head south. You belong only to yourselves."

The women stared at me, their faces rigid, their eyes hungry.

"Or," I said, and a ripple went through the crowd at my tone, "you can join us. You have the strength in your arms to fight; you have the will in your hearts to free others just as we have freed you. There are three more camps in the wasteland, all enslaved, all building the wall. Three more camps, just like this one." Lia's eyes were closed, listening; I remembered her doing that, listening to me practice my violin, a lifetime ago.

"We are the Lupi, the wolves, because we hunt as a pack; because we fell on the sheep who called themselves our captors and tore them to pieces. We will fall on those other camps, one by one. We will march in like the tide, and no one will stop us. We will sweep in like fire, and nothing will be left in our path." I was breathless, pacing, as the crowd of half-starved women watched me in total silence.

"Are you with me?" I demanded.

"Yes," the women whispered, the hiss rippling through the crowd.

"You are *wolves*. Find your voices. You don't need to whisper now because you are *free*," I shouted. "Are you *with* me?"

"Yes. *Yes*. YES!"

"We march at noon," I said. "Meet on the north hill in two hours."

The crowd started to disperse, and I turned to regroup my own people. I should have asked Lia who to put in charge of the Chirani; I had no doubt that most of them would be coming with us. I saw Felice watching me quietly from the shadows by the keep. "The young lady with the lute said she wanted me to give this to you," he said, looking slightly puzzled. "It's sealed."

Lia must have lifted the heavy parchment from Demetrio's office, along with a pen and the seal. I broke the seal and read the page quickly. It was not a letter; it took me a moment to realize it was musical notation. One of the songs we'd found in the cabinet? No. *Lady's tits,* I thought, reading it over.

The tune was fairly close to one of the folk songs I'd played with Mira, but the words were different—and very catchy, I had to admit, humming it over to myself. It was the ballad of one Eliana, who had discovered the Circle's deadly secret and now sought to keep them from destroying all of Verdia, whatever the cost.

In the name of the Mother, Her Son, and the Light,
We are fire and water and God's open hand.
I have freed you and now I will lead you to glory.
I'll trade my own blood for the life of the land.

At the bottom of the last page, Lia had written neatly, *more to come.*

Lady's tits, I thought, *how embarrassing,* and went looking for Giovanni. I found him saddling Demetrio's horse, and held out the sheet with a bit of trepidation.

"What's this?" Giovanni stepped away from the horse and took the parchment, looking it over. I saw a glint of annoyance cross over his face, and then he shook himself and laughed mockingly. "The heroine of ballads! I hope you'll still stoop to sharing a tent with the rest of us."

"What do you think of it?" I asked, not willing to ask the real question: *Does it bother you that this is about me, and not about you?*

"It's not bad. It's better than 'The Wicked Stepmother.'" I must have looked puzzled because he laughed again and said, "You know. 'I've brought a gift of honey, bright as sun and sweet as wine.' The reformers wrote that."

"That was you? One of my friends spent hours in the library looking up references to honey in old ballads, trying to figure out what that damn song meant."

"Yeah, I'm not surprised. I'd tell you that I argued for a more transparent meaning, but I don't want you thinking I'm just trying to get in good with the heroine of the ballads." He gave me back the parchment with a little mocking flourish, and mounted his horse. "See you back at camp."

CHAPTER TWO

*To some I bring a sword; to some
I bring a lamp. There are many
ways to face the darkness.*
—The Journey of Gèsu, chapter 12, verse 25.

You're wrong," Giovanni said. "Dangerously wrong."

I threw down the map Felice had carefully drawn out. "*Dangerously wrong* would be dividing our forces!"

"Isabella agrees with me."

"Isabella also thinks she could run the Lupi better than I could. It's no wonder she likes the idea of her own little army."

"Look." Giovanni nearly grabbed my shoulders, then thought better of it. "If you don't trust Isabella to get her men up to Cuore without you, why did you make her a commander?"

I ignored the question. "It's a stupid strategy."

"What would you know about it? You know *nothing* about strategy. You know nothing about *tactics*. I do. So why won't you listen to me?" He glanced past me. "Lucia. Talk some sense into her. Maybe she'll listen to *you*."

Lucia shook her head. "I am not a strategist."

"Neither is she," he said.

"We're not dividing the Lupi," I said. "Discussion ended."

Giovanni looked past Lucia at Felice, who was sitting quietly in the corner of the tent. "You. *You're* supposed to know something about strategy. If this were a mock battle with your tutor, what would *you* do?"

"I'd keep the Lupi together when we left the wasteland," Felice said. "Like Eliana is doing."

I nodded, satisfied, and Giovanni shot Felice a venomous look. "Remember," he muttered as he stomped out. "He only won nineteen out of twenty-five."

He returned moments later. "The scouts are back," he said, and held the tent flap open for Camilla.

It was far too soon for the scouts to have returned—had something gone terribly wrong?—but Camilla was grinning broadly. "They're gone," she said. "The soldiers pulled out of the camp; it's just the prisoners."

"Are you *sure*?"

"Positive. We ended up going into camp and talking to some of the prisoners. The soldiers packed up the day before yesterday and headed out of the wasteland."

"Then let's head in," I said. If we waited much longer, the prisoners would disperse. Camilla saluted, and I sent Vitale to get my horse.

This was the last camp. Though we'd feared it would get harder and harder to liberate them, after Chira it had gotten easier: the camp commanders were demoralized and understaffed. Apparently Clara's attempts to arrange for reinforcements were having little effect.

We had no need to be covert, so in the last light of the afternoon, we massed on the hill overlooking the camp. Below us, people were pointing and shouting;

some were waving red banners. I looked at Giovanni and nodded, and we rode in slow procession down to the camp, the rest of the Lupi following.

The refugees surrounded us as we entered the camp. Men and women reached up to clasp our hands, pressing in so tightly that Forza began to sidle nervously. A small girl, maybe six years old, saluted us from her father's shoulders; other children had scrambled onto the roof of the vacant stables to get a better view.

Someone shouted a welcome, and this cheer was taken up, raggedly, by the refugees. I shouted a greeting back, then wheeled my horse to speak. "We came here expecting a fight," I said. "I guess we can't complain too much that the soldiers didn't have the stomach to face us."

The Lupi cheered that; the refugees joined in, but feebly. Their eyes were desperate, hungry, like the eyes of the refugees at Chira, like the eyes of everyone I'd seen in every camp we'd liberated. "From here, we ride north," I said. "The soldiers were our keepers, but it was the Circle who enslaved us—who created the wasteland, killed our families, imprisoned us here. We are going to sweep in on the Circle as we swept into the wasteland camps—like fire, like the tide, like the incoming storm. If you would join us, be ready to march at dawn tomorrow!"

Smoke still rose from the stone hulk of the keep. The retreating camp soldiers had loaded up what they could carry, and torched everything else. Including all the food. The refugees had stayed where they were in part because they were too weak to flee the wasteland and they hoped that the Lupi would bring them something to eat. After inspecting the ruins of the keep, I sent for Rafi to arrange for a meal for both the Lupi and the refugees.

Giovanni rode up next to me. "No grain," he said. "That's not good."

"It means that wintering in the wasteland is definitely not an option," I said.

Giovanni opened his mouth, as if he were going to restart the argument over our next course of action, but he thought the better of it. "We can't leave before tomorrow. Let's talk about it after we eat."

Felice was helping to serve the food when I arrived for my portion. He almost looked like one of the Lupi now—he was dirty, at least. He saluted and then served me some porridge. "Council meeting later," I said. "Be there. I want someone on my side." He smiled and nodded.

Giovanni also spent his time before the meeting marshalling allies. When I stepped into the tent, not only Felice but Isabella, Giovanni, and Rafi waited for me. Lucia followed a moment later. I sent for tea for all of us and sat down, waiting for the onslaught.

It started with Rafi. "I think you should disband the Lupi," he said.

This wasn't what Giovanni had expected him to say, either—that was obvious. "What?" Giovanni said. "What would be the point of that, exactly?"

"You don't know how to fight magefire," Rafi said. "Neither do I. Neither does Eliana. That's why you've been arguing for the last month over what to do next."

"So you think we should just give up?" I said.

"What would be the purpose in riding out of the wasteland, just so that we could all be killed?"

During the war with Vesuvia, opposing mages stood

at either end of the battlefield, hurling lethal fire back and forth. The armies were mainly there to keep the other side's swordsmen from walking up and skewering the mages. Of course, some skirmishes were fought without magical support, but on those occasions when one side had mages and the other side did not, the battles were typically over *very* quickly. We had no mages in our army—and for obvious reasons, we were not likely to get any. But just giving up and going home—not that most of us *had* homes—was absurd. "We're not disbanding, Rafi."

"So how do you plan to face the Circle?" Rafi asked.

"Use the land for protection," I said. "Strike from under shelter, preferably from behind. The Circle won't move against us all at once. If we draw them out a handful at a time, I think we'll have a chance."

"How many mages destroyed your village?" Rafi asked.

I felt a flush rise to my cheeks, and a lump rise to my throat. "I don't know."

"It wasn't many, though."

"Probably not. But Doratura was not an army; they were not prepared."

Rafi spread his hands. "Granted. So how do you propose to draw out the Circle?"

"I think we should take some tempting targets," I said. "Pluma, for one. We could fortify the town . . ."

"Pluma is a *stupid* target," Giovanni said.

"It's walled," I said.

"Walls don't stop magefire! If we're going to draw out the Circle, which I still think is a stupid idea, we should send one of the units to fortify a hilltop. An uninhabited hilltop."

"In other words, you want to set up some of our *people* as decoys?"

"Why is this a problem? *All* armies do this. What kind of generale are you?"

"The kind who stands *by* her people," I said, "and doesn't set them up to get *slaughtered*."

"You could make it a small unit," he said. "You could even ask for volunteers."

"*No,*" I said, "and that's the *end* of it."

Isabella leaned forward. "Giovanni may be an arrogant twit, but that doesn't mean you shouldn't take advantage of his strategic ability. And in this case he happens to be right."

"What if it was your unit I sent to be the decoy?" I asked.

"That would be stupid," Isabella said. "One of the less-experienced units would make more sense." I opened my mouth in fury and she cut me off. "*But,* if you did send us, we would go because that's a *strategy* that makes sense."

"I won't use my people that way," I said.

Vitale arrived with the tea and we all paused to sip and glower at each other.

"We should split up the army," Giovanni said. "Divide it up into its units and have each one make its own way to Cuore. If we keep the Lupi together, one bad skirmish could wipe out the entire army."

"The whole purpose of this," I said through clenched teeth, "is to get them to divide *their* forces. You want us to make the same mistake?"

"Our strength is in numbers?" Giovanni taunted.

"Don't compare me to Beneto," I said. "If anyone here is acting like Beneto, it's you. He viewed our lives as worthless, and you're acting as if you see them the same way."

"That's not true and you know it," Giovanni said. "You act as if you don't trust your own seconds."

I ducked my head to take a sip of tea, and Giovanni slammed his own tea down. "That's it, isn't it? You don't trust your seconds to lead the units up to Cuore without you."

My face was hot; I wished Isabella, at least, were somewhere else. "Half of the commanders can't even divide up the undesirable chores without a brawl erupting."

"But most of their fights are with other units," Giovanni said. "They get on well *within* each unit."

I glanced toward Felice, who hurriedly set down his tea. "I agree with Eliana," he said.

"About *what,* exactly?" Giovanni said.

"I think we should keep the Lupi together," Felice said. "As for Pluma—maybe it would help if we had some additional intelligence. The best information we've gotten in months was in those letters Demetrio had in his study. We need to know where the winds are blowing *now*—whether the residents of Pluma will support us or fight against us, whether people view our cause as just or cursed." Felice picked his tea back up. "Send Camilla, me, and maybe Tomas up to Pluma. I can talk to the reformers there and we can bring back some *current* information. If we ride, we could be there and back in less than two weeks; the food will hold out that long. Meanwhile, you can move the Lupi toward the center of Verdia, where you can strike out toward Pluma if you decide that's best."

I looked around the tent. Giovanni reluctantly nodded. "More information might help us."

Isabella was still glaring at me. "It won't change the fact that it's a bad idea to keep the Lupi together."

"We'll send Felice, Camilla, and Tomas," I said. "We can discuss this again when they get back." I turned to Felice. "You'll leave at dawn."

*   *   *

We moved the Lupi, along with our newest recruits from that last camp, to the edge of the wasteland while our scouts were gone. They returned well fed but not terribly well rested. Camilla brought back a small sack of apples, which I shared out among all of us as she gave her report. They were crisp and sweet; I savored my portion and licked the last of the juice from my fingers.

"They're singing your songs," Camilla said with a wry grin. "Tomas and I went around to different taverns, trying to get a sense of how people felt about the Lupi. They're singing Lia's ballads everywhere."

"During the war with Vesuvia, there was a battle outside Pluma," Tomas said. "Things don't grow well there; in a sense, they're in their own little wasteland. They definitely know about the Circle's secret now, and they're angry."

"And they like *you*," Camilla said.

"That's good news," I said. At least it was good news for me; Giovanni didn't look quite so pleased.

"What did you learn from the reformers?" Giovanni asked Felice.

"Apparently the Circle has almost entirely withdrawn to Cuore," Felice said. "The reformers believe that the Circle is planning to sit tight and wait to see just what the Lupi do. If you want to strike at a large target like Pluma, there's no better time."

Giovanni scowled. "What did Cilo think?"

"Cilo agrees that the timing is right for the Lupi to strike out of the wasteland."

"I don't believe it," Giovanni said. "Cilo *never* thinks it's the right time to act."

Felice gave him a sheepish grin. "Well, I was doing a little interpretation, because you're right, of course. But he sounded more positive about action than I've ever heard before—and coming from Cilo, that's really something."

Giovanni sighed deeply, out of arguments.

"What about those letters?" Isabella asked. "Last we heard, the Circle was planning to pounce on us as soon as we left the wasteland, because they couldn't hit us while we stayed down here. What happened to that plan?"

"I couldn't tell you," Felice said. "I don't think the reformers know. But for now at least, they've pulled back to Cuore."

"We leave the day after tomorrow," I said.

*   *   *

It didn't quite happen that way. The next morning, there was an outbreak of dysentery among the Lupi. It had started with the weakened refugees from that last camp. Many of them were already ill when we freed them. The morning after Felice, Camilla, and Tomas returned, scores more fell sick, and by morning on the day we'd planned to ride out, half my army was seriously ill. There isn't much you can do for dysentery but wait it out. Most of the Lupi were reasonably healthy after a summer of constant travel and reasonable rations, so I expected most to pull through, but an army that's up to its knees in runny shit is not exactly a fit fighting force. We'd have to wait until the worst of the illness was past.

I was not among the ones taken ill; I've always had a stomach of cast iron. Giovanni apparently did too, as he also stayed healthy. Lucia was struck down, though, and I spent a few days nursing her, giving her sips of cooled tea in between bullying the healthy Lupi into digging fresh latrines and covering over the filthy ones. We lost about two weeks to the illness. I'd have waited longer, but I'd seen our food stores and knew that we were almost out of time.

Still, as a concession to Giovanni's fears, as well as to the weakness of some of the Lupi who were only just beginning to recover, I left a detachment behind in the wasteland, under Tomas's leadership. This made an excellent excuse to keep Vitale, the youngest of the Lupi, out of danger. I decided that Felice could stay there, too. Though he had been a surprisingly patient teacher, and useful in councils, he had yet to make himself useful during an actual battle. And he'd had a particularly bad case of dysentery. The wasteland detachment could join us in Pluma once we'd secured the town, and at Giovanni's insistence, I agreed that we'd discuss dividing our army at that point. I wanted my troops to have a real victory under their belt, a real accomplishment. After two weeks shitting in the mud, we needed something to lift morale.

As we rode north, the land came back to life even as the plants were dying for the winter. The weeds were brown, the flowers gone to seed; we could let the horses forage now, which eased the burden on our food stores a great deal. The Lupi stared open-mouthed at the climbing weeds, the thistles, the last of the autumn wildflowers. I told myself that I remembered what grass and flowers looked like, but I couldn't help staring at the creeping bug that startled me, crawling up my leg during dinner.

The first night we slept in a meadow again, Lucia celebrated a special Mass, leading us all in the dance to celebrate the fertility of the land. It was danced in the spring planting season, she said, and at the harvest. It seemed appropriate. I thought about asking her for a dance to ask God to hold off the coming of real winter; I desperately hoped we could be done with what we were doing by the time winter came, although I was doubtful about our chances. Camping in our flimsy tents on bitter winter nights could easily kill half our army without the Circle Guard ever taking a shot at us. If we needed to, we could send people off to the reset-tled towns, but I feared that the Circle would hunt us down over the winter months—and if they didn't, peo-ple would grow comfortable, reluctant to leave their new homes and families in the spring.

We moved a little slowly the first full day back in green Verdia, staring at the trees and the bugs and the sparrows. We let our horses forage, and cut some real tent poles. I called a halt early in the day to let people relax a little, and sat down under a tree to practice my violin, with Michel standing watch nearby. Just as I started to unlace the ties of my violin case, I heard hooves crashing through the brush. I looked up to see Vitale throw himself off the horse.

"Generale Eliana," Vitale gasped. "Tomas sent me." He struggled for breath to speak.

I put my hand on his shoulder, glancing past him. "Get Giovanni and Lucia," I ordered one of my soldiers, but only Giovanni appeared in time to hear Vitale's message.

"Felice. Is he here? Have you seen him?"

I shook my head. "No. I haven't seen him. He was supposed to stay with Tomas."

"He's gone. He took a horse and disappeared."

It took a moment for this to sink in. "Why? Did he have a fight with someone?" I asked, but that was ridiculous. Except for that first day, Felice got along with pretty much everybody.

"No. No one. He spoke to no one—took the fastest horse—" Vitale was white, staring at our faces. "Don't you *get* it? Tomas said—he said—he's gone to the Circle. He *must* have gone to the Circle. Once he knew our plans—"

"Impossible," Giovanni said, but his face had gone pale. "Felice knew the password; he'd met Cilo—"

"Your bloody password! Giovanni, if he was a spy, what could he know, what could he *tell* them ..."

"We have to retreat," he said. "Get back to the wasteland *now*. Eliana. Trust me on this one—"

And I would have, but that was when the fires came down.

I grabbed for my whistle, blew *retreat, retreat, retreat*. The first wave had not hit the area nearest me, but I could see flames rising from farther in the woods. White sparks streamed toward the sky like fleeing stars and I heard screams of agony. "Oh my God," I said. "Lucia. *Lucia.*"

Giovanni took off at a run—I didn't see to where, but I stood frozen for a moment next to the still-gasping Vitale, looking around uselessly. I turned, and in the twilight, I could see a handful of figures on the hill behind us, clasping hands, silhouetted against the darkening sky and the bright burning forest. I counted. Five mages—that was all it took. Five of them. As I watched, they turned toward us, scanning the field we'd camped in. Michel grabbed me, whirling me so that he stood between me and the mages, as if he meant to shelter me with his own body if he could.

Over my head, I saw the fire spring into life like a billowing gold cloud. The color darkened to red, and the cloud slowly unrolled. As the edge of the cloud touched the tops of the trees, they burst into bright white flames. The cloud of fire paused for a moment, and I could almost feel the mages taking a collective deep breath. Then the flames flashed down toward me and I closed my eyes tightly, knowing that in an instant I would feel my flesh burning around me, and there was nothing I could do about it.

I heard a child's cry of agony and opened my eyes to see Vitale consumed in flames. "No," I screamed, and tried to move toward him, but Michel was still holding me, more out of fear than protection. I stared down at his hands and mine, whole and unburned. Vitale's scream ended as his body crumbled into ash.

The woods were flaming around me; the very air seemed to have turned to pulsing fire. Yet even the grass I stood on was untouched. I turned, dragging Michel around after me, and stared at the hill. At first I could see nothing but the fire, but as it burned everything there was to consume, I saw that one mage stood with arms outstretched to the sky—in summoning, not in supplication. Even with the flames to provide light, the face was shadowed, but I knew with cold certainty who it was. *She* was protecting me. Even as she killed everyone around me. Killed Vitale. Killed *Lucia*. My hands moved to cross myself. *Oh, God, spare Lucia.*

Michel still stood with his arms around me, protected by my nearness. At least I could save Michel. As the flames died down to rolling waves at our feet and then faded to nothing, I dragged him through the blackened field with me. Remembering my whistle, I blew *retreat* again and again, though the Lupi in the outer ring that had not been blasted in the first attack were already fleeing as fast as they could.

Five mages. How many mages sat in the Circle? Nearly two hundred? Yet our entire army fell to five. Yes, it was an ambush, but *five mages. What were we thinking?* What was *I* thinking? I knew what mages could do. *Of all the people here, I should have known what mages could do.* How could I possibly have thought we could face them?

God wants us to win, so we will. Somehow. Lucia's words rang in my ears. I had held on to those words through all these months, letting the easy victories against isolated, demoralized soldiers fool me into thinking we could win this war. *All those people dead. Vitale, dead.* And it was my fault; I had led them here, and because of me, they had died.

I should have never trusted Felice, or the information he brought back from Pluma. I should have taken Giovanni's advice and split up the army. *It was my fault.* Michel sobbed into my shoulder as we walked. If I'd reached for Vitale, if I'd tried to protect him as Michel had tried to protect me, he would have lived as well.

It wasn't until we had almost reached the wasteland that I realized the one other thing I had brought with me, still slung over my shoulder: my violin.

And so we returned to the wasteland, defeated, to take stock of who was left.

Giovanni, of course, had survived. Somehow I had expected to see him greet me at the edge of the campsite, grim and bitter and still pale with fear. He blamed himself for trusting Felice, and he blamed me for refusing to divide the army. Michel had survived with me shielding his body. Isabella had come through untouched as well, and had brought two of her own out with her.

Rafi, who had urged me to disband the Lupi because I had no way to fight magefire, was dead. Camilla the scout leader—dead. Martido and Fiora, the irritating couple that had quarreled over the bracelet—both dead. Perhaps half of those who had been in the woods that night survived, and I was amazed that it was that many.

My grief over the people we'd lost, and my fear for Lucia who was still missing, alternated with bitter, gut-twisting anger. *How could she,* I thought, again and again, as I sat alone at the north end of our makeshift camp, watching the road to see who returned. All these months, though I knew Mira was with the Circle, I had thought of her as their slave, as the Lupi had been their slaves. They had *forced* her to do magery; they had dragged her back to Cuore. Surely—I had thought— surely, she would never *truly* serve them again. But I knew that Mira had been the focus that night. She was the only reason I was still alive.

Lucia. Please, God, I prayed. *Bring Lucia back to me.*

It took two days for the survivors to straggle back to our makeshift camp. Some of them greeted me as they arrived; others wouldn't look me in the eye. I hardly cared. *I'll do anything you want, God,* I prayed, again and again. I knelt and whispered the words out loud, when no one was nearby. *Anything. Just let Lucia return alive. She's the only one I have left.*

At the very end of the second day, I saw one person straggling down the road, limping and alone. I shaded my eyes, then started walking toward her, then running.

Lucia caught me in a tight hug. "You're alive," I said into her hair as I pressed my face against her shoulder.

"Yes," she said, and embraced me for a long moment. Finally she whispered, "Eliana, I have a message for you. I think it's God's will that you relinquish control of the Lupi to Giovanni."

I went from relief to anger. "Because I was wrong about dividing the Lupi?"

"No," Lucia said. "Because what you want, more than anything, is to protect your people. But we can't fight this war that way. Giovanni understands that. You do, too, but you can't do it without destroying yourself." She stared into my face, her eyes bearing into mine. "Eliana. You have to give the army to Giovanni."

"What am I going to do if I'm not leading?" Not that I really knew what to do now; how could I rally the troops, tell them we could fight and win, when I no longer believed it myself?

"There will be something," Lucia said. "Please, believe me. I know. There will be *something*. Trust in God."

I had made a promise. *I'll do anything, God, just let Lucia return alive.* Was this the price? "All right," I said. "I'll go tell Giovanni that he's in charge."

*   *   *

Giovanni didn't gloat; in fact, he looked almost shattered, but he quickly agreed that I was probably right. I went to tell each of the surviving seconds that they would report to Giovanni now. We had always theoretically been equals, but everyone knew who was really in charge. I didn't find Isabella right away; Michel had seen her leave the camp, walking into the wasteland. I followed in the direction he pointed, and saw her as I came around the edge of a hill. She didn't see me; her eyes were closed as she knelt, her arms upraised. I had never been quite sure of Isabella's beliefs, but this was the posture to pray to the Lady. I held back a moment and watched.

Isabella was speaking, but too quietly for me to hear. I could see tears glint on her cheeks. Then she pulled a small sachet from a string around her neck. My mother wore one of those; it held a lock of hair cut from each of her children, even the two who had died. All mothers kept them, to bless and pray for their children when they were distant. It was one of the oldest traditions given by the Lady to Gaius.

As I watched, Isabella unlaced the pouch, took out a lock of dark, soft hair, and laid it on a rock. With a flint and steel and a bit of tinder, she set fire to the hair. I smelled the acrid smoke from where I stood, and choked back a cough. Isabella watched the smoldering ash for a moment.

"Now," she said. "Now you are truly dead to me." She closed her eyes for a long moment. Then she crossed herself, and I heard her mutter, "God forgive me."

I should not have seen this. I would talk to her later, I decided, and slipped away.

A few nights later, Lia arrived without warning. She found me with Giovanni and Lucia; I was still included in war councils, still addressed as Generale, just as Giovanni had been. "I've got something you might be interested in," she said to me without preamble. "Here."

The letter she handed me was sealed. "Don't open it," she said.

"Lia, what is this?"

"It's the letter of introduction for one Daniele, a premier violinist of the Pluma conservatory," she said. "He was just accepted into one of the ensembles in Cuore—playing within the Imperial enclave, in fact." She handed me another paper. "Here's the paper offering him the position."

I read it over quickly. I recognized the name of the ensemble; it was one of the many small ensembles that provided chamber music at court. "So where is this Daniele?" I asked.

"Dead," Lia said. "He died of a fever. But the Circle doesn't know that. Nor do they have any particular idea of what he looks like. Come on, Eliana, you know what I'm thinking! Don't you think there's anything you could accomplish if you were within the enclave of the Emperor? The enclave of the *Circle*?"

Giovanni's eyes lit up as mine went wide with alarm. "Oh no," I said. "Lia, I'm not that good. I'm out of practice. And anyway I'm a *woman*. Daniele was not."

"Cut your hair short again. No one looking at you ever knows you're a girl."

"My voice—"

"Is deep enough to pass," Lia said. "There are boys your age with voices squeakier than mine." She clasped my hand and looked at me eagerly. "You'll pass, Eliana. Maybe if you stayed there five years they might suspect your lack of a beard, but not now. And you won't be staying there for five years, will you?"

"Eliana, you've got to do it," Giovanni said. "We're never going to get this sort of chance again."

"What am I supposed to do?" I demanded. "Spy on them?"

"Well, yeah," Giovanni said. "And maybe more. Look, we know that the Circle is afraid of the army. Well, maybe they have *reason* to be afraid. Or maybe you could *give* them reason. You could gather information, win allies, you could even assassinate people in their beds! Well, maybe not that. But—"

"Giovanni, you're talking about court intrigue. What do I know about intrigue?"

"What did you know about leading an army? What did you know about training fighters? What did you know about *strategy*? When has not knowing what you're doing stopped *you* from doing anything?"

"You're just trying to get rid of me. To get me out of your way."

"Why would I bother? You've been *staying* out of the way. Eliana, no one else can do this!"

"I can't either," I said. "Giovanni, there are members of the Circle who *know* me, two of them. They will know that I don't belong there. There are Fedeli who could recognize me—"

"Eliana, I've spent most of my life with people like this. Trust me, they will never recognize you because they will never *look* at you. People like the men of the High Circle never look in the faces of their inferiors, and that's what they'll consider you. For all intents and purposes you will be *invisible*. Can't you see how useful that is?"

"What about Felice? We never caught Felice, and we *know* he was working for them."

"Court is huge, Eliana. And why would they be keeping a spy like Felice there? The chances are miniscule."

"*If* I go, how long do you expect me to stay there? What am I supposed to come back with?"

"The secret that will win the war," he said, then laughed. "I don't know, Eliana. Use your own judgment. Something will tell you it's time."

"Yeah," I said, "like I'll find out I've been recognized. Or it will finally sink *in* that palace politics are just not my cup of tea."

"Eliana, you'll be good at it. I mean that. Don't tell yourself you can't do it, because you can. You'll win this for us, because you know what? I'll lead the Lupi as far as they'll follow me, but I think this is the best chance we've *got*."

I thought about it.

"I'll need a haircut," I said softly. "And a different violin. The sound—violins are very distinctive. A musician could identify me from that alone."

Lia had brought the dead boy's violin, and I spent some time that afternoon practicing with it, getting used to the new sound. It was a better violin than mine, with a fine tone, but I decided to bring my own bow.

In the evening, Lucia cut my hair short and used a less-ragged blanket to make me a new tunic. "You make an attractive boy," she said, inspecting her handiwork.

We had a spare leather belt, and I folded my red sash and put it away. My neck felt chilled when she'd finished cutting my hair, and I pulled Bella's cross off and tucked it in with the sash. "I suppose I'd better leave this behind," I said.

"Yes," Lucia said. "It's what's in your heart that matters, anyway." She turned me around to face her. "I think God wants you to go," she said. "And I really think this is important. Take heart, Eliana. Gèsu will always give you the strength you need, to face anything. He's with you, Eliana. Always." She kissed me. "I will pray for you every day that you're gone."

"Thank you," I said, and I knew, *this is the price*. And I knew, as I kissed Lucia good-bye, *it was worth it*.

PART TWO

Are You As I Am

CHAPTER THREE

In my Mother's house there are many rooms.
—*The Journey of Gèsu, chapter 4, verse 13.8*

What's your name?"

"Daniele."

"Where were you born?"

"Mirago."

"Don't look so stricken." Lia punched me gently in the arm. "No one will question your story if you look like you believe what you're saying. Let's try again. What's your name?"

"Daniele." *This will never work,* I thought. *It's crazy to think it could.* "I am from Mirago. I just graduated from the conservatory in Pluma."

"Good. Say it again."

"My name is Daniele." Even though I was telling myself that no one would believe me, my voice was getting steadier, more confident. "I was born in Mirago, but I've been living in Pluma and going to the conservatory there."

"Again."

I repeated my name, my hometown, and my most

recent history until Michel returned to our camp with the paints he'd gone to buy at the apothecary's shop. "Now pay attention," Michel said. He dabbed paint first on my face, then on Lia's so that I could see how it was done. "Your skin needs to look a little rougher, and you can use these to add a little shadow to your throat, like this."

Lia peered at me. "Michel, you did an excellent job. She really looks like a boy."

"You don't," I said, blinking at Lia.

"I have a girl's haircut and girl's clothing. You're dressed as a boy." With Michel peering over my shoulder and advising me, I practiced putting the paints on myself until both Lia and Michel pronounced my efforts adequate.

"Where did you get so good at this, anyway?" I asked Michel as we rolled the paints up in a cloth and shoved them deep into my pack.

"Mascherata is my favorite festival," Michel said. "I love disguises."

I bound my breasts, and Michel helped me add a little padding to my shoulders to make my build look more masculine. "Don't worry too much about the shoulders," he said. "Lots of boys your age are skinny. Just make sure your breasts don't stick out too much."

Lia hunted down a calm pool of water where I could see my reflection, but I couldn't see myself well enough to be reassured. So the next time we passed through a village, she made me go in with Michel to ask for a meal. "Good practice."

We approached one of the larger outlying farms; we could smell fava beans and root vegetables cooking as we approached. I let Michel knock on the back door.

"Good morning, signora," he said to the woman who answered his knock. "We are traveling to Cuore. Would it be possible for us to purchase lunch from you?"

The woman waved aside Michel's purse. "It may have been a hard year, but we're not so poor yet that we'll take money for hospitality. Come in and have a seat."

The woman's name was Celsa. I mumbled my alias as I sat down next to Michel, feeling deeply uncomfortable in my false identity.

"Why are you going to Cuore?" Celsa asked as she started frying up wheat cakes.

Michel poked me. "I've been attending the conservatory in Pluma," I said, indicating my violin case. *What if she knows someone at the conservatory? This is a mad idea; we should head back to the wasteland now.* "I won a position in one of the ensembles at the Imperial Court."

"Good for you!" Celsa turned away from her cooking briefly to give me a friendly smile. "But *you* don't look like a musician," she said to Michel. "Why are you traveling?"

"To take care of my brother here," Michel said, giving me a punch in the arm. "We're twins—hard to believe, isn't it? He got all the talent. I got the muscles."

A young woman about my age came in with a bucket of water, and poured some of it into a kettle to make tea. "This is Partena, my eldest daughter," Celsa said. Partena brought us tea when it was ready, and sat down across from me.

"So you're going to play at court?" she asked. "That must be exciting!"

"I suppose it is," I said. Something about the intensity of her smile was making me nervous.

"I've always wanted just to see Cuore. Have you been there before?"

"No," I said. "I'm from Verdia. I was born in Mirago, and I went to the conservatory when I was twelve—and I graduated last week."

Partena laughed a little as if I was very amusing, and tossed her head so that her dark hair caught the sun that slanted through the open door. Her hair was very long, and she wore it unbraided. She had a very pretty face, I noticed.

"They kept you separated from the girls there, didn't they?" Partena asked.

I nodded. Michel leaned forward and said, "This is why I'm glad that *I'm* the one who got the muscles, instead of the talent!"

Partena laughed again, but turned back to me a moment later. "Didn't you ever ... break the rules?"

"Partena," Celsa said. "Set out bowls for the meal, please."

Partena stood up reluctantly and turned with a flounce that made her skirt swirl a little around her hips. She set the table and rang a bell to call in the rest of the family from the fields. Everyone came in a few minutes later, setting down baskets of harvested beans and freshly dug turnips. It was a large family, with several hired hands; the table was crowded. Partena took the seat next to me.

The oldest man—Celsa's husband, I assumed—made the ritual offering to the Lady, and everyone ate. The stew was thick and tasty, and I took a second helping but had to refuse a third. "Thank you very much," I said when the meal was done and Michel and I stood up to go.

"You don't *have* to go on today, do you?" Partena asked. "You could stay here for the night. We have plenty of extra space."

"We really need to keep going," I said. "But thank you for your offer." Michel tried again to give Celsa payment, and after refusing again, she agreed to have Michel and I do a quick repair to a broken door-hinge, which her family was too busy with the harvest to see to. Michel lifted the door into place ("I'm so glad you're the one with the muscles," I said) while I drove in a fresh peg to hold it at the right angle. Partena expressed copious admiration for our skill and tried again to convince us to stay the night, then we were on our way.

"There," Michel said, as soon as the farm was behind us. "Did *that* convince you?"

"Convince me of what?"

"That you can pass as a boy?" I must have looked at him blankly, because he slapped his forehead and said, "I can't *believe* it."

"What?"

"I can't believe you didn't notice! Partena was *flirting* with you."

"She was not!"

Michel put on a dopey expression and batted his eyes in a poor imitation of Partena's manner. "Did you ever ... break the rules?" he asked in a squeaky voice. "Why don't you ... stay the night? It must have been a very, *very* long time since you've had the chance to really spend ... *time* ... with a girl."

"Oh, come on, Michel. She ..." I paused. "Just because Partena ..." I paused again.

"She was flirting. Come on, El— Daniele. Admit it."

"All right," I said. "She was flirting with me."

"See?" Michel said. "You look like a boy. And no one at court is going to have *any* reason to suspect otherwise."

*   *   *

Michel would not be my bodyguard in Cuore, of course. Giovanni had told him the passwords to gain the trust of the university reformers. He'd serve as a liaison, and more important, as a messenger between me and the Lupi. Michel knew where the Lupi would be spending the winter. To provide some margin of safety, if I were recognized and arrested, I did not. It gave me an odd feeling, as if I were shut in a room with no windows. What if I wanted to leave, and Michel refused? Not that I thought he would, but still ... Worse, what if something happened to Michel?

As we traveled toward Cuore, we camped out most evenings—we were used to the cold, and wanted to savor the last of our privacy. Lia wanted to teach me the songs that she'd written about me, since she swore I *would* have learned them if I'd been living in Pluma that summer. There were other new songs, as well, some political and some not, and she taught me those as well. Michel lay on his blanket, his head propped on his hand, listening drowsily as we sang.

"How popular are your songs, really?" I asked, late one night as Lia packed away her lute.

"Very popular," Lia said. "I haven't been out of Verdia, but I think the songs have ranged a lot farther than that. You're becoming a folk hero."

"Folk heroes don't lose their armies."

"I'm working on a song right now that emphasizes the fact that you *survived* that night," Lia said. "Folk heroes don't win every battle."

Michel had been lying on his back—I'd thought he'd fallen asleep—but now he rolled over and propped himself up on his arm. "Hey, Daniele," he said. "Do you suppose Felice really met with the reformers in Pluma? I remember when he came back with Camilla and Tomas, they brought news of how popular those songs were, and he said that he'd met with the reformers in Cuore. And that the Circle had withdrawn to Cuore."

I thought back to the conversation with Felice. "I don't know if he actually met with the reformers, or if he was bluffing us. Do you remember what exactly he said?"

Michel paused for a moment, trying to remember. "He said that the Circle had withdrawn to Cuore, and that the reformers thought they were going to sit tight and wait to see what the Lupi did. And he said, 'If you want to strike at a large target like Pluma, there's no better time.' "

"That's right," I said.

"And Giovanni asked about someone named Cilo. Felice said that Cilo agreed with the plan, and Giovanni said he couldn't believe it, because Cilo never thought it was the right time to act. And Felice said—I remember this line, because I thought it was funny—'I was doing a little interpretation.' "

I tucked wool in around Daniele's violin, to cushion and protect it. "I remember that now. I bet Felice never met with the reformers."

"If we'd thought of it, we could have had Giovanni ask him about someone who didn't exist," Michel said. " 'What does Daniele think,' if there wasn't anyone up there named Daniele."

"If Felice had fallen for it, he'd have just claimed that someone named Daniele had joined," I said. I mimicked

Felice's voice: " 'But there *is* a young man named Daniele—perhaps he joined after your most recent trip. He's quite young, just sixteen, and he stands about as tall as Generale Eliana.' " I buckled the violin case. "We'd probably have believed him."

"Yeah." Michel rolled back onto his back.

I wrapped up in my blanket and stared up at the sky. It was a clear night, with a thin crescent moon; I could see almost as many stars as I could back at Ravenna. I closed my eyes, remembering the rolling flames that had filled the evening skies a few weeks earlier.

"Don't blame yourself." It was Michel's voice. "I never suspected Felice, either. Neither did Giovanni."

I sat up. Michel was still on his back, looking up at the sky. "You know what's really sad?" I said. "If he'd walked into our camp and said, 'I've come to join you,' I might have suspected. But no. He came saying, 'I've come to take over from you.' *That's* why I never suspected he was a spy."

"Remember that," Lia said, curled up on the other side of the fire. "Felice fooled you, and you'll fool the people in the enclave. If you run into trouble, brazen it out, like Felice did."

How would someone like Felice handle it, if he were a girl pretending to be a boy, and someone suspected the truth? If it were a woman who was suspicious, he'd probably offer to prove his sex by bedding her. Despite my bitterness, I found myself smiling a little. *I'll have to keep that strategy in mind.* I pulled my blanket over my face and fell into an uneasy sleep.

*   *   *

After a week of walking, I knew the songs Lia thought I should know, so she insisted that Michel and

I take a riverboat the rest of the way. We would be in Cuore much sooner. I agreed with some reluctance; my false identity was still as uncomfortable as a new pair of boots. Still, I couldn't believe it would be significantly easier even after another month, so Michel and I boarded the boat and said good-bye to Lia, who was staying in Verdia.

We arrived in Cuore on a damp, cold day a month and a half after the Autumn Equinox. The boat docked a mile outside the city, and Michel and I disembarked and joined the other travelers jostling their way along the muddy road. There were merchants with wagons loaded high with bolts of cloth, and finely dressed men and women on horseback, and filthy beggars in rags.

Unlike Pluma, Cuore had no walls. When we got off the boat, I'd have said the city had already started. There were houses and shops clustered along the road. Old women sat outside with apples spread on a blanket, selling them to the travelers. The houses became more closely packed as we drew closer, and then, when we stepped into the city itself, the dirt road ended. The streets of the city itself were paved with brick and rock.

"I should go by myself from here," I said. It wouldn't be a good idea for Michel and I to arrive together at the Imperial enclave. "Can you find your way?" Michel was heading to the university district.

Michel nodded shortly. "Can you find yours?"

"I'll ask for directions if I need them."

Michel reached out and clasped my arm. "Take care of yourself, brother. Stay in touch." Then he was gone, hidden in the press of the crowd.

The Imperial Enclave was supposed to be at the center of Cuore, but the city had grown unevenly, and now it was actually in the northwest quarter. I figured that the widest, busiest streets would eventually take me there. It took me several hours to walk the whole way, mainly because the streets were so crowded. It is not an exaggeration to say that I had never seen so many people in my life; Cuore made Pluma look like a backwater village. I passed through a district of cloth merchants, where I could smell dye, dirty wool, and greasy smoke. There were shops that had bolts of bright cloth piled under their awnings; I also caught glimpses through open doors of shadowy warehouses, where business was done only between merchants.

From the district of cloth merchants I passed through a district of rug merchants, and then spice merchants. The wares of the spice merchants were too precious to be kept anywhere but under lock and key; I could see locked chests and tiny brass scales, and the customers here seemed very wealthy. Still, they couldn't lock up the smells. I smelled something like a cross between garlic and freshly cut wood, lilies and wood smoke, honey and fresh-turned earth. This was also the district of the perfumeries; next to the brass scales in some shops, I could see rows of tiny bottles of colored glass. From the spice merchants' district, I crossed a bridge over a narrow canal; the stench of sewage was so thick I could taste it. Around me, people pulled their cloaks over their faces, so I did the same, but it didn't help.

Then the road passed through a neighborhood where every building seemed to house a tavern, and then suddenly high walls rose up in front of me. Walls surrounded the enclave, with a vast gilded gate at the front, and smaller, simpler doors along the sides, all heavily guarded. The wall was there to keep out riffraff, and even though I had a letter that would grant me entrance,

I found myself bristling quietly as I walked along the perimeter to the shining front gate. "Good day," I said to the guard, and presented my—Daniele's—letter of introduction, still sealed. *God,* I thought. *Please don't let anyone look at me too closely.*

The guard glanced at the seal and at me, and let me step through to wait just within the walls. He sent a boy running off with a message; there was an entire corps of young servants who did nothing but carry messages within the enclave. "You'll be waiting a bit," the guard said, and gestured for me to take a seat on a bench near the gate.

As the guard predicted, I was waiting for nearly an hour. Few people used this grand entrance; I found out later that most of the enclave inhabitants found it easier to use one of the smaller gates along the edge. There were a few well-dressed nobles who used the front gate, and I watched them come and go. None glanced in my direction, nor even really looked at the guards. I began to feel slightly more hopeful. Maybe Giovanni was right, and no one really would look at me.

The boy came hurrying back, finally, with an older man. "Daniele?" he said. I nodded. "I'm glad to see you're finally here. I am the Master Conductor." He took the letter of introduction from the guard, broke the seal, and looked over the letter quickly. "Everything seems to be in order. Follow me and I'll get you settled in."

The Master Conductor's office was a congenial mess. The room was cozy, with a fire on the hearth, and worn rugs covering the floor; bookshelves lined the walls, but he seemed to be in the habit of taking books down to read and never putting them away, because there were stacks of books on the floor by his chair, and the shelves seemed half empty. His desk was piled high with precariously balanced papers; one drifted to the floor as we came in.

"Have a seat," he said, and gestured to a chair by the fire. I sat down, and he unlocked a small, heavy chest and took out a silver medallion stamped with an eagle and strung on a leather thong. "You can feel free to replace the thong with a chain, but you should wear this medallion at all times," he said, and gave it to me. He pulled his own out to show me; his was on a long silver chain. "This proves you belong here, and will get you in when you come to one of the gates."

I nodded and slipped it over my neck. It settled against my chest where Bella's cross had lain.

"You'll be in Fabia's quartet; I'll send her a message that you've arrived. I'll have a boy guide you to your room; you'll have some time to get settled, as Fabia won't have you rehearsing for another day or two." The Master Conductor looked me over and gave me a fatherly smile. "In the meantime, you should buy yourself some new clothes. Here." He unlocked his strongbox again and took out a small bag of coins. "I keep some coin on hand for young musicians from the provinces," he said. "Don't worry about paying me back. Once you've settled in, you'll earn money by playing engagements; food and housing are provided, but you should save some of your money for clothes. It's important to present a good appearance here. The guard at the gate can direct you toward the tailors; I'd suggest tunic and hose in dark blue, or gray."

"Thank you," I said.

"We're glad to have you, Daniele." The Master Conductor rang a bell, and one of the messenger boys came to guide me to my room. "I know it all seems very strange, but you'll settle in quickly, don't worry, and you'll fit in just fine."

You have no idea how much I hope you're right, I thought as the boy led me to my room. It had started to rain, and I pulled up the hood of my cloak, shivering.

My room seemed very cold and dark after the warmth of the Master Conductor's office. "You can have a servant build you a fire, signore," the messenger boy said. Apparently he'd dealt with provincials like me before.

"How do I send for one?" I asked.

"You ring." The boy pointed to a rope beside the door. I rang and shyly requested that a fire be built. "Would you like me to show you how to get to the tailor?"

"I look that bad, huh?"

The boy flushed. "The Master Conductor *always* sends new musicians to buy clothes," he said.

I wasn't terribly enthusiastic about going out in the rain, but it was clear that without new clothes, I would stick out like a farm crow in an exotic aviary, which was definitely *not* a good idea. "Yes," I said. "Tell me where to find a tailor."

With some reservations, I left my violin in my room; it would be suspicious to carry it around with me, but I couldn't shake the fear that it would be stolen if I turned my back. Besides, as long as I carried all of my possessions with me, I could leave Cuore at a moment's notice. I shook myself—I *wasn't* leaving anytime soon, and I might as well get used to that fact—and carefully laid my violin across my bed. I wrapped up well and went out to the tailors' district.

It wasn't until I was walking past the first tailor's shop that it occurred to me that I would have to be *measured*.

At Michel's suggestion, I had padded the crotch of my trousers, but I didn't think they'd fool anyone who actually put their hand there. Just how personal did a tailor get with a young man being measured, anyway? I was going to have to buy hose, so my guess was pretty personal. I wandered the tailors' district anxiously for a while, finally settling on a tailor named Acilo, who looked old enough to be my great-great-grandfather. I hoped his eyesight was failing. And sure enough, to my immense relief, he did a poor job of measuring me; in fact, I was afraid that the clothes would fit so poorly I'd be out the money and *still* need to have new clothing made. Well. It couldn't be helped.

Back in the enclave, the fire had warmed my room, and the servants had made my bed, setting the violin carefully back on top of the covers when they'd finished. I rang the bell and sent for food; I would stay in as much as possible, I decided, until my clothes were ready. There was no sense in attracting more attention than necessary.

*　　*　　*

My clothes arrived two days later, while I was practicing the violin. Acilo's apprentice brought them to my room. I laid the bundle on my bed and left the boy waiting in the doorway as I fetched my purse, counted out five coins, then another for the boy. "Aren't you going to try the clothes on, signore?" he asked as I gave him the coins and gestured for him to leave. "Alterations are free."

"I don't have time now," I said. "I'll send for you again if I try them on and they don't fit." I shooed him out the door and closed it.

I had taken the Master Conductor's advice and bought several tunics in gray and blue—velvet, with matching hose. I laid them out on my bed, then barred my door and tried them on. Despite Acilo's sloppy measuring, they fit perfectly, or at least as well as I wanted them to. I padded the crotch of the hose carefully, wishing I had Michel here to advise me. I hoped if anyone put their hand there they'd snatch it away in embarrassment before they noticed anything amiss.

My chambers had a mirror—everyone's chambers did here—and I studied the effect of the new clothes. I looked like a peasant in gentry's clothing, but this was probably not unusual for a new arrival. And I did look like a boy, I told myself. I did. A pretty boy—I made a much prettier boy than I had ever made a girl—but a boy. No one had questioned that yet. Not the guard, not the Master Conductor, not the tailor.

With my new clothes, I no longer had any excuse to hide in my room. I looked in the mirror one more time and straightened my shoulders, then unbarred my door and left my room.

The walls and door of my chambers were thick enough to block out most sound, but I was greeted with a musical cacophony when I stepped out into the corridor. It was rather like wandering through the practice hall back at the conservatory. I closed my door behind me, swung my cloak over my shoulders, and headed out into the afternoon drizzle.

The interior of the Imperial Enclave was almost its own little city. The big Imperial Gate at the south end

opened onto a walkway that led past the Imperial
Palace and into the central gardens. The area west of
the gardens belonged to the Circle; they had their own
building, larger than the Imperial Palace, and the west-
ern gate into the enclave was used only by mages. The
Imperial Chapel, which was almost as large as the
Cathedral of the Lady that stood just outside the enclave, was at the north end of the central gardens, and
the Fedeli's citadel occupied the north section of the enclave. The citadel opened directly onto Cuore, and was
possibly the most well guarded of the buildings within
the enclave, as they kept prisoners in their dungeons.

The southeast corner housed the East Court—the
overflow palace, for the nobles who weren't quite noble enough to rate quarters in the Imperial Palace itself.
North of the East Court were a whole series of smaller
buildings. These housed the guards, the imperial advisors, the servants, and the musicians. There were three
more gates along the east wall, unassuming doorways
used for errands and other mundane tasks. The streets
and paths that led through the enclave (and through
the huge central garden) were paved with rocks. The
buildings were well built out of brick, and even the musicians' quarters had glass panes in the windows.

Musicians couldn't go into the Imperial Palace, the
Circle's palace, or the Fedeli citadel without an invitation or an engagement to play. But this was also true
for most of the people staying at the overflow court, so
on my first day with proper clothes, there were a lot of
people out walking in the gardens, despite the damp
chill. I walked around for a while, then sat down by
one of the fountains to watch the world go by.

Despite my self-imposed isolation, I could already
identify people's places by their clothing and other adorn-

ments. The ladies and gentlemen of the Imperial Court wore dresses and tunics in bright, striking colors, adorned with jewelry and gems. No one wore red. There were a few dressed in blue or purple, but most of the nobles seemed to dress in either green or a dark golden yellow. People generally seemed to wear the same colors as their friends; I wondered if it was simply a matter of taste, or if the colors had some other significance. All the nobles wore one of the eagle medallions, although some wore eagles made of gold, and many wore additional jewelry with eagles stamped onto it.

The Circle mages and the Fedeli also used the gardens. The mages wore robes; they were easily identified, but in part it was simply their air of utter assurance. The Fedeli wore black robes, always silk or velvet, with a small gold or silver pin on the left shoulder—two linked circles, the symbol of the Lord and the Lady. The Fedeli who wore silk made a rustling noise as they walked, as if they shuffled through dead leaves.

Nearly everyone at court with wealth and power— or who wanted to present an image of wealth and power—wore perfume of some kind. Passing by a cluster of well-dressed ladies and gentlemen was like passing through the spice-merchants' district again: I could smell honey, lilies, cedar smoke. The noble ladies favored floral perfumes; the men preferred spicy ones. The Fedeli chose from a wide range of scents, but seemed to prefer cloyingly sweet ones; Circle mages tended to select smoky scents. Remembering what Lucia had told me once—that the war with Vesuvia had been over the perfume trade—I wondered which scent was considered important enough to fight a war over.

In my classes on court etiquette, last year at the conservatory, Domenico had mentioned that people at court often carried flowers to mask unpleasant odors. It was hard for me to see how a flower could stand up even to just the perfumes people wore—let alone the stinking canal I'd crossed. Still, even in the chill damp of late fall, I could see that he was right. Both men and women carried flowers; some women wore a little bracelet of tiny blossoms around one wrist. Others carried elaborately embroidered sachets, presumably with dried flower petals inside. One forgotten flower was crushed on the edge of the fountain, as if someone had sat on it.

I could hear music from my seat by the fountain—several groups, in other parts of the garden. I could identify at least one string quartet, plus a small ensemble of flutes. Music was everywhere here. Back when I was a student at the conservatory, some of the teachers who'd played at court would sigh nostalgically and tell us that the nobility at court really *appreciated* beautiful music. My old teacher Domenico had hinted at the real purpose of this once, and Giovanni had spelled it out: cover.

"If you're having a conversation at court," Giovanni had explained, "and you don't want anyone overhearing, you can hire one of the ensembles to play for you. That way, anyone who tries to hear your conversation will just hear the music." Giovanni had thought this would give me an excellent opportunity to spy, but unfortunately, I'd suffer the same problem as any would-be eavesdroppers. I wouldn't be able to hear conversation over my violin.

"Learn to lip-read," he suggested then, ever-helpful. Damn Giovanni, anyway. If anyone belonged here, it was him.

Beyond the hedge, I could hear two people talking. "I really don't think he'll try it," a woman's voice said. I edged closer to the hedge, straining to hear. "I mean, really. She's above him. Don't you think, Clara?"

"You never know." Clara? I wondered if it was the same Clara who was the sweetheart of Demetrio, the commander at Chira. I leaned closer to the hedge. Her voice was a cool alto; she spoke in the tones of a woman of rank. "I have better things to worry about, in any case. We'll deal with it if it happens." They moved off. If this was the best I was going to do, I'd *really* wasted my time coming here.

One of the noblemen glanced at me incuriously as he passed by, and my nerve wavered: surely he knew I was a girl. But he glanced away without pausing for a more careful look. I wished I could see Michel, just for a few moments of reassurance, but it would be risky to go to the university during the day. Still, I was too jumpy to stay out in the gardens anymore that afternoon, so I headed back to my room.

I heard the dinner bell ringing a short while later, and movement outside in the hallway as people headed toward the dining room. For a moment I was tempted to send for a servant to bring my meal to me privately again—surely my trip out around the gardens was enough for one day—but then I shook myself and went out to join the other musicians.

The dining room was rather like a very grand conservatory dining room, but with the men and women sitting together, and much better food. I arrived slightly late and took a seat where there seemed to be space, across from two young men who looked about my age, one fair-haired and one dark.

"You're Daniele, aren't you?" the fair-haired boy said. "I'd heard another violinist had arrived." He clasped my hand briefly across the table. "I'm Valentino, and this is Quirino. You'll be playing in the same quartet as me. Not Quirino, though, he plays clarinet, not strings."

"Nice to meet you," I said. "Yes, I'm Daniele."

"Don't try to change the subject," Quirino said, and it took me a second to realize he wasn't speaking to me. "Valentino! Are you listening to me? You're going to get yourself in trouble again."

"Oh, Quirino. You take everything so seriously! I won't get in trouble. I wasn't in trouble the *last* time you thought I was in trouble. Or the time before that."

"Or the time with Clara?"

"So she threw wine in my face. She wasted a cup of an *excellent* vintage." He turned back to me with a shrug. "Did I mention that this is Quirino?"

This time Quirino turned to me. "It's a pleasure to meet you, Daniele," he said. He had a deep voice and the beginnings of a beard; he looked like he'd be taller than me once he stood up. Valentino, on the other hand, was short and awkward, with the persistent charm of an overfriendly terrier. I stopped worrying about my lack of a beard or a deep voice; Valentino didn't have them either.

"Where are you from?" Valentino asked.

"Verdia," I said. "The conservatory at Pluma."

"Oh!" Valentino said, obviously intrigued. "Hey, if you've been *down* there, maybe you can tell us—ow." He broke off. "Quirino, why—"

"Eat your dinner, Valentino," Quirino hissed, "and shut *up*. You can ask *later*."

Valentino gave me a baffled, hurt look across the table. I could only assume that Quirino had kicked him.

I glanced at Quirino. "Would it be best if I refrained from mentioning my home province here?"

"Most Verdiani simply say they are from the south," Quirino said.

"Ah," I said, and we left it at that.

We went back out walking after dinner. Despite the chill, most of the enclave was out for an evening stroll, wearing richly colored wool cloaks. Each person cupped witchlight to light the path; hundreds of globes of light shimmered like stars in the moist veil of mist. I'd forgotten how beautiful those tiny lights could be. The damp paving-stones reflected the lights, and the fountains flickered with stray gleams.

"There she is," Valentino breathed.

"Just don't, Valentino. Don't even think about it," Quirino said.

They were staring at a young lady who loitered idly by one of the fountains. She was a pretty enough girl, in a giggly Giula sort of way—high cheekbones and a turned-up nose. Her long, satin-dark hair was held in place with a jeweled band, and she wore a dress of buttercup velvet. Valentino sauntered over to her, Quirino and I trailing in his wake. From under his cloak, Valentino produced a fresh flower, which he held out to the lady as he approached. "Excuse me, signora, but did you perhaps drop this?"

"Oh!" The young lady looked up, feigning surprise. "Lady bright, I suppose I did. Thank you, Valentino, for getting it for me." She tucked the flower into her sleeve and took Valentino's arm; he led her to the edge of the fountain, sitting down there to use the sound of the falling water to cover their conversation.

"That's Sura," Quirino said in my ear. "Cute little thing, isn't she?"

"Adorable," I said.

"Valentino certainly thinks so. Never mind the brilliant yellow dress ..."

"Is there some significance to the yellow dress?"

"There are two factions at court—one wears yellow, one green. And Valentino's dear friend Ulisse favors green."

"What are the factions?" I whispered.

Quirino shook his head. "Does it matter? I'll tell you later. The important thing is that Sura is of great interest to Signora Clara, and Signora Clara can't *stand* Valentino."

"She threw wine in his face," I said.

"Yes. I'm not actually sure if it's that incident or the friendship with Ulisse that's the problem. But either way, Sura is trouble, whether she knows it or not. And whether Valentino wants to admit it or not."

"Isn't it *supposed* to be up to Sura?" I said. "And the Lady?"

"Well, yeah, but who's going to press *that* point? Other than the Fedeli—and bringing *them* into it would just open up a whole *new* crate of trouble."

Valentino and Sura were just talking, cheerfully oblivious to us—and to a grim-faced older woman in a yellow dress who glared at them from across the garden. "Sura!" she called after a few minutes. "It's time to go in."

"Is that Signora Clara?" I asked.

"Her?" Quirino snorted and shook his head. "I don't think Valentino would have tried to flirt with *her*! No. Clara is younger, and very beautiful. Watch out for the pretty ones," he said. "They're *all* trouble." Sura slipped the flower out of her sleeve as she jumped up to trail obediently after the older woman, and dropped it discreetly into the fountain. Valentino did not try to return it to her.

The following morning, I rehearsed with the quartet for the first time. Fabia, the leader of the quartet, played viola. Valentino was the other violinist, and the cellist was a man in his forties named Naldo. Valentino was brusque and professional at the rehearsal, all his flirtatious manner gone. Fabia clearly ran the quartet. I was surprised at what a pleasure it was to play in a group again. To my relief, I slipped easily back into the habit of following someone's lead to play in harmony. We finished up our rehearsal close to noon; Fabia seemed pleased. She drew me aside briefly to tell me that generally we rehearsed together in the mornings and did our own practicing in the afternoon. Solo engagements were at my own option, so long as they didn't conflict with ensemble rehearsals or performances. She'd held off scheduling any performances for a bit to let me get settled in, and was pleased with how well I blended. With a warning against spending too much time chasing after the ladies—I assumed, correctly, that she had seen me eating with Valentino the previous evening—she let me go to the noon meal.

Valentino pulled me aside after lunch. "I want to talk to you," he said. "Come back to my room."

I had never seen the inside of a boy's room at the conservatory, and I was shocked at the mess in Valentino's. He didn't appear to actually use the wardrobe that stood in a corner of the room, but just draped any clothes he wasn't presently wearing over the furniture. I wondered briefly if I should go mess my room up once Valentino let me leave, but decided I wouldn't be able to stand living like this. Besides, Giula would have created just as much of a mess if she'd had the opportunity; it probably wasn't just boys.

Valentino wanted to know about the war. I started to talk about the Vesuviani advance, but he shook his head and cut me off; he wanted to know about the *new* war. The Lupi. "You know," he said. "Are they a threat? Pluma is so *close* to the wasteland."

My breath caught and I hoped that my face hadn't just blanched. But this was ridiculous; I'd planned what to say if the subject came up. "The soldiers in Pluma insist that they'll be able to protect us," I said. "At any rate, the Lupi suffered a major defeat last month. I was never worried. Besides—" I lowered my voice further. "We weren't their targets."

"What do you know about them?" Valentino asked. "We don't hear much here, other than those songs—"

Valentino's door banged open and Valentino jumped up off his bed. It was Quirino, glaring across the room with an expression that could sour wine. "You are such an *idiot,* Valentino," he said. "Come on. We're going into town."

We walked out of the enclave, Valentino furtively protesting that no one would have overheard. "*I* did," Quirino said. "Lucky for you."

We walked through Cuore for a long time. I realized we were heading for the university district. Quirino led the way to a loud, smoky tavern. "Here?" Valentino said.

"Here," Quirino said. We went in and found our way to a vacant table near the back. I thought I glimpsed Michel as we made our way through the tavern, but he looked away without a flicker of recognition on his face.

Quirino pulled his chair in and leaned across the table. "So," he said. "Keep your voice down. What do you know?"

"I had noticed that no one here talks about the trouble in Verdia," I said, "or wears red. But I hadn't realized that it was quite *this* secret—"

Quirino shrugged. "It's not so much talking about Verdia," he said, "although that's easy enough to get yourself in trouble with. But Valentino was going to bring up the *songs*—"

"Which songs?" I asked. "The ones about the Lupi? *I have freed you and now I will lead you to glory/I'll trade my own blood for the life of the land*?"

Just the lyrics made Quirino nervous. "A month ago, a man named Protego played that song where he could be overheard—I'm not sure if he was mad or stupid— and three days later he was *dead*."

"Executed?"

"No, of course not. Probably poisoned. We got the message. Of course the song's been passed around anyway ... I think we all know the words, whether we believe it or not." Quirino shook his head.

"Hey, Valentino," a strange voice said. "I heard you were here." The boy joining us was tall, a little older, and dressed as a noble—in a green tunic.

"Ulisse," Quirino said, and introduced me, noting that I was from Verdia and they'd brought me here so that we could talk about the troubles without attracting attention. We'd attracted it *here*, obviously, but apparently Ulisse was all right. He pulled up a chair, obviously interested.

"So what exactly do you already know about what's going on?" I asked.

"They're peasants," Valentino said, ticking off on

his fingers. "Their emblem is a red belt and they call themselves the Wolves. They've been terrorizing towns along the edge of the wasteland—or something—and their main grudge is against the Circle."

"And there are the songs," Ulisse said. He looked at me. "Daniele? How much in those songs is true?"

I shook my head. "Pluma isn't in the wasteland," I said. "I don't know *that* much ..."

"If you think about it," Valentino said, "magery has been used for *centuries,* for *thousands* of years. Why would it cause a famine *now*? And if it was going to cause trouble anywhere, why wouldn't Cuore be affected?"

"Only one thousand years, and it wasn't until recently that the strongest magery has been used," Ulisse said. "The last war was particularly intense. And *no one* makes anything like magefire in the skies over Cuore."

"Are you saying you believe the songs?" Valentino asked.

"No," Ulisse said, in perfectly even tones. "Of course I don't believe them; of course none of us believe them. So, Daniele. You were going to tell us what *you* know."

"Some time back the Circle sent soldiers to keep the displaced farmers in the wasteland from migrating north," I said. This was common knowledge in Verdia, but Valentino looked surprised.

"Are you sure that was why they were sent?" Valentino asked. "Maybe there was another threat from Vesuvia ..."

Ulisse snorted. "Vesuvia is in no position to threaten us anymore—if they ever were."

I wondered if he knew something about conditions in Vesuvia that I didn't. "What are you saying?"

Ulisse shrugged. "I'm just saying that maybe the war wasn't fought for the reasons we're all supposed to believe." I knew that was true; Lucia had told me that the war was fought over a perfume ingredient, and they'd told us otherwise at the time. "Anyway, Daniele, go on. The Circle sent soldiers."

"Right. We actually knew it couldn't be for a new war, because there were no mages with them; they couldn't have been planning to challenge the Vesuviano Circle. Refugees who tried to go north past the soldiers—well, some were killed. Others were rounded up and taken somewhere, no one was quite sure where. According to what I've heard, they were taken to camps near the border with Vesuvia and enslaved."

"That's illegal," Valentino said. "Who was enslaving them?"

"The soldiers," I said, "on the orders of the Circle. The Circle wanted the prisoners to build a wall along the entire border with Vesuvia, since the border can't be defended magically anymore. You know—and this is something I've heard on very good authority— magery doesn't work in the wasteland."

"We'd heard that," Ulisse said, "though the Fedeli still deny it."

"Well, it's true." I paused for a moment, then went on. "That's where the uprising started, those camps. And that's what the Lupi did for most of the summer— they freed the camps. Then just as the summer was ending, we heard they were heading north. Then almost immediately after that, we heard that mages had destroyed their army and they'd retreated to the wasteland. Then I came north; that's all I know."

"Well, it sounds like we don't have anything to

worry about, in any case," Valentino said. "It made me *more* nervous that no one was talking about it, you know? Like, there must be something we *should* be worrying about."

"Worry about Sura," Quirino said. "Or Signora Clara."

"Do you know any more of those songs?" Ulisse said.

"I know them all," I said. "If you want to know the truth, I kind of liked them."

Ulisse hummed the tunes quietly, and it turned out he knew them all, as well. He even had them memorized. I was impressed, as he wasn't a musician. "Ulisse's got a crush," Quirino explained.

Ulisse turned bright red. "That's not true."

"Oh really? When was the last time you flirted with a lady and *didn't* compare her to the mythical Eliana? Could it be, say, a couple of months ago? Maybe before you ever *heard* the songs? Give it *up*, Ulisse; she's probably dead."

"No," I said. "She's alive—or so the rumors said." I glanced at Ulisse and bit my lip to conceal my amusement. "I don't think you'd like her, though. You know, she used to be a musician, at the Verdiano rural conservatory."

"That's *right*," Ulisse said. "Did you ever meet her?"

"No," I said, "but I met somebody who knew her, and trust me, she's not what you're picturing."

We finished our drinks not long after that and headed back toward the enclave. Valentino, flushed with wine and irritated with Quirino for harping on Sura, started in on Silvia, some ex-lover of Quirino's.

"Why shouldn't I sleep with a mage?" Quirino said.

"Maybe if you slept with mages you'd get into less trouble."

"Excuse me," Valentino said, "but maybe *I'd* like to have children someday."

"I'd like to have children someday, too," Quirino said. "Just not nine months from when I was sleeping with Silvia."

"You had a mage as a lover?" I asked, trying to clarify the situation. "What was *that* like?"

Quirino snorted, looking me over—probably wondering if I'd slept with any of the girls back at the conservatory. I blushed, against my will, and he relented. "About like any other girl, I guess. Silvia's very beautiful."

"So what happened? You decided you wanted to have children?"

Quirino shook his head. "You know how they take mages young, even younger than musicians? They teach them to think a certain way, you know, and if you don't go along with them, they make you sorry. Silvia used to talk about that, a bit." He paused.

"So what happened?" I asked.

"Well, one of the things they teach mages to think is that they're better than anyone else. And *that* lesson she'd learned." Quirino gave me a rueful smile. "But," and he turned back to Valentino, "she was *not* someone who was going to get me into trouble."

Once we were back at the enclave, Valentino wandered off—to look for Sura, no doubt—and Quirino drew me into one of the smaller gardens. "I don't trust Valentino to keep his mouth shut," he said, "and I don't trust Ulisse not to share things with Valentino. But you can trust me, and the fountain should cover our conversation." We sat down on the marble edge. "You know a lot about the rebels," he said, "and a lot about their leader. Have you met them? Her?"

"No."

"You can trust me," Quirino said. "I don't know how to convince you, but—I want to know more. Anything you can tell me."

Well, I couldn't play it safe forever.

"Not their leader," I said, "but a party of scouts—at least, that's what I thought they were." I'd thought this story out, on my trip up the river. "The roads in Verdia are dangerous right now. I was traveling alone, which was stupid. I don't know what I was thinking except that when I first started at the conservatory, before the war with Vesuvia, it would have been safe. I was set upon by bandits, and a group of four men and one woman came to my rescue."

"Lupi," Quirino said.

I nodded. "I thought so, though I'm not absolutely sure. It wasn't like they had writing on their foreheads saying 'hey there, folks, we're rebel soldiers,' or anything."

Quirino laughed hesitantly. "No sashes?"

"No, of course not. This was just a handful—but they carried crossbows, and they looked like they'd been armed from the bodies of fallen soldiers ..."

"They must have been Lupi," Quirino said. "What did you think of them?"

"They were courteous," I said. "They took care of me until I could join a larger group to travel with. When they realized I was a musician, of course, they taught me all those songs; that's why I knew them."

Quirino nodded. "Do you know any of the other, you know, secret music?"

"Old Way music?" I whispered, despite the cover of the fountain. "Don't all musicians?" I smiled at him wryly. "I knew without being told not to play those here."

Quirino shook his head. "It wasn't always such a serious crime. Is it true that the Lupi are also Redentori?"

"Most of them."

"The Fedeli—well, it's not like they were ever very happy about Old Way superstition, but since the trouble in Verdia started—" He shook his head. "Maybe we can take a trip sometime, out of Cuore, and you can teach me a few of those songs, you know?"

"I'd trade," I said. "But I gather I shouldn't teach Valentino?"

Quirino looked exasperated. "Valentino thinks that his naïveté will protect him. So he's friends with Ulisse, and he thinks Sura is cute. Why should this be a problem?"

"Why should it? I still don't understand. You said you'd explain the factions to me—"

"—later, I know. I'm sorry to keep putting you off, but my ensemble's performing soon and I need to get back to my room to get my clarinet. I'll explain later, I promise."

Quirino headed off, turning back to make a final request—"Find Valentino! Get him away from Sura. This is ridiculous—he really is going to get into trouble."

*　　*　　*

I went out to meet Michel that evening, at another smoky tavern near the university. I was afraid Ulisse would spot me and demand to know why I was there, but this crowd seemed to be older. Michel joined me at my table a few minutes after I arrived.

"Was that you I saw today?" I said.

"Yeah," he said with a broad grin. "I did a good job at looking like I didn't know you, didn't I?"

"You did fine," I said. "Do you have any messages for me? I don't have anything to report yet."

Michel sighed. "I met with the guy who runs stuff, Placido."

"And?"

"Placido wants to know why *Eliana* didn't come up to meet with them, or Giovanni. I told him that we've got a spy at court—not who, of course—and he wants to meet you."

"Out of the question," I said.

"That's what I said. He didn't like that answer. They're putting me up and giving me cover, but they're not letting me into their counsels. I'm not *noble* enough for them." Michel glared at his wine cup.

"Tell them I'm not up to their standards, either."

"I don't think it matters. I think they just want to prove that we're at *their* beck and call, and not the other way around."

"Well," I said. "We're not. Michel, stand straight and look them in the eye! You're better than they are. You've led soldiers in battle, you've faced the Circle, while they've slunk around Cuore holding meetings and appointing generali." I punched his arm gently. "But don't worry about it too much. All we really needed from them was a way for you to stay safely in Cuore, so that you could carry messages if needed. They're giving us that, right?"

Michel nodded.

"So, if Placido takes his head out of his asshole, great. If not, he's the one who has to live with the smell."

Michel laughed, and poured me more wine. "You're right."

Neither of us had anything else to report, so I bid Michel good-bye and got up to leave. As I slipped through the door, I came face-to-face with a tall young man with beady eyes and a round, piglike face. Pig-boy gave me a poisonous glare, then shouldered me out of the way to enter the inn. He was greeted by several people who raised their wine cups enthusiastically and shouted, "Placido!" I turned around briefly to take a better look, but he'd already turned his back on me, moving into the tavern with a bright smile and a hand-clasp for all. If pig-boy was the leader of the university reformers, I decided, I was glad that Giovanni was the worst I ever had to deal with.

CHAPTER FOUR

*Take heart: I am with you in the night as in
the day, in your weakness as in your strength.
Wherever you are, look for my face, and it
will shine on you from the smile of a stranger.
Reach for my hand, and I will touch you with
the lost feather of a bird. I am ever with you.*
—*The Journey of Gèsu, chapter 31, verse 2.*

A page wearing the Emperor's sigil delivered a small scroll to my room the next morning. I took it to breakfast to show Valentino and Quirino. "Is this for real?" I asked them.

"Oh, the banquet?" Valentino peered at the scroll briefly. "Yeah, everyone gets invited to one of those when they first arrive. Don't get *too* impressed. It's nothing all that special."

"But with the Emperor—"

"Hey, what do you suppose he does all day? He goes to banquets." Valentino winked, then shrugged. "He might be there, he might not. At my banquet, he showed up long enough for us to raise our wineglasses and toast his health, and then he left."

"So how many people will be there? Are they all musicians?"

"Hundreds," Quirino said, "and no, they won't all be musicians. These banquets get held every week or two, and all the new arrivals with some status are invited—musicians, counselors, petty aristocrats, scholars, priests, Circle apprentices. It's quite a mix. You could end up sitting next to some noble from the northern border, or a fresh-from-university physician, or anything."

"I sat next to a young lady from Marino," Valentino said. "Lovely girl."

Quirino snorted. "Didn't she slap you?"

"No, of course not," Valentino said. "Or—wait, no, maybe she did. I forget. It was either her or that flute player I tried to get to know my first week."

"In any case," Quirino said, "you're expected to go, but fortunately there's a decent chance it will be entertaining. When is it?"

I checked my scroll. "Tomorrow afternoon. Do I—" I hesitated; would a boy ask his friends what to wear? I decided I'd better risk it, and hunted for a boylike phrasing. "Do I have to dress up for it?"

Quirino looked me over. "What you have on should be fine. You're *supposed* to look like a musician. Don't bring your violin, though, or someone might make you play and you'll never get to eat your dinner."

The morning rehearsal went well; after the noon meal, I walked back to Valentino's room so that he could put away his violin and get his cloak. It was draped over a chair, on top of several sets of hose and what looked like a Midwinter mask; he picked up the cloak, then froze.

"What is it?" I asked.

"It's not mine," Valentino said. "I swear by the Lady! It's not mine! I don't know how it got here!"

I strode over to the chair and looked. Under the

cloak, someone had tucked a simple wooden cross on a green ribbon. Valentino threw his cloak down over it and backed away.

Quirino appeared in the doorway, his own cloak draped over one arm. "What's wrong?" I gestured toward the chair; Quirino closed the door behind him and came over to look. He grabbed up the cross in one hand and turned in fury on Valentino. "This is Clara's doing," he said. "I *told* you Sura was trouble!"

"It's not Sura's fault," Valentino said. "She wouldn't do anything to hurt me."

"Maybe Sura wouldn't, but Clara would," Quirino said. "*Now* will you believe me? *Now* will you stay away from her? This is just a *warning,* you idiot; she left this where you would find it. Do you have any *idea* what the Fedeli would—"

"Yes," Valentino said.

"Then stay *away* from her." Quirino pocketed the cross. "I'll take care of this. Why don't you stay in and practice this afternoon? It'll do your playing some good."

Valentino flung himself onto his bed, still upset. Quirino left him to his misery, and I decided to follow Quirino. Back in Quirino's room, he built up his fire, barred the door, and slipped the cross into the flames.

"You promised me an explanation," I said.

"Right." Quirino poked at the fire a bit; the cross was already almost unrecognizable. "The big dispute at court these days is what the army should do about the trouble in Verdia."

"You mean what tactics they should use?"

"Not exactly." Quirino went over to peer out the window, then came back and sat down. "The Circle prevented the army from crushing the rebellion this summer. The general suspicion is that the Circle is afraid that the army has gotten ideas about being able to defeat an enemy without the Circle's help. The Circle told everyone that they'd crush the Lupi in their own good time—of course, no matter what the Fedeli said, everyone knew that meant, 'once those dogs leave the wasteland, where they're safe from us.' And sure enough, the Lupi came out of the wasteland and the Circle destroyed half of them. But not all, and not their leaders, and now they're back in the safety of the wasteland. The Circle seems to think this was good enough, that after that blow, they'll go limping back home. But the Fedeli don't want to take any chances. They want the army sent in right *now*. And if the army isn't strong enough to do it, they want a new army raised. The army answers to the Emperor, and nobody knows for certain what he wants. For now, though, he hasn't sent the army down."

I nodded, thinking about Giovanni's plans to move what was left of the Lupi to one of the ruined villages. I hoped that he was able to keep their movements secret.

"So. There are two factions of the nobility—the ones who want to send in the army immediately, or the 'golds.' And the ones who want to wait, or the 'greens.' Ulisse is a member of the green nobles; Clara is a ringleader of the golds. Since Valentino is good friends with Ulisse, he's assumed to be a member of the green faction."

"Oh," I said. "What does Sura have to do with it?"

"Not much, except that her father is also a gold, and Clara has plans for her. There are a lot of alliances sealed at court through the Lady's coerced blessing. You tell the young lady in question who to sleep with, and if you're lucky the Lady also thinks it's a good idea. The Fedeli don't exactly approve, but they wink at it. It's part of life at court. Clara does *not* want Valentino going and spoiling that."

"What about you?" I asked.

"I'm just a musician," Quirino said, "and unlike Valentino, I manage to *look* neutral."

"Is this something I'll need to worry about at the banquet tomorrow?" I asked.

"Depends," Quirino said. "If your table companions are wearing blue, you don't have to worry. Much."

The following afternoon, I dressed in one of my new tunics, arranging the high collar to hide my girl's throat. Tucking the scroll under my arm, I walked through the gardens to the Imperial Palace and showed the scroll to the gatekeeper. He glanced at it without much interest, then summoned a page to lead me to the banquet hall. Another page met us at the door of the hall and showed me to a seat at the table. I felt rather like a sheep being herded to shearing; it was clear that this was a daily routine for the palace staff.

Waiting for the other guests to arrive, I took a look around the room. The banquet hall was huge and brilliantly lit. I realized that servants lined the walls, holding witchlight in hands cupped at their waists, so that the guests didn't have to go to the trouble of making their own light. Only the ceilings fell into shadow; the room was windowless.

The man to my left was clearly an aristocrat, and was also clearly more interested in the young lady to *his* left. I listened in on their conversation for a few moments, but they quickly became so overwhelmingly boring I started passing time by checking out the fashion choices of the people on the other side of the banquet hall. A lot of the newcomers had already picked sides, although I saw one puzzled figure wearing a green tunic and gold hose.

I heard a rustle of silk and smelled cinnamon and rose petals, and glanced over my shoulder to see the page seating another guest to my right. It was a young woman with dark hair and piercing eyes, gleaming white teeth like a cat, and black robes with a silver sigil on her left shoulder. She sat as the page held her chair for her, adjusted her robes, and turned slowly to smile at me. A chill ran down my spine. "My name is Daniele," I said. "I play with one of the string quartets."

"What a pleasure to meet you," she said in a voice like cream and velvet. "My name is Rosalba; I am a priestess with the Fedeli."

"You are also new here?" I asked, reaching for my wine and almost knocking it over.

"Yes. I have been out of seminary for three years, but I have been working in Varena. Is this your first placement as a musician?"

"Yes. I've been attending the conservatory in Pluma."

"How lovely," she said and smiled again. I kept expecting to see pointed teeth. "I used to play the flute, before I heard the Lady's calling."

"Where are you from originally?"

"A village near Varena," she said. I glanced at her hands; they were smooth, but with the echo of calluses, a harder skin on her palms.

I smiled at her. "Like me, then, you're—" I gestured. "A farm sparrow that's stumbled into the aristocrat's aviary."

"Indeed," she said with a laugh, and at my urging

spent most of the meal describing her farm and her family. Family was possibly the *one* safe topic; the last time I'd seen my family, I was not a reformer and I was not Redentore, and while I was not a boy, either, most of the details could stay the same.

Rosalba's life was strikingly like mine in some ways, although she did have one sister, much older than she was. "I think my family hoped one of us would have a calling," she said. "More for the money than anything else, alas." She smiled into her wineglass. "But, the Lady forgives the baser motives for the correct desires."

I nodded knowingly, and looked down at my own wine. "My parents had to settle for a musician, but I know what you mean. They won't be displeased with the money I'll be sending home." A lump rose in my throat and I choked it back with a swallow of wine.

We concluded the meal by toasting the farmers. "The Lord and Lady bless your family," Rosalba said.

"And yours, Mother Rosalba."

The aristocrat to my left had still not said one word to me. Rosalba clasped my hand and we went our separate ways.

*   *   *

Valentino and Quirino were loitering by my door when I returned, and they followed me into my room as I hung up my cloak and pulled off my boots. "How was it?" Quirino asked, and Valentino added, "Did you sit next to anyone pretty?"

"It was an interesting evening, and yes, I suppose the young lady next to me had a nice face." I gave Valentino a dubious look. "I think even you would have had the sense not to flirt with her, though."

"Why?"

"The young lady next to me was a Fedele priestess."

Valentino blanched at the thought, and Quirino smothered a laugh. "Don't count on it," Quirino said. "He probably would've noticed the face and not the sigil."

"So what did you *talk* about?" Valentino asked.

"Our families," I said. "She's also originally from a farm." Now that the ordeal of making conversation with a Fedele priestess was over, I felt relaxed and almost giddy. I sat down on the edge of my bed. "What an evening. The gentleman on the other side of me ignored me for the whole meal."

"Was the Emperor there?" Quirino asked.

I tried to remember. "I don't know," I said. "I honestly didn't notice."

"I can see why," Valentino said. "Was she nice, at least?"

"She seemed like someone who would be very nice, so long as you stayed on the Lady's good side," I said.

"Did you—" Quirino started, but he was cut off by a knock at the door. I got up to open it.

There was a messenger boy outside; he handed me a sealed scroll. "I'm to wait for a reply," he said.

I broke the seal and opened it. *Daniele,* a flowing cursive script read, *I greatly enjoyed our conversation at dinner and am most anxious to engage your professional services. I am particularly fond of solo violin music. If you have no other engagement, I would appreciate it greatly if you would attend me at my office tomorrow; I would like you to play for me for an hour or so. Please come at an hour past dinner; the guard at the Citadel will show you the way to my office.*

"What is it?" Valentino asked.

"It's an invitation to a solo engagement," I said. "Does the quartet have any plans for tomorrow afternoon?"

"No," Valentino said. Then, "A solo engagement? *Already?*"

I decided I'd better get rid of the messenger before explaining to Valentino exactly why his jealousy was misplaced. "This is my reply," I said. "I know relatively little solo music, but if she doesn't mind my limited repertoire, I would be happy to play for her tomorrow." The messenger nodded and I closed the door.

Valentino was still gawking at me. "Who wants you to play?" he demanded.

"Mother Rosalba," I said. "The Fedele priestess," and if my blood hadn't just turned cold I would have laughed at Valentino's look of panic. "I guess she liked me."

*   *   *

There has to be a way to turn this to my advantage, I told myself as I walked up the steps into the Citadel of the Fedeli, showing the invitation from Rosalba to the guards. They summoned an escort who would take me to her office. *Some way. I'll think of something.*

"Daniele!" Rosalba said as I came in. "I'm so glad you were able to come. I certainly don't mind a limited repertoire. The truth is—" she lowered her voice, "I rejoice in serving the Lady in whatever way She can make use of me, but this is a rather boring job and doesn't require that much concentration. The hard part's been done by the time I'm brought in. The music will be a lovely diversion."

"Isn't it your first week?" I asked. "How can it be boring you already?"

Rosalba sighed. "I had the same job in Varena. I write quickly—that's my curse. Excuse me. I mean, of course, that this is the way that the Lady has blessed me to serve Her." She sat down at a large desk. "Sit or stand, as you like. I had them bring in a comfortable chair for you, if you want it. You'll have to play a little quietly, since I have to be able to hear the confessions, but ... well, you understand. Just remember," and she smiled, "for me you *aren't* playing for cover. I'm not doing anything *secret,* I just want music while I work and thought you might do me the favor."

I sat down in the chair and tuned up my violin. We were in a small, narrow room with two doors but no windows. One chair faced us, at the opposite end of the room.

The door opened and two guards came in with a thin, fearful woman. "Sit," Rosalba ordered her, and took out a piece of parchment. "What do you have to confess?"

The woman spoke in a quavering voice. "I, Faustina, do confess to the crime of heresy." Rosalba's hand flew across the parchment, writing as the woman spoke. "I said to friends that I did not believe the Lady could have possibly meant to bless the match between my daughter and her sweetheart, because I don't like him." She paused. "I don't like him because he *beats* her, because he leaves her with bruises all over her *body,* but of course the Lady knows best." Her voice dropped to dullness again. "I renounce my heresy. I make my confession."

Rosalba finished writing and looked up at the guard.

"Is this certified as sincere?" He nodded. "Stand up and come over here," Rosalba said to the woman. "Make your sign," she said, and handed the woman her quill. The woman drew a circle where Rosalba pointed. Rosalba signed her own name, then the guard who'd certified Faustina's sincerity signed. Rosalba blew on the ink to dry it, then dripped wax onto the paper and pressed the seal of the Fedeli into the wax. "Very good," she said, and gave the paper to the guard. "Take her to Penitence."

For two long hours, I played through my solo repertoire and listened to the confessions that Rosalba diligently wrote down. The heresies were largely trivial, the heretics mostly terrified but not injured. Arrest by the Fedeli was usually enough to persuade run-of-the-mill malefactors to confess and accept whatever penance the Fedeli decreed necessary—fines, most often; public flogging or some other corporal punishment, less frequently.

After the second hour, Rosalba took a break, and stood up to stretch and ring for some tea. "It's dull work," she said again. "But the music has made this afternoon go much faster."

"What would you rather be doing?" I asked.

"Oh—you know. Rooting out heresy at the source, perhaps, or bringing apostates back to the mercy of the Lady. Transcribing confessions is—well, it's boring. But someone has to, and I'm very good at it." The servant arrived with two cups of tea, and Rosalba handed one to me. We sat back down; I blew across the tea and sipped carefully.

Through the wall to the next office, we could hear voices, muffled but loud enough to be clear. "—have enough now to try him and burn him for apostasy, if we want to. I think—"

"Are you mad?"

"We've tried blackmail. It hasn't worked."

"He's no use to us dead."

"He's no use to us *alive,* if he won't do as we ask."

There was a muffled obscenity from behind the wall, and then one of the men laughed.

Rosalba set down her tea. "They'll be bringing the next one in a moment," she said. "I'll let you go now— I understand most musicians must practice in the afternoons—but I'd greatly appreciate it if we could make this a regular assignment. I could afford—oh, perhaps three afternoons each week? When you don't have anything else scheduled?"

There has to be a way I can turn this to my advantage. And no violinist would be likely to turn down a solo engagement. "Certainly," I said. "I play at your pleasure, Mother Rosalba."

That night, after the evening meal, I retired alone to my room and barred the door, then drew the window shutters closed. I had never prayed much, back with the Lupi; I generally figured Lucia prayed enough for both of us. I had asked God to spare Lucia's life, but that was pretty much the extent of it. But here, surrounded by the Fedeli and the faithful, watching people around me making the offering to the Lady at meals because they feared the Fedeli if they didn't, I suddenly wished I could celebrate Mass. I wanted to taste the wine-sweetened water we shared; I wanted to see the light in Lucia's eyes when she spoke of her God. Most of all, I wanted to play the forbidden music, and even alone in my room I didn't dare. It was ironic because, as Teleso had said, *all* musicians learned the music, sooner or later. And played it, quietly and secretly. But not here.

Once I was certain that no one could spy on me, I pulled my dagger from its sheath. The cross-piece formed a strangely proportioned cross, but a cross all the same. I laid the dagger on my bed in front of me, knelt, crossed myself, and folded my hands. *B'shaem Arkah, v'Bar Shelah, v'Nihor Kadosh.* Except for my urgent requests before battles, I never knew what I was supposed to *say* to God. So I closed my eyes, and thought of Lucia. I hoped God would know what I meant.

* * *

"*Gèsu went into the house of his enemy,*" Lucia recited. "*Do you think he wanted to do that? Don't you think he was afraid?*"

"*But he had God's Light in his heart,*" I said.

"*Yes,*" she said. "*But he was still one of us. So he was afraid. Just as we would be. Just as you will be. Just as you are. Just as I am.*"

I realized suddenly that I stood in Rosalba's office, Rosalba writing furiously next to me.

"*I am afraid,*" Lucia said. "*But I have my faith, and that sustains me. I have the Light, and that strengthens me. I have all that I need. Knock, and the door shall be opened. Ask, and you shall receive. I will never serve you again. I will never serve you again.*"

Rosalba looked up. "*Take her away,*" she said. "*Take her back to interrogation. We will lead her back to the mercy of the Lady if we have to break every bone in her body, if we have to burn away the last of her reluctant flesh. Take her away.*"

* * *

I woke up and for a moment I didn't remember where I was, and reached out in the darkness, not even certain who I was reaching toward. "Lucia?" I whispered, but it was Mira my half-sleeping self had hoped to find by my side.

I will never serve you again. I will never *serve you again.* My dream had been about Lucia, but the words were Mira's—spoken in the darkness of her own dream when she first came to the conservatory. "Fine words, my friend," I whispered. "But you served them well enough when you rained fire onto the Lupi."

I closed my eyes, but I could see Mira's gray gaze; against my will, I found myself thinking of the cold softness of her hand when I'd held it the evening after she arrived, in the darkness of the practice hall. I clenched my hands into fists, trying to will myself to think of Lucia instead, but I knew that I had trusted Lucia so quickly and so willingly in part because the light in her eyes had reminded me of Mira.

I turned over and pulled the blankets over my head, trying to dispel my thoughts. I didn't want to think about Mira. Mira had saved me only to leave me; she had saved me again only to destroy the Lupi. I never wanted to see her again, I told myself. I prayed to God that I *not* see her—it would be terribly dangerous, as she could recognize me. I had changed a great deal, but I didn't think that I had changed so much that Mira would not recognize me if she saw my face. *Miriamne,* I thought. *Her name is Miriamne here. And she is not the woman I knew.*

I dozed fitfully for a while, but it was a relief when a soft rap roused me. I scrambled out of bed, pulling on my robe and tying it securely, checking in my mirror to be sure that nothing about my appearance would betray me. It was just dawn. "Who is it?" I called.

"It's Ulisse," he said. "Let me in, I need to talk with you."

I checked the mirror one more time, then lifted the bar on the door and let him in. I was afraid he was going to start asking for details about the Lupi or, God forbid, Eliana, but he had more prosaic things on his mind. "Valentino told me about the—you know. Heretical icon in his room," he said. "Quirino is afraid that Valentino hasn't broken things off with Sura."

I shrugged sleepily. "I wouldn't know."

"His room's right near yours," Ulisse said, and his voice took on a wheedling tone. "Daniele, do you think you could follow Valentino? Watch to see if he slips out? We *really* need to know if he's trying to still see Sura secretly."

"Look," I said. "Isn't this Valentino's business? If you're so worried, why are you trying to get *me* to follow him?"

"He'd notice if I followed him," Ulisse said. "But he's my best friend, Daniele. If he came to grief because of his friendship with me, I could never forgive myself."

"So what is it you want me to do?" I decided to go along with it; if nothing else, it would give me a chance to practice my eavesdropping skills on an escapade that didn't seem likely to get me into *that* much trouble.

"Watch for him, tonight," Ulisse said. "After dark. If you see him leaving, follow to see where he goes. And *tell me* if he goes to meet Sura."

"Fine," I said. "But only *once*." I could always let Ulisse talk me into doing more spying if I decided it was to my advantage.

It was one of my days to play for Rosalba; when I

was done with breakfast, I made my way to her office and slipped in unobtrusively. Rosalba glanced up to give me a quick smile as I took my spot, then turned back to an old man who sat rigid in the chair in front of her. "What do you have to confess?" she asked him.

"I, Lecto, do confess to the crime of blasphemy," he said in a hoarse voice. "I took the Lady's name in vain. I would not afflict your ears with my blasphemy, but I repent and regret my words, and will never speak them again. I renounce my sin. I make my confession." He looked up at Rosalba anxiously. "Is that all right? Did I say the right thing?"

Rosalba finished writing and looked up. "Is this certified as sincere?" The guard nodded. "You did fine," she reassured the old man. "So long as you repent your sin; that's the important part. Come here and make your sign."

The old man could write his name, and did, at the bottom of the parchment, then hobbled off, escorted by the guards.

Rosalba sat back and cracked her knuckles. "I don't know how we get involved in that sort of thing," she muttered.

I finished the piece I was playing and lowered my violin for a moment. "Mother Rosalba? I have a suspicion that I know which phrase he used, and—uh—I've heard it used a lot over the years. And I'm just wondering, is that the sort of crime you hunt down? I mean, not that I *ever* take the Lady's name in vain—"

Rosalba turned to give me an amused look. "You can go ahead and confess your sin to me, Daniele. I promise, saying 'Lady's tits' is not exactly a capital offense."

"I'm just wondering how careful I should be should I, say, trip over a rock in the garden or something ..."

"Don't stay awake at night worrying," Rosalba said. She shook her head. "I suppose, as the Lady's Servants, we must guard the way to wrong on her behalf, and one sin leads to another. But really, I don't know how the Fedeli get involved in that sort of thing. It's the *major* sins that are really our domain."

"Like heresy," I said.

"Or apostasy," she said. "That man ... Lecto? ... probably swore *at* his priest; that's how he wound up here. Now—" she dropped her voice. "The Redentori, they're actually dangerous."

I tried to decide whether I ought to be familiar with the term, and ended up giving her a blank look. "Who?"

"You know. The Old Way apostates. A few years ago, no one had ever even heard of them. Then—" She dropped her voice again. "Would you believe there was an Old Way apostate at my *seminary*?"

I could believe it, actually. Rosalba's home city was Varena, and suddenly I had a strong suspicion that I knew exactly who she meant.

"There was this girl," Rosalba said, confirming my suspicions, "Lucia. She was a friend of mine, actually, when I could stand to be around her. She was one of those really *morose* people. You know, sad all the time and if you spent any time talking to her you'd be just as depressed. I tried, though, I *really* tried. I think—" she sighed. "I hate to judge this sort of thing, but I think the biggest problem was that she didn't *really* have a vocation. Maybe her parents pressured her into the seminary, for whatever reason; it happens. And seminary is a lot of work. You wouldn't necessarily know that, but it's a *lot* of work, and some of it's hard and dirty and unpleasant. If you don't *know* that you're serving the Lady, I can see where someone might hate it." She paused and glanced toward the door, but there was no sign yet of guards or a new prisoner, so she shrugged and went on with her story.

"Eventually the priestesses in charge of the seminary must have reached the same conclusion, because they sent Lucia to do a solitary vigil. That was their first mistake. Lucia came out convinced she'd heard the Old Way deity speaking to her. Their second mistake was that they decided all she really needed was a *nap*—" Her voice dripped baffled scorn, "—and left her alone, if you can believe it. She escaped, but not before trying to convince a half dozen of us that worship of the Lady was a stupid idea and we all needed to go learn the Old Way."

"Was she mad?" I asked.

"I actually think she was possessed," Rosalba said. "Their first step should have been to restrain her, and bring someone from the Fedeli skilled in casting out the Maledori when they have taken over someone's heart and mind." We could hear footsteps outside, and she hastily got out another sheet of paper. "In any case," she added, "that was when I realized that the Lady wanted me to join the Fedeli. Because when Lucia told me that I was worshipping a false god, I could *sense* the darkness within her. And I knew—" Rosalba's eyes showed deep regret, "I knew that if only I had the right words, the right ritual, the right prayer, I could cast out the Maledori and return her to the Lady. But I didn't; I wasn't one of the Fedeli yet." She sighed. "And now, of course, I record confessions. Thanks be to the Lady."

The door opened and a guard came in. Then two

more guards, because this prisoner had to be carried. I realized with horror that this was because there was very little left of his feet. The guards set him in the chair.

The prisoner wore a shapeless gray shift, and filled the room with the stench of blood and excrement. His cheeks were hollow and much of his hair was missing. His eyes were mostly closed. One of the guards nudged the prisoner and he began to speak. "I, Octavio, do confess to the crime of apostasy," he said. He spoke almost inaudibly.

Rosalba glanced over at me, and I quickly set my violin on my shoulder and started to play. At the sound of the violin, the prisoner looked up. His eyes were glazed and dull. After a moment he continued.

"I confess to the crime of apostasy. I have secretly been a Redentore, worshipping false gods and subscribing to superstition." His voice faded again.

"Your companions in apostasy," Rosalba prompted when he paused.

"Also practicing this crime with me," he said, and paused again, closing his eyes.

"Go on," Rosalba said.

Octavio was silent for a long moment. I realized that he was listening to my playing, and a slight smile came to his face. He opened his eyes again and looked straight at me. Where before his eyes had been dull, they were now lit with a dark fire. "No," he said.

"Go on," Rosalba said. "You have agreed to make a full confession. Do you want to be taken back to the torture?"

"I will not speak more," he said. "You have my confession. You may content yourselves with it. I have no one to accuse. I practiced alone; I worshipped alone. I know of no other Redentori."

"Octavio," Rosalba said, and set down her pen. She rose and strode across the room to face him. Her back was to me, but I could imagine her face, rigid as steel, her dark eyes gleaming. "Don't be a fool, Octavio. We will bring you back to the Lady's mercy sooner or later, one way or another. What have they done to you?" She jabbed a hand against his side and I could see his face contort in pain. "How long have you been here? One week? You might hold out another minute, another hour, but you will return to Her in the end. Why not return now?"

"No," Octavio said. "I have nothing more to say to you. In Gèsu is my strength. I recant my confession. I worship the true God."

"*Fool,*" Rosalba said, and slapped him. I saw a trickle of blood run from his mouth; he had already been beaten, many times, and she had reopened an old wound. "Do you think you can stand against us? Against the Lady?"

"We must be a threat to you," Octavio said. "Or you would not come for us; you wouldn't care so much that you'd wrest the spirit from my body just for a handful of names."

"You are no threat," Rosalba spat. "It is only out of mercy that we seek to return you to Her. It's to save *your* soul."

"My soul knows its true home," Octavio said. "You can tear my body apart, but my soul knows its true home."

"You will be put to the torture again," Rosalba said. "Is that what you want?"

"No," Octavio said, his hoarse voice breaking. "But I will not give you names."

Rosalba turned and went back to her desk. "Take him away, then," she said to the guards, and tore up the paper on which she'd started writing his confession.

My hands were shaking; I could barely hold my bow steady. I let the last note fade away and then carefully lowered my violin. Rosalba said nothing, crumpling the shreds of paper on her desk. Finally she spoke. "They will drive the Maledori from his heart eventually," she said, "but there may be very little left by then."

"And then?" I asked, lowering my violin.

"He'll be executed, of course, to prevent the evil from spreading, and the Lady will take him to Her." She sighed. "I'm sorry, Daniele; I know that was hard for you to see. Why don't you go to the chapel and say a prayer for Octavio before you go back to your room?"

Since arriving at Court, I had not set foot in the Imperial Chapel of the Lady—in fact, the last time I had been in a church was during my trip to Doratura, when Giula and I had taken shelter from the rain. The church by the roadside had been a simple building, wood and brick with a linen cloth on the altar. I found myself trembling slightly as I walked up the white marble steps into the Imperial Chapel, opening the heavy door to slip inside.

The chapel interior was shadowed and dark, even with the faded autumn sun shining through the windows of colored glass. The building was chill, almost as cold inside as out, and I tucked my hands inside my cloak, trying to warm them. I had no particular desire to pray, but I decided to walk Gaius's Circuit anyway, because I was afraid that Rosalba might have followed me or sent someone to watch me. I paused to meditate by the first altar, the Lady's Appearance to Gaius in a Vision, raising my hands and bowing my head in a prayerful attitude.

Gèsu forgive me, I thought, not willing to risk praying under my breath. *You know why I am truly here.* The icon of the Lady smiled benignly at me; this was one of the more insipid icons I'd seen, clearly designed by someone who strongly approved of the Lady as the Ever-Doting Mother of us all. Either that or a secret Redentore painted it to make trouble, but that seemed a little unlikely.

After an appropriate interval, I moved on to the next altar, Gaius's Return to the Old Imperial City. I wished Giovanni were here, so I could yell at him. *What am I supposed to do here? How much longer do I have to take this? How am I supposed to use what I know to do anything useful?* "You'll figure out a way," Giovanni would have said. "You're supposed to be so *clever,* aren't you? Uncorrupted by a *university* education."

I moved on toward the next altar on the Circuit— Gaius's Founding of the Circle—and then the next, the Lady's Victory Over Foolish Superstition. Still insipid, the smiling Lady rested her dainty foot on a broken cross. I closed my eyes. *Gèsu,* I whispered aloud, but very softly, *give your servant Octavio strength. Help him to know that he is not alone.* I knew I could never endure what Octavio had. And I wasn't sure whether to be happy or horrified that my music had given him strength to refuse them again. "There must be some way to turn this to my advantage," I whispered. "Help me find a way."

"How can the Lady help you, my daughter?"

I jumped in startled fear, but the priest was not

speaking to me. Of course not; I was already engaged in walking Gaius's Circuit. The priest—I sneaked a look at him from the corner of my eye—was addressing a young woman in robes who had just entered the cathedral. A young woman who now followed him down toward the great altar, her eyes downcast. I moved on to the next altar, taking a look at the young woman as I did so.

It was Mira.

I stumbled on the stones under my feet and nearly fell. The priest turned to stare at me as I recovered myself, but fortunately Mira did not. She continued on to the Great Altar without looking up.

"I am here only to pray," she said in a clear, even voice. "I don't need your assistance, Father."

He moved off as she knelt and closed her eyes.

The fourth altar of Gaius's Circuit is traditionally placed directly behind the Great Altar, and by a quirk of the furniture arrangements, when I turned around I had a perfectly clear view of Mira's face. Which meant, of course, that if she opened her eyes right now she would have a perfectly clear view of *my* face, as well, but for at least the next moment or two, I didn't care. *Mira.* Miriamne. Her face was pale and thin, her eyes and cheeks sunken, as if she were living in Ravenna instead of the Circle's cradle of luxury within the capital city. Was she praying to the Lady with sincerity? Or did she secretly whisper prayers in the Old Tongue, like I did? I wondered if the Fedeli would dare to accuse a member of the Full Circle of apostasy. As Mira straightened her back, I flipped my cloak hood over my face to conceal myself, but she did not see me. Her right hand flicked in a tiny, almost undetectable gesture, drawing a tiny cross over her heart. Then she rose and strode quickly out of the chapel.

I decided I didn't care anymore whether I had been followed; I couldn't stay in here any longer. Abandoning Gaius's circuit halfway through, I fled back to my room.

CHAPTER FIVE

If you open your eyes, you shall see the truth.
—*The Journey of Gèsu, chapter 7, verse 12.*

*U*lisse had asked me to follow Valentino, so as night fell, I watched quietly from my window. I could readily imagine that Valentino might be visiting Sura in secret, although in truth I sympathized with him. Why shouldn't he flirt with any girl who would put up with him, and be friends with anyone he chose? *That just goes to show your naïveté,* I could almost hear Giovanni saying; *yet another thing you know nothing about.*

It was a long, boring wait. The last of the stragglers slipped inside from their evening strolls, and the enclave became quiet. I could hear the gentle splash of a fountain near the edge of the garden; then, farther away, I heard the sound of a single trumpet.

There! Someone was leaving the building. I slipped out of my seat by the window, tossed my cloak around my shoulders, and went out into the night.

I caught up with the shadowy figure quickly enough, but I couldn't tell whether or not I was following Valentino. Whoever it was headed for the nearest exit, and I quickly checked to make sure I had my badge around my neck. I did. It made sense, I supposed, to have a secret meeting outside the enclave; it wasn't as if we were prisoners here. We wound our way through the city streets. I realized, too late, that I was never going to be able to find my way back. Well, if necessary, I could hole up somewhere and then ask directions in the morning. Everyone else in Cuore doubtless knew the way to the Imperial enclave.

I was expecting to arrive at a seedy tavern, but instead the person I was pursuing made his way to a quiet street of dark buildings—warehouses, I thought. I could smell the earthy smell of unwashed wool, and the acrid smell of dye; I thought we were probably in the textile merchants' district. The man I was following stopped, and I ducked back behind the edge of the building as he tapped lightly on a door several times. I could see the faintest flicker of candlelight from the doorway as he went inside, and I moved around to peer through a crack at the bottom of the shuttered window.

I had not been following Valentino—looking at him in the candlelight, I was quite sure of that. I wasn't sure *who* it was, though, because he—like everyone else in the room—was masked. There were eleven people in the room, and every one wore a white veil that covered the lower half of their faces, obscuring their features. My first thought was that they were preparing a performance for Mascherata, which was only a few weeks away, but they seemed much too nervous to be involved in something that innocent. Then one of them lifted the candle from the table, and I saw a small plate with a white cloth over it, and a chalice of wine. *Redentori*.

I knew I shouldn't be watching this. If they had any sense, they'd check for observers before they started their ritual, and I doubted a spy would be treated politely. I slipped back out into the street, and collided with a tall man in a black cloak. His hood fell back and I saw that he, too was masked.

"Sorry," I said, and started to dodge aside, but his hand closed on my arm and he jerked me in to the room through the open door.

"Weren't you watching the alley?" he said sharply to the woman with the candle. The cloth over his face muffled his voice slightly. "Look what I found." He shoved me to the floor. "Spying on us."

My mouth went dry. "I've seen nothing," I said. "I don't know who you are."

The woman with the candle slammed the door and barred it. "What are you doing here?" she asked.

"I have a friend who's in trouble with a lady, that's who I thought I was following—"

"You followed someone here?" The man who'd caught me looked around the shadowed room, his eyes narrowing.

"We have to kill him." It was the man I'd followed who spoke. I stared up at him; I didn't recognize his eyes or his voice, but presumably he was one of the musicians. For all I knew, *he* was a spy. Revealing myself as Redentore—let alone as Eliana—could get me killed even if they believed me and let me go.

The man I'd followed drew his knife. "I think he followed me. It's only just. I'll do it."

"Wait!" I said. "Don't hurt me. I swear I won't tell anyone what I saw."

"What good is the vow of a Della Chiesa?" said the man who'd dragged me in, speaking more to his comrades than to me.

There was a hush, then the man I'd followed lunged

at me with his knife. I rolled aside, drawing my own knife and throwing myself back into the corner. They'd be able to take me if they wanted to, but maybe I could bluff my way out of this somehow. I pushed myself to my feet, my back against the wall. The man who'd tried to kill me was keeping his distance with a glare. If he was a musician, which seemed likely, he wouldn't know any more about knife-fighting than I'd known before I started lessons with Giovanni.

"Just let me leave," I said. "If you try, you'll be able to take this knife from me, but blood will be shed, and it won't all be mine. I don't want to hurt any of you. I'm no danger to you—I don't know who I followed, nor who any of you are. And I *wouldn't* turn you in even if I could."

The man who'd caught me moved toward me slowly, his hands empty, palms up. "Our brother drew steel quickly," he said. "We don't want to hurt you."

I relaxed slightly—and with a jerk and a flash of reflected candlelight, his sword was at my throat, pinning me to the wall.

"Drop your knife," he said.

I dropped it.

"It's clear you know what we are, and why we're here," he said. "Why did you come?"

"I told you the truth," I said. "My friend Ulisse asked me to trail his friend Valentino, to make sure he wasn't meeting a certain girl secretly. Stupid enclave political goatshit. I'm just a musician. Valentino's just a musician. Why would—"

"Shut up," the man said, pressing the sword a little harder against my throat. "You're 'just a musician' like this sword is just an eating-knife. Where did you learn to fight?"

"From my brothers," I said. "Growing up."

The man made a sound of disgust and I saw his grip on the sword tighten.

"Wait!" I said and my voice cracked. "Don't kill me. I'm one of you. I'm Redentore."

"Nice try," the man said, "but I think we've heard enough of your lies."

"Stop," I shouted, and to my surprise, he did. "If I were Fedele—as you obviously think I am—why would I be sneaking around in an alley? I would have *infiltrated* your group. I would have arrived on your doorstep with something to make you trust me. I would be pretending to be one of you right now and you *would not be holding a sword at my throat,* you'd be celebrating Mass and you wouldn't even *know* that the knife was already in your back."

"If you are one of us," the woman with the candle said, "why did you wait till now to tell us?"

My gaze swept around the room. "Every one of *you* is masked," I said. "I am not. For all I know, you know who I am—and one of you probably *is* Fedele, sent to spy. And you know that, or why the masks? I had hoped I could persuade you to free me, and I wouldn't have to reveal my *own* secret."

The man with the sword shook his head. "It's too late to make claims like this." I saw his hand tighten again, and I looked around the room desperately, searching for sympathetic eyes.

"Wait." One of the men spoke—a short, stout man with a gentle tenor voice. "You judge hastily, brother. The boy's story sounds plausible enough to me." He stepped forward into the circle of candlelight and laid a restraining hand on the other man, then turned to me. "If you are what you say, sing the opening prayer for the Mass."

The sword eased back, and I took a deep—shaky—breath. For a petrifying instant, my mind went blank, but I formed the violin fingering with my left hand and could remember again. "B'shaem Arkah, v'Bar Shelah, v'Nihor Kadosh," I sang. I started the melody too high, and had to switch to the lower register, and my voice broke three times, but I made it through the opening prayer. I remembered just as I finished that I was supposed to be a boy. I hoped I hadn't sung too high.

There was a long, uncertain silence when I finished.

"Let him go," said my defender. "He's telling the truth."

"The Fedeli could learn our prayers," said the man with the sword.

"The Fedeli, yes," said my defender. "But not a random passerby who hoped to betray us for a rich reward. And he's right. The Fedeli would be in our midst, not peering in through a crack in the shutter." He laid his hand on the other man's sword-arm. "Let him go."

Reluctantly, the man lowered his sword and put it away.

My defender turned to me. "You are welcome to stay and celebrate with us, brother," he said.

My knees were shaking too badly to dance. "I will stay if I must, but normally I provide God's music; my dancing is clumsy."

"Go in peace, then," he said.

I clasped his hand. "Thank you, brother," I said, and fled the house as fast as my shaking legs would let me.

*   *   *

"Gèsu went into the house of his enemy."

I turned, expecting Lucia, but it was Mira. She looked at me with her gray eyes, and she did not smile. *"Do you think he wanted to do that? Don't you think that some mornings, he woke with every bone in his body screaming for him to run?"*

"The only place you ran was back here," I said, and I realized suddenly that we were in Rosalba's office. I looked around for Rosalba, only to realize that I was sitting at Rosalba's desk, her pen in my own hand.

"Do you condemn me?" Mira asked.

"Yes," I said, and my voice was shaking.

"I am unrepentant," Mira said. *"A confirmed heretic and apostate. Do your duty, then."*

I stood up, hearing Rosalba's robes rustling around me, and smelling her scent. "Take her away," I said. I remembered most of what Rosalba would say, but the words stuck on my tongue like ashes, and my voice fell to a whisper. "Take her away."

*   *   *

I woke with a start, my hands shaking. I made a witchlight, and put a kettle on my fire to make tea. It would take some time to dispel the dream, and I didn't think I wanted to go back to sleep right away, even if I could. My window was shuttered for the night, but I suspected it was nearly dawn in any case.

Trying to think about anything other than my dream, I made sure my appearance was in order in case I had any unexpected visitors, and made my tea. My room had a small table, and I sat down to drink tea and think about the events of the previous evening.

Redentori in Cuore, and at least one from the enclave. No, wait. I thought back to the room of masked people: they were all wearing medallions, all stamped in silver or gold. They were *all* from the enclave.

It wasn't surprising, really, when I thought about it. The Old Way had been making a resurgence throughout Verdia, not just among the Lupi; of course there would be Redentori here as well, and of course they'd be far more cautious. I wondered how many were spies— I could almost imagine repeated infiltration creating a secret Redentore cadre made up entirely of Fedeli spies. But, no. If they were all spies, they'd have killed me. I wondered if I were in danger, since any spies at that meeting had seen my face and knew I was a musician. I hoped they'd consider me too small a bird to bother hunting. I couldn't imagine leaving already; I hadn't learned, or done, anything *useful* yet.

Redentori in the enclave—some musicians, but some important enough to rate gold medallions. I *ought* to be able to find a way to use that. The Emperor controlled the army, and the Circle feared a strong army; the army without the Circle was nothing, except in the areas drained of magic, where the Circle was less than nothing. Perhaps one of the nobles I'd seen last night was close to the Emperor.

Outside my window, I could hear the cacophony of birds that meant that dawn was well and truly breaking, and I padded over to open the shutters. I leaned out to latch them open, and noticed something bright on my windowsill.

A spray of pink rosebuds. I picked it up, puzzled. Was this a token of love from a secret admirer? I sincerely hoped not; someone's romantic interest in me could make my life much more complicated. But it seemed more likely that someone had mistaken my window for someone else's, or that the flower had been set aside briefly during a flirtation and forgotten, my windowsill only a convenient shelf. I left the flowers on my table and went to find some breakfast.

Ulisse knocked on my door while I was practicing that afternoon. "Can I come in?" he asked. "I don't want Valentino to see me."

I stood back and gestured Ulisse in. "I don't have anything to tell you."

"He didn't go out?"

"I don't know. I saw *someone* leave, and I followed. But it turned out not to be Valentino." Ulisse started to say something in a wheedling tone, and I shook my head. "The man I followed almost killed me, Ulisse; I am *not* trying this again."

Ulisse fell silent, abashed. "I'm sorry, Daniele. I didn't mean to send you into danger. Valentino would have been annoyed if he'd seen someone follow him, but he wouldn't have tried—well, of course not. I'm sorry."

This seemed to be a good time to ask Ulisse some questions of my own, while he was off-balance and feeling guilty. "Quirino tried to explain the 'gold' and 'green' factions to me, but I'm not sure I really understood. You oppose sending the army into the wasteland against the Lupi because you're on the side of the Circle?"

Ulisse flashed me a grin. "I think Quirino made it sound simpler than it is. All the greens oppose raising a new army to crush the Lupi. Some of the greens *are* Circle loyalists, and want the Emperor to keep the army out of the wasteland because that's what the Circle wants. And others want the Emperor to keep the army out of the way because they are perfectly willing to hand the Circle a shovel and let them dig their own grave. You can probably guess which group I'm in."

"And the golds?"

"The golds want the Emperor to raise a new army right away to crush the Lupi. Some are Fedeli supporters. Some are Circle supporters who don't want to take any chances and don't think the Circle knows what's in its own best interests. And some are hoping that the Circle is right to fear a powerful, confident army."

"Which group is the dreaded Signora Clara in?"

"You know, I have no idea," Ulisse said. "She keeps her dice well hidden. I suppose if I had to guess, I'd say she's a friend to the Fedeli; she threatened Valentino with a heresy accusation, after all."

"If it was Clara who left the heretical icon in his room."

"If it wasn't, it was someone acting on her orders," Ulisse said. "I wish I knew if Valentino was behaving himself."

"I did my best," I said, and sighed, a bit theatrically.

"I know, I know. And I appreciate it."

"I had another question about the factions," I said. "What does the Emperor think? Does anyone know?"

"Well, so far he hasn't sent the army down to the wasteland, so he's siding with the green faction," Ulisse said. "Of course, no one knows why. Is he on the side of the Circle? Is he secretly wearing the colors of the Lupi? Is he just more afraid of the Circle than he is of the Fedeli? No one knows."

"What does the Emperor have to fear from the Circle *or* the Fedeli?" I asked.

Ulisse looked startled. "You don't know? Well, of course. You were at the conservatory. Emperor Iago died last year—you heard *that* at least." I nodded. "He died of a very sudden illness, and he was not a weak man, or an old one. It is commonly believed that he was poisoned by a political enemy. Of course, no one knows who. I think the Fedeli did it, personally, but I've heard it argued persuasively that it was the Circle. At any rate, Emperor Travan has plenty to fear, and no way of knowing *whom* to fear. I don't envy the Emperor."

"Have you ever met him?"

"Me?" Ulisse gave me a broad grin. "I've seen him from a distance, but we've never been introduced." Ulisse shrugged. "Mostly, the Emperor tries to stay out of the way of both the Fedeli and the Circle. I've heard some rumors implying odd things about the Emperor's sexual appetites, but I think those are just someone's idea of a good dirty joke. He's a very quiet man, very reclusive. Even when his father was alive, when I'd see him at a court event, he'd be avoiding the other people there as assiduously as possible. So if he *does* have unusual sexual tastes, they probably tend more toward the solitary pleasures, eh?" Ulisse chortled at the look on my face, then elbowed me and nodded toward the flowers on my table. "Nice roses. I hope *you* aren't planning on offering them to a pretty girl in a yellow dress."

"Oh ... no." I actually found myself blushing. "I found these on my windowsill this morning."

"Really?" Ulisse arched his eyebrow. "You've certainly become a heartbreaker quickly."

"It was probably intended for Valentino."

"Maybe it was that Fedele priestess you play for. Isn't her name Rosa?"

"Rosalba," I said. "And I very much doubt these are from her."

Ulisse shook his head. "Well, thank you for your

efforts, and I'm sorry again that you nearly got into trouble. I'll leave you to your practicing."

I stepped out later that afternoon to play in the garden: I stood beside a fountain and chose the tune of a romantic ballad, which attracted a number of sweet young couples. I didn't see Sura anywhere; with any luck, Clara was keeping her mewed up inside East Court, where she couldn't get Valentino into trouble. I did catch a glimpse of Rosalba, who gave me a friendly wave; I dipped my head in response.

When evening came, I sat down to put away my violin, and noticed that a yellow flower like a lily had been left on the edge of the fountain, close to where I was playing. I dismissed it as a flirtation device that had been accidentally mislaid, and left it behind when I headed to dinner.

*　　*　　*

I had intended to go down to the university district after dinner, just to give Michel a quick report. I didn't have that much to tell him, but I wanted to see a face I could trust. But as I was taking a second piece of bread, Fabia came looking for me and Valentino. "Egidio's quartet was supposed to play for the Emperor's banquet tonight, but Egidio sprained his wrist today, so we're filling in. Go get your instruments and meet me by the fountain." Valentino crammed the slice of meat he was eating into his mouth, and I resisted the urge to do the same with my bread; if I was hungry later, I could send a servant for a snack.

Fabia led us to the Imperial Palace. I had been impressed by the welcoming banquet I had attended, but this party made that one look shabby and informal.

Everyone in attendance here was among the nobility, high-ranked enough to live in the East Court if not the Imperial Palace itself, and people were dressed in their best clothing—dark green velvet with a pattern woven in with red thread; heavy yellow fabric that reflected the light like glass. The nobles had separated out by color, moving to opposite sides of the banquet hall, and very few seemed to have chosen neutrality tonight.

"That's Clara," Valentino whispered as we took our places in the gallery. I peered down at the lady he had indicated. It's difficult to judge appearance from above and I could not see her face from where we were, but even from above I could see the straightness of her back and the set of her jaw and shoulders. This was a lady who knew and appreciated power.

I turned back to Valentino after a moment. "You *flirted* with her?"

Valentino shrugged. "I was new here."

I shook my head. Only Valentino.

Fabia tapped lightly on the rail and Valentino and I took our places and tuned our instruments.

The Emperor's entrance was announced with a blast of trumpets. I rose with everyone else as he came in, studying him curiously. He had not in fact attended my welcome banquet; this was the first I'd seen him. He wasn't as tall as I'd expected; of course, no one described Emperor Travan as "short," but he was. He was richly dressed in dark blue, with a golden eagle clasp holding his cape at the shoulder. He flicked the cape neatly out of his way as he sat down. I took my seat on Fabia's signal, then struck up some lively dinner music.

From where I sat, I had an excellent view of Emperor Travan, and I studied him throughout the meal, paying just enough attention to Fabia to stay on the beat. Various nobles attempted to attract the Emperor's attention throughout the meal, and he gave each the barest attention, shrugging off the servile smiles everyone seemed to have for him. My first thought was that he was cold and unfriendly, but as the meal wore on, it became clear that he was simply miserable, going through the motions because that was what was expected of a monarch.

I could hear the general murmur of conversation and the occasional high-pitched giggle, but I could make out no conversation from the musicians' gallery, even during our breaks. I suspected nothing of consequence would be discussed at such a meal anyway, but it would have been nice to have that confirmed.

Toward the end of the meal I moved my attention from the Emperor to his guests. They had seated themselves along color lines, with the gold-clad nobles to the Emperor's left and the green-clad to his right. I recognized some of the faces from my visits to the gardens. Valentino's erstwhile lover Sura did not appear to be in attendance. However, as I scanned the gold-clad nobles, my eyes met those of one of the ladies. Her eyes glinted slightly as she looked at me and I realized that I was looking into the face of Signora Clara. My own eyes widened involuntarily as I waited for her gaze to move on, but she held my eyes—she had been watching me, and was not displeased to have been discovered. I had rehearsed the piece we were playing enough times that my hands and fingers continued to play, even as my face went hot and cold and I almost panicked. Then Clara dismissed me, turning away to talk quietly with the man next to her at the table, and my arms went watery with relief.

The rest of our performance passed without incident. We had only been engaged for half the banquet, to provide the guests with some variety. As we packed up our instruments to move out of the gallery and let in a small ensemble of woodwinds, I noticed one other person looking at me—the Emperor. He looked away quickly when our eyes met, so quickly that I almost thought I had been mistaken. I looked up hesitantly as I tightened the last of the buckles of my violin case, and caught him looking at me again.

"Did you see Signora Clara staring at you?" Valentino asked as the servants brought our cloaks to us and escorted us to the palace door.

"No," I said. "Was she?" *Why was Clara staring at me? Did she suspect? Why was* Travan *staring at me? What on earth did they want?*

"I bet Signora Clara was trying to decide if you'd warm her bed nicely," Valentino said. "You know, she isn't married."

"I can't believe I'm her type," I said. *Could I use the Emperor's interest in me, somehow? If I hadn't been imagining things?*

"You should give it a try," Valentino said. "You'll never know if you don't."

"I don't think I want wine tossed in my face," I said. "I don't have many sets of clothes."

"Nothing worthwhile is ever accomplished without risk," Valentino said grandly. "Just think—Signora Clara as your lover!"

You know what you have to do, Giovanni's voice echoed Valentino's in my mind. *You just need the courage.*

It was too late to go to the university district. I bid Valentino good night, and went into my own room. I went to drop my cloak onto my bed, and smelled something unexpected: a scent both delicate and heady. I looked down to see a sprig of winter jasmine on my pillow. And next to it, a carved wooden whistle, no bigger than my finger.

No, I thought. *Not possible.*

"I had to come see you," a voice said behind me, and I turned.

It was Mira.

CHAPTER SIX

A teacher of ethics who works as a carpenter?
A King who herds sheep? Who has ever
heard of something so absurd?
—*The Journey of Gèsu, chapter 4, verse 36.*

Discovered. *I was discovered.* My first impulse was to bolt back out the door, but if Mira intended to have me arrested, she would undoubtedly have guards outside. Drawing my knife would do me no good, either; I vividly remembered what Mira had done to the crossbow bolt shot at me, and I was certain she could annihilate a knife, or a person, just as easily.

Shaking, I turned away from her, and dropped the bar into place on my door. "What are you doing here?" I whispered.

"You think I've betrayed you," she said. She summoned witchlight with a flick of her wrist, illuminating her face with the white glow like moonlight. "You think I've set guards on you. I have not, *Daniele*." She spoke my alias with a slight emphasis. "Had I wanted to betray you, I would have done it last night, instead of leaving roses on your windowsill. Or this afternoon, when I left the flower beside you at the fountain."

That was you? I was silent.

"I should have stayed away. But when I knew you were so close—I had to see you."

I could not meet her eyes. I couldn't approach her. I turned my face to the wall and let myself sink to the floor by the door. "How did you get in?" I asked, finally. "Our rooms are supposed to be private."

"I bribed one of the servants."

"So all the servants will know that a musician had a visit from a mage."

"They'll think I'm your lover. It's not as uncommon as you'd think."

"Quirino had a lover who was a mage," I said.

"Silvia. I know her. She's close to my age."

I still couldn't look at Mira's face, so I studied the witchlight in her hand. It gave off a soft glow, dimmer than my own witchlight. Mira was doubtless skilled enough to adjust the illumination, to provide a moonlight glow or the sharp brightness of the sun, as she wished. After those many months seeing her avoid magery like poison, it seemed wrong to see her with witchlight—even knowing the truth. Even having the truth staring me in the face.

She knelt beside me on the floor. "Please talk to me," she begged.

"I don't know what to say to you." Mira tried to touch my hand and I pulled back, still unwilling to look her in the face. "You—" My throat closed, and I had to stop for a moment and fight for steady breath. "When you destroyed the Lupi, you killed the ten-year-old boy who had brought the message that Felice had betrayed us. He was standing in front of me. I saw him burn to death in the magefire."

"Eliana." Mira whispered my name so softly I could barely hear her. "I volunteered for the mission to destroy the Lupi. I called in favors, I pulled strings. Because the Lupi were going down in flames, whether I was there or not. And if I were the focus, the mage directing the power, I could protect *you* and as many of the other Lupi as I could."

I said nothing, and after a moment Mira went on.

"How many survived that night? I heard a rumor that said about half, is that accurate?"

I bent my head in a grudging nod.

"Had I not been there that night, please believe that I am not exaggerating when I say that at *least* nine in every ten Lupi would have died. I couldn't protect all of you. I protected as many as I could—and the people I knew were especially close to you, like Lucia and Giovanni." Her hand closed over mine too fast for me to draw away. "I love you. I spared you as much as I dared."

"If you love me," I whispered, "then why did you leave me?"

Mira pulled her hand back. "You couldn't understand."

I jerked away from her, leaping to my feet and whirling to face her. "To hell with you. I may not be a mage, but that does not make me your inferior in the eyes of— in the eyes of anyone who counts." The words spilled out of me like wine from a cut wineskin; with effort, I forced my voice back to a whisper. "Do you know what I understand? The Circle killed my family, destroyed Verdia, enslaved me and thousands of others while mouthing loyalty to the Lady, and slaughtered my army. And *you* are one of them."

Mira had bowed her head at my onslaught. When I had finished, she said, "You're here to spy, aren't you?"

"Do you *really* think I'm going to discuss that with you?"

"No."

"I think you should leave now," I whispered. "You shouldn't have come." I unbarred my door and stepped back.

Mira's head was still bowed, and she kept her face turned away from me as she picked up her cloak and threw it around her shoulders. She didn't say good-bye.

My head was spinning. It was far too late for a casual visit to Michel, but I needed his counsel. Should I run now? It was true that Mira could have turned me in if she'd intended to. But would she turn me in now, after I threw all my anger and hatred into her face? I shook my head as I picked up my own cloak. *She wouldn't. Mira wouldn't betray me.* I needed to talk to Michel. I pulled up my hood and went back out into the night.

As I made my way through the silent midnight streets, I was reminded of the previous night, when I'd trailed the Redentore to his clandestine meeting. What if Mira were following me now? Perhaps she *had* betrayed me. Maybe the Circle Council had told her to come to me and see if I'd be willing to resume our friendship, with the idea of winning information from me willingly. I was fool enough to fall for Felice, after all. What if someone was following me now to see who I met with, to catch Michel with me in the same snare?

I paused for a moment to listen for a footfall. And heard one, softly, a short distance behind me; then no more, as if the follower had frozen when I stopped.

I *was* being followed. I whirled and ran back the way I'd come, drawing my knife. A cloaked figure had pressed itself into a doorway, hiding in the shadow. I grabbed the cloak and threw back the hood, and found myself face-to-face with Mira again.

"You followed me," I said.

"It's not safe to talk in the enclave. I wanted to find you outside."

"Then why did you approach me in the enclave in the first place?"

"I was *hoping* that you'd agree to leave with me once you saw who was there." Mira's gray eyes were rimmed with red, but her voice was steady now. "But even if you do hate me—I had to hear you say my name one more time. My true name." She swallowed. "Say my name, Eliana, that's all I ask. I swear on all that's holy, I'll kiss crossed twigs if you like, I won't bother you again."

I licked my lips and looked down. "Mir—" My throat closed. I thought of Vitale, dying before my eyes—of Rafi and Camilla and all the others who'd died. But Mira stood before me, and when I looked into her face, though I could not forgive her, I couldn't sustain my rage, either.

"Let's go for a walk," I said.

Cuore was never completely quiet; even late at night, there were people coming home from taverns, or out on other errands. Mira steered us through streets of closed shops and warehouses; the homes of the merchants, above the stores, were mostly dark and quiet, though we could see the glow of witchlight or the flicker of a candle in a few of them. I found myself thinking of the conservatory, in the hours before dawn, the night after Bella's murder. When Mira was ill the second time. My hand strayed to the eagle medallion, which hung where Bella's cross should have been. At any rate, no footsteps followed us; for all practical purposes, we were alone. We could talk freely.

"What do you think would have happened if we'd jumped the wall that day?" Mira asked.

I didn't need to ask which day she meant. "Well, I'd probably have wanted to go home to visit my family," I said. My throat tightened. I let out my breath; when I spoke again, my voice was calm, flat. "That's where I went after you left."

"I heard a song about that."

I forced out a sharp little laugh. "Lia makes it sound more heroic than it was—swearing vengeance on their graves and all that. Really, I gathered up what I could find, and buried it. I played the funeral song. That's all. No vows, no vengeance. Not then, anyway." I turned my head to look at Mira's face. "Do you happen to know which mages did it?"

She stopped in the street and turned to face me. "No."

"You say that with a lot of certainty."

"I could have found out. When I first heard the songs, and realized they were about you, it would have been easy enough to ask around. I didn't. Because I didn't want to know. I have to see these people every day. And once I knew—" Her face was pale; her gray eyes, hard. "I'd have killed them. All of them. As comforting as it would have been to take vengeance on your family's killers, I guess I thought I was more use to you alive. I guess my willful ignorance is another thing you can hate me for."

I shrugged and we started walking again. I wanted to hate her for it, but my anger had spilled and spent itself, at least for now. I tried to imagine waking every morning at the conservatory knowing that some of the other girl musicians had done unspeakable things, and fearing to ask who, lest I find out it was Bella, Celia, Flavia, or Giula. *I'd have left,* I thought.

"If we'd jumped the wall that day, I suppose that after we buried my family we'd have gone down to Ravenna together," I said. "The survivors of the fight were all taken there; I went because I hoped someone in my family might still be alive." I shook my head. "I didn't find anyone I knew, but I found some of the reformers from the university. They were trying to lead a breakout, but they weren't going about it very well, so I took over."

"Good for you," Mira said. "I've encountered Placido, and I don't much like him."

I bit my lip and looked at her. She arched an eyebrow and for an instant I saw a flash of the smile I remembered from the conservatory. "Oh yes, I know who leads the reformers. It's not a very well-kept secret. I think the Circle and Fedeli leave him in place because he's more damaging to his cause than helpful. If they had him executed, someone competent might take over."

"Teleso made that mistake," I said. "The commander of the refugee camp. He executed the two leaders, and that gave me the opening I needed. If you'd been there with me, it's hard to say what would have happened. Teleso underestimated me; then he decided to court Guila, and she kept him distracted. If you and I had both gone to Ravenna, we might have died together, like Jesca and Beneto."

"Maybe."

"Don't think your magery could have gotten us out of it, either. You can't do magery in the wasteland."

"I know."

"A friend of mine at Ravenna told me the real cause

of the war with Vesuvia," I said. "She told me that all it was *really* over was the perfume trade."

Mira's hands clenched. "Be careful of phrases like 'all it was really over,' " she said. "I, myself, fought because my family's village could have been the next victim of a raid from Vesuvia. Those raids really happened, and if they meant nothing to the mages of the Council— well, they meant something to many of the mages. And the soldiers."

I bit my lip, suddenly outraged by her flash of anger. "Thank you so much for your *protection*, Miriamne. The Circle protected us from the Vesuviani like the Fedeli at the conservatory protected us from the Maledori."

"We didn't know." Mira's eyes were wide and angry. "How could we have known what would happen? No one knew until it was too late."

"And then you covered it up."

"Not me."

"The Circle did it, and you're one of them."

Mira's eyes were bright with fury, but she bit down on whatever she had meant to say, and fell silent. I suddenly found myself remembering our fight at the conservatory, that day that I'd reminisced about the kind mage who'd tested my aptitude for magery, then given me apples even though I'd failed. Today, here, Mira and I were separated by a rift that couldn't be bridged by a sprig of winter jasmine.

We reached the river after a few more minutes of silent walking, and sat down on a slab of stone at the water's edge. The winter rains had raised the river's level; dark water lapped against the wall built to keep it from flooding Cuore. There was debris in the river, but thanks to the rainwater, the smell was tolerable. "What are you thinking about?" Mira asked.

"I'm thinking about the nice mage with the apples," I said, knowing that she would know what I meant. "I suppose you had a test like that, too."

"Oh, yes," she said. "But I was older than you were, because my parents had not sent for him. It was a neighbor who sent a message, and the mage came to our house with an escort, two guardsmen, to ensure that my parents behaved themselves. He took me for a walk, and he was kind—very kind! He knew that my parents might have warned me to fail the test on purpose.

"So first, he asked me about my family's farm. My parents were typical farmers, so of course, there was always something we needed and couldn't afford, or couldn't take the time for: a flock of goats, an apple orchard, new boots, a new roof. So the mage told me how much money the parents of a mage-child were sent each month. It was a lot. Enough to pay for everything I had ever heard my parents wish for.

"Then he spoke a little about Cuore. I was always a restless one. When I was ten, what I most hoped for was the opportunity to go to the conservatory, because it would mean leaving my home village and perhaps someday traveling a lot more. I think he sensed that, so he told me about going to Cuore, about the adventures mages had. Then, and only then, did he test me. He had me make a witchlight first, and of course I did that easily. Then he had me light a piece of wood. Then he gave me a stone, and asked if I could burn that.

"You actually don't have to set the stone on fire to be accepted as a Circle initiate. Just being able to make it hot to the touch is considered good enough, and being able to make it glow is a fair accomplishment. But I was an older child, and I had at least a little sense of my own abilities by then. So did the neighbors, for that matter; that's why they'd sent the letter to Cuore. I laid my hand on the rock and left my palm print. Rock doesn't burn, of course. It melts. I already knew that, because I'd experimented to find out what I could set on fire."

"And so you became a member of the Circle."

"Yes. And my mother . . ." Mira let out a deep breath. "Oh, she was angry. So, so angry. Initiate mages usually stay with their parents for several years, while a tutor comes to stay with them, but let's just say I was not a typical case."

"I read your letters," I said.

"Liemo 'forgot' those, damn him. I suppose I'm lucky he remembered to bring my violin."

On the far bank of the river, I could see someone moving around, dim witchlight in his hand. The figure picked through some of the debris that had washed out of the river, then moved on, apparently not finding anything worth keeping.

"There were nights at the conservatory when I dreamed about the war," Mira said. "I used to wish I could sit down by the wall, or in the north practice hall, and talk to you about it." Her voice blurred a little, then steadied. "It was worst in the months after Bella was killed. I wanted so badly to tell you everything—"

"Why didn't you?" Mira didn't answer right away, and I heard the edge in my voice when I asked, "Or wouldn't I understand?"

"Oh, I think you'd understand." Mira's eyes glinted. "I hate to admit that part of it was that I didn't entirely trust you. Not—" she raised her hand to cut me off.

"Not that you'd have told anyone who mattered. But few secrets were kept at the conservatory. You'd have told Bella. Bella would have told Flavia. Someone would have written to her parents. When I left Cuore, the Circle was trying to suppress the knowledge of what caused the wasteland by killing as many people as they had to. I was afraid that as the word began to leak out, they'd trace it back to the conservatory and kill everyone there." She shook her head. "And telling you just part of the truth—I didn't trust *myself*. Once I started talking, the whole story would have poured out."

I was silent.

"But those nights I dreamed of the war—of the mud, and the fire, and the fear—it was hard."

"I had no idea."

"I know."

"And during the war—" Mira tossed a pebble into the river. "We thought of magery as inexhaustable. Like the ocean, not like a well that could someday run dry. Even now, there are mages who sincerely don't believe we caused it. After all, the Circle lives in Cuore; beyond the Circle, there are thousands upon thousands of people who use magery every day. Why wouldn't Cuore have become a wasteland?"

That was a good question. "Well, why not, then?"

"I think that somehow something replenishes the energy, as rainwater replenishes a well. When the well is drawn on for ordinary things—witchlight, fires, even fireworks—there's plenty to go around. It's only the great magery that drains it dry."

"If the Circle had known, would it have made a difference?"

"Of course it would have," Mira said. "The mages

of the High Circle aren't idiots. They're terrified of the wasteland, of what it means. They'd have found a way to end the war if they'd known."

"They must have had some idea, though. The wasteland is all along the border. It couldn't have happened all at once—it must have gotten harder and harder to draw out the energy."

Mira was silent.

"They didn't know because they didn't want to know," I said.

" 'I can't help those who will themselves to blindness,' " Mira murmured. "That's a line from the Redentore holy book. The Journey."

"The only other person I know who can quote that is Lucia."

Mira nodded. "There used to be a copy in the Circle library. In the restricted collection, of course. That's where I read it. I don't know about Lucia."

"Is it still there?"

"I don't know. I've been afraid to look. I'm sure someone watches to see who goes to read it, these days, if it's even still there. Maybe they gave it to the Fedeli to burn it."

I nodded, but I was thinking about Lucia, not about the book—her hands, her smile, the light in her eyes when she talked about God. I suddenly wished more than anything that I could talk to her about Mira. Would she be able to forgive what Mira had done?

"I wish I could meet Lucia," Mira said, as if she'd read my thoughts. "I suppose Giula did meet her, if she was in Ravenna."

"Yes. She and Lucia didn't really hit it off. Giula hated Giovanni—well, at the time, so did I, but Giula really hated anyone associated with him, too. And Lucia didn't think much of Giula."

"What is Lucia like?" Mira asked.

There was a fallen branch in the river, with water swirling around it; I stared at the swirl of white water, considering my answer. "She'd have gotten along very well with Bella," I said. I tried to decide what else to say. Lucia was a dancer, a believer, a former initiate, a daughter of privilege who threw it away to chase her God. But when I turned my head to glance at Mira, I said, "She's not like me."

Mira nodded, not asking what I meant.

"Are you Redentore?" I asked.

"Here in Cuore? Are you mad?"

"There are groups that meet secretly."

"Do you think they'd welcome a mage into their midst? It's not as if I can abstain from magery."

"I don't think most Redentori here do. Too dangerous."

"I know you're Redentore," Mira said. "It's in the songs."

"Oh, yeah," I said. "And after all, they're accurate in every detail; we've established that, haven't we?"

"Are you saying you're not?"

"No, I'm not saying I'm not. I'm saying that you think you know me now because you've heard the songs. But you don't, because those songs aren't about me. They're about someone who's never confused or afraid, and who never hesitates, and who's never lost. They're about someone a lot more heroic and a lot more *certain* than I've ever been."

In the east, the sky was streaked with gray; the sun would be up soon. "I really need to get back to the enclave," I said, standing up. I summoned witchlight to light the path and was shocked to see a red stain on the ground where I had been sitting. "What the—" I twisted around and realized that my clothes were wet with blood. No, *soaked* with blood. *I'm wounded,* I thought. But I hadn't felt any pain. "Lady's tits," I said, my voice shaking. "Where is this coming from?"

Then I realized: my courses. They hadn't come in months and months—not in Ravenna, not in the wasteland. I'd heard people say that they'd stop if you weren't getting enough to eat, so it wasn't surprising. Now at the enclave I was well fed, and here they were, back for a visit. I groaned. "Daniele" would hardly suffer from this problem. It would be day by the time I reached the enclave. Could I hide this? I took off my cloak and looked—no, there was no way to hide this. They'd returned with a vengeance. I'd have realized hours ago that I was bleeding except that the ground was so damp ...

"Let's get a room at an inn," Mira said. "I'll help you clean up."

There was an area of seedy taverns and inns close by; some never closed their doors, no matter what time of day it was. Mira paid for a room and carried up a bucket of water. I could hear someone snoring in the room next to ours; there were people close by, some sleeping, others maybe not. We would need to watch what we said here.

"I'll see if I can get the stain out," Mira said, setting the bucket on the table in the corner. "You may have to walk home wet."

"I don't care," I said. "If anyone asks I'll say I slipped and fell in a puddle. I'll act embarrassed and let them assume I was drunk. It's a lot easier to explain than blood."

"Give me your cloak," she said. "If we can get the stain out of this, it won't really matter about your tunic and hose."

"I should have bought a black one," I said. It was gray wool, and showed the blood like spilled black ink.

Mira dunked the stained part in the bucket and rubbed the cloth together. I started to sit down on the bed, then looked at my blood-soaked hose and sat on the floor instead.

"I'm sorry if I assumed too much, based on those songs," Mira said softly. "For so long, they've been all I had of you."

I felt my face flush and I mumbled something dismissive.

"When I first realized—" Mira rested the edge of the cloak on the bucket for a moment, thinking back. "I heard just a snatch of one song. Of course, they're forbidden, and no one will knowingly sing them for a mage, so I put on a dress and went to the university district to hear them. It took me weeks of visits to hear them all. My first thought was that my prayers had been answered. I had wanted so badly to hear news—" Mira paused, glanced at the door, and lowered her voice. "I'd wanted so badly to hear news of Eliana, and here it was. But then I was horrified when I heard everything she had gone through. For those around me, Eliana was a folk hero—an abstraction, not someone they knew and cared deeply about."

I swallowed hard and lowered my eyes.

"I suppose it's silly," Mira said, "but until I heard the songs, I had imagined her still at the conservatory, with Giula, Celia, and Flavia."

"You really thought she'd stay?"

"The Eliana I knew was always—" Mira paused "—very practical."

There wasn't much I could say to that. So I asked her the question that had been burning inside me since the day she rode away with Liemo. "Why did you leave?"

Mira wrung out my cloak and examined it in a flare of witchlight, then dumped it back in the bucket and came over to sit beside me. She took my hand; her hand was very cold, like the water she'd been washing out my cloak in. "Make a witchlight," she said.

"Why?"

"You'll see in a moment why."

I cupped my free hand, willing a tiny glow into the palm.

Light exploded in my eyes as I felt a surge of raw power shoot through every limb of my body; my fatigue vanished in a blur of exhilaration. The witchlight flared up like a torch, then went out as I gasped for breath. "What—" My vision was starting to clear, but I still felt as if I had a thousand pinpricks of light across my body. "What was that?"

"That was magery," Mira said. "That's what it feels like to be a mage, to channel real power."

My head was throbbing: *more, I want more, tell her to do it again.*

"To make matters worse," Mira said, her voice matter-of-fact, "if one of us *stops* doing magery, we get sick. You saw that happen to me twice. Once when I first arrived at the conservatory, and once after the Fedeli forced me to summon witchlight to prove I wasn't a Redentore."

I thought of Mira vomiting and convulsing on the floor of the practice hall. "I remember," I said.

"That's why Liemo forced me to use magery. He knew that once I did, my need for it would drag me back to Cuore." She squeezed my hand, then released it. "Now do you understand why I left?"

I did, but I didn't. After a moment, I shrugged, and she rose to go back to scrubbing at the cloak.

"So what happened after that?" I asked. "After you left?"

"I followed Liemo back to Cuore like a whipped dog," Mira said, not looking up from her work. "It was a quiet trip. He didn't gloat; he was afraid that if he did, I'd kill him. My rooms here in the enclave were exactly as I'd left them, and when I stepped out my door the next morning, Silvia greeted me without surprise—it was as if I'd never left. I was expecting that my absence would at least have been a bit of a scandal. Perhaps it was, but the gossip when I returned was all about a mage who'd adopted a baby." Mira laughed a little.

"Why is that so scandalous?"

"Well, you know we're all barren. All mages. The priests say it's because our sterility increases the fertility of everyone else—this is goatshit, of course. We burn out our own seed just like we burn out the land. Anyway, this one mage wanted a baby really badly, and I guess she found one. She was the talk of the Circle, when I came back."

"Is she still?"

"Oh, no." Mira wrung out the cloak, and turned to look at me. "No, for quite some time now, the Circle has had more pressing concerns."

"The Lupi."

"Or as most of the mages like to call them, the Cani. Dogs."

"Of course."

Mira laid the wet cloak on the bed and held up a light. "Come look and tell me what you think."

I stood up to look. The stain was faded but still visible. "Maybe we should ask for soap," I said.

Mira sighed. "I'll go look for some. Wait here a moment." She returned a short time later with a cake of yellow soap. "You know, I think we might have more luck getting the stain out of your hose."

I felt oddly self-conscious as I shed my clothes. It was ridiculous; I had shared a room with Mira for six months. The bed had a blanket, and I wrapped myself up in it for warmth. It smelled like old spilled beer. Mira dunked the hose in the water.

"Most of Cuore believes that Eliana is all that sustains the Lupi," she said. "The Fedeli would have her assassinated if they had the slightest idea where she was."

"Assassinated, hell," I said. "They'd have her arrested." I shrugged. "I think they're wrong, anyway. Giovanni has his problems, but he could lead the Lupi. He *is* leading the Lupi. Eliana is expendable."

Mira shrugged. "Maybe." She held up the hose: still stained. She picked up the cloak again. "In any case, I knew that the Circle would strike as soon as the Lupi left the wasteland. I thought about trying to get a message to them, but I couldn't think of a way to do it that wouldn't be too dangerous. Besides, I told myself, surely Eliana would *know* that the Circle would wait for her and strike as soon as she led the Lupi out."

"Surely," I said, through clenched teeth.

"What happened?"

"There was a traitor, Felice. He brought false intelligence."

Mira nodded, her eyes on the stained cloak.

"Did you know about him?"

"No. At some point during the summer, the conflict between the Fedeli and the Circle subsided a bit; that must have been when they agreed to send the spy down. I didn't know about it. Only the Circle Council would have known." She wrung out the cloak again, then shook her head. "You know, I think you should just take my cloak, and deal with the clothes later."

I pulled the sodden hose back on and then draped Mira's cloak over my shoulders. Mira was shorter than me, but the cloak was generously cut and I thought the short hem would be a great deal less noticeable than a bloodstain. Mira shook her head. "I should have thought of that immediately. Now you'll have to walk home in soaking hose; I'm sorry."

I laughed. "Well, if I get sick from running around in wet clothes, like my mother always insisted would happen, I'll send you the physician's bill."

"Well, I'll pay it—though I was *trying* to be helpful." She fastened the cloak around my shoulders. It was made of a much finer wool than mine, black instead of gray, and was lined with indigo wool flannel.

"Do you want this back?"

"Not worth the risk of contact. I have extras."

I bundled up my own cloak and tucked it under my arm, and pulled my boots on over the sodden hose.

"If I had sent a message," Mira said, and she was not talking about the cloak. "If I *had* sent a message, it could have been traced back to me—and then I could not have volunteered to go with four other mages to destroy the Lupi. I wouldn't have been able to protect my friend." She raised her eyes to meet mine. Her face was very pale, and her hands were shaking. "I had to protect Eliana. If I hadn't, my sacrifice at the conservatory would have been for nothing."

"I know," I whispered, but I couldn't erase the image of Mira raining fire on my army from my mind. I hesitated a moment longer, then said, "We can't meet again. It's too risky."

"I want to help you," Mira said. "I want to help the Lupi."

"Then tell me a way to turn back magefire."

Mira was silent.

I touched her hand, and then left to return to the enclave.

CHAPTER SEVEN

But what will you find behind the mask?
—*The Journey of Gèsu, chapter 5, verse 10.*

idwinter's Night was approaching: Mascherata, the festival of wild revelry honoring the Lord's victory over the Maledori. Of course, Cuore's celebration was rumored to be particularly debauched, but I was sufficiently distracted that Valentino took me by surprise when he asked, a week before the festival, if I had my mask yet.

"No," I said.

"You haven't celebrated Mascherata outside the conservatory, have you?" he asked.

"Well, I did as a child—"

Valentino waved a hand dismissively. "If you haven't celebrated Mascherata in Cuore, you haven't celebrated Mascherata." He glanced at Quirino. "I'm right, aren't I?"

"Definitely," Quirino said. He looked at me speculatively. "Did you have a costume in mind?"

"Well, you know." Something discreet and inconspicuous, but nobody wanted to be discreet and inconspicuous at Mascherata. I tried frantically to think of something acceptable. "Um, something bright—velvet—with feathers. Why, what were you going to wear?"

"A red sash," Quirino said with a wicked smile. "We're both going to dress as Lupi."

My jaw must have sagged. Valentino said, "It's Mascherata! Lots of the nobles will be dressing as Lupi, too. It'll be fun!"

"Are you going to dress as a woman?" Quirino asked me. Dressing as a member of the opposite sex was always a popular costume theme at Mascherata.

"I hadn't been planning to," I said.

"Oh, come on," Valentino urged. "You've got so little beard, you'd make a great woman. We could get you a wig when we get your mask—"

"You've got barely more beard than I do," I said, trying to hide my panic. "Are you going to dress as a woman?"

"I'm already dressing as a Lupo," Valentino said.

"There are women among the Lupi," I said. "Their leader, for one."

"There's a thought," Quirino said to Valentino. "Dress as Eliana. A Lupa with a violin—don't you think that would work?"

Valentino looked at me. "Daniele would make a better Eliana."

This was a really, really bad idea, and I thought frantically for an idea, *any* idea, that they might like better. Or, failing that, an excuse. "I'll go as a Lupo *or* a woman, but I don't want to dress as Eliana. I'd have to carry my violin around all night, and that would be a nuisance."

"I suppose that's true," Quirino said. "It could get stolen in the crowd."

"Exactly," I said. "Actually, you know, I'd been kind of thinking I'd like to dress up as a noble. That stupid gray conservatory robe wasn't that long ago for me, you know?"

They laughed. "All right, Daniele," Quirino said. "Just so long as you dress as a noble *lady*. You have to have *some* fun with your costume."

The next day, they took me out to one of the shopping districts near the enclave. Every shop had turned into a costume shop, with masks, face paint, and flimsy but luxurious-looking gowns, tunics, and cloaks. With Quirino and Valentino inspecting the dresses over my shoulder, I picked out a dark red one—the color of the Lupi would be acceptable on Mascherata, clearly—with an elaborate fake brocade that turned out to have been painted on. Then it was on to the wig maker. Mascherata wigs were not made from real hair, but from an assortment of materials including yarn, feathers, and—for the extravagant—strands of glass beads. At Quirino's urging, I tried on the wig of glass beads. "Glass from Varena," the merchant said, frowning because he suspected I wasn't really going to buy it. He held up a mirror.

The glass caught the light from the late-afternoon sun, sparkling red and blue and yellow. The beads were tiny, threaded on strands of silk as long as my arm, and they clicked against each other like pebbles spilling from a cup.

"You should buy it," Valentino said, but I handed it delicately back to the wig maker and bought a cheap wig made from black yarn instead.

Our costumes and masks tucked under our arms, we went down to the university district to have a drink with Ulisse. Valentino waved his mask at Ulisse. "We've got our costumes. What are *you* wearing?"

"Guess," Ulisse said with a broad grin, pulling out a chair to sit beside us. We ordered a round of drinks. Quirino and Valentino discussed the relative merits of two of the soprano vocalists. I didn't really think either one was pretty enough to mention, and I watched the crowd, not really listening, trying to decide whether I should come back to the university district that night to see Michel even though I had nothing new to tell him. Valentino tried to get me to take sides in the argument, and I demurred; Quirino took this opportunity to ask which female musician I thought was prettiest, and I said I preferred not to name names until I'd had the opportunity to take a look at *all* the female musicians, and I was fairly certain I'd missed a few in my scant months at the enclave.

When we were ready to go, Ulisse drew me aside, away from Valentino and Quirino. "A lady asked me to pass this on to you," he said, and handed me a sprig of winter jasmine.

I froze, staring down at the flower. "Did she give you any other message?"

"No," Ulisse said. "She seemed to think you would know what this meant. Was that a tease? Is this some secret admirer?"

"I know who it was," I said, and forced a grin to my lips. "I just need to figure out what she meant by it." *Meet me,* presumably. Where? The inn we went to before, I supposed.

"You have interesting taste in ladies, Daniele," Ulisse said. I couldn't quite read his expression. I wondered if Mira's status as a member of the Circle had been obvious when she passed her "message" to Ulisse, but I didn't dare ask, and Ulisse volunteered no further comments.

Tucking the jasmine sprig out of sight, I stammered some thanks and followed Quirino and Valentino out of the tavern.

I went out that evening to the inn where Mira and I had tried to wash out my cloak. The downstairs room was loud, the crowd disreputable, and the company— so to speak—inexpensive. I waited uncomfortably, drink in hand, watching the door anxiously. Mira arrived an hour after I did; she had shed her robes and was wearing a dress. It was a simple dress of blue linen, but obviously well made, and it made her almost as conspicuous as the robes would have. She caught my eye, we paid for a room, and went upstairs to talk.

"I hope you aren't angry that I sent you a message," Mira said. "I wanted to warn you, the Circle knows that the Lupi have left the wasteland."

My heart was suddenly very loud in my ears. "Do they know where they are?"

"No."

My panic eased a bit. "Good."

"They've sent out searchers, to the areas near the wasteland. I don't know precisely where they're looking. But I wanted you to know that they *are* looking."

"Thank you," I said, although this information did me very little good. Especially since I didn't know where the Lupi were, either. I could pass it on to Michel, but it was unlikely he'd feel he could do anything with it either. "Was there anything else?"

Mira hesitated and looked a little embarrassed. "It's a little thing, but—" From under her cloak, she brought a pair of slender scissors. "You need a haircut," she said.

I touched the ends of my hair. "Why?"

"You don't have a beard. That implies that either you aren't growing facial hair yet, or you're very careful about shaving it off. If you were fastidious about shaving it off, you'd be getting your hair cut regularly."

I touched my cheek. "I've kind of been hoping to pass as a late bloomer."

"Oh, I think you do. But if you keep your hair trimmed, it's less likely that anyone will stop to look and wonder."

"You're right." I dropped my cloak on the bed and sat down. "You've got scissors; I assume that means you're willing to take care of it."

The bed frame creaked as Mira sat down behind me. As she leaned forward, I smelled Rosalba—cinnamon and rose petals—and startled so violently I almost fell off the bed.

"What is it?" Mira's hand held a comb with tiny, even teeth, carved out of bone. She had frozen to stillness when I jumped. "Did you hear something?"

"Rosalba," I whispered. "The Fedeli priestess. I smell—" I looked around, realizing it was absurd. "For a moment, I thought I could *smell* her."

"Oh." Mira laughed self-consciously. "She must wear—you know the perfume that caused the war with Vesuvia? I thought you might like to know what it smelled like, so I put some on. Rosalba must wear the same perfume. Sorry, I didn't realize it would inspire that sort of reaction."

I settled back down, laughing a little shakily.

"Does she frighten you?"

"I'd be an idiot if she didn't." I breathed in the scent again; knowing that it was Mira, I realized that it smelled subtly different. More cinnamon, and less rose. "It's too bad. It's a nice scent." I shook my head. "Not nice enough to fight a war over, but a nice scent."

Mira dipped the comb in water and combed my hair

out carefully. I found myself thinking about the morning of the Viaggio festival back at the conservatory, when Mira had combed my hair for me, patiently easing out each tangle. My cropped hair barely gathered tangles now, but Mira's hands were as gentle as I remembered. Her fingertips brushed the back of my neck. The last time we'd touched her hands had been ice cold, but today they were warm. I could feel the calluses on her fingertips catch in my hair, and she smoothed my hair back down with her thumb. From the bed, she picked up the scissors.

We'd had a pair of sheep-shearing clippers in the wasteland; that's what Lucia had used to cut my hair. Mira must have bought hers from a toolmaker who normally supplied barbers; they were perfectly made and very sharp, and snipped through the ragged ends of my hair with a soft click. Mira stroked her fingers around the tops of my ears and along the nape of my neck, tracing the line as she cut it.

"There," she said finally. "It's done."

"I wish I had a mirror," I said, touching my hair tentatively. "I could admire your work."

"Take a look when you get back to the enclave. I think I did a good enough job, but if you don't agree, you can always take yourself to a real barber." Mira tucked the scissors away in a pouch.

Back in my room at the enclave, I examined my appearance in the mirror; Mira had done an excellent job. I touched the ends of my hair where it curved around my ears, remembering Mira's deft work, then barred my door and took her cloak out of my wardrobe. When I pressed my face to the lining, I could smell something like new-cut wheat and faint wood smoke—

Mira's scent, without Rosalba's perfume covering it up.
Mira had smelled like this at the conservatory, too. It
was her own scent, and not a perfume.

I lay down on my bed, stroking the velvet-soft lining
and trying not to think about anything at all.

*   *   *

*I was sitting in a meadow with Giovanni and Lucia,
the other Lupi surrounding us, chatting with each other,
rolling out blankets to sleep on, staring at the birds and
the leaves and the creeping bugs.*

*Then suddenly I heard shouts, and I looked up: the
sky had turned to rolling, seething flames, churning
over our heads like a red and orange sea.*

*I leaped to my feet. There, on the hilltop, I could see
them: five mages, one with her hands stretched to the
sky.*

*"Don't do it," I screamed. "Mira, Mira, please, don't
do it . . ."*

*   *   *

I woke, breathing heavily, my face still pressed to
the cloak. Had I shouted out loud? I pressed my hands
to my lips, wondering if anyone could have heard me.
It was very late, and the building around me seemed
silent; I pressed my ear to both walls, but heard no one
stirring. Even if I had shouted in my sleep, I thought,
trying to calm down, "Mira, please don't do it" wasn't
anything all that incriminating. If anyone asked, I'd
say that Mira was a bully from my home village, someone who'd hurt me as a child. *No one will ask,* I told
myself. *No one heard you.*

I lay back down, unwilling even after the dream to

put the cloak away, and closed my eyes. I imagined Mira in her own room, in the Circle's citadel. Was she lying awake right now, too? I rubbed the lining, thinking of the touch of her hands against my neck, the calluses on her fingertips catching in my hair.

No. Damn you. I got up and yanked the cloak from my bed, balling it up and stuffing it into my wardrobe. *You destroyed the Lupi. You killed Vitale before my eyes. You—*

I lay back down on my bed, breathing hard. *It's Lucia I wish I could see,* I told myself. *Not Mira.* But as I faded back into sleep, it was Mira's scent I thought of one more time, and the feel of Mira's hair under my hands.

But then I dreamed of fire again, and woke with my pillow wet from tears.

*   *   *

On the afternoon of the Mascherata festival, Valentino and Quirino insisted on helping me with the wig and the face paint. Before letting Valentino and Quirino into my room, I bound my breasts, then put on the dress and padded the chest with obviously fake material.

Quirino helped to arrange the wig on my head, and feathers in the yarn strands of the wig. I tied on my mask; below the mask, Valentino painted my lips and cheeks. Finally, I looked into the mirror. I was relieved; I would never recognize myself as Eliana, or as female, or even as human. Fedeli priests traditionally dressed as Maledori for the Mascherata festivities; I could probably pass for one as well.

Valentino and Quirino had both dressed as Lupi.

Valentino was also dressed as a woman, sort of—he wore men's clothing, but with a wig of long, dark hair. I decided not to ask if he was supposed to be dressed as Eliana. Quirino wore a rough brown tunic with a sash of wine-red velvet. When they were done with me, Valentino and Quirino both tied on their masks. Quirino's was tinted red, to match his sash; Valentino's was plain white, like mine. "Come on, ladies," Quirino said, offering his left arm to Valentino and his right arm to me. I watched Valentino carefully to see how he took Quirino's arm. This was ridiculous; I could give myself away by playing a woman too convincingly. Or, I could give myself away by failing to play a woman convincingly enough, and raising someone's suspicions enough to take a good hard look at me. It probably would have been best to get sick the week before Mascherata and stay sick until after the festival was over, but it was too late now.

The Mascherata festival was celebrated in the streets of Cuore; we all tucked our eagle medallions inside our costumes and left the enclave. The streets were brightly lit. Torches leapt and witchlight gleamed, and bonfires burned in the center of every intersection.

"Do they really run wine in the fountains instead of water?" I asked Quirino, shouting to be heard over the din in the street.

"No," he shouted back. "There's no shortage of wine, though," and he handed me a flask.

Yet another thing to worry about; drink myself to insensibility and get found out that way. Or draw attention by staying sober. I took a careful swig and passed the flask back to Quirino.

Back during Dono alla Magia, in Ravenna, Giovanni

had described the revelries that took place in Cuore. The Circle made colored lights in the sky, he said. As we rounded the corner, I saw what he meant; vast colored flowers bloomed suddenly in the dark night. "Oooh!" Valentino said, and stopped to look.

Three mages stood on the street corner, clasping raised hands. Two wore ragged tunics made of scraps of stitched-together velvet, carefully frayed at the edges. The third, a woman, wore nothing but her mask. "Isn't she cold?" I whispered to Quirino.

"Mages doing magic don't get cold," he said. "My old lover Silvia told me that."

When the colors faded, the mages bowed, passed a wine flask, and stumbled off down the street, already thoroughly drunk.

"Come on," Valentino said. "There's dancing in the market piazza. Ulisse said he'd look for us there."

"How's he going to recognize us?" I asked. Valentino just laughed.

The market piazza was ringed with masked men and women beating drums, mostly on a regular beat. Despite the masks, I thought I recognized some of them as musicians from the enclave.

"Dance with me, signora!" commanded a strange woman dressed as a man. I clasped her hands as she pulled me away from Valentino and Quirino. We spun back into the crowd. I thought of the time I'd danced with Mira, in the class on courtly graces at the conservatory. This woman danced with far more skill than Mira, but less grace. At least it was easy to follow her lead. She had drawn a moustache onto her upper lip, and played the rude rogue throughout the dance, squeezing the padding I'd stuffed into the dress to mimic a bosom. I slapped the hand away with a cry of mock indignation. We tussled briefly, then she dropped my hand, announcing that she would find a lady who appreciated a fine lusty gentleman.

I had lost track of Valentino and Quirino, which was just fine with me, since without them I could try to fade into the paving-stones. I started for the edge of the crowd, but someone else grasped my arm. This time, it looked like a genuine man. "Would you do me the honor of dancing with me, signora?" he asked. His velvet tenor was oddly familiar, but I couldn't place it. Perhaps he was a noble that I'd played for.

"But of course, signore," I said. "I am always happy to dance with a gentleman." I took his arm as awkwardly as I could, and he spun me back toward the center of the dancers.

My new partner was an excellent dancer; he danced rather as I imagined Michel would, if I had ever danced with him. He was confident enough to lead me in a complicated series of twirls and flourishes, and skilled enough to ensure that I never stepped on his feet. I worried, as we danced, that I should be more clumsy than I was, dancing the woman's part—but to deliberately misstep in the hands of such a skilled partner seemed like it would be more suspicious than decently competent dancing. Besides, I had danced both a girl's part and a boy's part, learning to dance at the conservatory. Undoubtedly the boys had done the same in their classes.

My partner wore a red sash with a black tunic, and a mask that covered almost his entire face. He was short and a little stout, with boxy shoulders. But he was unquestionably a nobleman; his hands were even softer than Mira's. I wondered suddenly if he might be a mage. Well, if he were, I'd give him the slip as soon as I could.

"Would you care to rest for a bit, signora?" he asked some time later. I nodded; I wasn't out of breath yet, but my legs were tired. He steered us through the crowd to one of the less-crowded streets. "You play the violin, do you not?" he asked me.

"Yes, signore," I said.

He held up my hand and brushed my fingertips lightly with his own. "I could tell from your calluses."

I gave him what I hoped was a boy's imitation of a girl's flirtatious smile. "You're very observant, signore."

"Sit and drink with me," he said, so I followed him to a quiet spot off the main street, and we sat down in the shadows. He gave me a flask of wine and I took a cautious sip. It was excellent wine, some of the best I'd ever had. I took another swallow, then another, then passed it back.

"I love Mascherata," he said. "It's my favorite night of the year."

"You love to hide, then?" I said.

"I hate to hide," he said. "It's only with the mask on that I can be my true self." He turned his head to look at me. With the mask that covered his whole face, I couldn't see whether or not he was smiling; it unnerved me.

"Strange," I said. The wine was strong; just the little I had drunk was making me light-headed. "My mask makes me feel exposed. I'm afraid of what I might reveal."

"What does it matter?" he said. "With your mask on, no one will know who you are."

I smiled at him and shrugged.

He clasped my hand and bowed to me briefly. "Dance with me, signora."

I stood up again and we danced slowly in the alley-way, moving to the pulse of the now-distant drums, as I had once danced with Mira. "Tell me who you are not," he said to me.

"I am not a Fedele priest," I said. "Nor am I gentle-born. Who are you not?"

"I am not a mage," he said. "Nor am I a musician." He traced my face with one hand. "Come with me," he said, and so I followed him again, as he led me through the alley, and through another alley, and another. We were alone in the darkness. He stroked my arms, running his hands along the velvet. "Tell me what you are," he said.

"I am a musician," I said. "Tell me what you are."

"I am a man who loves other men." He laid his hand on my face gently. "Are you as I am?"

I froze. "I think," I said, and my voice squeaked, "that I am not as you think me."

He dropped his hand and turned away. "Refuse me without fear," he said. "I'm a fool."

"No—" I said. The sadness in his voice was heart-breaking. "It isn't that. I find you very—" I paused. "I actually really am a woman."

The alley was dead silent for a long moment. Then witchlight flared in the man's hand, as he turned to study me. I couldn't read his expression behind the mask, and began to feel frightened. With the hand that wasn't holding the witchlight, he reached up and in one smooth motion pulled my mask off. "Daniele," he said. "I was right, it *is* you."

Someone knows. Someone knows my secret. My mind soared into panic, and I did the first thing that occurred to me. Ripping my knife from its concealed spot under my skirt, I launched myself toward the man. He was drunk and unsteady already, and I knocked him flat on his back in the alley.

"Wait—" he said, his words garbled with fear. "Wait, Daniele—"

Holding my knife to his throat, I tore his mask off. And stared into the face of the Emperor.

CHAPTER EIGHT

Knock, and the door shall be opened.
—*The Journey of Gèsu, chapter 4, verse 26.*

My stomach lurched. "Oh my God," I said. My words came back to me a heartbeat later and my stomach lurched again. Now I had *really* done it. My knife was trembling, and I couldn't tell if it was Travan or me that was shaking. I couldn't kill the Emperor; he was the one that I had desperately hoped for an opportunity to get on my side. But I couldn't let him live. He knew *everything*.

I held the knife-edge at his throat, paralyzed by fear.

"Wait, Daniele," Travan said. "Don't you know me?"

"You're the Emperor," I said.

Travan stared up at me desperately, shaking his head. "I am one of you."

I stared at him in disbelief.

Travan licked his lips and his voice sank to an even fainter whisper. "I am Redentore. You spied on the Mass when I was there. I kept the others from killing you."

I dropped the knife. Gathering my skirts around me, I climbed off of the Emperor. "Your Imperial High—"

"Shhh," he said. "There are people about, and anyone might overhear. Call me Travan."

My mouth was dry. "I'm so sorry—"

Travan sat up wearily and leaned against the building. With one hand, he clasped my skirt and tugged, urging me to sit again. I sat down beside him.

"I've been watching you since before you visited the Mass," Travan said. "I knew who you were when I approached you in the piazza. I'd thought for some time that you might be like me." He formed a light and studied me again, then flicked the light away. "You make a rather attractive boy, you know."

I swallowed hard and tried to convince my head to stop spinning long enough to let me speak. "Travan," I said. "You have the courage to defy the Fedeli, to follow your conscience and the true God. Do you have the courage to defy the Circle? If it's not for nothing?"

Travan turned toward me. "You're one of the Lupi," he said.

"Yes," I said. Travan was silent, so I took a deep breath, then another, and started talking. "You know that your father was murdered by his political enemies. And you know that could happen to you; both the Circle and the Fedeli are looking for ways to force your hand. You're caught between them but you don't *have* to be. You could rule in truth, and not just in name. You could take revenge on those who arranged the death of your father. If you have the courage to join us. If you have the courage to defy the Circle."

Travan met my eyes, and I saw fear in them, but also trust. "Who are you?" he asked.

Please, God, let this be the right thing to do, I thought. "Eliana," I said. "I'm Eliana."

"If you're Eliana, what are you doing here?" he said. "Why aren't you with the Lupi?"

"The opportunity presented itself to send a violinist," I said. "I was a conservatory student, once. And—before I left, the Circle had nearly destroyed my army."

"I had heard that," Travan said, and looked away. "So why should I join a losing cause—even one that offers me a true throne?"

"With you on our side, everything would be different," I said. "The army is loyal to you. And the Circle fears them—for good reason. Without soldiers for protection, mages are vulnerable. *We could make this work.*"

"If I take your side," Travan said, "the Circle and the Fedeli will cooperate in my murder."

"You'll have to leave Cuore," I said. "Tonight, if you're willing. I have people here who can slip you out."

Travan hesitated. "And if I'd like to think this over?"

"You are the Emperor," I said. "I will await *your* decision."

Travan was silent again for a few moments. Then, "Tell me this," he said. "Would the Lupi *truly* support me against the Circle?"

"I swear in Gèsu's name," I said. "We would support you."

Travan nodded. "Then I'll do it."

* * *

The tavern where I normally met with Michel would be closed for the evening's revelries, but with luck Michel would not have gone far. Travan and I tied our masks back on and made our way through town. My head was still reeling, and I knew that both my wig and my false breasts were askew.

The streets seemed to be full of Lupi, but if my soldiers had ever gotten this drunk, I'd have tossed the lot of them into the stockade. I kept seeing familiar people in the featureless crowds. Three times, I was certain I saw Lucia. Twice, I thought I saw Felice. And once it was my mother I saw, dancing with a young man in the street that ran past the tailor's shops. I nearly cried out, but then she turned and I realized that it was a man.

When we reached the streets near the university, I feared that Travan was losing his nerve. "Just a little farther," I whispered. "Wait here while I find Michel."

Travan nodded and slipped into a shadowed doorway. I could drag Travan out of the city myself, but Michel and Placido could provide us with horses, which we'd need to have Travan a safe distance away by morning. I realized with dismay that my violin was still back at the enclave. Well, if I didn't have a chance to go back for it, I'd leave it. The Emperor was more important than any instrument, and besides, my old violin was with Lucia.

Michel was nowhere to be found, but I spotted—of all people—Ulisse. "Ulisse," I hissed. He stumbled over, flask in hand, giggling at the sight of me. "Shh, this is serious," I said. "I need to talk to Placido. Do you know where he is?" Michel would probably be close by.

"Yeah, maybe," Ulisse said, looking vaguely around the crowd. "That's right, he's the next street over. Least he was a little while ago."

"Thank you," I said, and started to pull away.

"Hey," he said, pulling me back toward him. "Don't you have a kiss for the gentleman?"

I gave Ulisse a swift kiss on the cheek. "I'll see you later, Ulisse." Someday, Ulisse would find out who I really was. The thought made me smile.

The university reformers seemed to be celebrating Mascherata together. More than a few had jumped at the opportunity to dress as Lupi, with red-tinted masks like Quirino's. They were dancing to drum music, with some music provided by a violinist who was having trouble keeping up with the beat. The dancers had formed a circle, as if they were celebrating Mass, but they weren't dancing in unison.

Even masked, Michel was easy to recognize; no one danced like him. He had gleefully dressed as a Lupa, a wig of long dark hair held in place with red ribbons. I clasped his shoulder and he did a double-take. "El— Daniele?" he hissed.

"Yeah, it's me. Michel, you're not going to believe this, but I've got an ally who needs to get out of Cuore *tonight,* on the fastest horse we can find."

"Why wouldn't I believe it?" Michel was much less drunk than his companions. I drew him back toward where I'd left Travan.

I glanced past Michel's shoulder, then over mine, and leaned closer to him. "The ally is Emperor Travan."

"Tr—you're not serious!"

"I am."

Michel's face lit. "This will change everything."

"*Only* if we can get him safely out of Cuore *and* hide him well enough that we can keep him safe. I want to take him to the wasteland. We don't have to fear the Circle there, and the Emperor commands the army, so—"

"I don't know how you do it, Daniele," Michel said. "A horse? That's what you said you need? For this kind of support, I'd get you horses if I had to steal them from my grandmother."

"Can we just get some from Placido? We'll need six horses—two for each of us—or else three horses and money to buy three more."

Michel nodded. "Yeah. Placido's an ass but I think I can get him to do this. Stay here for a minute."

I leaned against the rough stone wall of a shop as Michel vanished back into the dancing crowds. My legs were aching, I realized, from too much dancing. What time was it? How many hours till dawn? Probably quite a few.

Michel was coming back with Placido at his side. Placido was dressed in a black velvet tunic with a flame-red velvet sash. Instead of a simple white mask, he wore a stylized mask made to look like the face of a wolf. It was probably the most impressive costume I'd seen all night, but I found myself suppressing a laugh. If this was how he imagined the Lupi, how did he imagine Eliana? Michel caught my eye as he led Placido toward me. "Daniele, I've told him that you're our contact."

Placido's beady eyes glared at me from behind his mask.

"Have you told him what I need?" I asked Michel.

"Yes," Michel said. "He says he's willing to provide horses, but he wanted to meet you."

I turned back to Placido. "It's a pleasure to make your acquaintance, signore," I said.

"I'd like to see your face, if I may," Placido said.

I took off my mask. He stared at me a moment longer.

"And your face, signore?" I said.

Grudgingly, Placido untied his elaborate mask and

took it off. His face was flushed red from wine and dancing.

"Since you're leaving so soon," Placido said, "would you be so kind as to inform me your real name? I may find myself needing to seek out your assistance myself, sooner or later."

"Ask for Daniele, if you need our help," I said.

Placido gripped my arm, shaking his head. "That's not good enough." His face was close to mine, and I could smell his dank breath, and feel the faint spray of his spit on my forehead. "If you wish any further assistance from us, you will tell me exactly who you are."

Michel had reached for his knife, and I shook my head at him. There was no point in alienating Placido, and my identity hardly mattered at this point; I was leaving Cuore as soon as we got horses. And I didn't think Placido was a spy. "I am Eliana," I said.

Placido's grasp sagged, then tightened again. "You expect me to believe that?"

"Believe it or not; your choice," I said. "It's true. Now," I jerked my arm free and straightened up, "go get our damn horses before someone comes to investigate."

Placido flinched back slightly, and his eyes narrowed. With careful precision, he tied his mask back on. "Six horses will be waiting for you at the southern edge of Cuore in one hour," he said, and walked away.

"Can we trust that?" I asked Michel.

Michel hesitated, then nodded. "Whatever else you can say about Placido, he's on our side. Even if he really doesn't believe you, he won't screw this up for us."

"Come on, then," I said. "Let's get Travan."

To my relief, Travan still waited where I'd left him.

He was masked, so it was hard to guess his expression, but his eyes seemed relieved to see me again. "Is everything arranged?" he asked.

I nodded. "Horses will be waiting. We'll take you to where the Lupi are wintering, then down to the wasteland, where the mages can't attack us. Let's head for the edge of the city; it will take us close to an hour just to walk there."

"Your violin?" Michel asked me.

I shook my head. "Leave it. It's too risky to go back in." I glanced over my shoulder and lowered my voice, so that just Michel and Travan could hear me. "Where *are* the Lupi wintering?"

"Lucia and Giovanni are in Montefalco," Michel said. "It was destroyed during the war, but it's not actually in the wasteland. It'll be a little out of our way to go there, but not too much."

"Maybe we should just go straight to the wasteland, and then I can double back," I said.

"That might be a good idea," Michel said. "So long as one of us has coin enough to buy food. There isn't going to be any down in the wasteland."

The streets were less crowded now; wine and exhaustion had claimed many of the dancers. The costumes changed as we made our way through town. In the university district, we were surrounded by drunken, velvet-clad Lupi. Beyond that, we found ourselves in a crowd of beggars clothed in scraps of red and purple. Then came a mass of Maledori; there were masks of hook-beaked birds and strange hybrids of dog and cat.

"Daniele!"

Michel and Travan fell back a step; from the corner of my eye, I could see Michel draw Travan into the shadows of a doorway, but I didn't dare look. The person who'd called to me wore ragged red robes and a mask with swirls of color painted on it. I wouldn't have known her by sight, but I recognized her voice: "Rosalba?"

"What are you doing here?"

There was only one answer to that. "Looking for a good party," I said.

Rosalba laughed, a light crystal tinkle. "You've found one!"

From behind the mask, I could see her eyes start to stray past my shoulder. *Oh no,* I thought. If she recognized me, she could recognize the Emperor. I dodged in front of her and clasped her shoulders to keep her still. "Actually—to tell the truth—I was looking for you."

I could see her smile even from behind the mask. "Really?" She ducked her head a little shyly. "I was rather hoping you were."

"You know—" I could hear Michel's breathing behind me, quick and frightened. "I'm kind of tired. Were you thinking of heading back to the enclave anytime soon?"

Rosalba's hand found mine. "I'll walk back with you now, if that's where you're headed."

When Rosalba turned away, I spared one quick glance back at Michel and Travan. *"Go,"* I mouthed at Michel.

Michel gave me the tiniest of salutes and nodded. Michel would make it work; I could trust him. If I couldn't catch up with them, I'd come up with something. Besides, this would give me the opportunity to get the violin.

The enclave was dark and quiet. Rosalba held my arm close to her as we ducked in through the gate; the guard gave only a cursory glance at our medallions. I'd hoped Rosalba might head off to her own quarters once we were back, but she followed me back to my room. "Could you give me just a moment?" I asked when we reached the door. "This is not the world's most comfortable costume."

"I'll wait out here," Rosalba said. "Just open the door when you're ready."

I closed the door and hesitated for a moment. Barring the door would be suspicious; why would I distrust Rosalba? But if she opened the door while I was unclothed—I slipped the bar into place, but very, very quietly. The bindings over my breasts were secure, so I pulled on a tunic and hose, quickly splashed the paint off my face, and checked my appearance in the mirror. Then I opened the door.

Rosalba had taken off her mask, and she held it by the string. The ragged red robe she wore was luminous in the witchlight that glowed in her hand. She smiled, a little shyly, as she came in and sat down.

I put the kettle over the fire and poked the fire up a bit. "I'll make us some tea," I said.

"Thank you," Rosalba said.

We waited silently for the water to heat. Rosalba tucked her legs up against her on the chair, studying me gravely as I stared at the kettle. I glanced at her after a few minutes, to see if she was still staring at me. She was, but lowered her eyes quickly. Finally the water was ready. I made the tea and poured a cup for each of us, sitting down on the other chair. "Did you have a good time tonight?" I asked.

"Oh, yes," Rosalba said. Then she shrugged. "Mascherata isn't my favorite holiday. I'm not really one for crowds."

"Me either," I said. "It's probably because we grew up in the country."

"That could be it," Rosalba said. She sipped her tea, and looked at me over the rim. "How did you celebrate Mascherata at the conservatory?"

Unbidden, the image of the Fedele priest cutting Bella's throat rose before my eyes. I turned away from Rosalba to poke at the fire, hoping that she hadn't seen my face. The Fedeli had come to the Verdiano Rural Conservatory last Midwinter—not to the conservatory in Pluma, where Rosalba thought I was from. "It's different," I said, when I thought I had control over my voice again. "We had a chapel service, and we all made masks, but boys and girls were kept separate. There wasn't a lot of wine. They wanted us to behave ourselves."

Rosalba nodded. "At the seminary, they kept a pretty tight lid on us even at Midwinter," she said.

Rosalba fell silent again, and I decided I was content to let the conversation lag. As long as I wasn't talking, I wasn't going to make any stupid mistakes.

Rosalba spoke again after a few minutes. "I heard a rumor the other day that I might get reassigned."

"To what sort of job?" I asked. "Can you talk about it?"

Rosalba shook her head. "No. But, it would mean leaving the enclave. And it would be *much* more interesting than transcribing confessions."

"Great!" I said, flashing her a bright smile. "That's what you were hoping for, right?"

Rosalba nodded. "I'll finally be doing what I felt I was called to do," she said. "But—" She sighed. "I'll miss you, Daniele."

"Oh—I'll miss you, too, Mother Rosalba. But I know—well, not that you didn't *like* transcribing. But there are so many people who could do it. And you—"

Rosalba smiled into my eyes. "Daniele, you know, I think you're the only person in Cuore who understands me."

"That can't be true," I said.

Rosalba leaned over and took my hand. Her fingers were surprisingly cold, as if she was nervous about something, and she stroked my hand gently. "I'm so glad you came looking for me tonight," she said. Then she leaned forward and kissed me.

Her lips were warm and tentative, and as soft as rose petals. I could smell her cinnamon-rose perfume. Her hand still gripped mine; her fingers were icy cold. For a moment I started to kiss her back—then panic swept through me and I pulled away so sharply that I nearly fell out of my chair.

"M-mother Rosalba, I can't," I said. "It would be wrong. I'm not a priest."

Rosalba pulled back. "No, it's all right, Daniele. One of the privileges of the Fedeli priesthood in Cuore is that we can sleep with who we please; we aren't paired, since we don't have churches. But if you don't want to, if you don't find me appealing—"

"Rosalba—" I tried to pick myself up with something resembling dignity. "Mother Rosalba, you're the most beautiful woman I've ever met. But I hadn't realized—I need some time to think about it. To pray about it." I found the excuse I'd been fishing for, and I heard my voice steady with relief. "I hadn't realized the rules were different here, I hadn't allowed myself to think about the possibility of—"

Rosalba was studying me carefully. "That's understandable, Daniele." To my relief, her eyes no longer showed hurt, although I couldn't quite read what they did show. She smiled tentatively. "I can always tell when a boy finds me beautiful," she said. "So I was a little startled that you pulled away. But that makes sense."

I sat back and took a gulp of my tea.

Rosalba looked around my room. "I don't suppose you'd play something for me?" she asked.

"I'd be happy to," I said. Playing would mean I wouldn't have to talk with her. Or kiss her. I tuned my violin and set it on my shoulder. "Any requests?"

"Play me some dance music," she said. "Like in the streets."

I struck up one of the tunes I'd heard earlier in the evening, and Rosalba rose to dance to my playing. She moved more slowly than the frenzied dancing I'd seen in the streets. She had a graceful, deliberate style, and she covered a lot of ground, using the whole room.

When I finished the piece, Rosalba sighed. "You know, I really am quite tired," she said. "I'm going to go home and sleep for what's left of the night. Are you going to come play for me tomorrow?"

I bowed deeply. "I play at your pleasure, signora."

"I'm honored. Well. I'll see you tomorrow, then." Rosalba took my hand, then very tentatively kissed my cheek. I smelled rose and cinnamon, then she paced quickly out of the room.

I closed the door quietly. *Thank God, thank God.* If I hurried, Michel might still be waiting. I buckled my violin into its case, barely slowing to loosen the strings, and threw in all my sets of spare strings, since they were impossible to get in the wasteland. It didn't take me long to pack; almost everything was gathered together neatly, since I'd known I might have to leave quickly. My money, my old clothes, my violin—there wasn't much else I needed. I bundled everything together, waited another few minutes to be sure Rosalba would be out of sight, wrapped my cloak around my shoulders, and headed out.

I walked to the gate as fast as I could without drawing attention. The gate I used wasn't far from the musicians' quarters. I could see the metal of the gates glinting a little in the last of the moonlight. The guard was even awake. "I'd like to leave, please," I said.

The guard stood. "You'll have to wait a moment, signore," he said, not unkindly. He looked past me into the shadows. "This who you meant, Mother?"

Rosalba stepped out. "Yes," she said.

I felt a cold wave of fear wash over me. "What's wrong, Mother Rosalba?"

She folded her arms and stepped forward. "Where are you going?"

"Back out to the party."

"Without a mask?" She poked at the bundle on my back. "That's more than just your violin."

I met Rosalba's eyes challengingly. "I'm meeting a young lady," I said. "I promised her I'd spend the night. I'm sorry. I didn't want to hurt your feelings."

Rosalba's lips tightened; her face was white. She addressed the guard. "I apologize, signore. There's a servant of the Fedeli whose services I need. Would you be so kind as to help me escort this man to the Citadel?"

"There's the gate—"

"There are other gates. Lock this one and come with me, on my authority."

I had a terrible feeling I knew who the "servant of the Fedeli" would be. Rosalba couldn't possibly have warned all the gatekeepers to watch for me, so as this guard turned away to lock the gate, I dropped everything I was carrying and started to run. I had run perhaps twenty paces when something solid and heavy hit my back, throwing me to the ground. I'd been tackled, the wind knocked out of me. The guard hauled me to my feet and pinned my hands behind my back.

"Citadel, you said?" he asked Rosalba. She nodded.

It was a long, cold walk. Someone was leaving the Citadel as we approached it. Rosalba quickened her step to intercept him—apparently, it was the "servant of the Fedeli" she'd mentioned before. He followed her over to where I waited with the guard—and, with a muffled exclamation, flipped back his hood. I stared into a pretty, boyish face framed by blonde curls. *Felice.*

Momentarily forgetting Rosalba, Felice stepped in closer. "Remember me?" he asked.

"You son of a *bitch*!" I shouted, and tried to tear my arms free. The guard jerked my arms behind me and I cried out involuntarily.

Felice laughed. "Rosalba, you've caught a bigger fish than I think you ever imagined. This is Eliana—*Generale* Eliana." He bowed toward me mockingly, then stepped in closer. "You'd better talk nice to me now, Generale. You're under arrest."

I leaned back against the guard, trying to make it look like I was shrinking away from Felice. He advanced one more step. That was all I needed. Leaning back against the guardsman for balance, I kicked out with one foot as hard as I could. "Hope you weren't planning on having babies, *traitor,*" I hissed, as Felice screamed in pain.

The guard yanked me backward so hard he almost dislocated my arm, then drew back his fist to hit me, but Rosalba put her hand on his arm. "No," she said, and her voice shook. "She's ours, and we want her in one piece." Rosalba turned to me, and her eyes were bright with fire. "So that we can properly return her to the Lady."

CHAPTER NINE

*Reach for me, and I will take your hand; I
will give you all that you need.*
—*The Journey of Gèsu, chapter 7, verse 22.*

The Fedeli guards pulled a hood over my head; I
wasn't sure if it was to disguise my identity as
they took me into the Citadel, to keep me from seeing
my route to the prison below, or just to disorient and
frighten me. I didn't know when Rosalba left me; Felice
stayed back on the steps of the Citadel, still hobbled. I
made a tentative effort to test the guard's grip on my
arms, and was rewarded with a blow so hard I thought
for a moment he'd cracked the back of one of my ribs.

We descended stairs, down and down and down. The
air was cold, and I could smell charred meat mixed with
human wastes, acrid urine, and sour vomit. I heard the
clang of a door, the rattle of a chain, and they snapped
something cold around my wrists. They were chaining me.

The hood was pulled off my head. I was in a cell, lit
with witchlight that hurt my eyes. "Hold still," the guard
said, and took out a knife. I drew away, but he grasped
the collar of my shirt and cut my clothes away from my

body, nicking me with the blade when he cut away the cloth I'd used to bind my breasts.

"Lady's tits," the guard said, studying me. "It is a girl, after all."

"I'm going to tell Rosalba you swore," I said.

"You do that, girl," the guard said with a short laugh, and they turned away, closing the door. I was naked, alone, in darkness.

Tethered to the wall, I could stand, but not sit. I hunched my arms as close to my body as I could; the air was achingly cold, and standing naked I could feel every draft. Beyond the door of my cell, I could hear activity—footsteps, murmurs of conversation, and then a long scream of pain that made my legs shake so hard that I had to lean against the chains for support.

What had raised Rosalba's suspicions? Obviously, seeing me leave when I did had confirmed them. But she hadn't seemed suspicious when she left my room. Was it that I hadn't jumped at the chance to sleep with her? Maybe she'd seen it in my eyes. Maybe she'd realized I was a woman. There were a thousand ways to be caught. I'd told Giovanni that.

From a cell close by, I heard a hoarse moan. I closed my eyes, wishing that I could cover my ears to blot out the sound. *Pray for me, Lucia,* I thought. Now that the worst had happened, my fear had ebbed to a dull ache in my stomach. They knew who I was; they were going to kill me. I tried to hold that thought in my mind, to summon the fear that ought to be there, but I couldn't focus on it for more than an instant. *I will never see Verdia again,* I thought, but I couldn't believe it. I couldn't imagine myself dead, or the world without me in it. I started to wonder if they would burn me, or if someone would have mercy on me and cut my throat instead. I heard the hoarse moan again, and shuddered from the cold. My back itched and I couldn't reach it with my hands chained; I rubbed it against the wall behind me.

I hoped Travan and Michel were well away. I trusted Michel to have enough sense to have gone on by now. I told myself that I had played my part; the others could take it from here. I was expendable. For some reason Giovanni's voice rang in my ears. *Expendable?* I could hear frustration and infuriation in his tone.

I wondered what Valentino and Quirino would hear in the morning. The Emperor vanished, Daniele arrested. Would they hear somehow that I was Eliana in disguise? I imagined Ulisse's reaction at learning that his drinking buddy for the last few months was actually the lady of his dreams in disguise. Only she'd be dead. And Mira—what would Mira think? It was too painful to think of Mira. I turned my face against the rough stone wall and tried to think of someone else.

In the Book of the Lady there were stories of villains who found themselves haunted by the people they'd killed. Teleso should come haunt me in this cell, I thought. I could handle that; I was proud to be able to say I'd killed him. I'd spit in the face of his apparition. But if a ghost were sent to *torment* me, it would be Vitale, the youngest Lupo who died in the magefire before my eyes. Or one of the other Lupi who had died that night—all the people who I had failed to protect. Who I failed. *You failed,* I could hear Giovanni say. *You were supposed to come back*.

Mario; he could haunt me too. Coughing up blood around the dagger in his belly. I wondered again how they'd kill me. Well, last I heard, the Fedeli didn't kill people by gut-stabbing them. My arms had gotten stiff in their chains, and I tried uselessly to stretch. My foot itched. I rubbed it along the floor.

I found myself thinking about my mother for the first time in months, and I realized that I wasn't certain I could picture her face. Had I really tried, up until now? Or had I satisfied myself with hazy images that faded like cloth in the sun? When I tried to picture my mother's face, all I could remember was the feeling of her arms around me as she held me on her lap, showing me the hair she kept in her sachet, a lock from me, from each of my brothers, and from the two children who died. My mind jumped to Isabella, praying to the Lady after the ambush. Burning one of the locks of hair from her sachet. *Now you are truly dead to me.* Isabella's face sustained me. I knew that if I were with the Lupi right now, Isabella would probably be complaining to me about some slight to one of her soldiers. I could hear her querulous voice, could even guess the precise words she'd use. I argued with my memory of Isabella for hours, passing time in the frigid darkness.

At some point I dozed, and was woken by the tearing pain in my shoulders as I slumped against the chains. I tried locking my knees, but I couldn't sleep standing up. I shook my head, trying to clear it, to wake myself up. I wondered how long I'd been down there—I felt as if it were horribly late at night, but for all I knew the night was long over and it was mid-morning.

Light flashed through the crack under the door. Witchlight—no, lantern light. The door swung open, and a gray-haired man came in. He wore black robes—wool, not linen. I heard no rustle as he walked. He carried a small wooden box with a handle, like a toolbox.

"Hello, Eliana," he said.

"My name is Daria," I said, since claiming to be Daniele was pretty much a lost cause at that point.

He shrugged. "We know you're Eliana," he said. "Felice identified you. Claiming to be someone else will only make this harder." He set down the box with a soft clunk and approached me. My heart knocked in my ears as I looked at him. He was shorter than I was. He stood just out of arm's reach, regarding me with a slight smile, for a long time. I tried to meet his eyes in a threatening glare, but he was not looking at my face; he was examining my body.

"This will be far more pleasant for you if you simply start by telling us everything you know," he said.

My stomach lurched. Somehow, in the night, I had managed to keep myself from ever thinking about what they would do with me *before* they killed me.

"Why you are here, for example. Where the Lupi are spending the winter. Who your allies are here. Who leads the apostate 'reformers' of Cuore. Anything else that would be of use to us. The more you can tell us now, the more pleasant this will be for you."

I locked my knees to keep from falling and raised myself as straight as I possibly could. "I would die before telling you anything," I said. My voice shook and I clenched my teeth, trying to force it steady.

"I'm sure you would," he said. "If you had the opportunity. You won't get one. You will die when *we* decide it's time for you to die, and that won't be until we know everything that you know." He regarded me again, still looking at my body. "And, as I said, this will be much more pleasant for you if you tell us everything now."

He paused and waited. I didn't trust my voice, so I was silent.

For the first time, he met my eyes. "Believe me when I tell you that you're going to tell us everything sooner or later. So why not just tell us now?"

I glared at him, forcing myself to hold his gaze. His eyes were a faded hazel-brown; harmless eyes. I couldn't believe, yet, that this man intended to hurt me.

He moved a step closer to me and took my hand, which I'd clenched into a fist. My hands were ice cold; his were very warm, and dry. He unwrapped my fist and spread my hand flat, palm up, against his. He traced the lines of my palm, almost affectionately, then each finger. "Musician's hands," he said. "Of course; they mentioned that you were a musician. Violin, yes?" I didn't answer. "Of course. You have the calluses." He brushed each fingertip. "You have lovely hands, my dear, perfect for playing the violin." I started to pull my hand away. Like a snake striking, he brought his other hand down to trap mine in a grip like a vise.

"We'll break your hands, you know," he said. "There are twenty-seven bones in each hand, and we'll break every one. First your left hand. Then your right, if it's necessary. I hope it won't be. It would be a shame to break such lovely hands." Still gripping my hand, he twisted; pain shot through my wrist. I cried out and he stepped back with a look of slight satisfaction on his face. "I don't think it will be necessary," he said. I shrank back without meaning to and he smiled for the first time. His teeth were yellow. I spat at him and he laughed out loud, then glanced over his shoulder. "Guard," he called.

The guards carried in a low stool, and set the man's

lantern on it. Then they shortened the tethers on my manacles, pulling my hands up over my head, then chained my feet, pinning me to the wall like a bug caught in a spider's web. *Gèsu will give you the strength you need,* I could hear Lucia saying. *Knock, and the door will be opened. Ask, and you shall receive.* But all the fear my mind had held off until now flooded me like burning poison.

"Felice," the man in black called.

Felice appeared in the doorway. I could smell his flowery perfume as he approached me. "Just once," the man in black said, indulgently. "And not her hands. Those are for later." He gave Felice a short stick, and in the flickering light I could see Felice smile. I closed my eyes and braced myself.

Pain exploded, so bad that for a second I wasn't sure where he'd hit me. My shin—he'd hit my shin. I wondered if he'd broken the bone. Was I going to be able to walk normally now? *It doesn't matter, I'm dead anyway. It doesn't matter if they break my legs, my hands, anything; I'm dead.* The pain had started to ebb when it exploded again. This time I screamed.

When I opened my eyes, Felice was gone, and the man in black stood regarding me. "Remember," he said. "This can go on for as long as it has to."

He opened his toolbox and began to lay out implements on the low stool, explaining some of them to me as he went. I couldn't bear to look, but I couldn't bring myself to turn away. I was shaking so hard my wrists bruised against the manacles, and I felt like I might vomit. The lamp gave off a dull red glow; it was heating some of the implements. The man in black held one up dispassionately, examining it. It smoked slightly in the reddish light. He blew on it gently as if to cool it, then set it back into the flame.

"Rosalba," he called.

Witchlight flickered at the doorway, and I heard a rustle of silk, caught the scent of spices over the smell of blood and fear. "Daniele," Rosalba said.

I looked at her, blinking past the witchlight. "My name is not Daniele," I said. "Obviously." I jerked my chin toward my female body.

Rosalba approached, dimming the witchlight slightly so that I could see her face. "Eliana, then," she said.

"Why are you here?" I said. I swallowed hard and turned my head to glare at her. "I suppose this is what you always wanted, isn't it? Torturing prisoners instead of recording their confessions? You said that's what you wished you were doing."

Rosalba's face was pale and uncertain; I could see a muffled horror in her eyes. "I'm not here to torture you, Eliana. I'm here to pray for you, that you will be freed from the Maledori that possess you and see the error of your ways."

"How did you know who I was?" I asked.

Rosalba's eyes flickered. "When I kissed you, I could tell that you lacked even the slightest trace of a beard. That made me wonder. So while you played the violin, I looked around your room. You had no razor. And I noticed—you had never truly moved in to your room. You were living out of your bags, like you thought you might leave at any time." She lowered her eyes. "So I watched your room. You behaved as someone guilty, leaving as you did. Sending for Felice—that was just a hunch."

I couldn't look at her face anymore, so I turned my

eyes away. "You know, I know Lucia," I said. "Your old friend from the seminary. I kissed her when I left her and I dream of her each night." It was Mira's face that rose before my eyes as I spoke, but I couldn't speak her name, so I spoke of Lucia. "She will never renounce her faith, and neither will I."

"The Lady waits for you with open arms," Rosalba said.

"I am Redentore," I said. "I believe in God, and Her Son, and Her Holy Light." I turned back and stared into Rosalba's eyes. "You can torture me until I say that I love the Lady; you can force me to foreswear my God, *Mother* Rosalba. But you can't change what's in my heart."

"If you have a prayer to say for her, say it," the man in black said.

Rosalba fell back a step. "Sweet and gentle Lady," she said. Her voice was shaking. "Touch Eliana, even within the darkness she is shrouded in. Let her find her way to you *quickly*. Bring her back to you without delay; may her pride not cause her to suffer too much, before she returns to you. So may it be."

The man in black bowed his head for a moment, then took a long, curved blade from the lamp. It glowed as red as the sun. He looked at it for a moment, then glanced back at Rosalba. "If you don't want to see this, you should leave now," he said.

Rosalba's eyes were still fixed on mine. "I'll stay," she said. Her voice was shaking.

I wanted to tell her to go away, that she didn't have to prove her devotion to the Lady by watching me tortured, but the man in black was there, smiling gently into my face. "In the name of the Lady," he said, and then I heard myself screaming, and I think Rosalba left sometime after that.

*　　*　　*

We had been dancing forever, in the darkness, around the fire. And then suddenly the music stopped. "Bella," a voice said. "Your heart is dark, Bella. You do not belong to the Lady."

I pushed my way to the front of the crowd. Bella stood alone, in her gray conservatory robes, facing Felice and Rosalba. "You must swear your loyalty to the Lady," Rosalba said. "The Lady loves you, Bella. She wants to forgive you."

I could feel the rising panic in my chest. Bella would not foreswear her faith. She would be tortured; Mira and I would be revealed. We would all be executed if we didn't recant, and Mira would probably be executed anyway. We should have run when we had the chance.

And sure enough, Bella spat on linked circles that Rosalba held out. "I belong to Gèsu," Bella said. "He will give me all the strength I need."

But instead of chaining her, instead of dragging her away to torture her, Rosalba shoved Bella to her knees, and Felice cut her throat.

*　　*　　*

Something stung my cheek, rousing me from darkness and delusions to a dim red glow, and terrible pain. I shook my head, *leave me alone,* and I was slapped again. "Open your eyes, Eliana."

My eyes were crusted over and I wanted to wipe them clean, but my hands wouldn't move. I managed to open one, and I saw the face of the man in black. "I thought you might like to know how long I've been down here. It's been a little under an hour. I want you to think about that, all right, Eliana? One hour." He smiled at me. "In any case, it's time for my dinner, so you'll have some time to think about this. *One hour.* Pain doesn't get any easier to bear, Eliana, and it's going to get a great deal worse. If you talk *now,* if you repent your sins *now,* if you return to the Lady *now,* I won't hurt you further."

I was silent.

"You were a simple musician once. You trusted the Lady, you did as you were told. There's another Eliana in there, someone who just wants to play her violin and let the world do as it will. I know there is. Eventually, she won't want to take any more pain."

I said nothing.

"You know that you're going to talk sooner or later," he said. "Tell us everything now, and save yourself the agony. You know it's what your mother would have wanted."

I forced my other eye open and met his gaze. "I—" My voice came out as a hoarse squeak. My throat was too raw to speak. I closed my mouth for a moment, and thanks be to God, felt a morsel of spittle moisten my tongue. I licked my lips, and jerked my head as if to say, *All I can manage is a whisper, come closer to hear.* He leaned forward, and I spit in his face.

His expression never flicked. "Well," he said. "I'll see you when I return from dinner."

He took the light with him. I was too disoriented with pain to summon witchlight, and my bravado was swallowed quickly in the whirlwind of fear and pain. "B'shaem Arkah, v'Bar Shelah, v'Nihor Kadosh," I said silently; it was too difficult to voice them aloud. I repeated the words, again and again. *Save me, please. Somebody. Anybody.* Even Giovanni.

I can't take what Octavio did. I can't. I knew I couldn't, and that knowledge buried me in fear. Mira had warned me that the Circle most wanted to know where to find the Lupi, right now. The evening before, I wouldn't have been able to tell them—but now I knew, and I didn't think they'd believe me if I said I didn't. And I knew plenty more they'd want to know— where Michel and Travan were going, and the likely route they'd travel to get there; that Mira was as eager to destroy the Circle as I'd been. I knew who led the Cuore reformers, although according to Mira that wasn't much of a secret anyway. I knew that Ulisse was involved in the reform movement, and that Quirino was a sympathizer. I knew too much. Far too much.

Hold out as long as you can, I thought. *You bore the lash without crying out. You can die for the Lupi. No matter how long it takes.* I couldn't clasp my hands, so I knotted my hands into fists and tried to pray. My mind was still whirling in fear, and I wet my lips and tried to focus. If only I had the faith that Lucia had—or Bella—or even Mira. *I've never truly believed,* I realized, *I've always had the strength I've needed.* I whispered the words—"Gèsu, give me strength, please, give me strength," but my mind kept falling back to the same plea. *Save me. Somebody save me. Anybody. Please . . .*

Rosalba's face flashed into my mind, speaking to Octavio, silk and steel in her voice and her eyes. "Don't be a fool, Octavio. We will bring you back to the Lady's mercy sooner or later, one way or another. *Fool.* Do you think you can stand against us? Against the Lady? It is only out of mercy that we seek to return you to Her. It's to save *your* soul. You will be put to the torture. You will be put to the torture again. Is that what you want? *Is that what you want?*"

I shook my head, to try to chase Rosalba out of my mind, and her fiery eyes were replaced by Mira's. But it was not Mira in her Circle robes I saw, but in the drab wool robes of the conservatory, held fast by the Circle Guards as Liemo ordered them to fire on me. Mira when she told me, after Bella's execution, "I can't do this again. I won't be able to let another friend die." The wild ecstasy on her face after her magic destroyed the crossbow bolt, and then the horror when she felt the burning need for magery close around her heart again.

Mira had sacrificed her life for me. She had sacrificed her dream of living free, on her own terms, instead of serving the cause she hated. She had given that up to spare me pain. And then to spare my life, she had shouldered the burden of my hatred. In the darkness, for the first time, I saw that clearly. I wished I could tell her, somehow, that I understood.

I thought of the night I'd spent on the riverbank beside Mira, and the night she'd cut my hair. I wished that I could retrace my steps, to take her thin, tense body into my arms and press my lips to her hair. *Forgive me,* I wanted to whisper. *Forgive me for hating you.*

I clenched my hands into fists. I couldn't speak to her, but I could die for her. And I *would* die for her, and for Lucia and Giovanni. I would hold out. *I would not fail.*

After a long time, I could see a light coming down the hallways and my mind spun with terror. "Gèsu," I said. "For your glory. Give me strength, for your glory."

Through the crack under the door, I saw a flash of

light so bright it almost blinded me. The door swung open and I blinked, trying to see past the dark spots swimming in front of my eyes.

"Eliana," a voice said.

It was Mira.

Mira opened the shackles on my hands and feet. I collapsed to my hands and knees, my joints stiff as a rusted latch. Mira knelt beside me. "It's all right," she said. "I'm not going to let anything else happen to you."

I'm dreaming, I thought, *just as I dreamed I was back at the conservatory.* Mira held a wineskin to my lips, but the wine burned my raw throat and I coughed. She wet a cloth and wiped my face. "I'm getting you out of here," she said. "But we have to hurry."

Mira had brought clothing with her—trousers, a simple tunic, boots. I pulled the clothing on as fast as I could, choking back a cry as the rough fabric rubbed over the burns on my body. When I was dressed, she wrapped a cloak around my shoulders and pulled up the hood. "Can you walk?" she asked.

I nodded. *I can do whatever it takes to get out of here.*

I followed her without question through a maze of corridors. No one stopped us; I wasn't sure whether this meant Mira had incinerated everyone in her path on her way in, or if she just knew the right path to take. I didn't really care. It took all my effort just to keep putting one foot in front of the other. My wounds burned with a dizzying pain, the bruises on my shins made each step hurt, and I still wasn't entirely sure I believed this was happening.

Finally, we emerged into the night. "It's almost dawn," Mira said.

"Dawn?" I said. "I thought it was dinnertime."

"They always leave prisoners alone for a while—it's to let you get scared, nothing to do with meals. You were arrested shortly after midnight; now it's dawn."

Mira led me out of the enclave through the mage's gate. In the streets of Cuore, there were a few last remnants of Mascherata—an old woman still beating a drum, and a lot of drunk people slumped over in doorways. Mira led me to an inn with a light still burning in the window—not the one we'd met at before, but an even smaller and seedier place, and one much closer to the edge of the city. She slipped in the door, latching it behind us, and led me through the inn and out back to a stable, where a horse stood saddled and ready. Mira began to check the straps and buckles on the horse's gear.

"The songs say you can ride, but I never asked you if that was true," Mira said.

"I can ride."

"That's good, because it won't take them long to realize that you're gone," she said. "I wish I could give you time to rest, but you need to set out right away. Everything you should need is packed on the horse." She finished tightening the straps and stood for a moment, looking away.

"Mira," I whispered. "Come with me."

"I can't." She turned back to face me, her eyes hard with resolve. "Eliana, the Circle *sent* me to free you. They deeply distrust the Fedeli's ability to drag information from you by torture, and they really only want to know one thing: the winter hideout of the Lupi. They're going to follow you. They're hoping you'll lead them there. If you don't, they think they can recapture you—or simply kill you."

"They won't take me alive," I said, and my voice shook. I couldn't go to Montefalco, then—or to Doratura, where many of the refugees from the camps still lived.

"Eliana," Mira said, and took my hand. "I didn't want to tell you this unless I was sure. And I'm *not* sure; I don't think I ever will be. But I think there's a way to turn back magefire."

I caught my breath. *"How?"*

"The songs. The Old Way songs. I don't know—" She bit her lip and looked away. "That's what I was trying to learn, at the conservatory, when I sent you to convince some of your friends to play the music with me. I thought there was a way, but I wasn't sure, and I'm *still* not sure. But I think Bella knew. I think that's why they killed her." She shook her head. "You need to go. The Circle wants you free—for now—but the Fedeli do not. And you're running out of time."

"I still think you should come with me."

"If I do, the Circle will know I betrayed them. They'll know you won't lead them to the Lupi; they'll ride us down and kill us both. Alone, you might escape."

I turned to mount the horse, and Mira caught my arm. "I think your magic is stronger than ours," she said. "Yours is stronger." She clasped my face and gave me a long, gentle kiss. Then she pushed me away. "Go."

I mounted the horse; Mira threw open the stable door, and I rode into the night. Not until hours later did I realize that I'd forgotten to tell her that I had forgiven her. I hoped she knew.

* * *

Your magic is stronger than ours. *Yours is stronger. Bella knew.* Mira's words rang in my ears as I rode through the night. I didn't know yet where I was going—south, of course, but whether to Montefalco or the wasteland, I wasn't sure. At dawn, I was tempted to take a short rest, but I was afraid that if I got off the horse I wouldn't be able to get back on. I slowed to a walk and dug through the most accessible saddlebag, finding cheese and water. I drank the water—I realized suddenly that I was terribly thirsty—and ate some of the cheese. There was a knife in the saddlebag as well; I slipped it into my boot, where I could get to it easily. The Circle was behind me, tracking me like a wolf tracks a rabbit; the Fedeli undoubtedly were looking for me, too. *They won't take me alive,* I thought. I'd cut my own throat, if it came to that.

That reminded me of Bella—Mira's statement, "Bella knew," and the dream I'd had in my cell. Bella had been murdered by the Fedeli. Not tortured, not burned, but simply murdered. I hadn't realized at the time just how strange this was, but now, after playing for Rosalba as she painstakingly transcribed confessions—now, I realized, the Fedeli did *not* normally kill people so quickly. They wanted a detailed confession, not merely a declaration of heretical faith. They wanted names, histories, repentance. Why, then, would they cut Bella's throat and let her choke to death on her blood in front of us? *Bella knew.* What was it they'd killed her to hide?

I thought back to that night. We had been dancing and dancing, to the drums and to Bella's trumpet. I'd felt a strange warmth, and then suddenly Cassio snatched the trumpet out of Bella's hands. And then she declared her faith, and they killed her.

I'd felt a strange warmth—like drinking hot wine, or playing the Old Way music. We weren't playing Old Way music—but we were dancing. I'd caught a glimpse of the power that night, just as I'd caught a glimpse of it while playing the Redentori songs with Mira and the others. I hadn't *really* known that power until the night that I played for the funeral in Ravenna, but maybe Bella had. *Bella knew.* Bella had realized something, and the Fedeli were willing to sacrifice the information they could drag out of her to ensure that whatever she had just found died with her, on the stones of the conservatory piazza.

Your magic is stronger than ours. Could I really do magic with the Redentore music? The idea seemed ludicrous. I thought about the surge of power Mira sent through me at our first meeting here, the sensation of light that flared the witchlight in my hand like tinder flaring into flame. *More, I want more.* I pushed the thought away, thinking about the power that I touched in the Mass, that I sent into the earth, that I used to stop the riot. That's what they killed Bella to hide. That's what we could use to defeat the Circle.

I rode through the day without stopping except to buy a fresh horse with the coins Mira had packed in my bag. *Your magic is stronger than ours.* I thought I had a way. I told myself that I *knew* I had a way, and prayed that I was right.

As I rode into the village encampment at high noon the next day, I heard the perimeter guards shout. "Who goes?" Then—"*Eliana?*" The voice was incredulous, delighted.

"It's me," I said. "And company's coming. Round everyone up and get them to the center of the village."

Lucia, Isabella, and Giovanni came running as I rode into the center of the village.

"Eliana!" Isabella shouted.

"What's wrong?" Lucia asked.

"I've been followed," I said.

"And you led them here?" Giovanni demanded.

"Listen to me," I said. "First of all, I need my violin. Then bring everyone to the village piazza. Hurry. I'm an hour ahead of them, at most." I turned to Lucia. "Do they know the Dance that Turned the Storm?"

"Yes," Lucia said. "But we haven't danced it recently."

"Teach it again. Isabella, gather all the children and the injured into the piazza. Shelter won't protect them from magefire—they need to be close to us. Giovanni, I'll need something to stand on, and so will some archers—they'll be shooting from *inside* the dance circle."

"You're mad," Giovanni said.

"No, I'm not," I said. "It's possible that I'm *wrong*, but I'm not mad."

"And if you are wrong?"

"Just hope I'm right," I said. "Because it's too late for anything else."

The preparations were completed in minutes. I stood at the center of the circle, on a kitchen table that had been dragged outside, my violin in my hand. The village children sat under it, the older ones trying to reassure the younger ones. A dozen archers stood on benches, looking a little confused. Everyone else stood in a circle around us, hands clasped. Giovanni glared at me from the bench where he stood with a crossbow; Lucia's eyes were closed, her face peaceful. Then I could see distant dust kicked up by swift horses; they were coming.

I played the opening notes to the dance on my violin. *"Rachamin Arkah,"* Lucia sang. "Rachamin Arkah. Rachamin Gèsu. Rachamin Gèsu." The dance began to move around me like a vast wheel. *Side-together-side skip. Front-together-front skip. Side-together-side skip. Back-together-back skip.*

God, I thought. *I'm trusting you. This had* better *work.*

My pursuers rode into the village. There were a dozen of them—eight guards, four mages. They hadn't brought along any soldiers, just members of the Circle Guard. The mages dismounted almost casually, clasping their hands and closing their eyes.

"Keep dancing!" Lucia shouted. "Don't look at them. Look at Eliana. *Keep dancing.*"

The mage in the center—the focus—raised his hands to the sky.

I gathered the fear and faith and motion of the dancers, feeling the power running through my body like blood, like Mira's magery. *Stronger than ours.* A calm came over me as I saw the fires coming down on us. *Back,* I thought, and focused the dance-energy *out.*

Red clouds of magefire rolled around us, breaking like water at a dam. The fire rippled toward the houses around the piazza; the clay walls melted like butter as the houses were consumed by the flames. One of the houses had brilliant red flowers out front; for a moment the flames and flowers merged, then only the fire was left.

But the magefire shimmered along the edge of our circle like a candle dancing along the edge of a glass.

Lucia's eyes flew open and I realized that she hadn't really believed this would work.

The clouds dissipated, leaving the burning houses; I could see the faces of the mages, eyes wide with disbelief. I took a step toward them. Perhaps I could extend the protection beyond the edge of the circle. *Out,*

I thought. *Go.* Another cloud of magefire came down, but this one broke at the edge of the piazza. The dancers moved faster and faster, their realization that this was working filling them with energy and flooding me with power.

The mages were frightened now. One started to break out of the line and was jerked forward again by his fellows.

"Shoot them!" I shouted. The archers jumped; they'd been staring dumbfounded at the magefire. Giovanni stood beside me and raised his crossbow. As the focus-mage raised his arms again, Giovanni loosed a bolt and the mage fell, clutching at the bolt in his throat, crawling desperately away from us.

"No," I heard one of the other mages cry. "This can't be happening. This is impossible!"

"Come on!" Giovanni shouted to the other archers. "Don't just stand there gaping! You are soldiers! You are wolves!"

The archers raised their shaking bows and fired a volley of bolts. Another mage fell, clutching at a bolt in his gut; one of their guardsmen cried out as he took a bolt in the arm. The two remaining mages dropped to the ground, still clasping hands. "Kill the dancers," one of them shouted to their guards. "Break their circle, and we'll take them out with fire."

The eight guardsmen charged toward the square. Giovanni rolled under Lucia and Isabella's clasped hands, drawing his sword as he rose. He kicked one guardsman in the gut as he caught the sword of another against his own. "Fire again!" he shouted. "Kill the mages; we can deal with the guards when we're done!"

One of the guards stabbed a dancer in the back with

his sword; as she fell, the people on either side of her clasped hands to continue. That was too much for the rest of the archers, though, and they dropped their crossbows and followed Giovanni's example rather than his orders, ducking out of the circle and drawing swords. One archer fired one more bolt toward the mages, but I saw the bolt sizzle and vanish in the air, like the bolt that had been fired at me at the conservatory. Unfortunately for me, with the archers out of the circle, I'd lost my bodyguards. I jumped down off the kitchen table, pretty sure that I could work the Redentore magic without being able to see outside the circle.

The Circle guardsmen were excellent swordsmen, but they were outnumbered three to two, and Giovanni looked like he thought he could fight two of the guardsmen all by himself. Watching from inside the circle of dancers, I realized that the guardsmen had trained much more with their crossbows than in close-quarters fighting; the Circle didn't usually want them too close to their opponents as it made it impossible to use magefire without killing the guardsmen as well. Normally when someone attacked at close range, it was a single, desperate person; no real threat to eight guards.

Beyond the piazza, I saw a movement. "The mages," I shouted. "They're running away!" Giovanni kicked away the guard he was fighting and tore after them. I tried to extend the power of the dance to where the mages were, but it hardly mattered; he tackled one mage and threw him to the ground, cutting his throat, while one of the other Lupi stabbed his sword through the other.

The piazza was suddenly very quiet, and I realized that we'd killed the mages and all of their guards. *Rachamin Arkah,* the dancers sang. *Rachamin Gèsu.* I ended the dance and looked around at the faces of the Lupi. Some people were too stunned to react; others had smiles of wild delight. Lucia's eyes were bright and her cheeks were flushed. Beyond her, Giovanni turned toward me, thumped his chest with his fist, and held it out in salute.

"The Emperor's army fights for us," I said. "And our faith is stronger than magefire."

PART THREE

Stronger Than Magefire

CHAPTER TEN

Trust not in the gratitude of the powerful.
—*The Journey of Gèsu, chapter 7, verse 33.*

The wasteland hills were gray in the thin winter sunlight. "Are you sure you're leading us in the right direction?" Giovanni asked again. "Everything looks the same."

"Not to me, and yes, I'm sure," I said. We crested the hill, and beyond could see a red banner flapping in the wind. I turned to Giovanni. "See? I was right."

"Luck," he said.

Michel had taken Travan to an old army barracks in the northern part of the wasteland. We had been in contact with him by messenger, but hadn't arrived in person until now. Giovanni and I had ordered the Lupi to regroup in the wasteland; the Emperor was setting up supply lines, and we could use the wasteland's protection from magefire while we recruited additional musicians.

Travan and Michel were not alone. Already, courtiers and minor nobles were defecting. Clara had been among the first to join them; according to Michel's message, she had embraced the Redentore faith with an apparent fervor that startled him. I found this fact oddly reassuring; surely, Clara would only join a side she thought would win. By joining us now, she positioned herself as one of the Emperor's most loyal advisors. Though there was also the fact that she'd been unable to marry her lover because of the Lady's withheld blessing. Clara had been joined promptly by that lover—husband, now—Demetrio, the army commander who had escaped our attack in the wasteland last summer. Demetrio was acting as a liaison to the army, and helping to set up the supply lines.

The shifting winds of politics had created unexpected bedfellows. Placido had also come south to join the Emperor's makeshift court, and despite their original affiliations, he and Clara had discovered that they had a great deal in common. Starting, no doubt, with a keen sense of their own self-interest and a knack for discovering which way the wind was blowing.

The Lupi army had made camp a day's ride away; I wanted to keep the nobles out of our hair. Also, although I trusted most of my army, there was always the possibility that we'd brought along a spy, and it was easier to protect Travan with only a handful of people around. Giovanni and I had ridden to the Emperor's court by ourselves, leaving quietly before dawn.

Michel came out to greet us, his face bright. We dismounted from our horses and I clasped his arms; Michel pulled me into a hug. "I thought you'd never make it," he said. "Are the Lupi close by?"

"Not far," I said. Beyond Michel, I could see others come out of the barracks. Placido, Clara, and another man—Demetrio, probably. Not Travan; presumably he was waiting inside.

"Hello, Generale Eliana," Placido said as I came up

toward the door. "What a pleasure to renew our acquaintance." His face showed anything but pleasure.

"I trust you are confident in my identity this time," I said.

Irritation flashed through his eyes, but he laughed as if I'd made a particularly amusing joke. "Of course," he said.

Clara regarded me with a faint speculative smile. "I believe we have also met before," Clara said, clasping my hand gently in greeting. "You were going by 'Daniele' at the time, yes?"

"I was," I said. "We were never exactly introduced, but I played for a banquet you attended." I remembered Clara's bright eyes studying me. She was studying me again, but I had nothing to fear this time and looked readily back at her.

"Let me present my husband," Clara said. "First Generale Demetrio of the New Imperial Army."

Demetrio bowed formally, offering me the ritual salute between military equals. I returned the gesture, though I couldn't help remembering what Lia had told me about his brutality. Well. Shifting winds could bring unexpected allies—for me, as well as for Clara and Placido.

"Let me present my second-in-command, Generale Giovanni," I said. Demetrio and Clara nodded as Giovanni bowed formally. Placido looked as if he had just bitten into a rotten fruit, and this clearly pleased Giovanni no end.

"I am honored by your welcome," Giovanni said. I had never heard him so polite, but Placido's pudgy face tightened even more. I'd have to ask Giovanni later what that was about.

"Shall we go in, then?" I asked. Placido turned away

with a final venomous glare toward Giovanni. Clara and Demetrio gestured toward the door and we went into the barracks.

There were a lot of people living there. The air inside was close and damp; the smell of horses mixed with incense and perfume. Tapestries and furniture had been brought from Cuore, far grander than the halls they adorned. The most absurd item I saw was a delicately carved wood box used as an apple crate.

The Emperor's audience chamber was in part of the old meal hall; it had been partitioned off. Travan was pacing the room impatiently when we came in. I studied him from the doorway as the servant announced our arrival. Travan had lost weight; he hadn't been fat when I saw him in Cuore, but there had been a softness that was gone after the long flight to the wasteland. His black velvet tunic was finely made but plain. He wore no crown or sign of his office, but a carved wooden cross hung around his neck. He turned eagerly at our arrival.

I sank to one knee and bowed my head; Giovanni did the same a pace behind me. "Your highness," I said. "It's good to see you again."

Travan crossed the floor in three steps and drew me to my feet. "Daniele—Generale Eliana." He kissed me on each cheek, and I could hear Placido's sharp intake of resentful breath behind me. "I'm so glad you've come at last." He gripped my hands tightly, then released them. "Still in boy's clothes, I see," he said.

" 'Still?' The last time you saw me I was in a dress." Placido coughed discreetly. "Your highness," I added.

"On Mascherata, dresses *are* boy's clothes," Travan said. "Well, it's good to see you. Whatever you're wearing. I'm glad you made it here safely."

"And how was your trip, your highness?" I asked.

Travan's eyes brightened. "Most exciting. But Michel took good care of me." At a rustle from Clara, Travan glanced past me and smiled resignedly. "I suppose we can save the visiting for later. Demetrio, would you be so kind?"

Demetrio showed us to a table at the end of the hall. There was a huge piece of parchment spread out on the table, with an elaborate abstract drawing of thin black lines. Circles and stars had been drawn all over, and small counters had been placed throughout—to hold the parchment down, I thought at first.

"This is Cuore," Demetrio said, pointing, and I realized that the parchment was in fact a detailed map. "Varena, and Pluma. Here's the wasteland. The Imperial army has divisions camped here, here, and here." Those were the tokens. "How many Lupi are there?"

"Several hundred right now, but I expect our numbers to increase significantly over the next few weeks. I trust we will be supplied with the lines you've set up?"

"That can be arranged," Demetrio said. He placed some tokens on the map in the wasteland. "Now, explain to me exactly how your defense against magefire works."

"I can direct the energy of Redentori dances to deflect magefire," I said. "I suspect other musicians could learn to do the same thing."

"Redentori musicians," Clara said.

"Presumably."

"How large an area can you protect?" Demetrio asked.

"More than just the area with dancers," I said. "It extends out a fair distance, but I'm not sure just how far."

"We'll need more musicians," Demetrio said. "And more dancers."

"We're going to try recruiting from the conservatories," I said. "I'm confident that the ability isn't restricted to violinists."

"This will help a great deal," Demetrio said. "But the walls of the Imperial Enclave will still pose an obstacle, unless we wish to recruit some mages of our own."

"Out of the question," Clara said.

"I thought as much. So." Demetrio looked around the table. "With only the Fedeli and the Circle Guard left to defend them, and with offensive magic rendered useless, the Circle's only possible strategy is to withdraw into the enclave and wait for us to come to them."

"If they have only one course of action, that should be an advantage for us," Giovanni said.

Demetrio gave Giovanni a patient look. "Unfortunately, they can predict our goals as easily as we can predict theirs. We must go to Cuore, sooner or later; they know that."

"We can't lay siege to them," I said. "Well, I suppose we could, if we had to. We'd need thousands of dancers, though, to take shifts—"

"No, I agree," Demetrio said. "We should avoid a siege if we possibly can. With your cooperation, Generale, I'd like to besiege them indirectly."

"What do you mean?"

Clara spoke. "The famine in Verdia disrupted Cuore's usual food supply. They've been supplementing it by purchasing grain from a country across the sea, bringing it in on ships. If we attack those lines of supply, this will deprive the Circle and Fedeli of food, and possibly augment our own supplies."

"Can we starve them out that way?" I asked.

"No," Demetrio said. "Many from court have fled or will soon, so there will be fewer people to feed from existing stores. But it will weaken them—and frighten them. Possibly enough to force them out from behind their walls to confront us directly."

"We'll be happy to cooperate with that effort," I said. "Tell me what you'd like my troops to do."

Demetrio outlined the precise routes where the grain was carried. I wasn't certain I understood, but Giovanni nodded enthusiastically, so I was fairly sure he'd be able to help me out with this later. "In addition," Demetrio said, "please think about any ways that you might draw the Circle out, or the Fedeli. You were a spy for several months, were you not, Generale? If you know of anything that we can use toward that end, be sure to let me know. If the Lupi don't have the manpower, we'll work with you."

"I'll try to think of something," I said.

"Very well," Demetrio said. "We'll be in touch. I'll go discuss the new information with my adjutant." Demetrio clasped my hand, bowed to the Emperor, and left the room.

"You must be tired from your trip," Clara said to me. "I assume you'll be staying for a few days?"

"For tonight at least," I said.

"We've made up some guest quarters for you. Would you like a chance to wash and have something to eat?"

"Yes, I'd appreciate that," I said. I wanted a chance to talk alone with Giovanni.

"Michel can show you where your quarters are,"

Travan said. "Generale Eliana, I'd appreciate it if you'd join me for dinner. I'd like a chance to talk again."

"I'd be honored," I said. With any luck, Clara and Placido would not be invited.

Back in our room, I closed the door and turned toward Giovanni. "Why doesn't Placido like you?"

Giovanni looked up, startled. "The Emperor greets you with a kiss, the First Generale of the Imperial Army salutes you as an equal, and your first question is about Placido's stupid grudge?"

I set my pack and violin case down on the cot. Our quarters were spare and we were sharing a room, though a curtain had been provided for modesty. Michel had gone to get some water for us to wash with. "I don't have any questions about the Emperor or Demetrio that I'd expect you to be able to answer."

Giovanni laughed and unlaced his own pack, taking out a slightly cleaner shirt. "Placido never liked me."

"There's got to be more to it than that."

"Really? I'd expect you to be able to understand that sentiment, even sympathize. Oh, all right," he said, laughing again at my infuriated expression. "I'll tell you the story. Placido's a few years older than me, and bigger than me, as you may have noticed. When I started at the university, we met at one of the taverns and he took an instant dislike to me—I can't imagine why, but some people do. Anyway, he pushed me around a bit—spilled my wine in my lap on purpose and insulted me. I challenged him to a duel, and he disarmed and thoroughly embarrassed me. I found out later this was all to impress a lady.

"So. I spent every waking moment for the next three months working on my swordplay. My best friend, Antonio, tutored me. We both did so poorly in our studies that we were nearly sent home from the university in academic disgrace. After three months, Antonio said I was ready, so I went to the tavern, picked up Placido's wine, and threw it in his face." Giovanni had a faint wicked smile on his face, remembering. "Placido drew his sword, naturally. We took it outside. I disarmed him before he landed a blow and gave him the thrashing of his life." His smile faded to a look of resignation. "This was perhaps not the best strategy to win his friendship. Which probably made things more difficult for you and Michel in Cuore. I'm sorry. That wasn't a consequence I exactly had in mind when I threw the wine in his face."

I raised my wineskin in salute. "There was another consequence you didn't foresee."

"What was that?"

"Having learned what you knew in three months, you were well prepared to teach me to fight—quickly."

"True enough! I hadn't thought of that," Giovanni said. "Well. You know that it was university scholars who made the connection between magery and what happened to Verdia. To suppress the knowledge, the Circle had the scholars responsible, along with their students, framed for heresy and executed by the Fedeli. Antonio was one of those students. And so I joined the reformers."

Giovanni's face was distant, but his eyes were soft. "Placido sent me down to Ravenna to get rid of me; he knew the commander had a reputation for being brutal, and hoped I'd open my mouth at the wrong moment and get myself killed."

"Some days I'm surprised you didn't," I said.

"Yeah, well, Placido probably figures I opened my mouth and got Jesca and Beneto killed. You know, the lady Placido was trying to impress the night he bullied me was Jesca, can you believe that? It didn't work. I think she may have gone to Ravenna to get away from him."

"I could believe it," I said.

"Anyway, that's why Placido can't *stand* that I'm a generale of the Lupi. Even the fact that I'm your second doesn't make up for it. I'm sure he hates you, too, but Travan likes you so he has to work a little harder at hiding it."

Michel knocked on the door, and we let him in. He had heated the water slightly, so it was tepid instead of freezing. "How on earth are Clara and Placido surviving hardships like this?" I asked, dunking my face and hair and then rubbing them dry as quickly as I could.

"They each brought a couple of servants," Michel said. "I'm sorry. I could go heat it more—"

"No, don't be silly; we'll manage." I took out a comb and started working it through the tangles in my hair. It was a good thing my hair was short. "So tell us everything, Michel. Did you have any close calls getting down here?"

"A few," Michel said. "But we got through all right. Travan is a good man, and courageous. He could be a good leader."

"That's a relief," Giovanni said. He had stripped to the waist and was splashing water on himself.

"We had about a week alone once we got here," Michel said. "Then Placido found us, and Signora Clara."

"How many others are here?"

Michel shrugged. "At least thirty, I think. There will be more once a proper supply line is set up. Right now the hardships down here deter all but the most ... ambitious."

"Or those on a mission," I said. "Have there been any attempts on the Emperor's life?"

"One," Michel said. "We identified and executed the assassin."

"Is there anyone else here who could serve as a bodyguard?" I asked.

"Some of Demetrio's soldiers," Michel said. "I didn't take down that first assassin alone, you know."

"Michel, I think you should stay here instead of returning with us to the Lupi," I said. Michel's face fell, and he started to protest. "The Emperor needs a bodyguard he can trust completely. I think at this point he knows he can trust you, yes?"

Michel nodded unhappily.

"But also, Michel, we need someone here who can counteract Placido's and Clara's influence. You're doing that already, aren't you?"

"Maybe," Michel said. "Sort of. But—"

"The Lupi need a voice here, and it can't be me," I said.

"What about Giovanni? He's got more experience with this sort of thing."

Giovanni made a choking noise.

"I'd sooner send Isabella," I said.

"Hey!" Giovanni said. "I can be much more diplomatic than Isabella."

"Michel," I said, "you're the right person for this. The Emperor likes you and trusts you—and I like and trust you, and I know you'll do fine."

"But I'd rather serve *you*," Michel whispered.

"You will be serving me," I said. "By serving Travan."

Placido and Clara—to their immense consternation, I suspected—were not invited to dinner with the Emperor. Neither was Giovanni. Travan and I dined alone, with Michel standing watch at the door. The food was very simple, just soup and bread. Travan ate distractedly, soaking his bread in his soup and telling me about his journey here.

"So the Fedele says to Michel, 'Why are you two traveling together?' " Travan said, imitating the priest's squirrelly, suspicious voice. "And Michel says, 'He's my elder brother.' And the priest's eyes get narrow, and he says, 'I heard you say *last* night that he was your *friend*. And now he's your brother?' And Michel slings his arm around the priest's shoulder and kind of takes him aside and says, 'Look at him, Father. Would *you* want to admit to being this man's brother if you didn't have to?' "

I laughed.

"This story gets better every time," Michel said from the doorway. "I'm starting to feel sorry for the priest. Are you going to tell her I ended up having to bribe him?"

"Granted, but you bribed him to overlook horse theft; he never suspected what was really going on."

"So how is life here?" I asked. "Not exactly as comfortable as the enclave."

"Oh," Travan shrugged. "My bed is soft enough and my stomach is full. This is exciting. Frightening, but exciting. It's strange to have people currying favor with me instead of trying to threaten me. I think I like it."

"Have there been any serious threats?"

"One," Travan said, and told me about the assassin. I nodded. "Your Highness, I was originally planning to take Michel back with me to the Lupi, but it's clear you need an experienced bodyguard. Would you be interested in having him stay with you on a permanent basis?"

Travan's face lit. "Yes," he said simply. "I've been dreading losing Michel."

"You have to promise to listen to his advice," I said. "He's been my adjutant as well as my bodyguard, and I don't want that going to waste. Even if Clara and Placido think he's an ignorant peasant."

"Of course I will listen to him," Travan said. "He's been my first and best friend since I left Cuore."

I gestured to Michel and he came over. His feet dragged, but his face was solemn and resigned. He touched his heart with his fist and held his fist out, saluting me. "On my honor, I swear I will serve the Emperor as I have served you," he said. He turned to face the Emperor, and offered him a salute as well. "On my honor, I swear I will serve you with all my loyalty until you release me from my vow." He knelt and bowed his head.

Travan touched Michel's shoulder lightly. "Stand, Michel; you never have to be formal with me. I accept your service, and I swear I will respect and value your loyalty."

Michel stood, meeting my eyes. They were oddly guarded now, and a little hurt. I hated to lose Michel—but I'd hate even more to bury Travan before we could take Cuore. Michel would understand someday.

When I returned to my room, I opened the door to find Clara sitting on my cot, talking with Giovanni. "Giovanni and I were discussing the supply line," she said.

"Specifically, what supplies we need most urgently," Giovanni said. "Food, of course. For us and for the horses. What else would you say?"

"Proper tents," I said. "With tent poles. Weapons for the volunteers that will be coming."

"You're quite certain that you will get additional recruits?"

"Our faith is stronger than magefire," I said. "That's a pretty strong indication of whose side God is on, isn't it?"

"Indeed," Clara said.

"Also, it's midwinter—farmers can afford to join our army now. In fact, if they send a son to join us, it relieves the pressure on *their* winter food stores. But mainly—God is on our side."

"Have you thought about how you will keep out spies?" Clara asked.

"We can't keep out every person who *might* be a spy," I said. "We assume that some of the Lupi are spies and take steps to minimize the damage they could cause."

"New recruits are supposed to have someone vouch for them," Giovanni said. "We're more wary of people who've come from towns. Most of the Lupi are farmers."

"How can you tell whether someone comes from a town?" Clara asked.

I held up one hand, palm out. "Calluses."

"But that's not going to be a completely reliable test," Clara said.

"There *is* no completely reliable test," I said.

"Well," Clara said. "As you try to think of ruses to lure out the Circle, I'll try to think of ruses to sort out the spies. I'll let you know if I think of anything."

"We'd appreciate that," I said.

Clara rose. "If you think of other urgent supplies, let me know in the morning. I'll see what we can do." She turned back at the doorway to look at me. "I was a little disappointed that your friend didn't come with you, Eliana—the dancer. Lucia, is that her name?"

"Yes," I said. "Lucia." Her name still felt strange on my tongue, after the months in Cuore where I couldn't speak it.

"I heard she is a long-time Redentore—perhaps one of the people who started the revival of the Old Way."

I nodded. "Yes."

"I'd very much like to meet her."

"I will relay your invitation when I return to the Lupi," I said.

"You might consider sending her here," Clara said. "For her safety, when the Lupi leave the wasteland."

"Lucia is a soldier, like the rest of us," I said, bristling a little without meaning to.

"Very well, then," Clara said, a hint of a smile on her lips. "Good night."

When the door closed behind her, I turned to Giovanni. "Why the interest in Lucia? Did she mention Lucia earlier?"

Giovanni shook his head, his lips tight.

"You have a theory?"

"She wants to know, for future reference, who can be used against you. Who you care about. She'd heard Lucia's name, and made a lucky guess. You confirmed her suspicions—you care for Lucia."

I shuddered. "You think Clara would hurt Lucia to get to me?"

"Only if it's to her advantage," Giovanni said. He met my eyes reluctantly. "You know Clara better than I do. What do you think?"

I thought about the cross Valentino found in his room. "I think you're right," I said. I pulled off my boots and crawled under the blankets of my cot. "If she ever hurts Lucia," I added as I arranged the blankets, "I'll have her head for a paperweight."

Giovanni smiled. "You'll have help getting it."

* * *

I was in the Great Cathedral in Cuore; it was a festival day, and I was surrounded by hundreds, maybe thousands of people. But instead of rose-petal incense, I smelled lamp oil and scorched metal. My stomach turned. "I have to go," I said quietly to the people sitting near me, and they moved aside to let me out.

As I reached the center aisle, I saw that Bella was chained to the Great Altar, her robe ripped open to bare her skin; the man in black stood beside her, humming quietly under his breath. "In Her name," he said, lifting a knife that glowed like an ember.

I realized suddenly that they thought Bella was me. I could stop this—if I turned myself in, I could free Bella, but I would have to take her place. I stood frozen in the aisle, unable to speak, unable to run, and then I heard Bella's scream of agony, and smelled burned meat—

"Wake up, dammit."

Giovanni's face glared down at me by candlelight, and I realized that my face was damp with sweat and tears. "If you're going to have nightmares, can't you have quiet nightmares? Sit up."

Shaking, I let Giovanni help me. I saw a red glow and cried out involuntarily, then realized that all I saw were the embers of the fire. I covered my face with my hands, trying to control myself and hating my weakness. "I'm fine," I tried to say, but my voice squeaked.

"I'll get you some tea," Giovanni said, but first he sat with me for a moment, his arms around me, steadying me. "You really need Lucia here; she's better at this than I am." He stroked my hair for a moment, then stood, still steadying me. "On second thought, I'll get you some wine." He poured me a cup. "It's not hot— sorry—but trying to find tea just now seems like more trouble than it's worth."

I sipped the wine. "It doesn't matter," I said. "I don't really want either."

"Do you want to talk about it?" Giovanni asked.

"No," I said.

When I was calm, I lay back down, and Giovanni went back to his own bed.

"I could never do it," Giovanni said. "I could never have endured what you endured."

"You could do whatever you had to do," I said.

Giovanni didn't answer. I blew out my candle and lay staring into the dark.

I got up at dawn and went outside to practice my violin. I was still shaken from my nightmare, as well as my reaction to it. I hated bad dreams—especially when they showed my weakness to anyone sleeping near me. Lucia slept beside me and had learned to recognize the signs and shake me awake early, so that I didn't disturb anyone else, but I felt bad enough about waking Lucia. I suspected this one had been triggered by my conversation with Clara—the feeling that I was being outmaneuvered in some way that I couldn't even guess at. Or maybe it was just that seeing Clara reminded me of being in the enclave.

I started by playing études, but I wasn't concentrating on them the way I felt I ought to. I thought of Mira, and her focus as she played. Perhaps I could use my connection with Mira to draw the Circle out somehow. But even if she had freed me on the orders of the Circle Council, the other mages had to suspect that she had some responsibility for what happened after that. If now she suddenly announced to the other mages that she thought it would be a good idea to attack Pluma, I couldn't imagine that she'd have a whole lot of credibility.

"... Daniele?"

I turned and almost dropped my violin. "Quirino! What are you *doing* down here?"

"I followed the Emperor when I heard what happened. When I heard who *you* really were. Assuming what I heard was true. It seems way too far-fetched ..."

"That I'm really a woman?"

"No, that I could believe. That you're really *Eliana*."

"That's also true. How did Ulisse take it?"

Quirino groaned. "With wine. Lots of it. 'She must think I'm such a fool,' he said. Again and again."

"I have to admit that it was hard not to laugh when Ulisse got misty-eyed at the mention of my name, but how was he supposed to know? If Ulisse had been able to figure it out, someone else would have, too. And I was trying pretty hard to avoid that."

Quirino nodded. "Still, I wish I'd known. I'd have helped you in any way I could."

"I couldn't put you in that sort of danger."

"Valentino's here, too," he said.

"Despite Clara?"

Quirino shrugged. "She seems to have dropped her grudge. Go figure. I'm sure it's just a matter of time before Valentino gets himself in trouble again. Ulisse's gone to join the Lupi. I think he's planning to disguise himself, to avoid humiliation."

"As a girl? Oh, don't tell me. I don't want to know. Quirino—" I gave him a sideways look. "There *is* a way you can help me now. We need musicians. *Lots* of musicians ..."

*   *   *

Giovanni and I left in late morning. More dust-covered and saddle-sore nobles had arrived, some accompanied by guards, others by servants. Clara and Michel were finding room for them in the barracks; another building would be needed soon. As I made my way through the crowd, a bony hand gripped my arm. A chill ran up my spine, and I turned. "Amedeo," I said.

"Watch yourself," the madman said distractedly, jabbing my arm with his long fingers. "Clara, she's trouble. Placido, he's trouble too. Watch yourself."

"You think I need a prophet to figure *that* out?" I said. "Thanks, old man. I knew that already."

Amedeo nodded vigorously. "You do know, you do. What did I tell you? You don't need me—you can see clearly for yourself, if you open your eyes." He stepped in close to me, gripping his hands into fists. I started to draw back, but he laid his fists gently over my heart. "Two hearts beat here, Eliana. Two hearts beat in your breast: one for your cause, one for your friends. Sooner or later, you'll have to choose. Be ready." He dropped his hands and walked away.

CHAPTER ELEVEN

Blessed are the music-makers,
for they hear the voice of God.
—*The Journey of Gèsu, chapter 2, verse 18.*

Giovanni and I were spotted by one of the perimeter guards as we rode in toward the Lupi camp. He had been lying just at the crest of one of the brown hills, his dirty tunic and trousers barely visible against the dust. He stood up and came running down the hill to meet us. It was one of the Lupi who had disappeared after the defeat near Pluma a few months earlier, returned now that victory seemed possible. Back in the heart of the camp, Lupi were lining up for their evening meal. Lucia greeted me with a warm embrace, and Giovanni and I told her about our trip to court over tea in my tent.

As I stretched out that night under my blankets, I found myself thinking about the conservatory. Flavia and Celia were probably still there; they'd be almost ready to graduate. Domenico, my teacher—undoubtedly still there. I wondered if they ever thought about me, if they had any inkling that the Eliana in the ballads (I was certain that the ballads had found their way there) was me. As word started to circulate that the Lupi needed musicians, it was possible that some of them would come join us. Flavia, at least; I thought that Flavia might.

Lucia was already asleep; I heard her murmur something in the dark and turn over. But Giovanni, on the other side of Lucia, wasn't snoring yet. "Giovanni," I said softly.

"Yeah?" He rolled over to face me.

"What do you think the Circle and the Fedeli will do when they get word that we're recruiting musicians?"

There was a pause, and then a long sigh. "They'll probably round up all the musicians they can find and hold them in Cuore 'for their own protection.' They may not really understand yet how we do what we do, but if we're looking for musicians, they'd be idiots to assume that we were looking for after-dinner entertainment."

"We'd better send messengers tomorrow," I said.

"Good idea," Giovanni said, and settled back into his blankets.

I heard Giovanni begin to snore a few minutes later, but I still couldn't sleep. What if something happened to the messenger I sent to my old conservatory? *Very well then*, I thought. *I'll send two. Three.* I tried to imagine my own reaction to the message. Would I have grabbed my violin and headed for the wasteland? I liked to think that I would have. Certainly Bella would have, and thinking it over, I decided that even without Bella there, even without Mira, I'd have gone to join the ragtag army to the south. Flavia, too. But Celia? How would Celia respond to the message from a stranger? And Domenico? I desperately wanted my old teacher to join us, I realized. What if he didn't believe that the Eliana behind the message was me?

Very quietly, I got up and dressed. I would have to

go myself. *It won't take long,* I thought. A few days to ride there, a few more days to walk back. Celia and Flavia would come if I asked, and Domenico; maybe a few others. I could handle this. The Lupi might be gathering to my banner, but I'd returned only recently from Cuore and they were quite capable of functioning without me. But I didn't think Giovanni would see it that way—or Lucia—so I dashed off a quick note and left them sleeping in their beds. Within the hour, I was riding east. The moon was waxing and nearly full, and my horse cast a faint gray shadow in the moonlight.

Giovanni caught up with me an hour later, furious. I wheeled my horse around to face him. "You must have woken up right after I left," I said.

"What in hell do you think you're doing?" he demanded.

"I'm riding to the Verdian Rural Conservatory," I said.

"You're needed with the Lupi."

"You all did just fine without me while I was in Cuore. This is only going to take me a week or two. Giovanni, *I* need to carry the message. The musicians at the conservatory know me. They trust me."

"Actually, when you're carrying an unpopular message—and trust me, Generale, this is going to be a *highly* unpopular message, 'join us or sit in prison in Cuore'—it's usually best if they *don't* know you."

"They're my friends," I said. "I'll know what to say to convince them to come." *And I have to at least* try *to protect them.*

"You couldn't have woken me up to discuss this with me before you took off?"

"I knew you'd make trouble."

"I should have brought your bodyguards to drag you back."

"You think they would?"

"I could ride back now and get them, and give it a try."

"You'll never catch up with me again if you do."

Giovanni met my eyes in an exasperated glare, then shrugged and looked away. "Then I'm coming with you," he said. "You're not doing this without someone to protect you."

It would have been pleasant to retrace my steps exactly—to pass through Doratura and visit Giula and Rafi, then through all the towns to revisit the families who had offered me hospitality on my way home from the conservatory, but it would have been far too risky. We would ride east through the wasteland, and then due north, or close to it, to reach Bascio.

We spent that first day riding across wasteland hills, stopping occasionally to rest on the hard brown earth and to feed the horses (we had three, since I had brought a pack horse). I wished that I could have done this entirely alone: Giovanni couldn't always be trusted to make a good impression. And I so desperately wanted to convince everyone at the conservatory to come with me.

The weather was dry, thank goodness, and my nightmares stayed away even after we crossed out of the wasteland. We had to spend one night in fertile territory, and it was a part of Verdia that was too thickly settled for us to camp discreetly. We would attract curiosity and suspicion, riding north from the wasteland, but we would attract far more if we skulked in the woods instead of asking for hospitality. We asked at an isolated farm, and were greeted with wide, nervous eyes; clearly, they knew we were Lupi, sashes or no sashes. Giovanni went out of his way to be charming at dinner, but the entire family seemed to be afraid that if they said the wrong thing, we were going to pull out knives and cut all their throats. There was an awkward pause at the beginning of the meal, and it occurred to me afterward that this was probably a family that made the offering to the Lady, and that they were too afraid of us to do it. It made me sad to realize this. If they wanted to make the offering, I certainly didn't mind waiting a few extra moments to eat, but I was too nervous to think to say anything until it was too late. Giovanni and I slept in the attic of the stable, with the sacks of apples, onions, and turnips the family had stored for the winter, and traded off watches.

During the long, dark hours of my watch, I tried to plan what to say when I spoke to Flavia and Celia. *Think of Bella.* That would be the point to hammer on, unless Celia had managed to justify Bella's murder to herself out of her own loyalty to the Lady, in which case I wasn't sure I wanted to recruit her anyway. *The famine was caused by magery; everything the Fedeli did here, everything the Circle has done since then, has been to cover this up. They don't want us to know what magery does, and they don't care how many people die to conceal their secret. Think of Bella—one more death was nothing to them. Bella was on the verge of discovering how to do the old sort of magery. If it had been you, it wouldn't have mattered if you'd fallen to your knees and sworn eternal fidelity to the Lady. They'd have found some excuse to cut your throat, just like they did to Bella.*

Flavia will come, I thought. Domenico will come. I was less certain about Celia.

It was still quite early when we reached Bascio the next day. "I remember this town," Giovanni said.

"What do you mean?"

"I came here to spread that song, The Wicked Stepmother. I was only here a few hours, though."

"That was you? My friend Bella saw you come in. And, it was my teacher you sang to. I think I told you, though, we never did figure out what it was about."

Giovanni shrugged. "If we'd made it explicit, it wouldn't have been a very good song, would it? 'La la la, don't do magery. La la la, that's what created the wasteland.' Not to mention the fact that the Fedeli would have hanged everyone they heard singing it."

"How long did it take them to figure it out?"

Giovanni grinned with a great deal of satisfaction. "I set out in early autumn spreading it. They figured it out ... oh, sometime after Viaggio."

"We thought maybe the Fedeli had written it, and the poison honey referred to a heresy."

"You actually thought the Fedeli would be that creative?"

"Hey, until they showed up at Mascherata, none of us had ever actually *met* a Fedele. Except for Mira. And she didn't object to the theory."

"Mira must have known what the song was about. She just didn't want to tell you."

"I'm sure you're right."

Bascio was located on a hill, and the conservatory was at the very top of the hill; the road wound around the hill like gut around a tuning peg. I could see the Bascio townspeople coming out of their homes to check us out, but they were used to strangers coming through because of the conservatory, and we attracted curiosity but not suspicion.

The conservatory gate was closed when we reached it; on the other side, I saw the Dean of the conservatory, Biagio, and a group of teachers, including my old teacher Domenico, and Nolasco, Bella's teacher. Domenico's eyes went wide when I threw back my hood, then he turned to Nolasco. "I told you we'd see Eliana again before long," he murmured as I dismounted. Beyond them, farther up the hill, I could see clusters of gray-robed students. We had been watched; we were being watched now.

I handed the reins of my horse to Giovanni and walked up to the gate. "Can we come in?"

"What if we say no?" Dean Biagio said sharply. "Will you batter down our gate and enter by force?"

"Does it look like we brought our army? Unless you've been building up your wall, we *could* just walk around to the back and hop over it. That's what Bella and I did when we went to Bascio on a dare."

The touch of humor worked. Dean Biagio smiled a little in spite of himself, and I hoped he was thinking, *well, so it is our old Eliana, and not some strange Maledore with her face.* He swung open the gate, and gestured for a servant to come take our horses. "Come, both of you," he said. "Whatever it is you're here to say, we'll discuss it in my study."

I could see gray-robed students watching me from windows as I followed the Dean; I shaded my eyes to try to see faces, to see if I recognized anyone, but I couldn't make them out. Inside, the flagstone floor was cold under my boots. As we turned down the corridor that led to the Dean's study, I saw a student flatten herself against the wall to get out of our way and realized it was Flavia. But no flicker of recognition crossed her face; she was looking at Giovanni, not at me, and he clearly made her nervous.

The Dean's study was warm and smelled strongly

of toasted bread and fresh tea; I could see a steaming cup on the edge of his desk, placed by one of the servants. His desk was clean and neat, and his shelves were stacked with musical scores, some brown with age. Along the back wall, there were instruments held neatly on racks: a lute, a violin, a flute, a drum. His window was glassed in, and the winter sunlight caught the dust flecks that spun up in the air when he sat heavily down on the cushion on his chair.

"Sit," Dean Biagio said to Giovanni and me, gesturing at the two chairs facing his desk. Domenico closed the door and took a seat off to the side. "We know you are the leaders of the Lupi," he continued, his voice heavy. "Why have you come here?"

"We need musicians," I said.

"By 'we,' you mean the Lupi, of course."

"I mean all those in the service of Emperor Travan. Lupi and Imperial Army both."

Biagio glanced at Domenico, who raised one eyebrow silently.

"And you fight against the Circle," Biagio said.

"And the Fedeli."

"Of course." Biagio looked down, a faint smile on his face. "Where exactly is it that you intend to lead my students, assuming any wish to follow you?"

"To the wasteland, initially," I said. "Then—" I hesitated, then plunged ahead. "You are familiar, I'm sure, with some of the Old Way music. You may also know that there are dances that go with the songs. A musician playing for dancers can channel the energy of the dance, and use it to turn back magefire. With that power, we can do battle with the Circle and win."

Biagio and Domenico exchanged glances. "So that's

what they meant when they said that your faith was stronger than magefire," Domenico said. "We'd heard some odd stories about what happened at Montefalco."

"And rumors that more musicians were wanted," Biagio said.

"Already?" I kept my face impassive as my stomach lurched. How quickly would the Circle respond to this rumor?

"So you don't believe that it's the Redentore God placing Her hand of protection over Her followers?" Domenico said. "You just think it's a different sort of magic?"

I turned to look at my old teacher. His expression was as impassive as mine, and I wasn't sure whether his tone concealed hope, contempt, or fear. "I don't think you have to be Redentore to make this work," I said. "And I think Mira came here to hide because she suspected this was possible."

Domenico lowered his eyes.

"You realize, I'm sure, that even if I do not assemble the students and faculty to let you speak to them, you have already accomplished your mission," Biagio said, his tone bitter. "I have no doubt that the nature of your visit has already spread through the conservatory, and some will follow you. Perhaps I should simply ask you to leave now, and let the eager ones go as they will."

"I'd prefer that you let me speak to a few people first," I said. "I'm sure the Emperor would prefer that as well."

"I'm sure you're right," Biagio said. "And I'm sure that our old friends Father Cassio and Mother Galeria, of the Fedeli, would prefer otherwise. And the man who rode in last spring, what was his name? Liemo?"

"He'd prefer otherwise as well," I said. "You're right. Actually, I'm sure that all three would be most pleased if you took the initiative to offer both of us poisoned wine."

"Or better still, took you both prisoner," Domenico said. "They'd probably be especially happy to get you alive."

I looked at Domenico, and realized that he was almost starting to smile. "Absolutely," I said. "But they'd settle for our heads in a sack. I'm sure you'd both be richly rewarded. For as long as the Circle and the Fedeli's rule lasted."

Biagio rolled his eyes. "I'm not going to give you poisoned wine—as if you'd drink anything I offered, now that the suggestion's been made. Not that I keep poison on hand to rid myself of uninvited guests in any case."

"If you did," I said, "you could have offered some to Cassio and Galeria."

"Quite right," he said. "At any rate, according to what you'd like us to believe, they'll be in no position soon to reward my faithfulness to the Lady."

"The Lupi and the Emperor stand together," I said. "Everyone in the Empire knows the truth about magefire, and now we have a way to defend ourselves against it. How long do you think they'll stand against us?"

"And in the meantime?"

"In the meantime, as soon as they hear that we're recruiting musicians, I imagine that they'll send some guardsmen to escort anyone they find here to comfortable new quarters in Cuore. If you bring our heads in a sack to offer them, they may trust *you* enough to allow you the liberty of the city."

"So we have the Lupi to thank for being in this position," Biagio said. "Is that correct?"

"I'd say that you have the Circle and the Fedeli to thank, actually. It was the Circle who destroyed much of Verdia; it was the Fedeli who spilled Bella's blood in the conservatory's courtyard."

Biagio lowered his eyes, and I saw that his hand shook as he lifted his cup of tea. I leaned forward and lowered my voice.

"I believe that we will win this war—the Lupi and the Emperor together. It's possible that I'm wrong about this, though; I can't say I know what the spring will bring. The one thing that *is* certain is that if you stand with us, you stand *against* the Fedeli. Since you can't know for certain which is the preferable side to be on, you might as well stand *against* the people who cut Bella's throat."

Dean Biagio looked up at me, and I saw a glimmer I couldn't identify in his eye. "Thank you," he said. "If you and your companion will step outside for a few moments, Domenico and I would like to discuss this in private."

Nolasco, the trumpet teacher, had waited outside the Dean's study; he escorted us to a small sitting room a short distance down the corridor. I wondered if he had listened in on the conversation; he had been Bella's teacher, after all, and I rather thought that he would not be a friend of the Fedeli. His face was rigid, though, and I wasn't sure. I also caught another glimpse of Flavia, loitering outside the Dean's study. This time, she met my eyes, and I saw her face light up with recognition just as Nolasco ushered us into the sitting room and closed the door.

"Do you think the Dean's going to let us recruit?" Giovanni asked as soon as we were alone.

"Yes," I said. "But he may do it by allowing me some time 'alone' to 'visit' my old friends. I'll take whatever he offers, frankly. I just hope he hurries."

We didn't have to wait long. Dean Biagio swung open the door a few minutes later. "We are the Emperor's loyal subjects," he said, inclining his head. "In what way can we best serve him?"

"Assemble the students and staff," I said. "I'd like to speak to everyone at once."

*   *   *

The chapel bell tolled, summoning students and teachers to an unscheduled service. The chapel was perhaps not the best location to recruit people to rebel against the Lady, but it was designed to accommodate all the students and teachers at once. As I faced my strangest audience yet, the girl students were on my right, the boys on my left; the teachers lined the walls and sat in the back. I scanned the aisle seats for Celia, but she must not have arrived soon enough to grab one of the "good spots." The students were breathless and bewildered; some of the younger students looked as if they'd been crying.

"Don't be afraid," I said. "I am not your enemy." *Great,* I thought as soon as the words were out of my mouth. *That would sure have made* me *feel better, back when I was a student.* "I am Generale Eliana of the Lupi, servant of Emperor Travan, but many of you probably remember me as simply Eliana, violin student, and friend of Bella."

I could hear someone's breath catch at the sound of Bella's name. I looked around the room. "Yes, you remember Bella, don't you? Probably better than you remember me. I heard once that she was one of the brightest students the conservatory had ever seen. On festival days when we played games to test our memory for obscure tunes and bits of musical lore, Bella would win every game until Nolasco made her sit down to give others a chance. She was kind, daring, fiercely loyal to her friends and what she believed to be the truth. And the Fedeli murdered her—cut her throat before our eyes, and forced us to continue dancing while she choked to death on her own blood."

In the front row, there was a girl I didn't know—she looked maybe a year or two younger than me, but old enough to have been in the courtyard that night. She had wrapped her arms around herself as I spoke and was trying to hold back her tears.

"We couldn't allow ourselves to cry that night," I said. "We couldn't allow ourselves to be angry, because we feared the Fedeli so much, and because we believed that they were an undefeatable, all-powerful enemy. *But they're not.* The Emperor has turned his back on them and joined the Lupi in the wasteland. We have joined forces against the Circle and the Fedeli, and we have a way to win, even against magefire. But we need *your* help."

I licked my lips and looked cautiously toward the teachers at the back of the room. Nolasco, Bella's old teacher, stared at the floor, his face hidden. Domenico's eyes were on me, his face solemn and half shadowed.

"You've *all* played Old Way music—songs from the Redentori rituals. After leaving the conservatory, I learned that there were dances that went with the songs. And when I faced mages from the Circle in Montefalco, I discovered that those songs have *power*." I raised my voice. "By the power of God, and the power of the music, I saw magefire extinguished like a candle plunged into cold water. Without magefire, the Circle is powerless. Without the Circle, the Fedeli are powerless. If you join with me, we can restore the Emperor to true power.

If you join with me, we will see that the Fedeli never murder another Bella."

"And if we don't?" someone called.

"I leave this afternoon," I said. "And I want only willing volunteers. If you choose to stay, though, you should probably realize that word is getting out that the Lupi are recruiting musicians. The Circle and Fedeli don't yet know why, but they will act quickly to round up musicians from the conservatories. Your prison, should they find you here, will be a reasonably comfortable one, but you will be their prisoners, nonetheless."

The girl in the front row was openly sobbing now, and other students had gone very pale. The fear in the room was palpable as they realized that the one choice that most of them probably wanted to make—*stay here, and let the world do what it will*—was not an option. I leaned forward and spoke gently. "If you do not want to join me, but you do not wish to be a prisoner, you can also simply leave and return to your home. Very soon, the Circle will be far too busy to seek out and round up every minstrel and former conservatory student in Verdia, no matter how much they'd like to." I raised my voice again. "But I hope that you will choose to join us. On one side, the Circle and Fedeli stand against Verdia—for it was the Circle's magery that drained the lands and caused the famine. On the other side, the Lupi and Emperor stand together. Join us, and serve the Emperor. Join us, and find out how it feels to *really* play the music you've always played in secret."

I straightened up. "We leave in two hours. If you wish to join us, meet us at the front gate with your instruments." I gestured to Giovanni, and he followed me out of the hall.

"How many do you think will come?" Giovanni asked.

I sighed. "I don't honestly know," I said. "It's funny, because I was pretty good at predicting how many of the prisoners at the camps we liberated would join the Lupi, but here I have no idea. I like to think that if I were still a student, I'd be off packing my bag right now, but I don't know that I would."

"You would," Giovanni said.

I sent Giovanni to the kitchen to negotiate for food—we'd need to feed our volunteers on the trip through the wasteland and back to the Lupi camp. Then I went to the north practice hall, where I used to meet with Mira, Bella, Giula, Flavia, and Celia to play the Old Way music. It was even colder and draftier than I remembered. In the slivers of daylight that came in through the cracks in the walls, I studied the one fresco that still remained. I had always thought it was Gaius with the Lady's Gift: it showed a frightened man clasping a tiny gleam of light to his breast. Looking at it now, I realized that it had probably been left intact because others assumed the same thing, but it wasn't Gaius. *Aral Chedvah,* I realized. The Archangel Gabriele, thief of God's holy Light. "Gabriele stole a fragment of God's holy Light," I remember Lucia saying, "and placed it in the womb of a pure young woman. And so she conceived a child, a son, and she named him Gèsu."

This was a church, I realized. *A Redentore church.* I had never even seen Mass celebrated indoors, except for the secret Redentori in Cuore. It was hard to believe that Redentori once had actual churches, and I felt the need to do something to acknowledge that I was on holy ground. I crossed myself, finally, and whispered a prayer in the Old Tongue. I wondered if Mira had known, if that was the real reason she'd liked coming here.

"Eliana?"

The whisper came from the doorway. I turned: Flavia. She came inside hesitantly, as if she didn't really know how to treat me, this strange firebrand who claimed to be her friend. I realized that I didn't really know what to do, either—would Flavia even want me to hug her? I had been gone a long time ... I hadn't even said a proper good-bye when I left that day, nearly choking on my grief and anger.

"I'm so glad you came to see me," I started to say, but Flavia was speaking at the same time. "—glad you came back," she said, and then laughed awkwardly. "Sorry," she said. "Finish what you were saying."

"I just said that I was glad you came to see me," I said. "On my way here, I was picturing myself talking to you and Celia alone, not making a speech to the whole school."

"It was a good speech," Flavia said.

"I've had a lot of practice giving speeches," I said, and then immediately felt like I'd said the wrong thing.

Flavia turned a little red and said, "Yeah, we've heard rumors. Songs."

"They're probably all lies."

"Except for the parts about you giving speeches."

"Right," I said. I sounded like a pompous priest; I wished we could just start this whole conversation over. "Those might be true."

"*Eliana.*" Another voice from the door. I turned to see Celia coming in at a full run; she threw herself into my arms with a shriek of delight. "You came *back*! You *hadn't* forgotten about us. You came back to ask us to *join* you!" She clasped my arms in her hands.

"You can't even imagine how many times Flavia and I have wished we went with you when you left, like Giula did. We'd have left a hundred times if we'd thought we'd have done you the slightest bit of good—and if we'd known where to find you."

Celia let go of me, and I took the opportunity to give Flavia a tight hug. "Is that true, or is Celia making it all up to make me feel good?" I asked.

"It's worse than you think," Flavia said. "She *wrote* a song about you."

"Oh, horrors," I said. "At least Lia started out with the story straight when she wrote her songs."

"This one's about your early life," Flavia said.

"It's actually more about Bella," Celia said. "Of course no one sings it publicly, but I think everyone knows it." She bit her lip. "No one was talking about Bella—or Mira—or you and Giula. It was as if none of you had existed. It made me angry to think that people were forgetting already."

"You've changed," I said.

"Maybe you just didn't know me very well before," Celia said, and tossed her curls. "Anyway, I'm coming with you, of course."

"And so am I," Flavia said.

"And so are we," a voice said from the doorway. It was Domenico; Nolasco was a pace behind him. "I should have looked for you here first; I remember this was where you had your secret ensemble." Domenico looked around. "I can't imagine why you met here. It's freezing." He clasped my hand briefly. "And so the student becomes the teacher. I am yours to command, Generale."

"Thank you," I whispered. "I will try to be worthy of your loyalty."

"I think my students will choose to come as well," Nolasco said. "All of them. It is their decision, of course, but—" his eyes glinted with a hard light. "We have not forgotten Bella."

Over a hundred students and teachers waited by the gate to the school when Giovanni and I were ready to leave, their instruments slung over their shoulders. I was stunned by the size of the crowd, and I realized that the trip back to the wasteland was going to take a lot longer than I'd expected. To my surprise, Giovanni seemed to have obtained enough food to feed everyone for the trip. He must have had more faith in my rhetoric than I had.

Domenico and Nolasco were coming with us; Dean Biagio was not. Nearly everyone I'd known personally was coming, but also many strangers—the percussion teacher, the flute teacher, a number of boy students. I thought about giving them another speech to inspire them for the walk, but something inside me was saying, *hurry, hurry, hurry.* So I discarded the speech and instead said, "I'm so glad to see all of you. Grab some of the food and let's get moving."

Giovanni had loaded my horse and his with food and supplies bought from the conservatory's kitchens, along with the pack horse, but they couldn't carry all of it; the musicians had to help, and I heard a great deal of grumbling as people shouldered sacks of food along with their instruments. Giovanni led all three horses, to free me up to wander among our new recruits and encourage any who seemed to need encouragement.

An hour after we set out, I sought out Celia, and discovered that she'd attached herself to Giovanni. "Are you *Generale* Giovanni?" she was asking. I fell in step a few paces behind them to listen.

"Yes," Giovanni said.

"I'm so excited to finally meet you! I've heard *so* much about you!" Celia tossed her curls, and set her hand tentatively on Giovanni's arm.

"Have you," Giovanni said, and looked at her nervously.

"Oh yes. You're in some of the songs. Those were always my favorite ones."

Celia was *flirting* with him. My jaw dropped, and then I grinned. Bizarrely, this seemed to make Giovanni nervous—more and more nervous as she persisted. Finally, when he was answering all her questions with monosyllables and grunts, she gave up and went to pester someone else. I smoothed out my face so that she wouldn't realize that I'd been eavesdropping, but I don't think she cared. She fell into step beside me and leaned close to my ear to whisper, "I had no idea that Generale Giovanni was so *handsome*. He isn't your ... your ..."

"He isn't my anything," I said. "Well, he's my friend and my fellow generale, but that's obviously not what you're asking about." She blushed prettily and tossed her curls. "Have at."

"I'm sure he'd be interested in *you*," she whispered.

"I'm sure he would *not*," I said firmly. "And if he were, he would be in for deep disappointment and a great deal of frustration."

That made Celia quite cheerful, and she moved off with a smile on her face.

"Thanks so much," Giovanni said as soon as she was gone. "I really did need a cute little companion; it'll make the ballads about me so much more popular."

"Celia's a very nice girl," I said, jogging a few paces to walk beside Giovanni.

"If you haven't noticed, Eliana, there are plenty of very pretty, very nice young women in the Lupi right now. Yet I sleep alone every night. Did you ever stop to consider that maybe this was because I think it would be bad for morale for either of us to take a companion from among our soldiers?"

"I had always assumed it was because you were still in mourning for Jesca," I said.

"Jesca!" Giovanni said. "Wherever did you get the idea ... In Jesca's eyes, I was a boy. No, Generale, I sleep alone for many reasons, but my deep affection for Jesca's memory isn't one of them." He shook his head. "Well, if Celia doesn't give up soon enough, I'll have her assigned somewhere far away from me. A woman can be more persistent than a wolf on a scent."

I snorted. "And a man can't?"

"Most men will give up when they get no encouragement," he said, and gave me an amused look through his lashes. "But lack of encouragement doesn't always deter young ladies like Celia. At any rate, she's taken herself off somewhere for now ... Do you suppose we can get them to move any faster?"

"Maybe a little," I said.

"I wish you'd taken a corps of dancers and a squad of Imperial guards when you decided to sneak off. It wouldn't have been exactly subtle, but since they mentioned they'd heard rumors that the Lupi were looking for musicians ..."

"I'm worried, too. I've been pushing things as fast as I felt I could."

"I know. That's why I wish we had soldiers to defend us." Giovanni handed me the horses' reins. "I'm going to scout ahead."

I nodded and took the reins without breaking stride.

Giovanni pulled the hood of his cloak up and set out at a slow run, down the slope we were on and then up the next hill, and then down again, hidden from view.

Flavia sought me out a few minutes later. "You spoke a great deal about Bella," she said. "But there's another from our quartet you never mentioned. Does it not bother you to lead a war against Mira?"

I bit my lip and looked away. I thought I could trust Flavia, but there were other people close by, and I couldn't risk Mira's treason being discovered. "*Miriamne* made her choice," I said.

Flavia nodded, her face troubled. "And Giula?"

I laughed. "Now *that's* a tale." I told her about our trip together as far as Pluma—then her reappearance at Ravenna, and her association with Teleso. "She ended up going to Doratura. As far as I know, she's still there."

Flavia sighed. "I would have expected better of her." She meant Giula, but I thought she probably expected better of Mira, too. And in the case of Mira, Flavia was right. I tasted bitterness in my mouth for a moment. Even though Mira had given me the key to the countermagery, and even though I was sure that she had cheered the news of our victory at Montefalco, part of me hated the idea of making war against her. Not because I had any hesitation about opposing the Circle, but because the idea of facing Mira across a battlefield again made my stomach churn. Shaking my head, I pushed the thought away and asked Flavia what she and Celia had been up to since I left.

"Off the road!"

Giovanni was running down the hill toward us. "Off the road!" he shouted. "Everyone, off the road *now*! Hurry! We need to hide!"

Confused, everyone plunged off the road to the south. The winter fields were muddy and bare, but a grove of cedar trees stood not too far away, and a tangle of brush beyond. Still, there were a hundred of us—and the musicians were not accustomed to hiding. "What's wrong?" I asked.

"There are twenty horsemen riding toward us," Giovanni said. "Fedeli or Circle guardsmen, I'm not sure. I didn't see any mages—they all seemed to be soldiers. But I'm guessing they're heading for the conservatory to take the musicians there into custody." He raised his voice again. "Hurry! Run, all of you! Once you're off the road, keep going!"

"Did they see you?" I asked.

"Maybe," Giovanni said. "From a distance. I don't think I'll have aroused their suspicions, though."

Our musical army moved with agonizing slowness, even though I could tell that everyone was trying to hurry. People were picking their way across the muddy field, trying not to slip. "Hurry!" I shouted.

We were crossing someone's farm, but if anyone could see us, they didn't come out to say hello. It was possible that if we asked, the family who lived here would hide us. It was also possible that if we asked, they'd promise us safe shelter and then trot off to find the guardsmen riding toward Bascio. There was no way to know.

"Down!" Giovanni shouted as we reached the stand of cedars. "Everyone, lie on the ground!"

I dropped without hesitation; around me, the musicians carefully set down their instruments and then huddled on the ground beside them. The horses, of course, were still standing, but I hoped the cedars would screen them well enough. We were in thick brown brush. I quietly blessed the drab gray robes, which would blend in reasonably well with the mud and bracken.

Beside me, Giovanni was crouched, watching the road from the screen of the cedars. "They're passing," he said. "They're going by. They didn't see us."

Around us, muddy musicians began to sit up.

"When they get to the conservatory, they'll know where we've gone," one of the boy students said. "Where we're going."

"We've got an hour or two," I said. "I think the Dean will stall them. Maybe mislead them. If I were him, I'd tell them some story about the Lupi riding in with a hundred soldiers, to explain why he let us recruit."

"If they look for us, they'll find us," someone said.

"Keep moving," I said. "Head south. They're not going to find us." I wasn't sure I was telling the truth, but for now, I wanted just to keep people moving.

"Do you know of anywhere we can hide?" Giovanni asked me quietly as we walked. "You've lived here, I haven't."

"I lived at the conservatory," I said. "I passed through this area twice—once coming, once going. They never let us leave the conservatory grounds." I picked a cluster of burrs out of my hair.

There was a delicate soprano-pitched cough, and Celia fell in step beside me. "I couldn't help but overhear you just now," she said. "My family lives only an hour or two from here. We can go to their farm."

"Are you sure they'll help us?" Giovanni asked.

Forgetting to flirt, Celia narrowed her eyes into a glare. "These are my *parents*. Do you think they'll turn *me* away?"

"Can you get us there off the road?" I asked.

Celia nodded. "There's a path. My mother comes to the conservatory to visit sometimes."

I gestured. "Lead, then."

Celia led us to a dirt footpath, and our army of musicians spread out into a long line, walking one or two abreast. I walked behind Celia, Flavia beside me; Giovanni brought up the rear with the horses, so that no one would have to walk in their leavings. Despite the danger, everyone still seemed to be in good spirits. Somewhere behind me, one of the boys started singing a marching song that I suspected he'd learned from a brother in the army; it was dirty enough to make a cowherd blush, but nearly everyone joined in on the refrain. *I'll lie in my bed, I'll sleep like the dead, I'll call for the milkmaid to bring me my bread. My heart will be fed, my lips will be red, my purse will be empty, my sweetheart I'll wed.*

Flavia didn't join in, nor did she pull her drum out to beat time. "The songs say that your family died," she said.

I nodded. "They got caught in the middle of a fight. The Circle destroyed the whole village."

"I've been worrying about my family. I didn't have a letter from them the last time the messenger service came."

I remembered the name of Flavia's village, a small town just outside the wasteland. "I haven't heard about anything bad happening there," I said. "But it's quite far south; I'm not surprised the messenger service didn't want to go there to pick up the mail."

"Yeah. I was supposed to be afraid that the Lupi were going to sack my village and kill everyone there, but I never believed you would."

"Good," I said. "Because we wouldn't."

"I'm sorry about your family," she said.

I clasped Flavia's hand. "The Lupi are getting volunteers now from all over Verdia. Maybe there will be someone from your village who will have news for you."

The trip to Celia's farm took two full hours, but we were not overtaken on the way. I had half expected Celia to lose confidence when she actually had to approach her family's home with a hundred hangers-on, but she marched up to her front door while we all stood in the front yard. The person who answered her knock looked like a younger sister; her mother and father came to kiss her and hear her explanation for why she'd abandoned her studies so close to possibly winning a lucrative position. I couldn't hear most of what she said, but I saw her point to me, and I caught the words *Fedeli* and *Emperor*.

She came back to join us a few minutes later, still perfectly composed. "Some of you will have to hide in the barn, some in the root cellar, and some in the house. There should be room for everyone, though."

"We are at your parents' disposal," I said.

The bulk of the recruits would hide in the barn, so Giovanni and I elected to stay in the barn with them. Celia insisted on keeping Flavia with her in the house; she would not hide, but would change into one of her sister's dresses and present herself simply as a daughter of the house. As Giovanni and I closed the barn door, I peered out through a crack in the wall and saw one of Celia's brothers taking off at a run; for a moment, fear flashed through me that he was going to turn us all in. But Celia's parents were unlikely to do anything that would get their own daughter into trouble, I thought, and I settled back against the wall to wait out the afternoon.

"If they find us anyway, you know, this is pretty much not defensible," Giovanni whispered as we settled down in the dirt and scattered straw. "They could burn this place down around us."

"Thanks," I said. "I really needed that image to think about. Do you have any alternative suggestions?"

"Not really," he said.

It was almost evening. Giovanni unpacked apples and cheese from the horse's saddlebags to hand around, since we could hardly expect Celia's family to cook for all of us. I kept watch through the crack in the door, though as Giovanni had pointed out, there wasn't much we could do if the guardsmen came other than to pray that Celia's parents were able to convince them there was nothing to look for.

We dozed as the sun went down. A few hours after sunset, we heard a noise that brought Giovanni and me to instant alertness—hoofbeats. I bit my lip, hoping that none of the musicians would instinctively summon witchlight when woken and give us away. The barn was very dark around me, and although I could hear some people snoring, I had no way of seeing who was awake and who was asleep.

Someone banged on the door of Celia's parents' house. The silence went tight around me; all but the most determined sleepers were awake now. I peered out the crack in the door. The moon was full tonight, and the rider carried a globe of witchlight. One rider, alone. He knocked again.

Celia opened the door. She was wearing a yellow

dress, her hair combed neatly; I hoped it didn't make him suspicious that she didn't look like he'd dragged her out of bed to answer the door. She shook her head.

The rider dismounted. He was close enough that I could see the insignia of the Circle Guard on his uniform. Celia said something over her shoulder, and a moment later her father joined her. She slipped her boots on and stepped out into the yard. Demurely and with perfect calm, she strode toward the barn, the guardsman a step behind her.

I caught my breath; Giovanni's hand closed on the hilt of his sword. Giovanni and I could almost certainly kill him, *if* he was alone.

When Celia was steps away from the barn door, I saw her father make a sudden move, and the glint of metal in the moonlight. The guard cried out once, very loudly, and I wondered with a sick feeling if the other guards were anywhere in earshot. In the darkness behind me, I heard someone whimper. Celia's father brought the knife down again, twice more, and the guard was still.

Celia opened the door. "It's all right," she said. "Don't be afraid, we've taken care of him."

I stepped out into the moonlight, looking down at the guard's motionless body. "What about the others? There were twenty—what if the other nineteen come looking?"

"Well, we'd have had to kill him regardless," Celia said. "He was planning to search. My brother ran out to tell the neighboring villages about the guardsmen, right after you arrived. My father thinks you should wait here a day or two, to let the other villages take care of the rest." She looked disdainfully down at the body. "They shouldn't have split up. Father says the Fedeli would have known better."

I looked at Celia's father. He had the same chestnut hair, though it framed a tanned, hardened face. He knelt, as I watched, to wipe the knife clean on the man's clothing.

"Did the Fedeli come through here last winter?" I asked.

Celia's father looked up, and his eyes were cold. "There was a burning," he said. "A foolish boy who opened his mouth at the wrong time. The Lady, and the Circle, had friends here once. No more." He sheathed his knife. "We are glad to help you, Generale."

"Would you like us to take care of the body for you?" Giovanni asked, stepping noiselessly out of the barn.

Celia's father nodded shortly. "You can bury him in our west field. We were planning to let it lie fallow this year, anyway."

Giovanni wrapped up the body in its cloak, and we carried it together to the field Celia's father had sent us to. We took turns digging; the ground was cold and difficult to shovel.

The blood had soaked into the dirt of the barnyard when Giovanni and I returned. No more guardsmen came, and after another day of waiting, Celia's father came to tell us that messengers had returned from the neighboring villages. Twenty guardsmen lay buried in shallow graves in the fields of Verdia.

"Let's move," I said. Celia's father moved the horse into the stable as we vacated it, and I thanked Celia's parents for their hospitality. Celia fell into step beside me, still wearing her sister's dress. For whatever reason, she didn't try to flirt with Giovanni again.

CHAPTER TWELVE

Is this the victory you seek?
—*The Journey of Gèsu, chapter 7, verse 12.*

From my tent, a few months later, I could hear the drums even when I couldn't hear the singing, like a distant heartbeat. When the wind shifted, I could hear the voices of the dancers, the flutes, the other violins. With Giovanni, I hiked to the crest of the hill and sat down to watch. Flavia stood in the center of the circle, and Lucia led the dance to the drumbeat. Flavia had cut her hair short; she still wore her conservatory robes, but had belted the robe with a red sash. "She's ready," Giovanni said.

It was hard to argue with that. I crumpled Demetrio's letter in my hand. "I don't like Demetrio thinking he can set our timetables for us."

"Granted, but he's right. We can't wait forever. The Lupi are getting restless."

Our army was camped on the shores of the Anira River. Thanks to the Imperial supply lines, we had real tents now and were generously supplied with food, but we were growing so quickly that space and food kept running short anyway. Demetrio's letter had urged me to send out musicians *immediately* to test their skills against magefire, to ensure that the ability wasn't limited to me.

"I had an uncle who thought the best way to teach children to swim was to throw them in the deepest part of a pond and let them figure out how to keep from drowning," I said.

"That *is* the best way to teach children to swim," Giovanni said.

I had sealed each of the musician recruits as Redentori, starting with Flavia, Celia, Quirino, and Valentino, but I knew that many still believed in the Lady. "We don't even know if you have to believe in order for it to work," I said.

"Magery was supposed to be a gift from the Lady, right?" Giovanni said. "But Redentori can still summon witchlight. Even if it's a sin," he added as an afterthought.

"You know, on our trip back from the conservatory, I used magery to light the fire one night," I said. "The tinder was damp; I decided the sin was on the soul of whoever gathered the tinder, which I think was you, Giovanni."

Giovanni laughed. "If you want to know the truth, when I'm not in the wasteland, I use witchlight whenever I have to get up to relieve myself in the middle of the night. I'll cheerfully endure whatever punishment God inflicts on sinners if it means I can avoid tripping and falling on my ass. So in other words, this is just the latest in a long line of petty sins, and not likely to significantly increase my divine punishment."

"I'll have to remember that," I said. "There are all sorts of sins I could probably pin on your soul."

"Consider it available," Giovanni said. "Within reason, of course. If, for instance, you are ever provoked to murder Clara and Placido, that sin goes on your own head."

In the valley below, the dance finished, and Lucia climbed breathlessly up to join us at the crest of the hill. "Flavia's ready," Lucia said. "As ready as she'll ever be."

"Take Demetrio's advice," Giovanni said. "Send them out."

We arrived back at the main encampment to find a new shipment of supplies. A half dozen Imperial soldiers waited, along with a clerk; I signed for the supplies and some of the Lupi went to work unloading and storing them. Another twenty-five new recruits had also arrived and were being sorted out by Severo.

A message from Michel had arrived with the letter from Demetrio. The makeshift Imperial city had been dubbed *Corte,* Court; Michel's latest estimate was that there were three hundred residents, including nobles, servants, and guards. Several musicians had arrived, but they'd been sent over to join the Lupi. The original army barracks had been added onto six times; the new buildings wound their way across the walled hilltop like a huge misshapen caterpillar. "Everyone but the Emperor and Placido are doubled up," Michel's letter informed me. "Placido doesn't have to share with anyone because he farts all night, according to rumor. There's talk of another building. They'd send the servants to sleep in tents, but the nobles are too worried that the servants will get fed up and leave, and they'll be left with no one to cook or clean the stables."

"We'd better finish this war fast," I said gravely to Giovanni when I had finished the letter. "Or the highest of our nobility might actually be forced to take up useful work."

* * *

There were several small groups of mages just across the border from the wasteland; they'd attacked some of the incoming recruits. We sent out scout teams of dancers, soldiers, and musicians, anticipating little trouble in finding confrontations. The Circle wanted to know the limits of our defensive abilities as much as we did.

"I hate doing this," I said as I watched the scouts leave.

"But look at them," Lucia said, pointing at Flavia. "They're eager to do it. They know it's a test and that they're the ones who will determine if it works, but they know they can do it."

"Besides," Giovanni said. "It's the only way to find out."

We sent the musicians we were surest of, like Flavia, but we couldn't be certain. If it didn't work, the scout teams would be killed. And we'd have to scramble for another strategy—fast.

"It *will work*," Lucia said.

The day after our scout teams left, two Redentori priests showed up. I didn't know them, but they carried a letter from Clara. "Generale Eliana," the letter said. "You mentioned concerns about spies. I have formed a group to combat the Fedeli and to identify their supporters; we call ourselves the Servi d'Arkah, the Servants of God. I have sent these two men to aid you in identifying Fedeli spies; they have been instructed to follow your orders. I urge you to take advantage of their services. You of anyone would realize how devastating even a single spy can be."

I looked up from the paper. One of the Servi was old, and had hunched shoulders that made him look like a vulture; the other had beady eyes and a shrill voice like a screech owl. "What is it you want from me?" I said.

"Just a few minutes of your time," the vulture said soothingly. "I beg you, think of us as advisors, not intruders. Sit with us a few minutes."

I sent Viola, one of my aides, for tea, and waved the Servi into my tent, clearing some of my papers off the table so that we could sit comfortably. "Are those papers of a sensitive nature?" the screech owl asked.

I looked down at the papers in my hands. Sensitive enough. "Why do you ask?" I said.

"Do you always leave them in the open like that?"

"This isn't the open," I said. "It's my tent."

"Still, many people must have access," the screech owl said. "Would anyone notice if someone came in, just for a few minutes, while you weren't here?"

"There is a guard on the tent at all times," I said. "Even when I'm not here. Do you think I'm a fool?"

"But," Vulture said, putting a placating hand on my wrist. His fingers were cold and sticky. "Are you certain you can trust every guard?"

"Yes," I said. "My aides have been with us since the slave camps."

"Who cleans?" Screech Owl asked.

"What do you mean, who cleans? Why would I need someone to clean my tent for me?"

Screech Owl shrugged and dropped the subject. We sat in silence for a few uncomfortable moments, then Viola came in with tea. She filled three teacups, setting them down in front of each of us. I picked up my cup and took a careful sip. Viola nodded politely to the Servi and left.

Screech Owl waited until the tent flap had fallen shut before speaking again. "Does she have access to your tent?"

"Obviously," I said. "And my tea, were she to want to poison me. Look, Viola escaped with me from Ravenna. If I can't trust her, I can't trust anybody."

"Does she ever use witchlight?" Screech Owl asked. "When you're not in the wasteland?"

"What does that have to do with anything?" I said.

"Does that answer mean the answer to my question is yes?" Screech Owl said.

"No, it doesn't mean the answer is yes!" I said. "My answer means I'd like to know why I should *care* whether my aides occasionally commit trivial sins in the name of convenience."

"No sin is trivial," Vulture said.

"Do you 'guard the way to wrong' on behalf of God?" I said.

The tent was very quiet for a moment. "No," Vulture said. "We find spies. And we've found that many spies retain loyalty to the Lady, and will honor Her when they can."

"Being a Redentore was never a requirement for joining my army," I said.

"Wasn't it?" Screech Owl said. "That surprises me a great deal, Generale. Does that mean that you don't believe?"

"Of course I believe," I said.

"Then why don't you wish for everyone to share in the true faith?" Vulture said. "Oh, but this is beside the point. The point is, any spies will *definitely* belong to the Lady. Identifying those who avoid Redentori practices will at least give us somewhere to start."

"I would expect spies, who knew their own treason, to be among the most fervent Redentori," I said.

"Were you a fervent worshipper of the Lady when you spied in Cuore?" Vulture asked. "I don't remember you from the chapel."

"No, I wasn't," I said. "But I was never a very good spy."

"You were good enough," Screech Owl said. "And you knelt in prayer when you could, didn't you? You quietly avoided church. *That's* the sort of thing we're trying to find here—but of the opposite variety."

I was silent for a moment.

"Never mind your aide," Vulture said. "We will trust in your trust in her. Do you have other people who use witchlight, when you're not in the wasteland?"

"I haven't ever noticed."

"Do you know of couples in your army who have sought the blessing of the Lady rather than marrying before engaging in—ah—affectionate relations?" Screech Owl asked.

"I don't keep track of those sorts of activities," I said.

"Well," Vulture said. "This is very unfortunate. What about attending Mass? Do you have people who don't attend Mass?"

"I don't take attendance," I said.

"That would be easy enough to change," Screech Owl said. "If you strongly encourage everyone to attend Mass regularly, and have the priests keep track of who comes, you could identify the weak Redentori—"

"Or those who have injuries that make it painful to dance," I said. "Or those who seek God's presence on their own. Or those who believe in the Emperor, and in our cause, but not in God! Are all these people assumed to be spies?"

"We're just trying to narrow things down," Vulture said. "That's all."

"I'm beginning to think you don't care about identifying infiltrators," Screech Owl said. "That surprises me a great deal, Generale. Especially given your own experiences with Felice. You trusted him on instinct, didn't you? He playacted a great deal of fervent belief in your cause, and you swallowed his lies. Didn't you?"

I was silent, glaring at them across the table.

The tent flap was yanked back with so much force it nearly pulled the tent down on us, and Lucia stood in the doorway, shaking with rage. "How dare you!" she shouted at Vulture and Screech Owl.

"The Priestess Lucia, I presume," Screech Owl said. "We have a letter for you from Clara." He handed her a sealed paper.

Lucia tore it in half without looking at it.

"Well, since you weren't interested in reading it, I'll tell you what it said," Vulture said. "Clara bids you understand that the Emperor has named you the heart of the Redentore faith, but Clara the head. And just as the heart must allow the head to decide in many matters, you must bow to Clara's will. And it is her will that the Servi exist."

"Get out of here," Lucia said.

"Isn't that for Generale Eliana to decide?" Screech Owl said.

Vulture and Screech Owl both looked at me. My eyes narrowed and I pointed to the door of the tent. "Get out of my camp."

"But—" Screech Owl looked as if he was thinking of attempting some further blackmail or threat.

"Get out of my camp *now*."

"It's almost nightfall," Vulture said.

I relented slightly. "I will arrange a place for you to sleep, then, and you can leave at dawn." I lifted the tent flap and summoned Viola. "Arrange a tent for these men, and an escort," I said. "They are not to roam the camp."

"You would throw us into the stockade?" Screech Owl said.

"I will not have you upset my soldiers with your nosiness," I said.

"We'll leave now," Vulture said, his voice colder than a winter lake.

I turned back to Viola. "In that case, see them to the border of the encampment."

The Servi mounted their horses and left without looking back. I stared after them, hoping that Giovanni would agree that tossing them out had been a good idea. Then I shook my head, half laughing at myself. Giovanni would have wrung their necks—first Screech Owl, then Vulture. I headed back to the tent.

Lucia was still there, alone, weeping. "They're gone," I said.

"They'll be back."

"We don't have to let them come back."

"Sooner or later," Lucia said, "we'll have to face them."

"Did you know about these people?" I asked.

"Yes. When I visited Corte, Clara told me about them. She was so proud! I said she was just trying to create her own little Fedeli and she got angry. I went to the Emperor; he'll let me in to speak to him because he knows I'm a friend of yours. I told him that petty enforcement was not what the Redentore faith was

about—that God doesn't want people *forced* to kneel
or dance or even to refrain from using witchlight. Our
faith is about serving God because we want to, not because someone says we're spies if we don't." She paused.
"The Emperor said he'd think about it. I guess he made
his decision."

I squeezed her hand, saying nothing.

"I guess I believed things would really be different,"
Lucia said, her voice almost inaudible. "I thought I
could really change things."

"Things will be different," I said.

"No," Lucia said, her voice soft and dull. "They will
paint Gèsu, and place him in the Great Cathedral, and
all that will change will be the decorations. Redentori
will go to Mass each week because they have to, and
will dance because they fear the Servi. The faces may
change, but the walls will be the same."

*   *   *

All but one of the scouting parties returned the next
week, exuberant. The music had worked; they had de-
flected the Circle's magefire and shot the guardsmen
dead. The Lupi hadn't been this excited in months. We
mourned briefly for the lost scouts—perhaps their musician had been unable to make the magic work, or
perhaps they had been ambushed. We'd never know.
The next day, we packed up our tents and loaded our
supplies onto wagons. It was time to advance.

Initial resistance was minimal. The Circle and the
Fedeli were unwilling to commit their forces to a futile
battle; they sent small groups of soldiers drawn from
the Fedeli and the Circle Guard, but not enough to put
up a serious fight or even to slow us down. The Lupi
were encouraged by our easy victories, but I knew that

this was exactly what Demetrio had feared; we were moving toward a showdown at Cuore, where the Circle and the Fedeli would be protected by the enclave walls. We couldn't simply secure the rest of the country and ignore Cuore; they would wait for our forces to disintegrate as Lupi left to plant their fields, then reemerge to attack us when we least expected it. Besides, taking Cuore would have a tremendous emotional advantage; it was the Heart, the center of the country, the seat of the Imperial throne. If we could take Cuore, we would have won, even if pockets of the Circle survived.

For a long time, I had continued to say my selfish prayers to the Lord, rather than to God—except for when I prayed for Lucia, after the Lupi were destroyed. It was hard to imagine that the Redentore God would care if my particular friends got hurt in battle. But toward the end of Mass one night as we approached the heart of the Empire, I found myself whispering a prayer to God: *let the Circle keep Mira in Cuore for now. Surely, after all that's happened, they don't fully trust her; let them distrust her too much to send her out to face us.* Of course, if they sent her out, that would give her the opportunity to escape, but if she was going to run, I was fairly certain she'd have done it by now. *God, keep Mira safe,* I pleaded silently. *Somehow, somehow, please keep Mira safe.*

The last major city before Cuore was Manico. We were perhaps two weeks south of Manico when the Lupi perimeter guards came to tell me that the Circle had sent an emissary to negotiate a truce.

I shook my head. "They're here to spy."

"If they're under a flag of truce, we have no choice but to treat them courteously," Giovanni said. He added to the guard, "Search them for weapons and keep them at the perimeter. 'Courtesy' doesn't preclude certain precautions."

I walked out to the northern perimeter of the encampment with Lucia and Giovanni. Three men had been sent. One wore a black wool robe with linked circles on his sleeve—Fedele. The second wore the uniform of the Circle Guard. The third wore no uniform, but a fine tunic of soft blue cloth. I felt my lips twist into a snarl when I saw his face. *"Felice."*

Giovanni grabbed my sword-arm and I shook him loose. "I know what a flag of truce means, Giovanni. I won't hurt him." I approached the messengers; in unison, the three men swung down from their horses. "If the Circle had any intention of negotiating, they would have sent someone else," I said, biting my words off as I tried to suppress the fury that rose inside my stomach. "What do you want here?"

Felice bowed low in courtly courtesy. "Generale Eliana, the Circle and the High Priest of the Fedeli send their regards."

"We extend our greetings to them," Giovanni said.

Felice straightened and looked up through his long lashes. "And how is your health, Generale Eliana?"

"I'm fine," I said. "Thank you so much for your interest."

He gave me an ingratiating smile. "Quite recovered from your ... detention?"

I met his eyes coldly. "Yes."

"Good," Felice said with an earnest nod. "It's always best when a *whole* body can be delivered to the Lady."

Beside me, I heard Giovanni's breath catch. I stepped

forward, pushing my hood back from my face. "Take your best shot, Felice."

Felice fell back a step and lowered his eyes. "I would never consider dishonoring a flag of truce."

"Good," I said. "So why exactly are you here?"

He cleared his throat. "I am here with an offer of clemency for you and for the other Lupi, should you cease and desist all hostile actions from this point onward."

I laughed. "How generous."

"I advise you to consider it, Eliana," Felice said. "Do you really think you're going to be able to pull this off? We still hold Cuore. You wouldn't want your friends to go through what you endured, would you? Think of your soldiers. Think of ..." His eyes flicked to the side, then back to my face. "Think of Lucia."

I heard a growl from behind me, and before I could stop him, Giovanni had drawn his sword and lunged toward Felice. Abject terror flashed across Felice's face; this was not an eventuality he had planned for. "Giovanni!" I shouted. "Drop your sword!"

Giovanni didn't turn around, but held his sword-edge to Felice's throat. "You dishonor the flag of truce with your insults," Giovanni hissed. He withdrew the sword and slapped Felice hard on the cheek with the flat of it, a duel-challenge. "We'll finish this some other time." He stepped back, shoving his sword into its sheath.

Felice rubbed his cheek, stunned. "I have a full offer from the Circle and the Fedeli in writing," he said, his voice quavering a little. "Do you wish to discuss it outside in the wind, or would you care to read it over at your leisure and discuss it when you have had some time to consider our offer? There are certain areas in which we are empowered to compromise."

I took the proffered scroll and handed it to Lucia. "Take them to an empty tent on the perimeter and keep them under close guard," I said to the Lupi. "We'll send for them later, if necessary."

"Why would they send Felice?" Lucia asked as we headed back toward the center of the encampment. "What could possibly be their purpose?"

"The only reason to send an envoy with that sort of offer would be to scout us out," I said. "Count our numbers, maybe overhear something useful. Felice is probably here to provoke us. Perhaps they think an angry opponent is to their advantage." I glanced at Giovanni involuntarily. Giovanni scowled darkly at the ground. "I don't think that worked quite as Felice planned, though."

"Perhaps they hoped you'd kill Felice on sight and dishonor the Lupi," Giovanni said. "That could create a rift between you and Demetrio."

"Demetrio's not exactly a close friend as it is," I said. "Still."

Back in my tent, I read the offer. Rosalba had drafted it; I recognized the beautiful handwriting. It was a more detailed and poetically worded version of what Felice had said at the perimeter: surrender, and we'll spare your miserable lives.

"There's no point in sending this," I said. "They must know we'll refuse."

"Perhaps it's a distraction," Giovanni said.

"Perhaps." I summoned a guard to order additional troops sent out to watch the perimeter, as well as a half dozen more to stand watch outside the tent of the "emissaries."

Lucia was pondering their offer. "Can we use this

somehow?" she asked. I looked at her, puzzled. "Demetrio said we should seize on any opportunity to draw the Circle out of Cuore. Is there some way we could use this to do that?"

Giovanni's head snapped up. "If they came here to spy—"

"—Maybe we could feed them some useful intelligence," I finished. "Like they did with us in Pluma. Like *Felice* did with us."

"If you think he'll fall for his own trick ... South of Manico is a good place for a battle," Giovanni said. "Maybe we could persuade them to meet us right where we want them."

"If we let them overhear—" I thought for a moment. "Perhaps that we're unconfident in our power to defend against a great *many* mages at once. I could say that I feel the shield weakening sometimes—that maybe fifty or a hundred mages working in concert could break through the barrier."

"What if you turn out to be telling the truth?" Giovanni said. "We've never faced down more than ten at once."

I sketched out a rough map on the dirt floor. "We'd bait the trap with some of the Lupi, but nowhere near all. If it turns out they *can* incinerate us, there'd still be plenty left to finish this. The road north leads through a large valley just south of Manico. We could send in the bait and wait for their 'ambush.' When they attack, more Lupi close in." I drew arrows coming over the hills I'd drawn. "Honestly, I think I could hold off any number. Especially since they aren't used to working in groups that large. But even if they *do* break through our defenses, they'll never be able to redirect their fire outward in time."

"I hope you're right," Giovanni said.

Lucia bit her lip. "This is the kind of opportunity we can't throw away. I think we should try it."

I looked at Giovanni.

"You're right," Giovanni said finally. "It's risky, but it's the best shot we have at avoiding a siege."

I nodded. "We need a 'traitor,' then. Someone Felice doesn't know—but someone we can trust ..."

*   *   *

"I have orders to take that one to Generale Eliana." Quirino held out the paper toward the guards.

The guard looked it over by lantern-light and shrugged. "He's all yours."

Quirino took Felice courteously by the arm. "If you would come with me, signore." He led Felice into the shadows of one of the larger tents, then unfolded an extra cloak and draped it around Felice's shoulders. "The generali intend to reject your offer, and to send you away without speaking to you again," Quirino said in an urgent whisper. "Cover your face with the cloak, signore."

Felice pulled up the deep hood. "Who are you?" he asked.

Quirino flashed a piece of hidden jewelry—two linked circles. "One who is loyal to the Lady, and would die for her."

Felice nodded slowly.

"Come," Quirino said.

Quirino led Felice through the maze of tents. ("Try not to let him see a whole lot," I had requested. "But make sure he wouldn't be able to easily find his way back.") Finally he stopped, and gestured for Felice to be absolutely silent. In an adjacent tent, Flavia was watching from a hole in the seam; when she saw that they were in place, she gestured, and Valentino abruptly stopped practicing his violin.

That was the signal. Inside the tent, I lit a fresh candle. Lucia and Giovanni looked at me expectantly. "At least the weather should be good," I said. We needed some chitchat first, to make this less suspicious.

"Only if you trust Severo's skills as a weather-caller," Giovanni said.

"He's right five days out of seven," I said.

"Yeah, well, predicting 'rain and a cold wind' every day in late winter will be right, five days out of seven," Giovanni said.

"But he's not predicting rain and cold, he's predicting sun and warmth."

"Tea?" Lucia asked, pouring herself a new cup. She spilled some on her lap. "Damn," she muttered, wringing out her skirt. I picked up a cup and took a sip.

"In any case," Giovanni said. "There are more important issues at stake here than the weather."

"I don't see what you're so worried about," I said. "Everything's gone as planned so far. The dances *work*."

"Against *five* mages, yes. Against *ten* mages, yes. But what if they send the whole Circle?"

I rolled my eyes and slammed down the teacup. "That's *not* going to happen, Giovanni, and you know it. They're going to stay safely penned up in their rabbit-hole until they run out of food. They're *certainly* not going to send more than a dozen mages when we've killed every mage they've sent our way so far."

"Just for the sake of argument, Eliana, how many mages do you think it would take to get through your defenses?"

"Mine?" I pursed my lips and picked up my tea-cup for another sip as I considered. "At least fifty—probably a hundred."

"There are enough mages alive for the Circle to send more than that," Giovanni said. "This could *happen*, Eliana. I think we should split the Lupi. Are you going to *listen* to me this time?"

"Giovanni, Demetrio has *asked* us to secure Manico. That valley is the only logical staging ground."

"That's exactly the problem! They know where to find us."

"Giovanni, I spent two months spying on the Circle—at your request, as you might recall. Two months! I *know* these people. I know how they think. And they are *not* coming out of their hiding place until their lives depend on it. So far as they've seen, we can wipe the floor with them anytime we want." I took a demure sip of tea. "I am generale," I said. "Are you going to follow me, or not?"

Giovanni picked up a cup of tea, then slammed it down so hard the cup broke. "You're a fool," he said. "But you're the fool the Lupi support. Am I going to follow you? What *choice* do I have? I'd follow you to hell—and I probably will." He stomped out of the tent.

I turned to Lucia, who was wiping up the tea. "Do you think Isabella is going to give me this much trouble?" I asked.

Outside the tent, Quirino watched Giovanni leave. "Quick," he said to Felice. "We need to get you back to your tent."

Felice followed Quirino without protest. As they neared where they had started, Felice gripped Quirino's arm. "Signore, you haven't told me your name."

"I think it's best you don't know it," Quirino said.

"Do you wish to come with us when we leave? The Fedeli will provide you asylum. You could meet us—"

Quirino shook his head. "You heard their plans. I am a musician, signore. I fully intend to be on that battlefield. And if the Circle attacks, they may rest assured that at least part of the field will be unshielded. My death will honor the Lady."

Felice fell back a step, stunned. "Your faith puts me to shame."

"You serve the Lady," Quirino said. "As do I. That's all I need to know." They were silent the rest of the way back to the tent.

Quirino made certain that Felice was well guarded, then returned to my tent, a broad smile on his face. "Felice didn't just take the bait," Quirino said. "He swallowed the fishing pole."

"Now we just hope that we really were lying," I said.

Giovanni clasped my shoulder. "I would truly follow you to hell," he said, "if it meant kicking Felice's ass."

"Let's hope it doesn't come to that," I said.

*   *   *

We kept just enough Lupi in the valley to make it look crowded. I was in the valley, along with Lucia, but Giovanni would lead the reserve troops. We didn't tell the Lupi what we knew was coming until the Circle was almost there; some were probably spies, and could spoil the ambush. The attack came an hour after dawn. My scouts had returned exhausted. Just over a hundred mages, with guards and Fedeli soldiers, were approaching from the north. We formed dance-circles and prepared for battle.

The Fedeli crested the hill and held their position. I had ordered our perimeter guards to fall back with only a token struggle; if the Circle and Fedeli took our bait, there would be far more soldiers than our perimeter guards could fend off. I couldn't see the mages beyond the Fedeli, but I knew they were there. *This is for you, Mira,* I thought, and raised my violin.

The dancers knew how many mages had come for us today; I could feel their fear around me like smoke. Still, they clasped hands and never stumbled in their dance. I closed my eyes and the power flowed into me; I breathed it in like a vapor and drank it like wine. I whirled to face our enemy, feeling the spinning, blinding light of the dance soaring around me.

I opened my eyes; the sky had turned to fire. The morning had been brilliant blue and white, as Severo had predicted; now the sky rolled with flames. The fire seethed overhead like a swollen river, and for a moment I felt nothing but fear.

"Ask," Lucia whispered from the circle. "Ask and you shall receive."

God, give me the power.

The flames arced down upon us like hawks diving on their prey. I felt the power explode upward from my feet, rising to meet the flames like a wall of water, like a blinding storm of light. The curtain of flame shattered like glass, and ashes rained down softly over us, but no fire.

That was when Giovanni's reserve troops rode in.

The mages never had a chance. The reserve troops broke their line. The scattered mages tried desperately to band together, but most were too panicked to summon magefire. The handful that managed created only the small fires that we'd dealt with before. The Fedeli stood their ground, but the Circle Guard broke and ran; they were as terrified as the mages at the idea of fighting without magefire.

Without their guards, at least half of the mages were cut down where they stood. The rest turned and fled. The second set of reserve troops were waiting for that, and met the fleeing mages and guards with a rain of crossbow bolts. Perhaps in the end, twenty-five mages got away, and a fair number of the Circle's guards. The Fedeli held their ground, refusing to flee or surrender. We killed them all. Felice was not among their number. No surprise there.

We suspected that the Circle mages who'd escaped would fall back to Manico and make another stand from the Fedeli's fortress there. We marched to Manico the next day, intending to attack the city before they could regroup, but we found the city empty, the gates to the fortress left open. We walked in without resistance. Within the fortress, we could see the preparations for a battle—crossbow bolts heaped in bales like straw, oil in cauldrons to heat and pour down. But the city was deserted.

"Maybe it's a trap?" I said.

Giovanni shook his head. "They're not in any position to set a trap—at least not one that starts with an open gate. They lost their nerve."

The Fedeli bastion in Manico was one of the most substantial in the Empire—larger than their Citadel in Cuore, which was constrained by the enclave walls. Just beyond their fortress was the Cathedral of the

Lady, which was even more impressive than Her cathedral in Cuore, since it had been built later.

"Raise our standard," I said. "Secure the city and search the Fedeli keep."

Minutes after the Lupi headed in, Severo reappeared at the door, an exuberant smirk on his face. "Look what we found," he said, and shoved a dirty, furious man out the door.

It took me a moment to recognize him. His hands were chained behind his back, and he wore the robe of a penitent. Nothing like the fine clothes I'd always seen him in before. "Felice," I said.

Felice stumbled back a step, only to run into Severo, who steadied him and then pushed him back toward me.

"Where's the key to the chains?" Giovanni asked. Severo tossed it to him.

"Where did you find him?" I asked.

"He was left chained in the first office," Severo said. He tipped his head, puzzled. "They must have meant for us to find him. Why did they leave him for us?"

"They were probably unimpressed by the intelligence he brought back," I said. "Weren't they, Felice?"

Felice looked like he'd like to spit at me, but his mouth was too dry.

Giovanni stepped forward and unlocked Felice's chains. "Severo, give me your sword," he said. Severo drew his sword and gave it to Giovanni. Felice fell back a step, his face white as paper. "I said we'd finish this later," Giovanni said to Felice. "And it's better than you deserve. You deserve to die kicking at the end of a rope. But I am no executioner—and *I* am going to be the one to kill you. You are under no white flag today. Defend yourself!" He threw Severo's sword to Felice.

Felice raised the sword and moved warily away from Severo and Giovanni.

"Lady's tits," I muttered, but backed up to let them fight. In the unlikely event that Felice won, I didn't think it would violate the rules of honor for me to hang him. And it would serve Giovanni right to get skewered for doing something this stupid.

"Your treachery killed hundreds of Lupi," Giovanni said. "You betrayed Eliana to the Fedeli. Do you have anything to say for yourself?"

Felice licked his lips, still circling. "Was not your beloved Eliana also a spy? We are the same, she and I. She served her masters, and I served mine."

Giovanni spat. "Eliana spied on the Circle. She does not betray friendship."

"Just wait," Felice said. He paused to smile coldly. "But thank you for reminding me that my quarrel is not with you." Without warning, Felice whirled and lunged toward me. I saw Giovanni's eyes go wide with alarm, but he moved quickly; before I had my own sword free from its sheath, he had drawn and flung his knife into Felice's back.

Felice stumbled. The sword dropped from his hand, but he fell heavily forward and into my arms. I could smell blood mixed with the lingering scent of Felice's perfume. Gagging, I shoved him away, letting him collapse to the ground.

Giovanni jerked his knife out of Felice's back. "Forgive me, Eliana," he said. "I took a foolish risk giving him a sword." He rolled Felice onto his back, but Felice's dying eyes were fixed on me.

"We'll meet again," Felice said.

"I don't think that's likely," Giovanni said, but Felice didn't hear him.

Lucia came looking for me as we returned to the keep. "This place is built like a maze," she said, clasping my hand. "We want to search the dungeon, in case they left prisoners behind, but we aren't sure how to get there. Do you know? Can you find it?"

"I'd be more use in the Fedeli Citadel in Cuore," I said, letting Lucia lead me into the building. "If this is anything like that, there should be passages into the dungeon through some of the offices. We'll need torches."

Giovanni rounded up some stray Lupi to help us search and to guard us, and I found an office that looked roughly like Rosalba's. The second door opened onto a narrow passage with a low ceiling. I shivered. "I think this might lead to the dungeons," I said.

I let Giovanni lead the way. The corridor ended with a spiral staircase; we headed down. I realized suddenly that the torch in my hand was flickering because I wasn't holding it steady. I clasped it with both hands, but it trembled harder. Lucia saw and took the torch from me. "We've found it," she said. "You don't have to come down." I shook my head and continued down the steps. It was cold at the bottom, and damp, and it smelled of blood and vomit. I found that I was having trouble taking deep breaths. Lucia put her free hand on my back as if to steady me. Giovanni glanced back; I expected an insult, but he gave me his most reassuring smile.

"Hello?" Lucia said. Her voice echoed off the stone walls, but there was no answering call.

"Maybe they took all the prisoners with them," I said.

The corridor opened up into a small guard room—empty, of course. Dice were still scattered on the table, and a half-finished cup of wine. I could hear a steady drip of water from somewhere down the hall, and the faint scrabble of vermin. We passed through the guard room and found ourselves in a cell block. Scores of cells were arranged in rows. The doors stood open.

I went to the first cell; Lucia held the torch up. In the flickering firelight, I could see a woman chained to the wall, but her head hung down limp. I took the torch back from Lucia and went in to kneel beside the woman. The floor was cold, and wet. I took the woman's hand in mine; it was cold and stiff. She was dead; her throat had been cut.

I straightened. "She's dead," I said. Lucia reached out for me as I went into the next cell. The next cell held the body of a man. He was naked, and had been tortured. The implements were scattered on the floor beside him. His throat had been cut, as well. The next cell held the body of a woman, chained down to a table; she had also been tortured.

My stomach rebelled. Lucia caught me as I fell to my knees. "Let's get you out of here," she whispered.

"No," I said. "No! We have to be sure. Someone might still be alive." I spat to clear the taste from my mouth and stood up. The Lupi were shaking their heads. Lucia was weeping. "Giovanni," I said. "Help me look."

Giovanni took one of the torches and went with me as we made a rapid circuit of the cells. Most of the cells were occupied. Every prisoner was dead. In the last cell, there were two bodies. Next to the body of the prisoner was the body of a Fedele priestess. She had driven the knife into her own throat, when she'd finished killing the prisoners—to avoid capture by us, presumably. Beside her body was a folded paper; I picked it up. FOR HER GLORY, it said, in an elegant, ornate script.

I recognized that script. I knelt by the body and turned the priestess's face toward the torchlight. It was Rosalba.

The anger rose around me like steam as we went up the stairs. "Why?" someone was whispering between sobs. "I don't understand. Why?"

" 'For Her glory,' " Lucia muttered. "These weren't the everyday heretics, these were the dangerous ones. These were the Redentori."

I still felt like I couldn't breathe; as soon as we were up the stairs, I went outside. The news of what we had found in the dungeon spilled through the city, and furious Lupi returned, looking for me, wanting orders, wanting a target for their anger.

It was late afternoon, and the sun slanted down, glinting off the stained-glass windows of the Great Cathedral. Lucia stirred beside me. "For the glory of God," she shouted. "Destroy Her Chapel! For the lives of the Redentori slaughtered in cold blood—burn the Cathedral of the Lady!"

CHAPTER THIRTEEN

The higher the flight, the farther the fall.
—*The Journey of Gèsu, chapter 30, verse 2.*

We gathered outside Cuore like dusk before a storm. From the peak of the hill to the south, I could see the camps of the Lupi and the Imperial Army, tents and campfires fading to the horizon. It was spring now, and the smell of wet dirt and new growth mixed with wood smoke and horse sweat and old blood. The defeat at Manico had been catastrophic for the Circle and the Fedeli. As Demetrio had predicted, the survivors of that battle retreated to the protection of the Imperial enclave. And so we'd still have to take Cuore, but at least it would be easier.

Back in the center of the camp, Placido had arrived. "Good afternoon, Generale," he said, bowing slightly. He'd brought two Servi priests with him—not the vulture or the screech owl, but Servi nonetheless.

Michel had also come with him. I grabbed Michel in a bear hug, which he returned enthusiastically. "How'd you manage this?" I asked.

"The Emperor gave me permission to fight this battle at your side," he said. "He knew I wouldn't want to miss it. Also—did you ever wonder how the Emperor got out alone during Mascherata? Demetrio and I finally got it out of him. There's a sewer tunnel that was built by the old Empire; it hasn't been used for centuries, apparently, and it leads under the wall. The Emperor told me how to find it, and I can lead people there to open the gates to the enclave."

Placido had brought a letter from Clara, which I pushed aside to read later. "Keep the Servi out of my way," I said. "I don't want them bothering my soldiers, not the night before a battle." Placido nodded a surly assent.

"I'm sure you want to speak with the Imperial Generali," I said. "So I won't keep you."

"Of course," Placido said, teeth clenched. He probably wanted a word with me, but he wasn't going to get it if I could help it. I might get lucky and die in the battle, and then I'd *never* have to listen to him.

"What does Clara's letter say?" Giovanni asked when Placido had gone.

"I don't know," I said, pulled it back out, and handed it to Giovanni. "You read it."

Michel dined that evening with Lucia, Giovanni, and me. He was doing well in the Emperor's service, although he missed us. The Emperor wanted Michel to stay on as a personal guard even after the war was won. "I'll probably do it," Michel said. "I lost my family to the famine. My former home is in the wasteland. I don't really have anywhere else to go."

"That's going to be true for a lot of the Lupi," I said.

"Doesn't that make you nervous?" Giovanni asked.

"I hadn't really thought past the end of the war," I said.

"Maybe you should start thinking." Giovanni slid

Clara's letter across the table to me. "Clara talks at some length about the Emperor's hopes that the Lupi will find something to do with themselves *outside* of Cuore once the war is over. I think somebody's getting nervous."

Michel looked up from his soup. "Are you saying that the Emperor—"

"I'm not saying anything about the Emperor," Giovanni said. "I think it's Clara that's getting nervous, and probably Eliana is the cause as much as the Lupi. They're loyal to you, Eliana, not to Emperor Travan. Clara's in a very nice position these days, and it's only going to get nicer when they return to Cuore. Anything that can jeopardize that makes her nervous."

I picked up the letter and read it. "She's trying to imply a threat, but it's not clear what she thinks she's going to do to us," I said. "Do you think she plans to send the Imperial Army against the Lupi to get rid of us?"

"The Emperor would never stand for that," Michel said.

"Clara and Placido," I said. "What a pair."

"You know what they say," Giovanni muttered. "Even in the worst flood, offal floats."

"Generale Eliana?" someone called from outside the tent. Placido. I clapped my hand over my mouth; Lucia started laughing silently. I ran through the last few minutes of conversation; damaging, but not damning. I was fairly certain he couldn't have been there for long, as my guards would have announced his presence. In any case, he was here now.

"Come in, Placido," I said.

Placido came into the tent. He looked annoyed, but

I had no idea whether it was because of Giovanni's insult or just because of Giovanni's presence. "I wanted to bid you good night," he said. "And to wish you God's grace in the battle tomorrow."

"May God smile on you, as well," I said. "Have a seat. We were just discussing Clara's letter."

"Indeed," he said. "What did she write? She didn't share the contents with me."

I was tempted to make up something shocking, to see from his reaction whether or not he was lying, but decided against it. "She raises the question of where the Lupi are to go once the battle tomorrow is won, assuming that God continues to stand with us."

"Have you ideas along those lines?" Placido asked.

"The Lupi who've joined us over the winter are farmers," I said. "They have lives to return to, homes, fields to plant. The ones who we liberated from the slave labor camps, though, their farms were in the wasteland. They don't have anything to go back to. But if the Emperor would set aside land for them, farms, they could go there."

"Where were you thinking?" Placido asked.

"My former village, Doratura, has already been re-settled by refugees from the slave camps," I said. "There are other villages like it; some have already been resettled, but a formal declaration would end any question."

"I'm sure the Emperor would be willing," Michel said. "That's certainly an easy enough request to grant."

Placido gave Michel a look that could curdle cheese. Michel took a bite of bread, not appearing to notice.

"And you?" Placido asked.

"What about me?"

"Do you wish to return to a farm?" Placido said. "What do you intend to do next?"

"I wish to continue to serve the Emperor, in whatever capacity he can best use me," I said.

"The Emperor wants you to join his staff as an advisor," Michel said. "He's said so."

Placido's glare could have lit Michel's vest on fire, except doing that sort of thing was a sin and Placido was probably afraid we'd report him to the Servi. "How delightful," Placido muttered. "Don't you want to return to your home?"

"My family was killed when the Circle destroyed my village," I said. "I have no home to return to."

Placido clucked his tongue with almost-genuine sympathy. "Clara worries about people with no family," he said.

Probably because we have no one who can be used against us, I thought. "It was terrible to lose my family," I said. "But I have found consolation in my service to the Emperor." I mentally blessed Michel's excellent memory for conversation. I'd have to remember to hint to him later that if he wanted to repeat this entire conversation to the Emperor, that wouldn't bother me at all.

"Have you ever had the opportunity to attend the university, Generale?" Placido asked.

That was a question I didn't see coming. "No," I said. "My education was musical."

"You should consider attending," Placido said. "For a time, to round out your education—if you're going to become an Imperial Advisor. I'm confident the Emperor wouldn't hinder such a plan."

"To learn what?" I asked.

"History," Placido said. "Philosophy."

"Why would the Emperor need me for such expertise when he has you?" I asked. "Not to mention Giovanni?"

Giovanni had been quietly enjoying the conversation from the corner; his head snapped up and he glared at me. "Michel, does the Emperor want me as an advisor?"

"I don't know," Michel said. "He hasn't ever said so."

"Good," Giovanni said. "I'd like to become a worthless layabout at court. I'm assuming that will be acceptable to him?"

Michel grinned. "I think he'll figure you've earned it, Generale."

"Did you have any other questions, Placido?" I asked.

"No," Placido said. "I just came to wish you good night, and God's blessing."

"Of course," I said. "Good night, then, Placido, and good luck to you tomorrow, as well." Not that Placido was likely to need it; I was confident he'd stay near the rear, assuring himself and us that he would only get in the way. University arms training prepared one to be a gentleman, not a soldier.

We finished our meal after Placido was gone. I wanted more wine, but it would be too easy to overindulge tonight, and I would need a clear head tomorrow. I sent for tea instead.

Isabella came to the door before the tea arrived. "Generale Eliana, may I have a word with you?" she asked. "Alone?"

Giovanni, Lucia, and Michel started to get up, but I waved them back. "You stay here," I said. "Isabella and I will go for a walk." My bodyguard trailed us at a discreet distance; Isabella and I headed out to the southern hills, past the perimeter of the camp, and sat down.

The sun was setting. I stared at the twilight sky, thinking that I should have brought a lantern for our walk back.

Something glittered at the edge of my vision. I looked up; Isabella had tears in her eyes.

"When you take Cuore," Isabella said. "I need you to protect my daughter."

"Daughter?" I said. "What daughter?"

"Miriamne is my daughter," she said. "The woman you call Mira."

Now you are truly dead to me. I remembered Isabella's ritual burning of the lock of a child's hair ... and how she had come untouched through the magefire, just as I had.

"I told you I had a daughter who was a violinist," Isabella said. "When we first met."

I remembered that, barely. "You said she died during the war. That was Mira?"

"She's still my daughter," Isabella said, and her voice turned salt and bitter from choked-back tears. "No matter how much I wish she were not, she's *still* my daughter." She turned to me. "She saved you. I heard you tell Lucia about that—how she saved you and sent you back to us. She can't help what she does; I understand that. *Please.* You're the only other person here who cares about what happens to her. If you can—"

"I don't know," I said. "Isabella, I can't make any promises."

"Please," she said. "If all the other mages are dead, there will be nothing more she can do. They need the power of many to create the magefire, to do the powerful magery." Remembering the incinerated guards outside my cell in the Fedeli Citadel, I was dubious, but kept silent. "Miriamne can be spared," she said. "She saved your *life*. She told us how to defeat them. She has been fighting for our side as hard as she can—"

"I know," I said.

"Save her, then!"

"I can't make promises."

"Promise to try."

"I will try," I whispered.

Isabella was silent. "I shouldn't have come to you," she said. "Not for this."

"It's all right."

"No. Go back to your tent. I know you'll do what you can." Tears glittered in her eyes again, and she gave me a fierce, hard smile. "Good luck tomorrow, whatever happens. I hope you come through alive."

*   *   *

Mira clasped my hand by the conservatory wall. "We should go on a trip," she said. "Right now."

I shook my head, though I couldn't bear to pull my hand away. "I can't," I said. "I have obligations . . ."

"Dance with me, then," she said, and I clasped her hands and leaned my head against her shoulder, breathing in the scent of winter jasmine. When I raised my head, she was gone; I stood alone by the fountain near the musician's quarters, in the Imperial enclave. There was no one else there; the buildings were empty, completely dark. It was night.

Suddenly, I was struck with the conviction that if I didn't find Mira then, I would never see her again. I kindled witchlight without a moment's hesitation and began to run, calling her name. Though I'd known my way around the enclave fairly well by the time I fled it, they seemed to have rearranged, or perhaps expanded; the building I entered was a maze of hallways and dark doors. "Mira," I shouted. "Mira!"

*   *   *

I woke with a start; for a moment, I thought that Lucia had shaken me awake, or Giovanni, but for once I seemed to have woken myself up without disturbing my companions. I wondered what time it was, knowing that I would not be able to sleep again that night.

Was there any chance that Mira had already fled the enclave? Alone, a mage could pretend to be just a frightened civilian, could slip through the noose and escape. Somehow, though, I knew that Mira wouldn't have done that. She would stay till the end—probably hoping that from her place in the battle, she'd be able to wreak havoc on the other mages' plans. Or perhaps just hoping that she could protect me. There was no guarantee that she'd be the focus-mage who faced me at the gate, but if she fled, she'd know without any doubt that she would not be able to save me.

In her place, I'd have stayed. So I knew she would be there tomorrow.

I wanted with all my heart to protect her, as Isabella had requested. But it was hard enough to protect someone in my own army, like Lucia or Giovanni. It was impossible to protect someone on the other side of the battlefield. Mira was a focus, a mage who could aim her magic with the precision of a hawk's dive; she had demonstrated her ability to choose her targets the night she spared me, Giovanni, Lucia, and Isabella while taking out half of the Lupi. I didn't have that power; I couldn't aim the tide of destruction I was about to unleash.

I closed my eyes, wishing that I could slip back into my dream. Wishing that I could embrace Mira, and run away with her, as I'd failed to do when I'd had the chance. There was no harm in spending my nighttime hours doing what I couldn't possibly do for real. *God, I whispered when sleep didn't come. Please keep Mira safe tomorrow. Somehow.*

*   *   *

We marched at the first gray light of dawn, Lupi followed by the Imperial Army. The sky was rose and gold as we knelt in the rocky hills just south of Cuore. "B'shaem Arkah, v'Bar Shelah, v'Nihor Kadosh," Lucia sang, drawing a cross and raising her arms as if to embrace the two armies. "Our sins are forgiven; God stands with us in our battle. We are the children of God's Holy Light. Amen."

"Amen." The word rolled through the army like water poured down a hill.

I stood and looked around. I couldn't see the ends of my army; soldiers knelt as far as I could see. They looked at me, with loyalty and fear, with contempt and reluctance, with eagerness and innocence. I took a deep breath; there was no way that the soldiers on the edges of the crowd would hear me, but I hoped my words would be relayed back and not garbled too badly.

"In the Name of the Mother," I said. "And Her son, and the Holy Light." I drew a cross, like Lucia. "God has shown us the way to victory. God has held out Her hand; it is for us to grasp it." I looked up at the sky. This wasn't very inspiring. I'd need to do better than this before sending people down this hill to fight and die.

"Some of us fight for our families, slain by the Fedeli

and the Circle in the service of their power," I said. "Some of us fight for the Emperor, and the vows we've spoken binding ourselves to his service." I stepped forward. "Some of us fight for ourselves, to avenge the pain we've endured in the name of the ones we fight. Some of us fight for God, for Her grace and for Her glory.

"We fight for so many reasons that sometimes it's hard to remember that we are all fighting for the same thing—for the same purpose. Because we are *all* fighting for our land. We're fighting for what we see when we close our eyes at night—a Cuore ruled honorably for the sake of the people, not brutally for the sake of power. We're fighting because we know there's a better way than what the Circle has shown us. We're fighting because we know what magefire does, what it will do if the Circle is not stopped. We're fighting because we love *honor,* because we love *justice,* because we want to wake to an Empire that is *ruled* with honor and with justice. We are fighting for *tomorrow.* We are fighting for the tomorrow that we *want* to wake to."

The armies cheered, despite the fact that if you'd asked me an hour earlier, I would have guessed that most of them didn't *actually* see that when they closed their eyes at night. Oh well; maybe they would now.

"God is with us because we fight for honor," I said. "God is with us because we fight for justice. God is with us because we fight for the land." I drew my sword and held it over my head so that even the soldiers in the very back could see it catch the first sun of the day. "God is with us, and with God, we will fight them. With God, we will *defeat* them. With God, we will *bring* the dawn of honor and justice to the Empire.

For the glory of God we will march into Cuore. For the glory of God we will dance in the Light. No magery can stand against us; no mage will stand against us. For the glory of God, today will see the *final* defeat of the Circle!"

The cheer of the armies became a roar like approaching thunder, and I knew that the Circle heard us in the city below. I sheathed my sword and mounted my horse, and the signalers blew a blast on their trumpets. There was no turning back now. It was time to take Cuore.

* * *

Giovanni claimed that walls had once been built around the whole city of Cuore, not just the Imperial enclave; they were used for defense, in the days before magefire. In the years after the fall of the Old Empire, the city grew and spilled past the crumbling fortifications, and the walls were slowly dismantled for building materials. "Good thing for us," Giovanni said. "It's going to be hard enough getting into the enclave, never mind breaching any extra walls."

We attacked the city from three sides, closing like a noose around the Circle and the Fedeli. Cuore rose slowly out of the edges of the valley, farms giving way to huts, then small houses, then shops and old stone buildings. The civilians of Cuore had fled in earlier weeks, leaving the city to the Fedeli and the Circle.

The enclave walls were not terribly high or thick. They had not been built to withstand a real attack; they had been built to keep out the riffraff of Cuore. Still, even with the Circle's magic neutralized, Fedeli crossbows could keep us from scrambling up the walls more or less indefinitely. They had walled up all but the main gate, which was strong enough to stand against anything we could throw at it. And an extended siege was not practical; the dancers would drop dead from exhaustion trying to protect us day and night. We would have victory in a day, or we would retreat and try again another time.

Michel was leading some of our best scouts through the Emperor's secret sewer tunnel. The rest of us, for now, were just creating a distraction—though if Michel and the others failed in their mission, the distraction might become the backup plan.

A university education turned out to have its uses; Placido's backup plan was evidence of that. In the days before magery, everyone had used walls for protection, and armies had been forced to find ways to deal with them. In one of his old books, Placido had found a picture and building instructions for a device called a catapult said to be good for breaking down walls when you hit your target, and killing a great many people when you missed. Builders in the Emperor's service had constructed several duplicates for us, and it seemed to work reasonably well in tests. I had watched a demonstration a month earlier. "Back my first year at the conservatory, I had a teacher who kept poor order at meals," I'd said, watching the catapult. "I used to take a spoon and smack it to throw bits of food at Bella."

"Yeah, I did that at the university, too," Giovanni said. "Same principle."

I accompanied the first catapult that we dragged in through the streets; its purpose was distraction, and my presence could only serve to make it more so. Giovanni accompanied us as well. Between the dancers and the catapult, our progress was slow but inexorable.

Heavy smoke choked me as we worked our way through the streets; Cuore was burning. It was the smell of the ashes of my family's village, but now it was my side that had set the fires, burning out pockets of enemy soldiers who had hidden in houses in the city, planning to attack us from behind. The sun was incongruously bright through the smoke-haze, casting sharp morning shadows on the paving-stones and glinting off the window-glass in the better houses.

We reached the center of town. Flames leapt from the high roof of the Cathedral of the Lady; the stained-glass windows were shattered from the heat of the fire. Dead soldiers and Lupi lay scattered through the piazza, including some dance-circles that had been incinerated with magefire when the musician had been shot. We moved the catapult into position. There were three dance-circles in the piazza already, giving us overlapping circles of protection. Along the wall, I could see Fedeli bowmen gesturing wildly for others to join them. Some seemed to be pointing at me. The catapult offered some shelter, and I ducked behind it, speeding up the dance. Giovanni stood beside me, watching the wall. "Who taught those people to fight?" he said. "They're running around like scared ducks."

A rain of crossbow bolts came down. "Some ducks," said one of the soldiers.

The arm of the catapult had to be cranked back, which took time. Six soldiers working together lifted a boulder into the cup of the catapult, then one blew a whistle to warn everyone to get clear. When the catapult released the rock, the catapult would be thrown backward. "Now!"

The catapult arm snapped forward, launching the rock high over the wall. "Damn," Giovanni said.

"It doesn't really matter if we hit the wall or not," I said.

At the edge of the wall, I was fairly certain I could see a mage. Fire suddenly blossomed overhead like a swirling red flower. I focused the power of the dance up and out, and the fire scattered like leaves in a wind, fading to yellow and gray.

"Rachamin Arkah," the dancers sang, breathless. "Rachamin Gèsu."

The soldiers had loaded a second boulder. This one missed the wall as well, flying just over it. We were aiming high, not wanting to risk taking out our own troops. "We'll get it next time," the soldier said to me. I nodded. Crossbow bolts fell again; some of the dancers fell this time, and the uninjured dancers scrambled to re-form their circle. The faces around me grew rigid and set, but no one broke and ran. From the sheltered area behind the piazza, more dancers joined us.

Where's Michel, dammit?

"Come on," Giovanni urged the soldier cranking back the catapult arm.

"Shut up, Generale," the soldier said.

The soldier blew on his whistle and launched the third rock. The aim was true, and Fedeli bowmen scrambled frantically out of the way. The boulder smashed into the wall—but bounced off, leaving the wall still intact.

"This will work. It'll just take a few more," the soldier said.

But that was when we heard shouts, and the triumphant blast of a trumpet. Michel had opened the gate.

"Go," I shouted.

I thrust my violin into its case and slung it across my

back, drawing my sword. I had yet to become more than barely competent at swordplay, but I felt better having it in my hand during battles. Giovanni waited, his eyes flicking urgently along the wall. "With the dancing broken up, any mage who keeps his head will head straight for this wall," he said. "You have to hurry."

"I'm done," I said, and we started to run around the edge of the enclave toward the open gate. I felt like I had after I started the uprising in Ravenna—swept along by a river of anger and excitement, no more able to command my army than I could command a storm. I was not Eliana la Generale, I was wind, or lightning.

"Hey, Eliana," Giovanni called, and then whatever he was about to say was cut off in a cry of pain. I whirled to see Giovanni collapse to the ground, his knees folding under him.

"Giovanni!" I shoved my sword back into its sheath and dropped to the ground beside him.

Giovanni's eyes were closed, his breath coming in shaky gasps, but he was saying something, and as I leaned close, I could hear it: "Lady's tits, Lady's tits, Lady's tits—"

There was a crossbow bolt deep in the muscle of his left arm. "I've got good news for you, Giovanni," I said. "You're going to get a chance to repent your blasphemy."

Giovanni swallowed hard. "It's minor?"

"I know it doesn't feel minor."

Giovanni forced his eyes open to squint up at me. "You're laughing at me."

"No. It hurts like hell and it missed your heart by inches, right? I'm not laughing at you. *All* my injuries have been minor and they still hurt like hell. Grab my shoulder." Giovanni obeyed, and I hauled him to his feet. "Let's get you over to that corner." The edge of a smoke-drenched building would give us something of a screen from the bowmen. Giovanni let me drag him over, and I lowered him to the ground again as gently as I could.

Giovanni still clasped my shoulder. "Hold still," I said, and snapped off the shaft of the arrow. Giovanni screamed and his hand clenched around my shoulder hard enough to leave a bruise.

"I'm going to have to push it through," I said.

"Can't someone else—"

"Don't you trust my healing?"

"I trust you," Giovanni said, managing to meet my eye with a faint smile. "But don't you want someone else to get bruised this time?"

"There's no one else handy," I said, and put my sword hilt in his hand. "Squeeze that, if you'd rather."

"I'd rather make you suffer along with me," Giovanni said, but he kept his hand on the sword hilt. "Do it, then."

It was a good thing he said that, because I was about to lose my nerve. I pushed the shaft through with the flat of my palm, as fast as I could. Giovanni screamed again. I pulled the last of it out. The arrow had broken cleanly; there shouldn't be any splinters left in the wound. I ripped a piece off my tunic and bound up his arm.

"It's too bad you didn't get shot back when I still hated you," I said. "It would've been a lot more fun to hurt you."

"Yeah, I'm sure," Giovanni said. "Does that mean you don't hate me anymore?" He opened his eyes again; they glinted with tears of pain.

"I haven't hated you for ages," I said.

"Do you like me?" he asked.

"Don't push it. You need to move; we're still in the middle of a battle, you know."

Giovanni stood shakily and drew his sword. "I can fight," he said. "It wasn't my sword-arm that was hurt."

"Trying to prove your manliness?" I asked.

"Oh, shut up. Some of us have a battle to win."

We swarmed into the enclave like wasps, terrified Fedeli priests scattering from our path. The trumpeter blasted a signal, *to the Circle's Citadel*. We made our way through the smoke. My eyes were watering, and I saw the gardens through a blurred haze. I hardly recognized where I was, but the Circle's enclave would be ahead and to my left. I touched my violin once or twice to be sure that I hadn't lost it.

The Circle had fortified their building as much as they possibly could, and laid in supplies for a siege, just in case we could come up with a way to wage one. Placido's machine was not going to work against these walls, but that was all right; I had another idea. I ducked into one of the circles of dancers that danced by the edge of the Circle's fortress. The piazza was thick with dancers. We spread out around the fortress, making room as more circles arrived. Frustrated mages occasionally threw magefire at us, but it sparkled harmlessly off the edge of our circles.

"Now," I said, and raised my whistle to my lips, blowing a single long blast. Every circle dropped hands, flattened into a line, and reclasped hands to form a single vast circle around the entire building.

Flavia pounded out a drumbeat that echoed through the streets, even over the noise of the battle, and I started to play. *Rachimin Arkah—Rachimin Gèsu*. This was the dance that turned the storm; this was the dance that turned back magefire. *Rachamin Arkah.* The power surged around me and through me, like a river, an ocean, a hurricane. *Rachamin Gèsu.* I stretched out my arms, holding my violin and bow out like dagger and sword, my fists to the sky, and I focused the power on the walls. *This is the dance that crumbles walls.* I heard thunder, or the roaring in my ears. The barricaded doors and windows of the fortress blew open with force enough to knock back anyone who'd stood too close, with the crack of split wood and broken stone. *Burn,* I said to the walls, and I could smell bitter smoke, hear cries of fear from inside. *Burn, like you burned my family. Burn, all of you, burn.*

We broke our circle to let soldiers into the building. I shoved my violin into its case and drew my sword, following the soldiers in. The Circle had designed their fortifications to keep us out, not to provide themselves with escape routes. They had worked out strategies to fight us if we got inside, but the strategies were easy to guess and exploit. If they used magefire, they'd kill their own. If they didn't use magefire, they'd never stand against us. They were trapped.

The hallways were narrow and so at first I found myself behind a knot of people, with more pushing from behind. Members of the Circle Guard had blocked the hallway; the knot broke loose as they turned and fled. I was swept quickly past the remains of the fight, scattered bodies and slippery blood. The mages would be upstairs, with the guard down here to protect them. I headed for the staircase, backing off as a gout of sudden flame billowed down the stone spiral. It was only one mage, maybe two, but I frantically gestured the approaching soldiers to stand back. I yanked out my violin and started to play, loud enough for the sound to carry upstairs. Some of the soldiers formed a clumsy dance circle, but it hardly mattered. The mage couldn't see around the curve and fled at the sound of the music.

Dancers and other musicians arrived and began forming dance circles in the Circle's Great Hall, so I shoved my violin away and drew my sword again, charging up the steps. The mage had fled ahead of our advance, and the staircase opened onto a long hallway of closed doors. "Knock them down," I ordered.

The doors had been barricaded, but one after another they collapsed in on themselves. I ran to the end of the hallway, following Lupi through that door. The room was dark and quiet, and richly furnished. "Is there anyone here?" the man beside me asked.

"Search," I said.

That room led to another room, and then another, this one brightly lit. I came in and saw a blue-robed man raising his hands to summon magefire, his eyes closed. It would take a moment for the fire to come, and I ran forward, slamming my sword into his gut. He cried out, his fire dissolving like red mist. I pulled my sword out and he slipped to the floor.

"Give me a clean death, damn you," he choked out. "Don't leave me like this."

I drew back my sword to cut his throat, then paused. "Open your eyes, old man," I said. "Look at me. *Liemo.* Look at me."

The mage who had held me hostage—who had forced Mira to return to the Circle—opened his eyes and squinted at me through his pain. "Do I know you?"

"You should," I said. "You made me your prisoner.

You tried to have me maimed. And you took from me the woman I loved most in the world."

Liemo's eyes widened slightly. "You're Miriamne's friend, aren't you?"

"I am Eliana," I said. "Generale of the Lupi and, yes. Mira's friend."

Liemo's lips twitched into almost a smile and he motioned for me to bend closer. I leaned down. "Do you want your friend?" he whispered. "She's not here. She slipped away just before the battle. I don't know where she went."

"What makes you think I want to find her?" I said.

Liemo laughed, then flinched from the pain. "The woman you loved most in the world?" He shook his head. "Do as you please, girl, but give me a decent death first. I'm sorry I took your friend, and I'm sorry I threatened you. It was—necessary." He closed his eyes and turned his face away from me.

I braced my sword briefly against his chest, then thrust it into his heart. He gave a brief jerk, then was still. I wiped my sword on his robes and then stood, dazed. The Lupi waited, watching me.

"Search the rest of the room," I said. "Kill any mages you find." I sheathed my sword and stumbled back down the stairs.

Outside, the air was gray with smoke and dust. I had seen enough battles now to know we would win. There were Fedeli soldiers and Circle Guards stumbling through the haze, crying threats and searching for their fellows, but most had fled or fallen. I wandered toward the gardens. They had been trampled in the fighting; I could see scattered bits of rosebush and leaves of flowers that would have bloomed yellow and white in a few weeks. As I looked around at the devastation, I heard music. It was just a few notes, very faint, on a wisp of a breeze that stirred the dust and blew more choking smoke into my face. There was music all around me, but this was not a Redentore song. Straining to hear, I caught another snatch of music on the breeze.

I wound my way through to the other side of the gardens, into the shadows of the buildings that had once housed guards, servants, and musicians. The fighting had left this part of the enclave almost untouched. No one was here, though I saw a terrified guardsman who cried out and fled when he saw me. I ignored him. The doors of the musicians' dormitory stood open; inside was shadowed and hazy with stray smoke, but oddly peaceful. The music was louder here—I could identify the music now. Finger exercises. I stepped carefully around the corner, as quietly as I could, but Mira heard me, and the music changed. *Rachamin Arkah. Rachamin Gèsu.* I slipped the door open.

Mira was alone.

She stood by the shuttered window, her back to me. She finished the song and lowered her violin and bow, holding them slack at her sides. "Hello, Eliana," she said, still not turning around.

"Mira," I said.

Mira turned, and met my eyes. She set her violin and bow down and reached her hands out to grip mine. I stepped forward, grasping her hands with my own, and she pulled me toward her, her lips soft against mine. I wrapped my arms around her, my heart pounding. Mira broke the kiss and pushed me away. Her eyes were frightened but resolute, and they burned with dark fire.

"Go ahead and kill me," she said. "Just make it fast."

I shook my head. "I'm not—"

"You have no choice. Please." She closed her eyes for a moment, then opened them to look at me again. "I mean it. I'm as much a prisoner to magery as you were to the Fedeli. You have no choice. If you want to destroy the Circle, you have to kill me." Her eyes scorched through me to the soles of my feet.

I drew my sword. Mira clasped my face and pulled it to hers again. I felt her breath mix with mine, the heat from her cheeks. Touching Mira was like drawing the power of a thousand dancers; my head spun and I could see light like a million stars. She took my hand and drew the tip of my sword to her heart. I felt her tense, and brace herself—

I jerked my sword back as Mira threw herself forward, catching her with my other arm before she could fall. "The destruction of the Circle is nothing to me if it doesn't mean your freedom. Mira. I will not kill you. If you have the will to die for me, you have the will to defeat magery again. I know your heart. Some things are stronger than magefire."

Mira swallowed once, and I saw her cheeks grow pale. I picked up her violin and bow and put them in the case that lay on the floor. She made no move to take the case, so I slipped the strap over her shoulder. I would need to hide her robes somehow; I glanced around the empty room, then opened her violin case again, shaking out the blanket that padded the violin inside and wrapping it around her shoulders. "You'll have to carry your violin in your arms," I said. Mira took the violin as I handed it to her, but made no other movement. "Come on," I said. "I'm getting you out of Cuore."

The enclave was awash with smoke, dust, and blood; the haze rose red from the streets. I slipped one arm around Mira, pulled her arm over my shoulder; I would look like someone assisting an injured companion. I ducked my head to hide my face, but I didn't see anyone looking at us. Mira played the part of a wounded soldier well enough, stumbling through the streets like someone drunk and blind.

The fight was in the center of Cuore; the edge of Cuore looked like the battlefield's frayed hem. Fleeing Circle guardsmen and Fedeli, terrified Lupi and Imperial soldiers, had flung themselves down here to catch their breath. The air had begun to clear, and you could see that Cuore was cloaked in swaths of thick smoke. Most important, there were riderless horses that had found their way here from the battle. They were skittish, but I managed to persuade one to come to me, and to let Mira take the reins.

"Go," I said.

Mira started to mount the horse, then turned back. "Why did you save me?" she whispered.

I took Mira's face in my hands and gave her one last gentle kiss. "You know why," I said. "Go."

*   *   *

By evening, the dust had settled, and a gentle rain put out the smoldering fires. The enclave was secured. The mages and Fedeli, slaughtered. I went to find Isabella, and discovered that she was among the dead; so were Severo and the mad prophet, Amedeo. I felt as lost as I had the night I returned to the ruins of my village. We had won.

PART FOUR

Then Follow Me

CHAPTER FOURTEEN

*Those that live by the sword will
die by the sword.*
—*The Journey of Gèsu, chapter 11, verse 23.*

"Clara, a word with you."

The enclave's gardens had come through the battle for Cuore surprisingly well. Two months after the war had ended, there were no flowers in the garden, but many would bloom again next year. In the meantime, damaged benches and fountains had been repaired, to allow for precisely this sort of informal mingling, maneuvering, and toadying.

"Of course, Eliana, I'm always happy to spend time with you." Clara sat down at the edge of the fountain, gesturing for me to join her. She wore the dark blue dress that had become the uniform of the Servi, with a huge jeweled cross. Though it was a hot day, she seemed perfectly comfortable: no sweat on her dress, and not a hair out of place.

"I understand Valentino has somehow gotten in trouble with the Servi again," I said, sitting down.

"Has he." Clara's eyes were distant as she toyed with her cross.

"Yes. It seems that someone interpreted the phrase

'Lady's tits' as a fervent prayer. That seems odd to me. Is this the sort of enforcement your people usually engage in?"

"I imagine there were some ... less-than-mitigating circumstances, perhaps?" Clara said.

"I'm confident that it was all just a misunderstanding," I said. "Would you look into it for me?"

"I'd be glad to," Clara said.

"Also, you know," I said, "this is the third or fourth time that Valentino has been in trouble? It was only two months ago that we took Cuore. Each time it's been for something truly petty. I'm sure the vast majority of the Servi don't use their office to pursue personal grudges, but ..."

"Are you saying that Valentino is being targeted?" Clara said, her bright eyes widening slightly.

I raised my hands in a calming gesture. "All I'm saying is that Valentino is a boy who is skilled at raising the ire of powerful people. Not that anyone would *mean* to target him, of course, but perhaps in Valentino's case, there might be someone who genuinely doesn't realize that they're motivated by personal dislike?"

"Perhaps," Clara muttered.

"Well. I'm sure you can resolve it. There's no need to bring this to the attention of the Emperor."

Clara's head jerked toward me. "I'm sure you don't really think it's so serious?"

"Servi misusing their power for personal gain? I would think *that* would be serious, don't you? But so long as this doesn't come up again, I'm sure we can assume that's not it."

"Of course," Clara said. Her voice could have frozen hot tea. "Was that all, Eliana?"

"Yes," I said. "That was all."

"Then perhaps you might take a moment for me," Clara said, her manner becoming ingratiating again. "People have noticed ... well, as you said, it's been two months. Yet you continue to dress in men's clothing."

I looked down at my wine-red tunic and hose. I'd traded in the trousers and rough tunic that I'd worn as a soldier for soft fabrics in rich colors, but I had indeed continued to wear men's clothes. "Yes," I said.

"I was wondering if you might like the name of a good dressmaker? Mine is excellent, and ..."

I laughed out loud, and quickly controlled myself. "Excuse me. No, Clara, I don't think that's necessary. I'm really quite comfortable in these."

"I only raise this because it's begun to cause a little bit of trouble," Clara said.

This was new to me. "What sort of trouble?"

Clara considered her words carefully before she continued. "Some twenty of the younger ladies of the court have taken up your fashion."

I'd heard rumors about these women, but nothing clear. I stifled a smile. "How is this trouble?" I asked.

"They are refusing to wed," Clara said stiffly.

I raised one eyebrow. "Show me where Gèsu says marriage is required," I said. "He never married."

"That's what these young women say."

"I'd say they've got a point," I said. "If they don't want to marry, well, I hate to disappoint you, Clara, but I'm behind them all the way. Now if you'll excuse me, I'm meeting some people for lunch." I headed back toward the palace.

There was a low chuckle from the shadows as I rounded the edge of the garden, and I turned to see Giovanni. "You'd better watch your tongue around her, Eliana," he said. "Just think how much it would please

Clara to have you prosecuted if you ever say 'Lady's tits.' "

I glared at Giovanni. "She wouldn't dare."

"If she thought she could get away with it, she'd do it in a heartbeat," he said.

"Are you coming up for lunch?"

"Of course. I came looking for you and was fortunate enough to overhear your conversation."

My room in the Imperial Palace looked out over the gardens. I arrived just as the servant brought up our lunch: a tray of cheese, bread, and cold roast mutton. Lucia helped herself to bread and cheese while Giovanni sliced the meat. I looked out at the gardens; they were still crowded, despite the heat of the day.

Lucia finished her lunch and leaned back in her chair, fanning herself with a fan of woven palm fronds. "Did you get Valentino out of trouble again?"

"Yes," I said. "This time."

"Thank God we have the Servi to protect us from threats like Valentino, eh Lucia?" Giovanni asked.

Lucia shot Giovanni a bitter look. "Not all the new Redentori religious orders are like the Servi. Flavia's order is nothing like them."

"The Cantatori," I said. Flavia and some of the other musicians and dancers who had served with the Lupi had started a religious order of their own.

"Well, maybe if Flavia ran the Servi they'd be less of a pain in the ass," Giovanni said.

"Much less," I said. "Flavia would tell them that as committed Redentori, they should dance the Mass at least once every day, and not worry about what everyone else was doing."

"Would they even be the Servi if they weren't sticking their nose in everyone else's business?" Giovanni asked.

"Not for long, and I think that would be a good thing." I pushed my chair back from the table. "Is summer in Cuore always this hot? I could swear it never felt this hot at the conservatory."

"Go get yourself a fan," Lucia said. "There was a boy selling them just outside the gate yesterday."

From a distance, I could hear bells striking the hour. "Maybe later," I said, standing up. "Council meeting today."

"Oh, lucky you," Giovanni said. "You get to talk to Clara twice in one day."

"And Placido; don't forget Placido."

"You can have my fan if you'd like," Lucia said. "I can go get another one."

"Oh, no," I said. "I think it would be too tempting to use it to swat Placido."

The Imperial Council was a council of advisors; the Emperor did not have to take our advice, which was just as well since we never agreed on anything. I had come to really hate Council meetings. Clara was on the Council, of course. So were Demetrio and Placido; there were also three others who I hadn't met before the war ended: Romolo, Manlio, and Benvenuto. Benvenuto was a scholar from the university, but much older than Placido; he was reedy, with thin lips and white hair. Manlio was from a merchant family on the coast, and Romolo was from some noble family that had supported Travan early on. Clara and Placido were by far the most vocal Council members, and I felt outnumbered and outargued. Half the time I suspected that Travan agreed with me but didn't have the backbone to stand up to Clara and Placido. The person I most often found myself agreeing with was Demetrio, but Demetrio was married to Clara, and his initial agreement often turned out to be part of her strategy.

The Council chamber was lavishly furnished, with a thick patterned rug on the floor, velvet-covered chairs, glass windows, and a long table topped with inlaid marble. Today the windows had been propped open, but the room was stiflingly hot, and I immediately wished I'd accepted Lucia's offer of a fan. Clara was already there when I arrived, still looking perfectly composed. She had a fan of jet-black feathers, and she fanned herself gently, lost in thought. I pressed my damp palms against the cool marble, wishing I could just lay my whole face down on it.

Demetrio arrived just after I did. I sat to the Emperor's left; Demetrio sat to his right. Clara sat at the opposite end of the table. Demetrio greeted me politely and then sat down with a barely suppressed yawn. "Sorry," he mumbled. "It's the heat." Benvenuto came in, deep in conversation with Manlio, and Romolo came in a few moments later, carrying a fan like Lucia's. Placido arrived last, his face so red from the heat he looked sunburned. There was a rustle at the door: Emperor Travan. In unison, we stood; Travan came in, sat down, and nodded, and we all sat back down again.

Most of the day's business was tedious beyond words: a pair of noble houses in Varena were squabbling over something involving restrictions on certain imports. I barely understood why these imports were restricted in the first place, though Placido seemed to find this deeply interesting and had a long argument over it with Manlio. Demetrio, at least, looked as bored as I felt. I wished

Giovanni were on the Council; he would actually have some understanding of the trade issues we discussed, and he could back me up against Clara and Placido.

Watching Travan as he listened to Placido arguing with Manlio, I thought that he had aged in the last two months. I wondered if the privilege of leadership had been more appealing in the abstract than in reality. I had to duck my head and compose my features at the thought. Travan wasn't the first person to discover that leadership wasn't always as much fun as it looked, and he probably would not be the last.

A fly was buzzing around the room; it kept trying to land on my sweaty head. When it buzzed around the Emperor's head, he made a gesture of annoyance and a servant came in to try to swat it. At least this gave me something more entertaining to watch than Placido's increasingly red face. The servant chased the fly around the room twice before finally shooing it out a window. Of course, a new fly found its way in moments later. I wondered if Travan was going to order the windows shut, but to my relief, he didn't.

My legs itched from my hose, and I found myself thinking longingly of the looser clothes I'd worn as generale of the Lupi. I wondered if maybe I should have taken Clara up on her offer of a dressmaker; a dress, today, sounded rather more comfortable than what I was wearing. I glanced toward the other end of the table. Clara's feather fan had sped up slightly, and her face and hair were starting to look damp.

The argument over the squabbling noble houses petered out, and Travan looked down at some papers of notes. "Demetrio," he said. "Did you have an issue you wanted to discuss?"

Demetrio nodded. "Vesuvia." He looked around the table. "We haven't heard any rumors about them moving toward the border, but we can't assume our luck will hold."

"What would they gain from attacking us?" Romolo asked.

"Well, revenge, for one thing," Demetrio said. "There was a great deal of bitterness over the last war, and it was our Circle that started it."

This was news to me and to Romolo; no one else seemed surprised. "What about the villages?" I blurted out. "The villages in Verdia that were burned?"

Demetrio's face was impassive. "There were burned-out villages in Vesuvia, as well. It's hard to say who started the raids, but the first major blow was struck by our side."

I sat back, remembering Mira's flare of anger when I said the whole war had been over a perfume ingredient. I wondered if she'd known that our side started it. *All that suffering,* I thought, *for something so trivial, and we were the ones who started it.*

Demetrio was speaking again. "Without mages to defend us, they will assume we are easy prey. So far as I know, they still have a Circle."

"We beat our own Circle, we can beat theirs," I mumbled.

"They must have heard stories about what our faith can do," Clara said. "Don't you think their mages will be too frightened to approach us?"

"I don't think we can count on that," Demetrio said.

"They'll have to cross the wasteland first," I said. "Our Circle was terrified of the wasteland; I can't imagine that their Circle feels differently."

"Now, if we could just make the wasteland a bit harder for their army to cross," Clara said, thoughtfully.

"What are you talking about?" I said. "The wall? It was nowhere near complete."

"Our ancestors built far more complex roads and canals," Placido said. "Certainly if *we* wished to complete the wall, we could see it done."

"Are you volunteering to go build, Placido?" I asked. Everyone laughed, even Clara; Placido's red face turned purple and he forced out a laugh as well. Then he shot a look at Travan.

"Tell me more about the wall," Travan said. "How close is it to done?"

I spoke before anyone else could answer. "It's barely started," I said. "Seven short lengths have been constructed. There are miles and miles between each length. The slave camps were at work for about half a year. It would take a very long time to complete at that rate. If the Vesuviani move against us any time in the next ten years, it will not be sufficient protection."

"It couldn't hurt to *try* to complete it," Placido said. "If we devoted more resources to the construction, we could move up the timetable significantly."

"It wouldn't hurt whom?" I said. "Who, exactly, were you thinking of sending?" I remember Mario's comment, back in Ravenna—that if the Circle wanted a wall, they should hire laborers to go build it. With a high enough wage, I had no doubt that they would get volunteers. However, after war, famine, and civil war, the Empire's treasury was not exactly filled with piles of glittering gold.

"I realize that this is a painful subject for you, Generale Eliana," Clara said cautiously. "And of course the wholesale enslavement of the farmers on the border was entirely wrong. However, the war against the Circle has left us with a certain population of people who find themselves with very little to do ..." She paused and tapped her fan against the table thoughtfully. "I think some time in the wasteland, where the futility of depending on the Lady can be fully contemplated, might be deeply beneficial to certain people."

"You're talking about re-creating the slave labor camps, but enslaving the priests and priestesses who served the Lady," I said. Clara smiled and began to fan herself again. "And anyone else who refuses to convert, no doubt. And when that's not enough, anyone who fails to embrace the Redentori faith at your level of orthodoxy."

"If we need to imprison people, I see no reason that we shouldn't get useful work out of them," Clara said. "Do you, Your Highness?"

I turned to the Emperor, biting my lip to resist the urge to interrupt. He saw my agitation and nodded, giving me permission to speak.

"Highness, it may begin with the priests and priestesses of the Lady, but there won't be enough of them to complete this task. There won't be enough open Della Chiese to complete this task. Sooner or later, she will be sending down people like—like the Priestess Lucia."

Clara laughed out loud "Oh, be serious, Generale Eliana. The Priestess Lucia and I have had our disagreements, but I hardly think it's fair to say that I would send her into exile."

Emperor Travan shrugged and turned back to me. "So how would you propose that we protect ourselves from the Vesuviani?"

"Well, first, I think we need more current and accurate intelligence than a suspicion that they *might* want to take revenge on us," I said. "I think someone needs to go down there."

"Are you volunteering?" Placido asked.

It was a measure of how much I hated court that for a moment, that prospect sounded appealing. But Travan shook his head. "No, Eliana is too recognizable to go as a spy. But it's not a bad idea. What if we find out that yes, they are massing against us?"

I paused to think about it. "When I was in Ravenna, I played for the funeral dance of the two executed reformers, Beneto and Jesca. This was before I knew the full power of the dances, but I remember the energy; to avert a riot, I pulled the energy down into the ground under my feet. That night, I realized that I could make a witchlight again—barely, with effort, but I could do it." I looked around the Council. "I think that the Empire should create some permanent installments in the wasteland, but not prisons. Create communities for dedicated Redentori; so long as they're housed and fed, I think you'll find volunteers." It occurred to me that Flavia's order, the Cantatori, would probably like this idea. "They can dance each day to restore the wasteland; over time, perhaps plants will flourish again. And in the meantime, they can keep watch on the border and fend off enemy magery. They would need detachments of soldiers as well, of course. A few communities like this, dotted along the border, would be far more protection than a wall."

"What do you think of that idea, Clara?" Travan asked.

Clara opened her mouth. "I think it's a terrible idea," she said immediately. She paused to gather her thoughts—or, I rather suspected, to dredge up some reasons. "It's a terrible risk for the Redentori, living right on the border like that."

"These would be volunteers," Travan said. "Your protective feelings are admirable, of course. Go on."

"You're talking about the creation of an entire religious order," Clara said. "A new one."

"Or the expansion of an existing one, like the Cantatori," I said.

"I don't think that's a good idea."

"Because they might challenge the power of the Servi?"

"Of course not!" Clara was pricked into vehemence for a moment, then sat back and summoned her kindest smile. "The proliferation of orders was something that weakened the Della Chiese. I think we can learn from their mistakes."

"To be sure. Why do you think it weakened them?"

"There were rivalries," Placido said, coming to Clara's rescue. "Factionalism. Precisely the sort of problems that the Servi were created to prevent."

"God forbid that any of us should disagree, after all," I said.

"Well, exactly," Placido said. "I don't think God wants us to disagree."

I shot a look at the Emperor, wondering if he saw how self-serving Clara's argument was. I thought he probably did. Lowering his eyes, he plucked at the braid on his sleeve. "Priestess Clara, I understand your concerns, but Eliana's idea seems to be so beneficial in so many ways I can't possibly disregard it."

I was hoping that Travan would appoint someone like Flavia or Lucia to create the wasteland guard posts, but Clara immediately said, "Well, though I disagree with the idea, of course I obey your command, Your Highness, and the Servi will begin setting up communities of Redentori immediately."

Travan's eyes flickered to me; I wanted to protest, to say that the Cantatori were far better suited to the task than the Servi, but he said, "As you wish. Demetrio, I will ask you to find someone who can spy out the territory of the Vesuviani. In the meantime, I think this meeting is concluded."

We rose as the Emperor left, then made our own way out. As I straightened my tunic and fought the urge to pluck at the hose, which were sticking to my legs in a really awkward way, I noticed that Clara was looking at me. It was not a venomous glare, of course; Clara would never have been so careless. It was a cool look of veiled patience. Like a cat, I thought. Stalking her prey. I bit my lip and looked away.

* * *

I couldn't sleep that night, and after a while I got up and lit a candle. I was very careful not to use witchlight in Cuore, though it was tempting sometimes. The ceiling of my room seemed very high at night, with only candlelight to flicker into the vaulted corners. The darkness frightened me when I woke from dreams full of blood and fire; I found myself wanting to summon witchlight, to see my room in a pure steady light that shone in every corner and didn't dance in the breeze of my breath. Since I couldn't do that, I stumbled out of the huge soft bed and went to sit in the window, instead. The moonlight comforted me, along with the knowledge that the garden was there.

There had been no nightmares that night—no sleep at all. *It's the heat,* I thought, fanning my linen nightshirt as I stood by the window. *Maybe I could sleep if I went and lay down next to one of the fountains in the garden.* I laughed a little at the thought.

I liked my room fine during the day, but at night the palace was too quiet. The stone walls deadened sound in a way that cloth tent walls hadn't. Living in the Lupi encampment, I was always surrounded by thousands of people, and some nights I thought I could hear most of them snoring. Even at the conservatory, except for the three-month gap between Lia and Mira, I'd always had a roommate. Mira had talked in her sleep on occasion. Lia had snored.

After a while, I blew out my candle and curled up in the window seat. It was strange, but sometimes I wished I could have just gone on living with the Lupi. Not that I would have wanted a never-ending war, but if I could have somehow created a village of my closest friends and allies, and spent the rest of my life living in a tent— well, it was a strange thing to find appealing, but I would have liked it better than court. Of course, once the war was over, the Lupi had scattered. The ones with homes had returned to them. Of the others, some had gone to resettle villages like Doratura, as I'd suggested. A few had settled in Cuore—Giovanni and Lucia, of course, and Michel, who was still the Emperor's bodyguard. There were the Cantatori, of course, and some Lupi had joined the city guard. But for the most part, my army was gone.

I felt guilty for feeling such a loss; we'd won the war, after all, and they had the right to enjoy the fruits of their struggle. Still, as I drifted off to sleep in the cushions of the window seat, I wished I could hear birds, at least, and the wind through the trees.

*   *   *

"Let's run away," Mira said. "You've got your violin with you, I've got mine. What more do we need? We could just jump over the wall and go."

I looked out over Bascio. But instead of the tiny village I remembered from the conservatory, I saw the Imperial gardens and the tightly packed buildings of Cuore. "Run away?" I said. "But everyone I know is here. Lucia and Giovanni, the Emperor—"

" 'If you would journey with me,' " Mira quoted, " 'Turn your back on your home, on your comforts, on all that you know. Then follow me.' "

I shook my head. "I don't know."

"It would be an adventure, Eliana!" Mira said. "We could see the world together." She clasped my hand and fell silent, looking into my eyes. My heart started knocking in my ears as I returned her gaze. Then she dropped my hand and clambered over the wall. "Let's go."

I started to follow her, but my feet wouldn't move. I couldn't cross the wall. Mira was already heading down the road. "Wait!" I called after her, but she didn't turn back. I knew it was useless, but I called again, "Wait! I want to come with you!"

*   *   *

I woke in the darkness, convinced beyond reason that if I hurried, I would find Mira waiting in the garden below. Unwilling to question my own conviction, I threw a light cloak over my nightshirt and thrust my bare feet into my boots. My heart pounding, I eased my door shut and ran down the stairs and out into the garden.

No one was there. I sat down at the edge of the fountain and waited for a long time, listening to the splash of the water. I finally made my way back up to my room just before dawn.

CHAPTER FIFTEEN

*There is no greater love than that of the one
who gives his life for his friend.*
—*The Journey of Gèsu, chapter 45, verse 29.*

It was perhaps a month later that I first heard the rumor from Giovanni. The heat had eased somewhat, and we had met early in the morning for a practice session at the enclave training ground. This was not a part of the enclave I'd ever seen as "Daniele," but noblemen could practice their skills as swordsmen in the comfort of an enclosed courtyard. Giovanni tossed me a sword and we worked together for an hour or so, stopping when the sun rose high enough to really get uncomfortable. Sitting down in the shade, we drank cooled tea and watched some of the others who were still at work. By virtue of regular practice, I was—according to Giovanni when he was feeling magnanimous—almost as good with a sword as he'd been when Placido had kicked his ass back in his early days as a student.

"I don't know why I do this to myself," I said, putting down the cup of cold tea and stretching until my back cracked.

"It's for my scintillating conversation," Giovanni

said, slouching next to me and refilling his cup. "Or else you're keeping yourself in good form in case you get to lead another war. I can't decide."

"Maybe it's in case I ever have to fight a duel with Placido."

"Better have me fight it for you, if this comes up anytime soon," Giovanni said. "He may look like a pig, but he's faster with a sword than you'd expect."

"He beat you, after all."

"Exactly. Though that was a long time ago."

Giovanni took another swig of the tea, then checked carefully to see if anyone was close enough to overhear our conversation. "There's a rumor going around about you," he said. "Supposedly you were seen, toward the end of the battle for Cuore, spiriting someone out of the city."

I bit my lip and looked away from Giovanni, watching the men who were still training out in the sun. "Really," I said, when I trusted my voice to stay even.

"Yes, really," Giovanni said. "Who was it?"

"I don't know what you're talking about," I said.

Giovanni stood up abruptly and went to put away the training equipment. When he returned, he sat down closer to me and said, "The person I heard it from seemed to think it was a Fedele priestess—someone you kept company with while you were here before."

"Rather an odd way to put it, but the priestess I 'kept company with' was Rosalba," I said. "She's dead, remember? We found her body in Manico."

"That's what I told the person who told me the story," Giovanni said.

I thought back to the night of the battle. I hadn't thought anyone had seen me, but I hadn't really taken steps to disguise myself; there hadn't been time. "What are people making of this?" I asked.

"The story I was told apparently illustrated your gallantry," Giovanni said. His voice was sour. "Risking your life to save a lady who'd fallen in love with you, thinking you were a man."

I snorted. "Rosalba betrayed me to the Fedeli."

"Yeah, well, maybe that was supposed to be a lover's spat? *I* didn't come up with the story." Giovanni slouched back against the wall, relaxing slightly. "I'm probably worrying over nothing," he said.

We got up to go and walked back to my room, chatting about nothing in particular—gossip about other people, how the rebuilding efforts were going, the weather. When we reached my room, Giovanni said, "It was Mira, wasn't it?"

I didn't answer. Giovanni's face was rigid as he walked away.

The extent of my friendship with Mira was not widely known beyond my closest associates; it simply wasn't something I had liked talking about. Lia had kept it out of the songs she wrote, and fearing for Mira's safety, I'd tried to make sure only a few people ever heard the full story of my escape from the Fedeli. Giovanni and Lucia knew, of course, and obviously Isabella had known. Flavia and Celia knew that we'd been close friends at the conservatory; so did Giula, but she hadn't ever joined the Lupi, even when we'd put out a call for musicians. So far as I knew, she and her family were still living in Doratura.

Nonetheless, a week later Lucia told me that she'd heard a rumor that I had helped a mage escape Cuore. Her face was puckered with worry as she leaned back in her chair and plucked at the fabric of her skirt. "I thought you should know," she said.

I leaned back in my own chair, looking out the window. It was dusk, and the garden was in deep shadow. "What do you think I should do about it?"

"Deny it," Lucia said. "Find out who's spreading the story and put a stop to it."

"The only way to kill a rumor is to start a better one," I said. "Denying it, pursuing the people spreading it—these are just fresh logs for the fire."

"I think it's Clara who's spreading it," Lucia said. "But I can't prove that."

"Clara's too smart to spread the rumor herself. If I were her, I'd arrange for someone who liked to gossip to overhear the most damaging information."

"Still, it's her doing."

"You're probably right," I said.

Lucia's hands were twisting the fabric now. "Is there anything to the rumor?"

"Would you think less of me if it were true?"

"Of course not," Lucia said, and then raised her eyes to meet mine. "I mean that. I know you, Eliana. If you helped a mage escape Cuore, you had a good reason to do it."

I laughed a little at that. "You're a priestess. You should probably be telling me that I sinned and ought to go turn myself in to the Servi right now."

"If I ever reach the point of telling *anyone* to go to the Servi for anything, I hope God strikes me dead."

"Whatever would Gèsu say about that?" I tried to make my shaky voice take on a teasing tone, with mixed success.

Lucia's hands relaxed their grip on her skirt and she leaned forward. "He'd say that redemption is open to all who seek it, even Clara, and that I ought to remember that."

I could genuinely laugh at that. "I don't think you need to worry about Clara seeking redemption anytime soon. She thinks she's doing the work of God."

Lucia shook her head. "No. No, she's not. But I think you were. Redemption is open to all who seek it—even a mage. That's why you saved Mira."

Had Lucia followed me that day? I turned to meet her eyes, shocked, and she simply shrugged. "I know you, Eliana, and I know what you've told me about Mira. That's all."

I nodded a little.

It had grown quite dark while we talked, and I went to light a candle. "I would rather die than tell any of this to the Servi," Lucia said. "But Clara is going to start asking around soon, and she'll know better than to rely on my testimony, or Giovanni's. Be careful. Giovanni's right. She hates you, and she's afraid of you. Please be careful."

I nodded again, and Lucia left.

Outside, it had grown quite dark. I settled into the window seat; I could see a few stars and a sliver-thin moon. Back at the conservatory, when the Fedeli had come to investigate, Mira's secret ensemble had met and sorted out what to do—to deny, to keep our secret. I could seek out my friends at the enclave and ask them to lie on my behalf—to give each of them a consistent story to tell Clara. They would do it, I was fairly certain. I mulled over that possibility for a while, and then discarded it. The truly damaging information—that I had smuggled someone out of Cuore—was already common knowledge. I had no idea who it was who had seen me, so I couldn't very well ask them to change their story. Clara was no idiot; she knew when she was being lied to. A unified brick wall from my friends would only convince her that I was hiding some terrible secret. The truth was bad enough, I thought, but I had no doubt that Clara could twist it into something even worse if she wanted to.

Clara came to visit me a few mornings later. I poured tea for her as she settled into a chair, her fan of black feathers flicking back and forth. With a look of grave concern, she told me that people were saying that I'd helped a mage to escape the fall of Cuore.

"Are they," I said. Clara was toying with the jeweled cross she wore, and my own fingers strayed to Bella's cross, which I wore around my neck now on a silk cord.

"You don't seem surprised," Clara said. "Is there something to this rumor?"

"I first heard this story a few weeks ago," I said. "I know how gossip travels on the lips of the malicious. It's said I helped someone to escape, so naturally there are some who assume the worst." I tightened my jaw to keep myself from spitting out my suspicion that it was Clara herself who had started the rumor that the lady I'd helped was a mage.

Clara relaxed slightly into her chair. "Then of course you'll welcome an investigation," she said. "To clear your name."

"For you to investigate this slander will only give credibility to it," I said. "Is that what you want?"

"Do you have something to hide?"

"Are you going to tell me next that 'innocence doesn't *need* to hide?'" I asked.

Clara wet her lips. "I'm not going to quote the Book

of the Lady to you," she said. "But it does seem to me that if your conscience is clear, then you'll know you have nothing to fear from me."

I met her green eyes. "It hardly matters whether I approve or not. You're going to investigate the story regardless."

"It's for your sake, Eliana," Clara said. "We can't have people believing that *you,* you of all people, would be planning to create your own Circle to depose the Emperor."

Create my own Circle? Depose the Emperor? I had turned away from Clara; now I whirled back to face her. "For the love of God, Clara, if I had intended to depose the Emperor, wouldn't I have made my bid for power *before* the Lupi were disbanded? An army would have been a hell of a lot more use to me than one mage, don't you think?"

"I agree completely," Clara said, with a smile as full of false warmth as the midwinter sun. She stood up and put a friendly hand on my arm. "And I'm confident that's what my investigation will find."

"You were right," I said to Lucia over lunch. "Clara has decided she needs to investigate the rumors. Apparently now the story is that I've created my own Circle to depose the Emperor."

"That's absurd," Lucia said.

"Oh, I agree," Giovanni said. "But this is a game Clara can't lose. Even if she 'clears' Eliana of all suspicion, the fact that Eliana was investigated at all will be reason to distrust her."

"Do you think she knows about my friendship with Mira?" I asked softly.

Giovanni shook his head. "No. None of your old

friends have joined the Servi. Right now, Clara—and Placido, I'm sure he's in on this—are just trying to stir up suspicion and distrust. You have influence, popular support, and the Emperor's ear; if they can erode any of those even a little, it's well worth their time."

I nodded, then lowered my eyes. Of course, the "worst" was true—I *had* saved a mage from the fall of Cuore, though not for the reasons that Clara had implied. *Maybe I should flee,* I thought. Clara was highly unlikely to send people to hunt me down. But if I did, everyone, not just Clara, would assume that I really *had* saved at least one mage, maybe more, in an attempt to create my own Circle and take power for myself. My reputation would be utterly destroyed, but more important, so would that of all my friends and allies, from Giovanni and Lucia down to the young ladies who dressed in men's clothes and refused to wed.

If worse came to worst, I thought, I could confess— that I had saved Mira because I was in love with her. I wasn't sure what punishment would fall on me for that, but I was fairly confident that at least my friends wouldn't suffer for my carelessness in allowing myself to be seen.

*   *   *

A few days after my conversation with Clara, Flavia came by my room for a visit. Along with a fair number of the Cantatori, Flavia had remained in Cuore. As Flavia had done throughout the war, the Cantatori wore gray robes styled like conservatory clothes. Though initially the Cantatori were made up solely of musicians and dancers who had served with the Lupi or the Imperial Army, now they were attracting members who had not joined during the war. Those who had served with the Lupi or the army belted their robes with a red sash, like Flavia had; those who had joined after the war left their robes unbelted. Flavia's sash was red wool, but in the heat of the summer she wore a linen robe rather than a wool one. I invited her in and poured wine for both of us.

We chatted first about the outposts that were being set up in the wasteland. Flavia and the other Cantatori were eager to participate but reluctant to put themselves under the control of the Servi. "We're thinking of building our own," she said. "Do you think we'll be able to persuade the Emperor to supply us with food like he's going to supply the Servi?"

"I don't know," I said. "Sometimes I think he doesn't like Clara any more than I do, but he often does as she says, even so. And certainly Clara won't want him to."

"I don't understand it." Flavia fidgeted with her wine cup. "We're talking about outposts in the *wasteland*. Why would Clara want to control something so remote, somewhere so desolate?"

"Well, *she's* not going down there," I said. "And this is Clara: if she could control the moon and the stars, she would."

Flavia laughed, but averted her eyes. "Speaking of Clara," she said, her voice heavy, "she summoned me yesterday. She wanted to ask me questions about you."

"That's not surprising," I said. "What did you tell her? If you don't mind my asking?"

"I don't mind *you* asking," Flavia said. Her face was red. "She wanted to know how you felt about the Circle, first of all. I told her you hated them. Everyone knew that. The story going around, that you tried to set aside your own Circle—the only person *less* likely to do that, I think, would be Lucia. And I told Clara that."

I nodded, and Flavia's flush deepened.

"So then she asked if you'd ever known a mage. I figured that I'd better not lie about this—if she already knew about Mira, she'd think you had something to hide. So I said yes, there was a mage hiding at the conservatory. Mira. We *all* knew Mira; Mira was the one who organized the first group of secret Redentori."

"Mira didn't organize Redentori exactly," I said. "We were just playing the music. . . ."

Flavia waved her hand dismissively. "Mira knew what she was doing. Bella was the first one of us to really convert, but don't try to tell me that any of us were *just* playing the music. Anyway, I told Clara that, and her face—well, it was like I'd just given her a present. Eliana, I have a terrible feeling that I gave her just what she was looking for."

She probably had, I thought, but I shook my head. "She would have found out from somewhere. You were right; if you hadn't told her I knew a mage at the conservatory, she'd have found out from somewhere, and then she'd have figured that I had something to hide, and that you were hiding it."

Flavia shook her head. "Yeah, but I thought about it later, and who else would have told her? Celia's moved back to her family's farm, Demetrio and Nolasco went back to the conservatory, and I don't think Clara would have gone all the way down to Verdia to question them. I was afraid she already knew, but clearly she didn't. I wish I'd talked to you, before I talked to her."

"Would you have had time?"

"Not really. But—oh, I should have come over here

when I first heard the rumor. I should have guessed that Clara—"

"How were you supposed to know?" I said. "Was that all she asked you about?"

"Then she wanted to know if you had any special connection to Mira. And I told her no, you didn't. I figured if she didn't already know you two were roommates, I wasn't going to be the one to tell her." Flavia paused, and sighed. "She had me swear that on the cross. I did it. I figure Gèsu probably understands about lying to human scorpions like Clara."

Valentino was the next of my friends to give Clara a piece of the puzzle. I heard about it from a thoroughly disgusted Quirino, who couldn't believe Valentino would have actually volunteered this information. "To *Clara,* of all people," he snarled, flinging himself into the chair by my fireplace. "Valentino! After all the times the Servi went after Valentino, I would have sworn that the only way Clara would get information out of him would have involved hot irons."

"Maybe that's what he was afraid of," I said.

Quirino rolled his eyes. "He might have at *least* waited until they were heating them instead of spilling everything he knew as soon as Clara had him alone."

"What did Clara ask him about?"

"The story about you, of course. Valentino fell all over himself trying to convince her that you never, ever would have freed Rosalba. 'She was the one who turned Eliana in to the Fedeli,' he said. 'Eliana never would have freed her.' Never mind that Rosalba was *dead* by the end of the war; if I know that, Clara certainly knows it and Valentino ought to have known it."

I nodded. "Did Clara leave it at that?"

"Of course she didn't. This is Clara. She wanted to

know how Valentino thought you'd escaped from the Fedeli. He said that he'd heard that after you vanished, the Circle said it was a priest—someone like Rosalba— and the Fedeli said it was a member of the Circle. And Clara pounced on that. 'A member of the Circle, Valentino? Think carefully: did you ever see Eliana meet with a mage?' "

I thought back—somewhat frantically—over my months in the enclave. Could Valentino have known about my meetings with Mira?

"Valentino said no, of course not. So then Clara asked about the priestess, and he said that she wouldn't have been the one who freed you, since she was the one who turned you in in the first place." Quirino sighed. "I think that was basically the end of the conversation. Valentino said that the thing that really worried him was that Clara seemed so pleased."

I lowered my eyes.

"Eliana?" Quirino said. "How *did* you escape from the Fedeli?"

I poured Quirino some tea, to give myself time to think about whether I should give him the honest answer, then took a sip from my own cup. "Well, you know, I think Rosalba rather regretted turning me in." I remembered her prayer, her shaking voice, and her pale face.

"Was she the one who helped you, then?"

I shook my head. "No. Valentino was right. It was a mage, Mira."

"Why would a mage have freed you?"

"The Circle ordered her to. They were afraid the Fedeli wouldn't be able to break me, so they planned to follow me back to where the Lupi were wintering."

"But that didn't happen."

"No. Mira warned me. And she told me how to defeat magefire."

Quirino shook his head. "A mage told you that? Why?"

"That's a long story," I said. "The short version, I guess, is that we were friends."

Quirino went a little pale, and swallowed hard, but he nodded, and drank the rest of his tea in silence.

Ulisse was the next of my old friends to come by for a visit. He had avoided me since our victory; apparently time hadn't significantly eased his humiliation at discovering that his old drinking buddy was actually the lady he longed for, in disguise. Still, today, he seemed to have regained a little of his old confidence. "Clara was asking me questions about you," he said as I poured him some wine.

"She's been asking lots of people questions," I said.

"Yeah, well, she asked me—" Ulisse lowered his voice to barely above a whisper "—about *Mira*. Miriamne. The renegade mage. She wanted to know if you and Mira had had any contact while you were spying in the enclave."

Ulisse had carried a message for Mira once—a sprig of winter jasmine that had meant, *meet me*. I knew, looking at him, that whether or not he'd known at the time, he knew *now* who he'd carried the message for.

"I told her no," Ulisse said. "Absolutely not, you hadn't."

I felt my face go hot and then cold. How would Ulisse have known for certain that I *hadn't* had contact? He was a student—he hadn't even lived in the enclave. To make such an emphatic denial, he had to be lying, and I knew Clara would reach the same conclusion.

"Thank you for being such a loyal friend, Ulisse," I said softly, and let him out.

Late one afternoon a few days later, I heard Clara's voice in the corridor outside my room, and stiffened, expecting a knock. But she was not coming to see me; a moment later I heard Lucia's voice and realized Clara was speaking to Lucia, in the room next to mine. "Good day, Priestess Clara," Lucia said, her voice very clear. "What a pleasure to see you. Please come in."

After a moment's hesitation—Lucia, at least, was my friend—I pressed my ear against the wall, straining to overhear their conversation.

They exchanged mutual pleasantries for a few minutes over tea, then Clara got down to business. "I'm afraid I need to ask you some questions about Eliana," Clara said. "I realize that she's a good friend of yours, but your first duty, as I'm sure you're aware, is to God, and your second is to Emperor Travan."

"Oh, of course," Lucia said so implacably that I shivered. "I'm happy to help you however I can."

Clara paused for a moment—surprised by Lucia's willingness to cooperate, perhaps—and then asked, "What can you tell me about Eliana's feelings toward the mage who called herself Mira?"

"Nothing at all," Lucia said, her voice distinct and perfectly courteous. "I'm terribly sorry."

There was a sharp clink as Clara set down her tea. "Excuse me, Priestess Lucia. I'm sure you know a great deal about the subject."

"Perhaps. But as you mentioned, my first duty is to God. As Eliana's spiritual counselor, all our conversations on that subject are privileged. It says in The Journey—"

"I don't need you to quote The Journey to me,"

Clara said, her voice sharp. "Perhaps you can enlighten me as to Eliana's feelings toward Emperor Travan."

"Again, anything Eliana has told me about this subject is under God's seal. I would, however, point out that Eliana *did* put him in power."

"The Imperial Army and the Lupi put him in power," Clara said.

"Perhaps you should ask the Emperor who he credits—or blames." I could hear the hint of a smile in Lucia's voice.

"While serving the Lupi in Cuore, did Eliana meet with Mira at all?" Clara asked.

"Oh, my goodness, you must realize that I wasn't there. But Michel was. Have you asked Michel?"

"I have." Clara's voice was stony. "He refused to talk to me. Why do you suppose that was?"

"I couldn't imagine," Lucia said.

"How did Eliana escape after her arrest by the Fedeli?" Clara asked. "Is it true that Mira was the one who freed her?"

"Again, I wasn't there," Lucia said. "I think you'd better ask Eliana that question."

"Rest assured," Clara said, and I could hear a rustle as she stood up. "I will do that."

I expected a knock on my own door next, but instead she knocked on Giovanni's. His room was on the other side of mine, and I went to listen without hesitation. He swung his door open at the first knock. "Oh, good afternoon, Priestess Clara," he said. "Please come in."

Again, I listened to slightly strained pleasantries. Clara made herself comfortable and Giovanni poured wine. Giovanni broached the subject first. "I'm quite sure I know why you're here," he said, "And I'm very glad you came to me, because I can straighten all of this out."

"Really. Well, I must say, I'm delighted to hear it," Clara said.

"Eliana did help someone escape during the fall of Cuore, but it wasn't a mage, nor was it a priestess. It was a musician who panicked under fire, a friend of hers from the conservatory."

"Really." Clara set down her cup with a faint click. "Why didn't Eliana simply tell me this when I first began investigating?"

"Eliana is quite loyal to her friends," Giovanni said. "The musician who fled would be deeply shamed if her cowardice were known. Eliana has a great deal of confidence in your honor and fairness; she knew that you would investigate the rumor, find nothing, and close your investigation, her friend's honor intact."

"What was the name of this friend?"

"I'd really rather not say," Giovanni said.

"I'm afraid I must insist."

"Well . . ." Giovanni hesitated for a moment. "Giula," he said finally. "It was a young lady named Giula."

"Perhaps," Clara said, "she saved two people during the battle."

Giovanni laughed out loud, an easy, casual laugh. "You think she smuggled out the musician, then ran back into the burning enclave, found a mage, and smuggled her out, too? I spent much of the battle at her side, and take my word for it, she didn't have that kind of time."

"But she saved Giula out of friendship. Mira was a friend too, wasn't she?"

"Once she was," Giovanni said. "Eliana knew her at

the conservatory. But she never forgave her for leaving—
or for destroying the Lupi."

"Not even after Mira freed her from the Fedeli?"

"If it was Mira who did it, she did it on the orders of
the Circle."

"So she wouldn't have saved Mira out of sentiment?"

"Eliana is not a sentimental person."

"Interesting." There was a pause; I thought Clara
had probably picked up her cup again. "You see, I have
an eyewitness—a servant from the enclave—prepared
to swear that he saw Eliana smuggling the mage Miriamne, also known as Mira, out of Cuore."

"Impossible. As I said, it was Giula."

"Giula can ride a horse?"

"Obviously, if that was how she got out of the city."

"Was Giula the sort of friend with whom Eliana
might exchange a passionate kiss?"

"They were old friends."

"Just as Mira was an old friend." The cup clicked
down again and I heard a rustle as Clara stood up.
"But of course, Eliana is not a sentimental person. If
she did smuggle Mira out of the city, you have made it
clear that in your opinion, it would *not* have been a
gesture of friendship. Thus, the theory that the purpose
of saving the mage was to create her own Circle— Oh,
don't shake your head at me, Generale Giovanni, and
leave your sword where it is. I will overlook your blasphemy in considering a physical attack on a Priestess
of God, given your fondness for Generale Eliana. Thank
you, Generale. You've been *most* helpful."

The door clicked shut. There was no knock on my
own door. Through the wall, I heard a glass shatter
against the floor.

The snare was closing around me. I decided to go to the Emperor—to confess to him that I *had* freed Mira, but not to challenge his power. I had done it because I loved Mira and knew that we could trust her. Surely, I thought as I paced the floors of my room, Travan will understand. Surely he has loved the wrong person— and surely, he will understand that for those like us, sometimes there is no *right* person.

The corridor outside my room was empty, and I hurried down the stairs and through the courtyard to Travan's quarters. But I was met at the door by Michel. "He won't see you," Michel said.

I stared at Michel; for a moment, I couldn't quite believe what I'd heard. "Why?" I asked, finally.

Michel shook his head. He didn't answer right away, and I realized after a moment that he was almost in tears. "I don't know," he said.

"Does he believe—the stories that Clara has been telling?"

"I don't know," Michel said again.

"You have to let me in," I said.

Michel shook his head. "I can't," he said. "Please, just go. I can't let you in."

Clara was waiting when I returned to my room, with Placido and three Servi—witnesses.

"Eliana," Clara said, and her face was grave with a hint of triumph. "We need to ask you about Mira."

"I have nothing to say to you," I said.

"Then you will be charged with treason," Clara said. "Don't you at least want to defend yourself?"

I pulled myself up as straight as I could stand. "Mira saved my life twice," I said. "She saved me from the Circle; when they came to take her back, they used me as a hostage against her. And she saved me from the

Fedeli. Mira was the first person I knew who dared to speak against the Circle—who dared suggest that I could have a future that didn't require me to play the tunes they called. Mira was one of the Lupi, even if she didn't wear a red sash."

"One of the Lupi?" Clara said. "Mira was one of the mages sent to *destroy* the Lupi, was she not?"

"Mira volunteered for that mission to protect as many of us as she could," I said.

"So she told you."

"Mira saved my life," I said again. "When she saved me from the Fedeli, she saved us all—including Placido, since I knew he led the university reformers. I couldn't have held out against the Fedele torturer forever. Mira was the person who told me about the power of the Redentori dances against magefire." I stepped forward. "Mira renounced magery once. I knew she could renounce it again."

"That doesn't matter," Clara said. "What you knew—or you *thought* you knew. Mira was a mage—condemned by God." Her fingers touched the jeweled cross she wore.

I felt my face go hot and cold, and in a single furious gesture, I yanked the cross from the chain around Clara's neck and threw it to her feet. "How dare you decide for God whether Mira is condemned?" I demanded. "What have you risked for your faith? What have *you* sacrificed? You don't love God. You love your position, your comfort, your power. If God condemns anyone, it's *you*."

A faint smile flickered on Clara's lips. "On my authority as the head of the Servi," she said, "I place you under arrest, Eliana, on suspicion of treason." She glanced at the cross on the floor; one of her assistants quickly picked it up. "And blasphemy."

"You can rot in hell, Clara," I said. "To be accused by you of blasphemy is the highest honor I can imagine."

*   *   *

Because of my stature—and perhaps because Giovanni threatened to kill anyone who tried it—I was not imprisoned in the dungeon, but placed under house arrest and confined to my room. Wary of giving me a public forum for more outbursts, Clara decided that my trial would be closed. I would not be invited. Neither would Lucia and Giovanni.

"We have to get you out of here," Giovanni said.

"How?" I said.

"There are Lupi still in Cuore," Giovanni said. "We could break you out. Then run—head north, far enough away that it's more trouble than it's worth to come after you. I have family in Varena; my father owns ships. We could get you across the ocean if we had to."

"Along with the Lupi?" I said. "All the Lupi who'd helped break me out?"

"Sure," Giovanni said, though I suspected he wasn't as confident of that as he wanted me to think.

"And everyone else that Placido and Clara would go after? You know this isn't just about me, Giovanni. If I run, it will be taken as proof of what Clara claims—proof that I saved a remnant of the Circle to help me make my own bid for power. What would be the logical thing to do then? Purge Cuore of every person loyal to me, from Valentino and Quirino to the young women who dress like me." I looked at Giovanni in the candlelight. "Can you tell me this wouldn't happen?"

Giovanni was silent.

"It would happen," Lucia said.

Giovanni's head snapped up to glare at Lucia. "You aren't helping," he said.

"I don't think Eliana would want us to lie to her," Lucia said.

"No," I said. "I wouldn't."

Giovanni picked up a wineglass, took a swallow, then hurled the glass in frustration at the fireplace. It smashed against the stones, and Lucia closed her eyes and pressed her hands against her forehead, blocking him out. "Eliana, Clara wants you dead," Giovanni said. "And she thinks she can get away with it. She's *sure* she can get away with it, or she wouldn't have let it go this far."

"Why is Travan allowing this?" Lucia said. "Eliana, do you have any idea?"

I shook my head. "He wouldn't see me," I said. "I tried to go talk to him, but Michel turned me away."

"Then you have to run," Giovanni said. But after what Lucia had said, I couldn't do it. No matter what the price.

Lucia and Giovanni spent the night of my trial in my room. As dusk turned to darkness, Giovanni napped in a chair, and Lucia, at my insistence, took the bed. I took the cushions in the window seat for myself—not that I expected to sleep. Very late, as I stared into the wispy light of the candle, there was a very soft tap at the door. I opened it: Michel. "Can I come in?" he whispered.

I stood back to let him through and quietly poured us each a glass of wine. He sat down across from me, in the window seat. Giovanni stirred, then went back to sleep.

"Has Travan agreed to see me?" I asked.

"No," Michel said. His shoulders were slumped; his head was bowed. "And he won't."

"Why?" I asked. "Is he that angry about this?"

Michel shook his head and covered his face with his hands. "I came tonight because I thought you at least deserved to know why Travan has turned his back on you," he said. His voice was muffled.

I waited.

Michel dropped his hands to the table, but didn't raise his face. "Travan doesn't really like Clara or Placido any more than you do," he said. "He accepted them as allies early on because it was necessary; now, they've got far too much influence. But, he can't just throw them out of power; he needs people to turn against them." He swallowed. "Travan is hoping that Clara will order you executed. Once you're dead, he's going to pretend it all happened without his knowledge or consent. He'll use this to disband the Servi, because clearly they can't be trusted with power. He's hoping to use this to take down both Clara and Placido."

I shook my head, unwilling to believe. "Did he tell you this?"

Michel shook his head, then nodded. "Sort of."

"Are you sure?"

He nodded. "Very sure."

I closed my eyes and rubbed my eyes with the heels of my hands. "Michel, will you carry a note to him for me? If you don't think he'll read it now—" I broke off. If Clara meant to have me executed, it could happen as soon as the next morning. With effort, I finished: "—give it to him after I'm dead." Michel nodded, and I moved to the table, getting out a sheet of paper, ink, and a pen.

When you hear the news of my death, Travan, you can console yourself with one thing: I truly did save Mira on the night that Cuore fell. I saved Mira because I love her. She is a friend, and when I faced her with a drawn sword between us, I knew that I could never betray a friend for political expediency. Alas, it's clear to me now that you lack my compunctions.

I saw the night we met that you have the will and the spirit to be a truly great Emperor, like the Emperors of the old days, before the Circle. But you will have to lead. You will have to stand up to Clara and Placido and those like them— and believe me, even if Clara and Placido both died in their sleep tonight, there would be more like them soon enough. You've chosen to listen to them; you can choose to stop. You can send them away from Cuore, and dismantle the Servi. You can decree that everyone in the Empire may follow their heart, and worship the god they believe in. You are the Emperor. You are the one person here who can make that choice.

I've asked Michel to give this to you after I'm dead. You wouldn't listen to me in life, but perhaps you'll listen to me now. As I saved Mira for friendship, I appeal to you now as a friend to a friend: lead, Travan. For the sake of your people. We fought and died for you —not for Clara and Placido.

When I finished, Michel was still slumped in his chair, barely able to look at me. Once the ink had dried, I folded the letter and sealed it, then gave it to Michel. Michel stood up and finally raised his head; his eyes were full of tears. "Thank you, Generale," Michel said.

"For what?" I asked.

"For everything," he said. He touched his fist to his chest and held it out, then left the room as quickly as he could.

Giovanni stirred in his chair, and for a moment I thought he'd been awake the whole time—but then he settled back down and started snoring. I still didn't feel at all like sleeping, but I didn't have the heart to wake Giovanni or Lucia for the company, so I curled up in the window seat to wait for morning.

*   *   *

Darkness and agony and Felice's grinning face faded into the wasteland twilight. I felt a comforting hand clasping mine, and sat up, free of my bonds. "Mira?" I said, but I was in the valley that had once been Ravenna, beside the burnt-out remnants of the keep, a single fragment of cloth flapping like a lost banner in the night breeze.

Mario was beside me. "Don't be afraid," he said.

There were others approaching us. Isabella and Rafi; Vitale; Severo. There were hundreds here. All of them, Lupi who had died during the war.

"You all died because of me," I said.

"We all gave our lives," Mario said. "And we would give them again." Mario clasped my hand gently, and for a moment, I felt the touch of warm flesh against mine. "Don't forget that," he said. "It was our choice. Honor our lives by living for what we believed in."

*   *   *

I woke early in the dawn to find Giovanni sitting at the table across from me. "You look terrible," I said. "Maybe I should have had you sleep in the bed."

Giovanni didn't smile. "They've found you guilty, Eliana," he said gently.

"Oh," I said, and had a strange impulse to go back to sleep. Maybe if I went to sleep and woke up a second time, it wouldn't be true. I reached for the tea and almost knocked it over. "What are they going to do to me?"

"Clara has sentenced you to death," he said.

I swallowed hard. "How is she going to do it?"

"Beheading."

My hand, on the teacup, shook suddenly, and the hot tea splashed onto my hand. I yelped in pain and blew on the scald to cool it. "Well," I said, and was relieved to hear that my voice was perfectly steady. "At least that's always looked pretty painless. Fast. Not like hanging or burning. That's better than a lot of the ways I thought I'd die, this past year."

"How about dying in your own bed at the age of eighty, surrounded by your grandchildren?" Giovanni asked. "Did that ever occur to you as a possibility?"

"I never would've had grandchildren, Giovanni," I said, and gave him a wry grin. He summoned up a weak smile in return and poured me a cup of tea.

"So this is it, then," I said. "They should be coming for me soon, I suppose."

"You might be able to convince Clara not to kill you if you begged for mercy," Giovanni said. "It's the sort of gesture she'd go for."

I took a swallow of the tea. "If she were planning to burn me alive, I might be able to make myself do it," I said. "As it is—" I sighed and closed my eyes. "Michel told me last night that Travan is hoping to use this to shove Placido and Clara out of power—as an excuse to disband the Servi. Do you think it'll work?" Giovanni started to answer, and I looked up to fix him with a glare. "Truthfully. Do you think it'll work?"

Giovanni lowered his eyes. "It will probably work," he muttered reluctantly.

"It's worth dying if it gets Clara out of power." I took another swallow of tea; my mouth had gone very dry. "I'm going to come back as a ghost and haunt Travan, though. Do Redentori believe in ghosts?"

Giovanni blinked at me slowly and then shrugged. "I think the question is open to debate."

"I dreamed about Mario last night," I said. "It was a nice dream, though. He didn't haunt me."

"What did you dream about Mario?" Giovanni asked.

"He was there with all the Lupi who'd died, and he said that it was their choice, that I shouldn't blame myself," I said. "Now that I'm going to join them, I guess they wanted to reassure me."

Giovanni smiled and reached across the table to squeeze my hand. Then he pushed back his chair and stood up. "Eliana, I need to leave for a while. I promise, it won't be long."

"What?" I stared at him. "Where are you going?"

"Privy," he said.

I started to shake my head in disbelief. He turned toward the door, then turned back to me, slipped one hand behind my head, and kissed me on the lips. Then he broke away and strode out.

"What the *hell*," I shouted after him. "Giovanni! Get back here." He didn't turn around. "Giovanni!"

I knew within a few minutes that he hadn't gone to

the privy, not unless he got lost or fell in. I woke Lucia and asked her to go look for him, then paced the room, touching my violin as I passed it but not picking it up to play. It was depressing, to be alone like this, and frustrating to lack an audience for the morbid jokes I was coming up with to pass the time and distract myself. Much more than an hour passed before there was a knock at the door. I opened it to see Lucia, and a guard.

"Lucia," I said, "thank goodness. Did you find him?"

Lucia looked at the guard.

"You're free to go," the guard said.

I stared at him. "Giovanni said I'd been found guilty."

"You were," the guard said. "But your sentence was overturned. New evidence has come to light."

"What evidence?" I asked.

"Someone else confessed to freeing the mage," the guard said.

Lady's— "Where's Giovanni?" I said.

Lucia slipped her arm around my waist, supporting my weight as if she thought I might fall suddenly. "Giovanni went to Clara, and said that you delivered Mira as a prisoner to him, but that he was so taken by her beauty that he freed her."

Oh my God, Giovanni. "Giovanni, you're an idiot; you're an *idiot*," I whispered. "Where is he? I need to see him." Lucia shook her head. "I'm not going to let him do this," I said.

"He knew that," Lucia said. "Eliana, Giovanni's dead."

*   *   *

I'd spent the morning bracing myself to walk out of my room stoic and dignified; now that I was free to go, and safe, all I could do was sit down at my table and sob. This wasn't what I'd been ready for. How could Giovanni possibly be dead? I'd just *seen* him. *Damn you, Giovanni.*

"But they all knew I did it," I said to Lucia.

"Giovanni started by shouting his confession from the center of the gardens," Lucia said. "He figured that if enough people knew that he'd confessed, Clara would look pretty foolish executing *you*—and looking foolish is the one thing Clara can't stand. He said that you were protecting him." Lucia sat down beside me. "He wrote you a letter," she said, and slipped it under my hands.

Eliana, the letter read.

> *By the time you read this, I'll be dead. I know you'll be angry—I suppose that's part of what makes this worth it.*
>
> Typical.
>
> *I can't let them kill you. But you're right—it's worth dying to bring down the Servi. I know you would never let me take your place, so I'm going to request that sentence be carried out before they break the news to you. If they refuse, I'll attack Placido; with any luck, I'll take him with me. Save Travan the trouble of deposing him.*

I looked up. "Placido?"
Lucia sighed. "Dead."

> *I know you'll be angry at me for doing this, but as time passes, I hope you will remember me with fondness and not with anger. Because just*

*as you would die to save Mira, I would die to
save you. Because I love you.*

*I know neither one of us has ever believed —
not in the Lady, not in Gèsu. Not the way Lucia
does, or Michel. But if there's a power, whatever
name She goes by, I hope She takes good care of
you. Don't behave yourself too well, though, because I'm counting on seeing you again.*

My love forever,
Giovanni

I folded the letter so that my tears wouldn't make
the ink run, and laid my head on my arms.

*   *   *

Though Giovanni's death wasn't quite what Travan
had planned on, it worked well enough for his purposes. Declaring that the Servi had clearly lost their
way if they had turned on Generale Giovanni, hero of
the Empire, he removed Clara from her post and ap-
pointed, of all people, Lucia. Lucia had never bothered
to disguise her contempt for the very idea of the Servi,
and that, I concluded, was precisely what the Emperor
wanted: a leader who would dismantle the organization. I found a couple of extremely trustworthy former
Lupi to serve as Lucia's bodyguards; she'd need them.
Giovanni, I thought, would have appreciated the irony.

There was a Council meeting the following week. I
took my seat, cautiously. There were a few new faces—
one of the old reformers that Giovanni probably
would have known, one of the Cantatori, and Lucia, of
course. Lucia sat beside me, and we rose together as
Travan came into the room.

I had not seen Travan since the last Council meeting,

though Michel had told me that Travan read my letter. I had to fight down my anger when I saw Travan; my hands clenched into fists. Travan's gaze swept coolly over his Council, but he didn't meet my eyes. Nor did he meet my eyes, or acknowledge me in any way, for the rest of the meeting. I found that without Clara and Placido there, I didn't have to say all that much anyway. At least, I thought, Travan didn't bar me from the meeting; I was a little surprised that he had not. It didn't matter, though. Watching his back as he strode out at the end, I knew that it would take a great crisis to inspire me to go to another Council meeting. I might be a hero of the Empire, but I was no friend of the Emperor.

I tried not to think about Giovanni, because it hurt so much. But for the first few weeks after his death, I kept thinking things like, *I need to remember to tell Giovanni about this later* or *Giovanni will be amused by that,* only to remember a moment later that he was dead. I avoided both Court and company, unwilling to risk weeping in front of others. After the first wound of loss had started to heal, a few months later, I realized that I was desperately lonely.

Lucia's new responsibilities kept her away from me most of the time. Flavia had left Court: the Cantatori were staffing the border outposts, and Flavia was either in Verdia at one of the outposts, or traveling through the Empire recruiting people to join the order, I wasn't sure. Of my friends still at court, many were avoiding me—out of shame, I thought, that they hadn't done more to foil Clara's investigation. Or maybe it was because I had avoided people so assiduously right after Giovanni's death, and they didn't want to intrude. Regardless, I didn't know how to bridge the distance between us now, so I stayed in my room, and brooded.

I have to leave, I thought one morning when I woke, stiff and cramped, in my window seat. *I'm dying by inches. I can't stay here.* I could go back to Verdia. To teach at the conservatory, or to visit Doratura. Or perhaps I could join the Cantatori and play my violin in the wasteland with Flavia and the others. They would welcome me, surely. It might even be helpful to the order, if it were known that Generale Eliana had joined them.

There was an appeal to the idea, I thought, taking my violin and tuning it. I might not have a whole lot of faith, but I could play while others danced, and pull their energy down into those dark hills, so that someday grass might grow there again. I could lose myself in the music; maybe someday I'd forget what I'd lost.

But if I leave Cuore, Mira won't know where to find me.

I started to play one of the folk tunes I had learned with Mira, back at the conservatory. Giovanni knew how much I loved Mira; did Mira know? If she knew, and she was alive, why hadn't she come back to me? Maybe when she stopped doing magery this final time, the sickness had killed her. Maybe she was killed trying to escape from Cuore.

Or maybe she was alive, but she didn't feel toward me as I felt toward her. *Impossible,* I thought, remembering the way her hands had gripped mine. But I found myself unwilling to believe that she was dead, either.

Perhaps, I thought, she's alive and she knows that I love her, but she's afraid to come back to Cuore: she might be recognized, a message might be read. She could put both of us in danger. But the Empire was vast, and the world vaster still. I couldn't very well go buy a horse and set out searching, not without *some* idea of where to look. *It would take a miracle,* I thought, *to find her that way.*

*   *   *

A miracle. After breakfast, I went to the Great Cathedral. Unlike the cathedral in Manico, the cathedral in Cuore had not been burned. As Lucia had once bitterly predicted, the building was still in use, but for Redentori observances. There was a painting of Gèsu behind the Great Altar, and the pews had been removed so that people would be able to dance. There was no service in progress at the moment, and the cathedral was empty. I eased the door shut behind me and stepped forward into shadow.

I had come to pray, but now that I was inside the cathedral I had to admit that I wasn't quite sure who to pray to. During the war, I'd continued to say my selfish prayers to the Lord. I'd prayed to God when I'd truly feared that Lucia was dead, after Mira had destroyed the Lupi, but most of the time I felt deeply awkward asking for favors from God. In some sense, I equated the Redentore God with the Lady; the Lady was too important to bother with small things. Years ago, during the war with Vesuvia—when I was still a Della Chiesa—I had prayed to the Lady for victory in the war; I had prayed to the Lord to protect my own small family, on their farm near the border.

I had come to the cathedral half intending to pray to the Lord, but now, looking around at the ransacked interior, at the painting of Gèsu, I couldn't bring myself to do it. If the Lord was anywhere, He wasn't here.

I rather doubted that God spent much time here, either. It was dim inside, and damp, almost chilly. I felt like I should say a prayer, though, so I crossed myself and mumbled something in the Old Tongue. I fingered Bella's cross where it rested against my collarbone, and suddenly thought of someone I could ask for a favor.

Giovanni.

The Della Chiese believed in ghosts. Bella had loved to tell ghost stories: most of her ghosts returned to haunt those responsible for their death, to take revenge, or to give one final message to those they'd loved. The dead knew things that the living did not. They could deliver messages, sometimes—dire warnings, in most of Bella's stories, but still. Mario had visited me the night before my trial, I felt sure of that; he had brought me a gentler message. Perhaps Giovanni could do the same. I wasn't sure what the Redentori believed about ghosts, but I didn't care. I wanted to talk to Giovanni, and if I wasn't supposed to do it, I didn't want to know.

Not in the cathedral, though. I'd find God and the Lord playing dice together behind the altar before I found Giovanni anywhere near the place. I went back out into the sunshine, made sure I had my eagle medallion, and went for a walk in the university district.

Giovanni doubtless had a favorite tavern as a student, but I didn't know which it would have been. I went to the tavern where I used to meet Michel; Placido and Ulisse both spent time there, so chances were good Giovanni had as well. I bought two cups of wine and took them to a table near the back. Drinking one, I stared across the table, thinking about Giovanni.

He'd hate this place now, I knew immediately. He'd mock all the students drinking cheap bad wine and choking down the half-burned meals this tavern served. Well. It couldn't be helped. I took a sip of my own cheap, bad wine, and thought about how useless it had been to come here.

Over on the other side of the tavern was a slightly built young man, very young. Brushing past him, another student spilled his wine, laughing at the young man's protest. I was reminded of Giovanni's story about being bullied by Placido, but this young man—boy—just sank back down in his chair and gently righted his now-empty wine cup, his head bowed.

Giovanni wasn't drinking that second cup I'd bought, so I picked it up and made my way over to the young man's table. "Here," I said, and set it down in front of him. "A replacement."

"Thank you," the young man said, gaping, and as I left, I could hear *was that really* and *what was she doing here* buzzing at my heels.

I went for a walk along the river, thinking of the night I'd sat on the bank with Mira. I sat down to watch the riverboats make their way up the river. It was a warm day, and I could smell sewage and rotting weeds. The idea of talking to Giovanni, of asking a dead friend to carry a message for me, suddenly seemed absurd, and the "offering" of wine even more so; I was glad I'd given it to the student.

Well, let's think about this logically. I rested my chin on my arms. Mira could not be in Cuore: I'd reached that conclusion a long time ago. If Mira had been in Cuore, she would have heard about my trial in time to take some action—she would have sent me a message suggesting that I turn her into the Servi, most likely, and if I hadn't, she'd have turned herself in. Or she'd have mounted a rescue attempt. Since she hadn't done any of those things, I knew she was not in Cuore.

It's a big Empire, I thought. *And an even bigger*

world. But Mira ran away once before, to Verdia. "I was born in Verdia," I remembered her saying. "I felt like I belonged there."

But where within Verdia? Not the conservatory, surely not. Somewhere along the riverbank, I could hear music—someone was playing a trumpet. The trumpet made me think of Bella, and I rubbed her cross between my thumb and forefinger.

The Cantatori. Of course. Mira would have needed somewhere to hide, and she wouldn't have wanted to go through the mage-sickness alone. She was still a talented musician, and she had always loved the Old Way music. There would have been a place for her among the Redentori musicians who continued to play and dance after the war. And in addition to the new outposts along the border, the Cantatori had a household in Pluma.

I'll go to Pluma, I thought, standing up and brushing off my clothes. *It can't hurt to go look.* I thought, just for a moment, that I smelled winter jasmine, but when I turned my head to sniff the air, it was gone.

*   *   *

For my trip to Pluma, I decided to disguise myself as a man again. As a woman violinist in men's clothing, I was recognizable to far too many people as Generale Eliana, and I longed for some privacy. But I was thoroughly accustomed to men's clothing; disguising myself as a man sounded easier than putting on a dress.

I still had my clothes from my days with the Lupi, but they were threadbare and stained from ground-in dirt. I had new clothes made, simple clothes of plainer fabrics than my court clothes, and new boots. I purchased extra strings for my violin, and took the case down from a shelf and oiled the leather. I tucked Giovanni's letter in the case along with the letters from my parents.

I told Lucia that I was going to Verdia, but not who I was hoping to find. We had dinner together the night before I left. She was cheerful, but her new responsibilities were weighing on her heavily. Dismantling the Servi would take time, and Lucia was already sick of the job. She picked at her meal and pushed her food away with a sigh and a rueful smile. "I'm hoping to move to Verdia myself, once I'm done with this," she said. "It may take a while, though. At least six months. Maybe a year."

I nodded. I thought it would take longer than that.

"I don't blame you for leaving," she said. "You'll have to write to me sometimes, though, to make me laugh."

"I'll try."

She smiled, and just for an instant, I saw the light in her eyes that I'd seen in Ravenna.

"Don't stay too long here," I said. "You weren't meant for this."

"None of us were," she said, and the light faded like a dying ember.

Traveling as "Daniele," a musician who had served with the Lupi but was now returning home to Verdia, I took a riverboat back down the Anira River. On several occasions, I saw people covertly using witchlight; I hid my own smile and said nothing.

Toward the end of the trip, I roused briefly one night and heard someone speaking quietly out loud; propping myself up on my elbow and squinting in the dim light, I saw another passenger kneeling, her hands raised up to pray to the Lady. I ducked my head down as she glanced around nervously, and I thought that she was nearly as covert and frightened as the Redentori I'd accidentally encountered in Cuore. I felt a strange twinge, a longing that I had never felt sitting in church at the conservatory. I wondered if God always made Herself known in the hidden places, or if it was simply that I felt most comfortable seeking Her there.

The refugee camp outside of Pluma was gone. I stabled my horse and then made my way to the former inn that was now the household of the Cantatori in Pluma. The door was answered by a young woman who quickly invited me in when she saw my violin case. "I'm looking for someone," I said. "A young lady who I think might have joined your order."

She sent me to the office of the local head of the order, a young woman named Prisca who was addressed as "Dean." Though Prisca wore the red sash of a Cantatore who had served with the Lupi, I had never met her. She was young, only a few years older than me, and a little awkward in her own authority. Her bassoon rested on a stand in the corner of her office. "I am pleased to welcome you, Daniele," Prisca said. "What is the name of the lady you are looking for?"

"I'm not sure if the name I know is her real name," I said. "She's about your height—gray eyes and dark hair. She plays the violin and she might have been sick when she first arrived."

Prisca studied me for a moment and then turned abruptly to look out the window. "You might be describing Bella," she said.

"Bella?" My voice cracked and I swallowed hard.

"Isabella. One of the other violinists shortened it to Bella, and it seemed to suit her."

I nodded. "I don't want to intrude if she doesn't want

to see me. If you could tell her—" I considered my words for a moment. "Please tell her that Daniele is here, but if she doesn't want to see me, I will leave and not bother her again."

Prisca nodded. "I'll go find her."

I was too nervous to sit while she was gone. If Mira was not here, I had no idea where to look next. Well, that wasn't true. I could go down to the wasteland again and try the border outposts; she might have gone down there, trying to undo some of the damage she caused with the Circle. I went to look out Prisca's window. It opened onto an interior courtyard; a gray-robed man was watering a small herb garden. His robes were unbelted; he had not served with the Lupi. A breeze through the window wafted the scent of winter jasmine to my face.

The door clicked shut and I turned, and saw Mira.

She had gained a little weight since the last time I saw her—which was good, because when I saw her at the enclave, she looked half starved. She wore unbelted gray robes. Her face was pale, and I feared that she was steeling herself to tell me to go away. But then she said, "Eliana," her voice cracking, and crossed the room in two steps to grab me in a tight hug.

I pressed my cheek against her shoulder, feeling the scratchy wool of her robes, her hair brushing against my neck.

"I'm so sorry," she whispered. "By the time I heard about your trial, about Giovanni, it was too late."

I nodded, not able to speak.

"You were right, you know," she said. "Some things are stronger than magefire."

I pulled back to look into her eyes. "You once asked me to go with you," I said. "That day at the conservatory, when you tried to convince me to jump over the wall and go. Will you come with me now?"

"Where?" Mira asked.

"I don't care," I said. "As long as it's with you."

Mira smiled, and her gray eyes lit like witchlight. "Minstrel life is hard," she said. "We'd never know if we'd be sleeping in a bed or under a bush; some nights we might even go hungry."

"I've slept under a bush, and it wasn't so bad," I said. "I've gone hungry and survived. We could be free, my love. We could see the world together."

Mira pulled my face to hers and kissed me. I could smell winter jasmine and rainwater; her fingers laced in mine and she squeezed my hand like the hilt of a sword. I could hear my heart pounding in my ears; beyond that, I could hear the wind in the trees outside the window, and the sound of a trumpet.

"Come with me," I whispered.

"I will," Mira said. "The world will be ours."

About the Author

Naomi Kritzer grew up in Madison, Wisconsin, a small lunar colony populated mostly by Ph.D.s. She moved to Minnesota to attend college; after graduating with a BA in religion, she became a technical writer. She now lives in Minneapolis with her family. TURNING THE STORM is her second novel. Please visit her website at http://www.naomikritzer.com.